love - Ingrid

Leaping the Fire

A novel of the Russian Revolution and Estonia's Independence

By Ingrid Scott

1905 -1924

LEAPING THE FIRE
Copyright: Ingrid Scott
ISBN-13: 978-1539397502
ISBN-10: 1539397505
Published: 1st November 2015
Publisher: Kororā Press

Cover Design by
Taivo Org
Küpress OÜ, Estonia

Dedicated to the memory of my Great Aunt Emmy

Table of Contents

Map of Estonia and surrounding countries

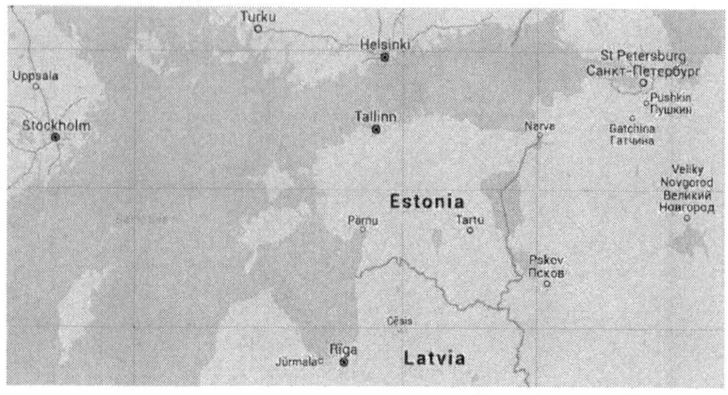

Jürimäe Family Tree

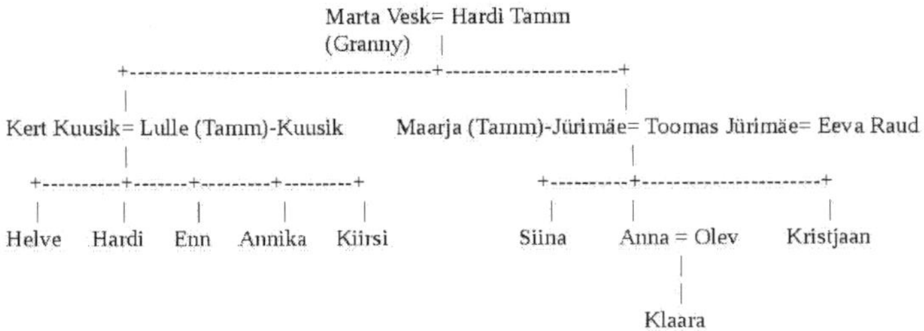

Feodorov Family Tree

1. *That Sunday* **9 January 1905, Petersburg**

The sky was a giant blue egg above us that day but the wind was colder than I'd felt in my life. Ice knives skidded along Gorokhovaya Street. Mama gripped my hand so hard it hurt. I knew if I let go I'd be swept away like a downy chick, fall into a canal, get pushed into a drain, who could say? I'd never see my Mama's face again. Masses of people plunged on and on – never ending. We were coming to the Palace Square and the River Neva.

That morning Mama had shaken me awake whispering in the early dark until I scrambled out of bed, caught up in her excitement. She plaited my hair, set out my wool dress, striped stockings, coat and hat before she slipped downstairs to pack ham and pickled cucumbers. She was never one to be cheerful at that hour on a winter Sunday but she joked as she tied my fur bonnet tight under my chin and wound my wool scarf around and chattered, breathless with anticipation. We told no-one where we were going, neither Papa nor our friend, Ksenia, none of the maids or servants, not the *ülemteener*, the butler, not a word. It wasn't the first time we'd been out secretly. I would never tell my brother or sister because however long the street: however sharp that wind, I would bathe in Mama's approval. I would see toys in the Nevsky shops and we would soon stop for hot chocolate. Gigantic signs hung along the street: spectacles over the optometrist, boots over the shoe-maker, a huge nutcracker shimmery with ice squeaked as it swung above the toy shop, but all the front doors were bolted shut. There were no carriages, no trams but I thought about the mug of hot chocolate I should get at the carnival.

"Warm are you, *karukene*?" The red felt flowers on Mama's hat trembled like summer poppies. We crossed the end of the bridge onto the giant curbs and iced pavements and I was still excited.

"Oh *jah*!" I said. Masses of people crowded, singing hymns, dirges, yelling, shaking fists or cheering. Russian words sound angry. I heard *strike, workers, rocks* and someone must have thrown one because something crashed and tinkled. Still I hoped we were going somewhere wonderful.

We'd walked from our friend Ksenia's house on Bolshaya Morskaya that morning and by the time the sun, milky-white, shone off windows and buildings the entire street was filled with people. The atmosphere was electric. There were other children too though none in a fur coat and hat like mine and no one as grand as my mother. I'd seen rag foot bindings and shrunken coats on the worst neglected people in Pärnu but never so many as here and I'd never felt so afraid. I kept close to Mama.

Banners crackled in the cold. Gold-haloed, painted saints in decorated helmets with despairing sad eyes flew over us.

As we crossed the Krásny Bridge I stopped and stared at the mermaids and serpents in the balustrades. Mama grabbed me with a frantic whispered, "Typhus!" so that I felt sick, not over the word, but her tone. The canal was a solid grey-yellow so we hurried over the bridge. My mittened hands were already tainted.

I could no longer feel my toes inside my precious mouse-fur lined boots and my fingers ached. I asked Mama if we had far to go. We had been walking forever since Bolshaya Morskaya.

"Wait. Wait and see," she told me. By then I could have cried with tiredness but I would not for Mama's sake. Children made faces at me and I became weary of the pushing and heaving. I longed to be back at Ksenia's sitting in the corner by the warm Dutch tiles sipping hot chocolate from one of her hand-painted cups with deer and swallows on the sides.

My mother said the march was for peace. She explained the banners as if I were adult. I listened but I searched for clowns and donkeys.

We neared the Great Square and Winter Palace. Mama livened up more while I watched the march of coats and laced-up basket slippers, *lapti*, felt boots, pass by. Mama gave me reasons and history while I listened to snow crunching and distant songs. At least there would be gypsies in red flared skirts, men with black moustaches, long hair and scarves. They'd play fast lively music on their fiddles and stamp to their drumbeats. There would be sad, sorry, chained-up bears, too. But there would be Grand Duchesses! In Pärnu every girl my age copied the duchesses and ran with a hoop and stick, rode a pony trap, and some even carried a box camera. I could do all that, plus knit with four colours, one after the other.

"He will listen," Mama insisted, though I was distracted when a furry head peeked from a man's coat pocket. I'd never before seen a ferret in a pocket. The man bared black teeth at me so that I tightened my hold on my mother's hand and snuggled into her side.

When my mother was cheerful the entire world was too. Now she was unafraid and bold. "The tsar will hear our demands, you'll see," she said as silver crosses and icons flashed and sparkled. I imagined Grand Duchesses silvered and glittering as well.

While Mama straightened my coat sleeves and tugged up my scarf I warmed up. The sun struck the boulevard. "It's about war.

Nobody wants war with Japan," Mama said.

"And duchesses?" I asked so that Mama smiled in the way she did for young children.

"Perhaps."

She indulged my sister Anna, my brother Kristjaan and me but in a moment she could completely forget us. I trusted Jutta, my nanny and Cook to know what I needed. Mama made decisions but it was Jutta who knew whether it was plums or strawberries that gave me stomach aches.

Mama would curl her hair, pluck her eyebrows or become engrossed in a romance novel and seem not to care for me. Some afternoons however, she drank from her crystal decanter with friends or else sat in her room with pills and bottles and told me to go away. That made me miserable.

The tsar, Mama would say, like everybody, had a job. Roosi brought us tea. Jutta looked after the children. Papa protected us, organised the factory, designed his beautiful inlaid furniture with rowan and cherry which he shipped beyond Danzig and Copenhagen. I had been in our factory. The smell of sawn wood reminded me of deep forests even if the glues made me dizzy. I held a piece of polished wood once, round and smooth as a bird, in the palm of my hand. I almost expected to feel its heart beat.

Mama's sister, *Tädi* Lulle's job was milking, planting, cutting the rye and hay, neither a day too soon nor a moment too late. With five children plus a crippled husband, even so she could pause, still as a painting, to find cloud berries at the edge of a marsh. Cloud berries, filled with goodness Lulle said, could keep her family well. If only they could pick enough to make jam to last through the winter. They were so blissful to taste that I could remember their scent and flavour.

I knew why Papa hadn't come with us that day; even so, I

begged Mama to explain why but she merely tossed her head and looked away. After a moment she said, “So, we disagree, Siina. Remember that a woman will do what she must. For goodness sakes, he is enjoying a ham omelette and second cup of coffee! Why should he mind?” She laughed so suddenly that the felt poppies bobbed on her hat.

Papa loved Mama’s attention – when it suited him. Otherwise he had no tolerance for being disturbed. He had been polite and cheery at Ksenia’s though he could burst into a rage and become silent and bad tempered as well. It made me feel bad when I couldn’t cheer him. Luckily Ksenia was a person who sensed what someone might say before they did. She calmed Papa and told him his feelings were cramped. I watched her caressing his fingers, soothing, saying it was his artistic nature. I adored Papa, I knew I always would, even though he and Mama had separate, opposite characters.

I became lost in my dreaming when I realised I’d let go Mama’s hand. There were black coats and shawls and felted boots in every direction. The poppies were gone. I panicked and began to cry. A Russian boy about my age, his blue eyes watering with cold, grabbed my arm, bold as brass, controlling me, shouting with a cracked voice, “This way!” I stumbled along with him until we saw Mama turning around and around in dread. She threw up her hands when she saw me, hugged me, then scolded me severely. I searched for the boy but he was gone.

I clung to Mama as we walked on together past a steaming heap of horse manure on the snow, sweet and rich, shining like black pudding. My legs turned to jelly, so close to the horses, and Cossacks! In battledress – magnificent, enormous men guarding the square, their great sabres clanking, their chests cinched with pistols and banded with bullets. We all knew about Cossacks, black-hearted men. They would whip anyone in their way, ride like centaurs and kill without flinching. They're the most loyal of guards, utterly, to the last breath, but they were not protecting us that day! Any Pärnu boy, older than me, a boy who could fight and swear and stay outside in the street past dark, after I was tucked up in bed, would run like a mouse if a Cossack were to gallop along Supeluse. I knew then there was to be neither dancing nor fairground and what Mama had said about Japan was true. War would come and we would get mixed up in it. When those huge horses snorted and stamped I almost let go my water in my pants inside all my underwear and wool and fur. I yanked Mama's hand and yelled as loudly as I could. I scampered from the square, fled from those horses and demon Cossacks and in my panic, tripped over my feet and nearly fell. Mama ran after me until between coats and legs I caught sight of the palace, its emerald green windows and cherry-red walls going on and on as far as a hundred school buildings, churches and barns together. Above all that, on the roof were statues, Greek or Roman: I'd seen pictures of such things. They wore armour vests or were draped and half naked. Mama was beside me, still and astonished as I. It was a *muinasjutt*, a fairy tale, crusted stone as decorated as an iced cake, more complicated than a lace shawl. From the rows of windows, below the fancy roof I willed a grand duchess to wave a hand or at least dip a pretty crowned head to us! On tip-toe I gazed, swayed, then crumpled, sprawling on the ground. Everything whirled and tipped around me. I looked up to a smiling, bearded face, a young man reaching his hand to me. He could have been one of Lulle's *sulaseid*, farm hands. His soft peaked hat shaded his eyes. His face seemed familiar. When he set me on my feet he tipped his cap to Mama. I should see how they liked one another, agreeing about the march, pleased there were so many, saying it was important and the biggest march ever. He said the great Petersburg factories were striking and hundreds, if not thousands of workers were marching. My mother kept smiling and nodding. He told her she was a rare woman.

"I don't blame them! I thought this would happen but even sooner," she said.

"You're an idealist!"

"I am."

He said he was Estonian, that he worked in Petersburg while at that moment the Kazan church bells rang for the end of the eleven o'clock service, so deafeningly that I couldn't hear another word until, "Pärnu. I used to work for the railways," he said.

"Ah, so. And we live near Ammende Villa," she said. Ammende Villa is a magnificent mansion surrounded by roses, begonias and trimmed lawns. There's nothing like it in Pärnu except for Katerina the Great's Kadriorg Palace, more grand yet. This man didn't care about it. He jack-knifed a bow, introducing himself.

"Juhan Priit," he told us, formal as any guest in our *saksatuba*, our parlour. He had a lot more to say to Mama about government, angry because so many were hungry and exploited and so on, for a long time. He was revolutionary. My mother agreed. She was mesmerised. She chattered on describing Russia's tragedy, mentioning Chaliapin who almost died in a gutter, while Juhan Priit talked about schools and poverty and workers without hope. Russia was obscenely wealthy, he said and I was sure that he looked at our clothes because we were not poor. I knew that we had woollen, lovely clothes especially my bonnet and my lined, German, mouse-skin boots.

"May I ask, Madame …?" he began.

"I am Maarja Jürimäe and this is my daughter, Siina." Mama

offered her hand and continued. “I come to Peterburg now and again with my husband. He arranges furniture sales for our factory,” she said and when Juhan took her hand and bowed again she said, “I believe in people’s rights and not war.”

“And we need more like you.”

“I admit it, and not the least because my cousins are fighting in Manchuria. Why should they go to war? They need to be planting and harvesting. That’s their work.”

By now the march had halted. We stopped and heard shouting though it was so distant it was more like a small piping bird. I leaned backwards and saw an angel on a great red pillar in the middle of the square. A fist of cloud blotted out the sun.

“Children and mothers are in front and we go in peace,” Juhan reassured us, nodded to Mama, and lifted me up on his shoulders so that I saw above the crowd. Juhan was tall so I could see a parade of guards around the red palace with its sparkling windows. It was incredibly beautiful but alas, there were even more soldiers, row upon row of them, kneeling, others, positioned behind, standing. I felt rather sick and I hung onto Juhan’s hat, my heart thumping away like a trapped rabbit, desperate to get down and run, only so afraid I couldn’t make a sound. A bugle blared.

“What now? What?” Mama yelled in her frightening voice.

The guards took aim. “Guns!” I screamed. “Shooting! Shooting!”

Mama grabbed at me but I clung to Juhan, too terrified to move.

Guns fired. People in the crowd fell. I saw them! It was killing and I would die. We were right there in front of those soldiers and guns. We would die. It was war! Bodies disappeared, shot, collapsing away. People stood one minute, the next, collapsed, bloodied and screaming. Cossacks galloped everywhere, swiping their deadly sabres above their helmets, arcing like fiery windmills, slashing and chopping, killing! I cried and screamed. I didn't want to die! I couldn't breathe but I screamed. I heard Mama calling me but I kept screaming until the strangest thing – the crowd roared in song. I imagined we'd escape but the truth was that people died, cut and bleeding. The Russian boy with watery blue eyes lay bleeding. His skinny body bled, dying.

Even Juhan didn't see what I saw, didn't understand my howling and panic at murder. I kicked and pulled his hat, his ears, his hair and yelled, "*Kasakad*! *Kasakad*!" until my throat ached and I saw a blade. "NO!" I screamed because my mother would lose her head like a sunflower in a hay field.

I can't remember after that. What I do remember was the angel on the top of the column showing her cross to the sky because that day many, many unready souls flew past on their way to heaven.

2. Hot Chocolate

Juhan must have flagged down a droshky from a side street off the Nevsky, I will never know. Somehow we got back to Bolshaya Morskaya through those murderous streets.

There was a great eruption at Ksenia's house. Papa furious; Mama collapsing still bleeding, Ksenia in charge; her mother-in-law in the way, breathless and tugging at us all, demanding to know what was to be done while my dying mother filled Papa's arms. I didn't notice when Juhan disappeared.

They took my mother into the front room, her blood trailing over Ksenia's precious carpets while Ksenia gave directions as if it was a performance, those ones when adults dressed as Egyptians and a murderer killed someone and disappeared. I had cried even though it was a play because Mama was killed. At the end she popped out from the curtain and we threw flowers. I was still full of sobs. Today was no performance and she would never get up to curtsey so I wouldn't let her go.

My father must have called the doctor while Ksenia and her maid pried me off my mother. The maid bundled me upstairs to get me warm, dry clothes. She was young and as upset as I, though when hot chocolate in a hand-painted cup arrived I was soothed. I had kept asking for it though I can't stand the sight or the smell of it since that day. I soon vomited chocolate all over the doll Ksenia had given me in the middle of all the jumble. I crushed it to my chest but after the sticky stinky mess, the maid tried to take the doll as well and I fought for it and pulled out some of the hair you could comb. In the end the maid cried too.

I managed to sneak downstairs, I was so desperate to see

Mama. Papa stopped me in the hall, his hands loose at his sides. He demanded to know where we'd been. I shivered with dread not knowing which secret to keep. He seemed to see into my heart. I was in shameful trouble but I managed to chatter about duchesses and he did not spank me.

"You are a child, Siina. What could you know?" he murmured at last, sadly, and reassured me that I was safe, his large grey eyes expressing forgiveness not reproach.

I feared Papa but also adored him. Had he been with us, Mama would never have been hurt. Even so I muttered lies.

"You went to Palace Square," he concluded. I felt weak and crumbly, afraid that Mama was dead in the front room, that I would be imprisoned for lying. Still I couldn't see her. My father stroked my hair and released me. The butler came to my side offering another drink. I held a hand to my mouth in case I should be sick while the maids huddled and whispered together about shooting and killing.

We stayed only a few more days with Ksenia. Mama rested. I wasn't allowed to see her. Every moment I thought she might die although I did forget her when I played with the wind-up-walking doll. To distract me, the young maid hit coloured balls with a little mallet in the hall.

Finally we were to go back to Pärnu.

Ksenia came into my room, her unbrushed ringlets bouncing, jasmine wafting from her white deep cleavage hardly covered in a purple burnoose. I imagined her a sun goddess even though she ducked in like a playmate. "Darling, you really are going. Shame. I love having you here." She kissed my forehead. "Take care of your mother. Be very good, yes?"

The brocade curtains had been opened and beyond layers of shutters, sleet drove at the windows. Icicles speared from the eaves.

"I will."

"I know. Thank god your Mama is progressing. She will be well. Next time you come we'll celebrate. You will yet see our wondrous sights!" Ksenia smiled brightly at me as if she had the power to heal with her blessings. "I thank the heavens every day that you're all safe," she said.

I hugged my quilt, struggling to sit up, wishing she would bend over and envelop me but she did kiss my forehead.

"Now you get downstairs because you're late for breakfast."

I didn't wait for the maid to come. I dressed myself in my favourite pink and yellow Muhu stockings and a soft knitted skirt and jacket with ribbons, ready for travelling. I would practically disappear by the time I got on my fur coat, hat and scarf and all the rest.

My parents sat together in the breakfast room. Mama was bundled into a dark blue cape to cover her bandages and whatever else was making her bulky. Papa set her food on her plate and cut it up and I heard them speak about the man who had brought us home, Juhan. Papa drew in a breath and paused, looking at me and I expected he would ask me a question but instead he picked up his coffee cup and gazed at Mama with hurt on his face.

I fidgeted with my ribboned jacket until at last Papa said, "Eat, *kullakene*," and waved me to the seat beside him. I was very glad to sit beside him from where I watched Mama, her fair hair twined with blue ribbons, her eyes dark and too pained to be interested in anything around her.

I took a little of everything onto my plate and ate like a mouse, furtively even when the table was covered with so much sliced boiled eggs, smoked fish, liver sausage, beetroot, rye and white bread rolls. Mama finally turned an anxious look on me and

I felt even more lonely and abandoned.

For the rest of the morning, maids and footmen bustled in and out of the hall with luggage. Ksenia's three dachshunds ran around yapping, and yelping whenever they got trodden on. Ksenia's mother-in-law, small and soft, with few words, drew me into the parlour, undid a box of draughts and we played a game. She asked about Kristjaan and Anna, whether we played chess, or snakes and ladders, and if I could ice skate or ride a bicycle. When I came to leave I was sorry to say goodbye. I thanked her and gave her a kiss on her wrinkled dry cheek.

Ksenia asked to see Mama and me before we left. She sat in a high-backed, studded chair in her dark-walled parlour. Something wooden, brass or marble filled every last space in that room. I stared around as we paused before our journey. Ksenia had tea poured and followed by listing all that we would do next time we came, when Mama was recovered. Despite Mama's silence Ksenia bubbled on, sure that soon we would return and all would be well. She would take us to the Fabergé shop filled with jewels, snuff boxes, emerald and ruby necklaces and studded eggs and to the bazaar of the Gostinny Dvor. We had to see the real, refined . Turning to me she described the toy shop on the Nevsky. A tiny train ran all the way around the room over bridges through tunnels and minuscule wooden towns with street lamps that lit up, under fir-covered mountains and farms with pigs and teeny chickens. I was sure to love it, Ksenia promised.

I was to keep the wind-up doll with its satin dress and a slot for a key to move its arms and legs.

When we said our goodbyes, kissing and hugging, Ksenia whispered, “Go safely. Be well,” and again, “Look after your mummy,” before puckering up her lips for a soggy kiss and giving me a hard hug.

LEAPING THE FIRE

"Come home to Pärnu," Mama said.

"In summer," Ksenia agreed although I didn't believe her.

By the time we stepped in the door at Supeluse, Mama's face was as white as an Italian mask and she needed powders. She had a headache, was hurt everywhere and shivered. I could not say goodnight nor kiss her. Jutta, my nanny, took charge of me and made sure of it.

"Your Mama must sleep. Now tell me about the lovely things in Peterburg, not the other."

Of course Jutta knew about Bloody Sunday and she forbade me talk about it but she did want to hear about the rest of Peterburg. My eyes watered and my words turned to *sült* when I thought back. I could no longer see Ksenia's ceilings, her carved Parisian mirrors or silver crusted icons without blood.

"Oh come. Tell me, *tibukene*. I've never been," Jutta encouraged.

I refused to tell Jutta about Peterburg but that didn't stop me remembering. I pictured cherry walls and emerald windows, the massive red tower with the angel and Cossacks charging with bloodied sabres. However much I tried to push away the memories I could not. Alone in our playroom I collected my brother Kristjaan's lead soldiers, took them to the outhouse and dropped them into the dark smelly hole, one by one, plop, plop, plop, plop. After, I felt rather better.

Even so, I hated bedtime and the dreams, the panic, the exhaustion from running. At least when my sister Anna was there I felt safe because I was definitely home.

Mama and Papa argued loudly so that I heard, and while I pretended it didn't matter it made me angry. I took Mama's scissors from her sewing basket and cut the wind-up doll's dress into shreds. I chopped off her hair too and hid the doll. After that I forgot about Ksenia as well.

After Mama recovered she held lunches and teas with friends. They drank tea from the samovar and dark wine from the decanter. Once again she worked on her embroideries in the bay-window of the *saksatuba* making table runners and serviettes. I watched her silver thimble flash but she would not pat the seat for me to sit beside her. Once she had explained to me about her silk stitches, the stars and crosses and how to make invisible joins. She had described Paris too, from where the silk thread came, and how women there strolled in the parks with parasols, their poodles and Afghan hounds on leashes. Couples would go coasting though the Bois de Boulogne in gleaming varnished carriages. Children in white lace dresses spun on carousels forever going in circles. We would go there one day, Mama said. Without Anna and Kristjaan because they were too small. Just Mama and I would go. But after that awful day Mama never talked about such things. She was unhappy with me.

When Jutta was upstairs putting Kristjaan down for a sleep one afternoon I tugged on my boots and coat and went outside. Someone had built a teetering snowman on the path. The mouth had softened into a sagging maw. I disliked the coal eyes. They were like Cossacks' eyes. I jabbed and stabbed with a stick I found. I gouged and kicked the snowman until Jutta came outside and scolded me for howling at a snowman. She shuffled me inside and reprimanded me. "Pneumonia, Siina! What are you doing, my child?" I hadn't put on my gloves. My hands were raw and red. Neither had I put on my hat and scarf. I cried that nobody cared about me but Jutta scolded me even further. I was lucky to have everything. I was naughty to complain and make a fuss. I should have listened but instead I stared at Jutta's slippers. They were embroidered by her aunt in Hiiumaa and there were angry colours of red and orange and vivid yellow.

"The tsar does NOT look after us!" I shouted back at Jutta.

"Well now, he's supposed to and it's a shameful disgrace! He is in charge, isn't he? And he did let all that murder happen! Still, now, you're just a little girl and you can't go telling me all that's wrong with our tsar, can you? You're to do as you're told, you are. So come now. Let's take off those wet boots and not be so silly. Let's forget it."

I sniffled and shrugged at Jutta and swallowed more tears but when she bobbed down and held me in her arms saying, "There, there," that simply made me cry all the more.

Ordinary soldiers appeared all over Pärnu after that, on horseback and foot, on Supeluse and *Aia tänav*, marching through the parks and gardens and standing on street corners smoking cigarettes because there were meetings in Pärnu. I heard whispers.

"Protesters will destroy the cellulose plant and there'll be huge trouble," Papa fumed. Protesters were disaster for our factory. At dinner Papa sipped fish and dumpling soup and dabbed his beard with Mama's embroidered serviette.

I hated fish soup but I ate it quickly because apple and rhubarb pie followed.

Mama became even thinner. "They're so organized?" she questioned my father. She'd lift the fine fair hair from an eyebrow and ask him to explain the logic of the protest when everyone would lose money, most of all the workers who needed it. She had become lighter and glassier. One day she would shatter into pieces.

"We don't trust anyone, Maarja, my dear. There's no telling a protester from a spy, a conservative from a capitalist, is there?

They have their arguments and each thinks they're right. Workers demand money, revolutionaries think they speak for all. Be careful, always."

Mama nodded and allowed a wrinkle to form on her pale brow.

"People go missing. Textile workers, teachers. Anyone," Papa said from the sideboard.

"I know," Mama admitted.

I understood *going missing*. We all did. We worried about friends, parents, a neighbour who might vanish. Still, we lived like anyone, anywhere, with excitement and disappointment, elation, frustration and sometimes, happiness.

3. The Meeting **Pärnu**

When I heard the shuffle and stamp of men coming in our front door I wondered if we were having a birthday party. I hadn't been dressed up to meet guests or bob a curtsey even though I sometimes greeted visitors before I went upstairs to bed. I would listen to their laughing and singing until I could no longer keep my eyes open. This night did not look like a party. I recognised no one, plus they were awfully serious. It was likely one of Papa's meetings and I didn't want to miss out. I crept downstairs and squeezed in the hall alcove before Jutta could notice. Men shrugged off coats and jackets, tugged away scarves and hats and kicked off galoshes. A bank clerk from Nikolai Street, a worker in a grey cap with no tie, a student in a dark navy uniform, the blacksmith I recognized from Rüütli Street, they all crammed into the hall through the glass doors into the parlour. A thin, monocled man noticed me and jerked his head, a one-eyed stork about to strike its prey.

"So," he whispered, bent double. His moustache was perfumed like a flower garden. "Ah so, you're the clever one." His voice was saw-edged and he spoke as if I were just a child. I was transfixed by his monocle in case it fell from his eye socket and swung on the black ribbon but I expected he'd pinch my cheek. "It's man-talk. Watch what you say," he joked but with a slipperiness that made my mouth sour.

In came a young man, blond hair falling from under his cap and down to his shoulders. Juhan! I barely stopped a squeal. My knight! My friend! Only he brought with him that day and the feelings I hadn't felt in a long time but which now sickened me. I shrank into the alcove between excitement and horror. Juhan never saw me. He went about greeting and nodding to the other men. He did not shake hands with the monocled man.

When I heard a thump on the stairs I peeked out to see. It was Mama, stumbling down the stairs, her hair loose, her dressing gown falling open, linen, white lace and curves, my mother. One knee led as if she were a ballerina preparing for a *rond de jambe* until she fell against the wall and Juhan bounded forward.

“I’m all right.” A hand went to her head, her eyes weepy, her skin paper-white. Juhan folded his arms around her. He was tall I remembered and she, small and light.

“Sir. Sir! I’ll take care of the *proua*. Thank you,” Roosi went pushing between them though Juhan didn’t let go of Mama right off and even as Roosi took her upstairs, Juhan kept hold of her with his eyes.

“Peterburg. If the water doesn’t kill you the police will,” the monocled man growled over his shoulder as he entered the *saksatuba*.

“What?” Juhan swung to him.

“In the Estonian contingent were you? Some want socialism, don’t they. Idiots. You know her?”

“Not at all. She needed support.”

I held my chin in my hands, wondering what they meant. Across the hall, through the glass doors, I could see into the *saksatuba* to a grey-haired man with a trimmed beard who managed a linen factory. I’d met him once. The man beside him I knew was a fisherman from Kihnu Island that lay low on the horizon, visible from Pärnu Beach. He’d go galloping home across the ice in winter. Sleighs packed with goods with families rugged up to their eyes would take the ice road, pass fishermen sitting still for hours, their eyes fixed on the holes they’d drilled, hoping to catch a seal.

Our neighbour was in the room too, in suit and tie, talking to our baker from Rüütli Street. I loved his egg-glazed bacon and cabbage *pirukad* and the honeyed soft white *sai* he baked.

When the men were all seated my father pulled the glass doors together but I could hear some of what they were saying. I'd find out what adventures they were planning.

"We're reasonable," I heard my father say after they'd talked for a time. They poured their own tea and vodka. "If Tõnisson says we can be as civilized as the French or the Swedish, I say why not? We're no hot-heads." My father looked around, chin angled, demanding attention, expecting agreement.

"You wouldn't expect anyone to be reasonable after Sunday. No one is! The country is in an uproar, not just me!" Juhan's argument came in quick, short bursts. "The *keiser's* done for, can't you see? We must move now!"

My father continued without raising his voice. "Perhaps so, but we're patient, young man. We will negotiate…we will become our own leaders, within the system. This is the way to improve life for us all, worker and farmer, so that we maintain what we have! Think Mr Priit! We'll go carefully and prudently." I saw my father hold Juhan's gaze.

"There'll be a bloody fight, that's what there'll be," Juhan burst. "There's no stopping the rage that's brewing, *härra* Jürimäe. And no wonder, don't you say? After so long that we've been held down!"

"No. Not at all. There'll be negotiation. That's what." My father continued as mild as ever as if he spoke for all.

I tugged the coat hems around my ears but I leaned forward. If only Juhan were my brother, and Papa and he agreed. If only they would not fight.

"But of course *härra,* we're committed to the same thing," Juhan reasoned. He sat back in his chair, his tone controlled, matching my father's.

"But not the same methods." My father circled his forefinger.

"But we will certainly discuss methods," Juhan replied.

Papa stood deliberately. He folded his arms and began to pace in front of Juhan. "We all have reasons for change. We each have views but let's not look at our differences."

"But we must act, now," Juhan said more forcefully, each word a stone in a sack.

"No, not confrontation. We work discreetly. We have resources and intelligence. We have what we need. But not with haste, *härra* Priit. We know the tsar tolerates Tõnisson. And our party. We can work together. This is far more productive. This will give us success."

Juhan jumped up now. He threw his arms in the air. "Not me. I stand for others here. We workers want, and need local autonomy. Rich factory owners, perhaps they can wait. They may have their resources but workers do not. Some families, *härra* Jürimäe, haven't a crumb on the table!" Juhan turned to his seat, reached for his vodka and downed it. He leaned over and took a handful of candied almonds from the centre of the table and tossed them down his throat.

"Yet there will be plenty for everyone when we reorganise. The land, the resources. We have the will. We have the power to do this. We will use our negotiating power, and not force an issue."

"But tomorrow, tomorrow when they cut the lights and power at the Dvigateli plant, all of Tallinn will seethe. What then, *härra*? What? Patience and understanding?" Juhan opened his hands to the men in the room daring anyone to disagree. "Do you really think so?"

I wanted to jump up and dash in and cheer for him but I was afraid for my father – afraid he might lose.

"No, *härra*. It's too soon," he said, composed as ever.

"But for solidarity, *härra*?"

My father waved his hand as though Juhan was a horsefly. "You shall have your moments for glory *härra* Priit, believe me. But not just yet."

"I'm not looking for glory. I mean to support my comrades!" Juhan retorted.

My father, , lowered his head. "But you're early! We will work the system and freedom will follow. Men in the Dumas are already listening. They know what we want. You'll simply get arrested, *härra*. So, you'll end up in Siberia faster than a bullet and what use will you be to us? Ah? We *must* maintain our ideals. A government with a say, a winning argument, that's the way to bend the *keiser*." My father sat, downcast, his hands folded in his lap.

I crawled to the glass doors. I had to warn Juhan. I had to tell him he could be shot in the heart or slashed to pieces in Tallinn. I thanked heaven Papa wasn't going. He might yet scold me. I feared him, but I ached for his affection too, to sit on his knee, to hear his praise. And I loved him for his wisdom.

"Juhan Liiv's *independence*, tomorrow!" Juhan thrust his glass in the air for our poet, he, Liiv who predicted that we would have our own state, while he, at times, thought he was the king of Poland.

The long-bearded man looked away from Juhan. The councillor stared at his drink. The Kihnu fisherman stroked his chin. My father took off his glasses and massaged his eyes.

"We need you, Juhan. We need you. Every man with a head

and a pair of feet must work for independence. If the police march you off with a pistol to your throat what use are you to our cause?"

I clutched my knees tightly to stop myself from leaping up.

"I'll have said my piece!" Juhan chinked his glass onto the table. I covered my ears.

"Stay for your dream, for all of ours!" Papa stepped over to Juhan, laid a hand on his shoulder and the monocled man stood up.

"Mr Priit, you're in the wrong meeting! The radicals and communists meet elsewhere."

"Such shit!" Juhan spat.

"But yes. The 'noses' are everywhere, *härra* Priit."

I gnawed at my fingernails.

"I'm no spy!" Juhan shook a fist, controlling his anger.

"Ah, but we know your type. You're in every meeting in every town, listening and recording."

"*Nuhk* yourself!"

"Oh no, I wouldn't care for it." The monocled man bowed like a stage actor and I wanted to hit him.

"And the rumblings have barely begun I tell you. *All the Russias* is doomed." Juhan's eyes rolled like a drunken man's. I was sure he would march to Tallinn.

"Papa!" I heard myself. "Härra Priit!" I cried as I fell against the doors, banging them open, as I went tumbling into the centre of the whole important men's secret protest meeting.

"What?" my father boomed.

"Don't …" I cried as he grabbed me around the waist and hauled me along the carpet. I struggled like a pig going to slaughter.

"What's this? What? First your mother, now you? In god's

name, what are you doing?" he fumed while I kicked, frantic because I should never disobey my father yet I was afraid for him, afraid for Juhan, and just as much, terrified for myself.

4. Lilacs

Papa did not go marching. There were meetings in our house every week but I did not see Juhan again. I was confined to my room for three days for eavesdropping. I dug out my wind-up doll and scolded her. I was to practise Gothic German script for hours as punishment. I folded a page in half and wrote a German word on one side, Estonian on the other. One day, I imagined, I could be a teacher. My work was precise and neat and Jutta admired it. She had been reprimanded too, for allowing me to sneak away.

I could hardly wait for Easter. Preparations began weeks ahead. We kept the usual customs though we didn't pray and hardly ever went to church but we recognised Shrove Tuesday, the day we farewelled winter. I saw summer spreading sunshine all over us like lingonberry jam on the centre of warm rye. We still wore stockings and scarves. On *Vastlapäev*, Anna and I went sliding with our friends down the small slope at the city park, as fast and far as we possibly could, because the further girls and women slid, the longer the flax would grow and the growers would get rich. Men cheered us on. After getting so hot and excited and worn out, I remembered that at home, were *vastlakuklid*, cardamom-flavoured yeast buns of white, flyaway flour, scooped out in the centre and filled with hazelnut paste and whipped cream. I had dreamed of *vastlakuklid* every day of the week but they were as sacred as eggs at Easter and candles at Christmas.

Snowdrops pricked green tips through the muddy earth, the

smell of old snow remaining. The next day the after taste of *vastlakuklid* was in my mouth. I followed Mama who led me around the garden. She had tied a print cotton cap on the way a farmer's wife did.

"What happened to *härra* Priit?" I asked her as I took lilac off-cuts from her gloved hand.

"What a question!" She tucked stray hair under her cap.

"Did he go to the protest?"

Mama lowered the secateurs. "Why do you ask about what you do not understand, Siina?"

"Why do you cut lilacs? Did he go to Tallinn? He could get killed. Did they put the lights out?" I scuffed back and forth on the path.

"He didn't." She snapped a twig.

"And Papa! He won't go." I stood still to stare at my mother.

"And I thank god for that." She snipped and snapped.

I tugged her linen skirt. "Mama, when they all stop arguing and protesting, can we go to the country? Can we stay with *Tädi* Lulle and my cousins?"

Mama smiled briefly. "You'd like that."

I nodded. She stroked my hair with her gloved hand. "We're all permitted to question sometimes. And reason."

It was that week when Cook wrapped eggs in onion skins, tied them up with rags and boiled them. Unwrapped, they were swirled soft gold-brown as if caught in waves and clouds. We children rubbed them with bacon fat so they shone like silk. Next, Cook gave us plain eggs and with tiny brushes, we painted stars and crosses, deer and chickens, though they looked more like snails.

As Cook and Roosi undid muslin bundles filled with drying

cottage cheese separating from the day before, they forgot about us sitting quietly at the far end of the table. They pounded the cottage cheese with great spoons, stirred in eggs, sugar and dried fruit, brought out wooden moulds to press it into a pyramid. They gossiped and chattered non-stop. A teacher on Supeluse, five doors away had been arrested. Secret police, I heard. No one knew why except he was a protester. I waited for the moment Cook would remember me, and the spoon and bowl she'd set aside that I could lick. Even more misery filled me as I listened. Papa might never come home and even if he did, he might be arrested before we set eyes on him. At last Cook looked our way.

"Here we are! You help clean the spoons and bowls. Lovely!" she said.

When the first *lumekellukesed*, snowdrops, broke through swollen earth, the days lengthened. My parents drank bilberry tea in the parlour, their voices lulling me to sleep. I dreamed they were saying *we will win.*

Like every child I longed for the end of snow although soon after there would be rain and fog. When green shadows tipped our trees I felt surges of happiness. Like every small plant and animal growing into spring a pulse rushed through me – summer was coming. Cornflowers mingled with rye in the fields yet our country boiled with rebellion.

Crows foraged for nests. Honey-scented narcissi crept through the borders of our paths. Mama was well, braided her hair and coiled it up, finished reading Schiller, took Kristjaan to Rüütli Street where she bought curling tongs and a book with a fat man sitting cross-legged drawn on the cover who, neither a god nor a philosopher, knew the path to peace.

"Buddhism," Mama said.

She also brought Max and Moritz for us and we laughed at the stories, regardless of the horror – two naughty boys trying to drown the tailor, and blow up their teacher, but who meet their end finally and properly themselves, ground in the mill for duck food.

When the sun hovered above the islands of Pärnu Bay my parents would sit between the raspberry canes, the night merely a shadow. Sometimes they played their gramophone outside and even danced. I would stir in sleep in the upstairs bedroom, aware of their murmurs and the gramophone starting up again.

Anna and I no longer wore stockings. We went barefoot in cotton skirts. Outside we lay on a rug on the lawn. If rain pelted down it was warm, summer rain.

October was the last chance to find *tatikud*, the best mushrooms.

"When can we go?" I asked Mama. "You love them."

"I think you love them, Siina. We'll get them at Lulle's. Or from the market."

That month Moscow railway employees went on strike, plus workers from across the entire Russian Empire.

"What now?" I heard Mama say. "What will happen?"

Papa closed his book. "The tsar will listen."

Hurrah! So, everyone would agree – if the tsar listened this time, the men in the Dumas would agree. *All the Russias* would not fall! Mama and Papa would be happy and there would be no more whisperings about men disappearing. Hurrah! We'd go and stay with my cousins in the country. Perhaps I'd ride Lulle's Tori horse! Hurrah! Hurrah!

A week later Papa packed his leather bag and called our

driver. A mass meeting was to be held in Tallinn. Another meeting. Another protest. If Papa believed that the tsar would listen, then he must! Anyway, the workers were permitted to protest.

I waited outside the parlour as Papa explained. “Gustav Suits believes we’ll be European *and* Estonian. We are that cultured.”

“Self-government!”

“Exactly.”

“You’ll be arrested.”

“No. No.”

“I’ll come too.”

“No. I’ll be back in a few days,” Papa said and kissed Mama on the forehead. “You go to your sister Lulle.” He took her hands and held them.

I scrammed upstairs to the bedroom. The tsar would listen, so I tried to believe but could not.

Three days later Papa hadn’t returned. I watched Mama to see what to do.

“We’ll go to Lulle,” she told me at breakfast. She laid her hand under her breast, the old wound. “I ache,” she said, took to her bed and stayed there the rest of the day.

We would go to Lulle and Papa would come home. Granny would be sure he would, and everything would turn out well. My cousins would take me on terrifying adventures and play daring games as always, and there were no soldiers and secret police on the farm. They were in Pärnu.

5. *Mustsada*

I dreamed I was flying without wings above thatches and forests, my cousins running barefoot in the snow below. Winter-coated horses, pigs, sheep and cattle raised their heads to look at me. I flew on and on, higher and higher until everything below became pinpricks. In one mighty dive I plunged, eyes streaming, ears popping.

I woke, leapt out of bed and without waiting for Jutta to warm my stockings on the Delft-blue tiles of our stove, I tied my hair up, pulled on layers of skirts and the felted cardigan Granny had made, and ran downstairs.

Aunt Lulle's farm in the far north of Pärnumaa, would be cold. It was hours from Supeluse.

In the kitchen, Cook was washing pigs' feet, laying them carefully side by side on the whitened pine table. "But no one told me you're going," she muttered. "I'd have had *sült* ready for your family and god knows they'd appreciate it." She circled the table, stirred porridge one minute, lifted the stove lid and checked firewood, returned to the pigs' feet and admired them.

"Are there ginger biscuits?"

"I'd have given you enough for them all if I'd known sooner," Cook grumbled and went rummaging in the pantry. "Salted herring, lingonberry preserves. Here -." She gave me a ginger biscuit. My mother was clicking along the hall in high-heeled boots to us. After skewering her hat with a pin she took me by the shoulders, inspected my hair, dress and boots.

"Your coat? Your books, your school work?" she said.

"I have them."

Cook passed the muslin package to us. "I hear the barons are leaving the countryside."

"And we're going there," Mama replied stiffly. "Come, the droshky. Say goodbye now," she said with a little smile. Her lips were glossy with glycerine and beeswax, her cheeks powdered. Cook swiped her hands on her apron and bobbed a proper goodbye.

Anna and Kristjaan sat on the stairs, Jutta between them holding their hands. They would see Papa return before I did. "We'll miss Papa when he comes home," I said to Mama.

"I know, I know," Mama said as we climbed into the droshky. We blew kisses, shouted goodbye and Merry Christmas to my sister and brother.

"Come back quickly," Anna shouted as Jaak stacked bags and blankets on the back, tied down the canvas flap and soon we juddered away over frosted cobbled streets, past parks and hushed schools, across Kuninga and Rüütli to the Tallinn Highway. I counted thirty seven soldiers, guns slung over shoulders though they were neither marching nor saluting.

"Mama...?"

"It's nothing." She stroked my cheek.

"But the barons ..?"

"Not for us to worry. No-one will bother us. No questions now."

The steel of our wheels bit ice as we jigged away. Soon there were houses asleep in the shining white distance from the road and smoke belching from sugared roofs set further and further apart across snow-covered meadows between forest stands. Horses in shaggy winter coats roamed fields or sheltered at hay-filled stalls. A farm woman reached into her earth cellar and filled a bag with food.

Four jet-black horses came at us from around a bend, a wide saggy carriage flinging from side to side behind. I grabbed Mama's hand. Robbers! Our carriage lurched close to a ditch. I saw the travellers – a woman in a green fur bonnet and a bearded man.

"Barons," Mama said squeezing my hand and after that the road was straight, with nothing but tired horses and carts, one full of sacks, another with sheep and pigs.

"But why are the barons…?"

"They will never own us," Mama said.

"Uncle Kert will still be in bed?"

"A broken back doesn't mend, *kallikene*. They tried every fern, herb and mud cure."

I'd never seen Uncle Kert on his feet though his children talked about when he mowed and rode and planted. Now he groaned from his bed. At hay making it was especially loud – when everyone pulled for all they were worth, Lulle, the children, a Polish worker, a girl from Kallaste, the sauna man, even me, I helped to get food ready. Plus we all watched in case it rained. We prayed for the sun to stay high, the sky to remain cloudless and the stooks soon to be dry. All day, from the milky morning, the dew still damp, until the sun hovered low above the horizon, everyone mowed, raked and sweated. Once Kert had cut graceful strokes for longer hours than anyone with Lulle, had harvested the wild summer meadows along the river and around the ancient trees, scything a rhythm together. Now he lay helpless, repeating his story of mending the roof thatch and falling. I dreaded seeing him but had to go in his room, stinky as an outhouse, however much Lulle and her girls cleaned and mopped. We all knew he was in pain and depression but he couldn't talk about it. I tried not to stare but I hated his complaints, the chords he played over and over, roaring drinking songs, moaning love songs until Granny would yell, "Enough!"

"You, too!" he'd return. Still, I kept believing that one day he would come walking out of his bedroom and all would be as it once was.

The fur rug slipped from my knees as our carriage jogged on and I woke from dreaming. Iced trees blurred past, a frozen stream wound around a barn, a stone bridge led off to the side. I wished something would move; a lynx, a fox, a wolf. Instead we came closer to windmill sails, frozen, hanging from a great wooden tower like a stuck ship, like nothing in my dream. Papa should be on his way home now. He should not stand up and make a fuss.

Soon I recognised the pole of Lulle's well spiking above fences, between trees, then the grain-drying house and a small building, the summer kitchen. To one side the farm house ran on and on, at one end the barn and further, the little house, the privy. I hated going there in dark driving snow. Frightening thoughts. Papa might be beaten or arrested. Mama and I would never see him again. I didn't say a word. I sat quietly, not to upset Mama and shook my legs awake. "Ponies!" I said "Look! Look! Are they ours?"

Mama smiled. "I think so!" The ponies, alongside us behind the diagonal fence, lifted and shook their shaggy heads. I wanted to ride. By myself.

We turned into the farm gate and there stood Lulle on her wooden porch, waving, layers of shawls wrapped around her and her baby. She was fuller in the hips and bosom than my mother, her hair heavier and darker. Her voice carried across courtyards and meadows unlike Mama's. Lulle was single-minded but so was my mother. Lulle spoke out quickly as if she had no need to think, more than Mama. Lulle and Granny knew everything about herbs to heal everyone in the *küla*. They prepared the dying, removing the feather pillow from under their heads.

I bobbed a curtsey to my aunt, who looked sideways at my mother. "*Saksa*! German!" Lulle remarked. She didn't approve but Mama did. Helve, standing back, tugged at her sweater, stretched her legs and mirrored me but avoiding my eyes even when I spoke. She flicked her pigtails, plaited with blue wool while our mothers gossiped, laughing, Mama taking Lulle by the elbow, turning her this way and that. My mother was always afraid that Lulle worked too hard and didn't eat enough but she looked wonderful, so did Helve and Annika. They looked mischievous as well.

"Yes but just for show," I explained though Lulle shook her head and hugged me off my feet and even Helve laughed as we stepped over the high threshold into the house to the familiar smells of hay and smoke and the family.

When Granny saw me her face folded in a toothless grin. She called me to her, her voice hoarse from smoking, her clothes reeking of tobacco. She was sharp as a knife and afraid of nothing. She expected her grandchildren to do chores without complaining, quickly and perfectly. I hung on what she said because she missed nothing and remembered everything. She had taught Lulle and Helve to weave, knit, sew and dye deep, fast colours. She led them to precious plants, mushrooms and herbs, describing each, the fatal and life-saving doses. I could never be sure of all the places snow berries and chanterelles grew or quite where watery channels shifted through the marsh but she reminded us, mostly at bedtime. Children drowned in marshes – sank, never to be found. I would call out every few moments walking through the *soo* with Helve and Annika. Even on the edge I would remember drowning stories. Grown-ups could lose their way, too. I was long cast under her spell and I loved her.

Granny's pin point eyes sparkled as she squeezed my fingers. "You've come for St Thomas's and you'll see Epiphany," she said as Helve stood over us, her hands on her hips, her little sister Annika and her brothers watching and waiting. She ordered me to follow, so Granny grinned at me and slipped my fingers from hers.

My cousins gawked at the shine of my patent-leather boots, the sheen of my silver buttons. Helve flicked her braids before grabbing my floral bag together with Mama's pigskin. I trailed after her to a room with a bright, striped rag rug on the wooden floor and fir branches tied to the window catches for Christmas. Helve dumped our bags on a pine trunk covered with poker work and stacked high with fleeces. The bed was smoothed flat with an embroidered blanket with yellow and orange flowers. The pillows were filled to bursting. I would share the bed with Mama as long as we stayed. I pushed my fist into the pillow and feathers drifted lazily. "We throw hay up in the rafters. We get a bigger harvest if it sticks there," Enn explained, laughing and jumping while Helve continued like a parish school teacher.

"Real silver?" She fingered my buttons.

I nodded.

"You can read Russian and German?"

"Yes!"

"Me too."

"I'll show you my books," I said, which made her smile such that I noticed her large white teeth.

"Work first, play after," she snapped and we all trooped after her to the main hall.

Mama and Lulle stood shoulder to shoulder, Lulle stirring the beetroot and meat soup, my favourite, Mama whispering in her ear. Their faces were red from the stove. I lounged with Granny as Lulle and Mama gossiped. “Barons are scuttling. *Mustsada*,” a poisoned word.

“*Mustsada*?”

“Talk, talk,” Granny muttered.

“Who are they?”

“Why care? You’re a little girl, Siina. Besides, nobody knows. I tell you, they won’t hurt us, don’t worry.” Granny bent away to search in her tobacco pouch, taking out her pipe.

6. Juhan

The wind howled in the pine trees and whistled over our roof. Shadows from the candles jumped around the moss-filled log walls. Thoughts of robbers and *Mustsada* filled my head. Hardi and Enn took out their knives and began whittling, I picked up my knitting, stripes of yellow and green, one day to be a thin lumpy scarf. I knitted two stitches together to make a hole, cast on extra for gathers and puzzled over the stitches. Granny opened her tobacco pouch and stuffed, then lit her pipe. Next to her box-bed she set down a potato drink.

Helve read *Tales for Alyonushka*, Mama and Lulle threaded mushrooms to dry in the smokiness over the fire. They whispered, smiling and nodding to one another. When Murri, Granny's dog, growled and bared her teeth, I lost a stitch.

"Someone outside." Enn jumped up. Lulle snatched the axe from behind the door.

A man's voice called. "Please! Open up!"

Hardi took down the scythe from the wall and stood to one side of his mother's raised axe. I didn't dare look outside, my legs were jelly.

"Who are you?" Lulle's voice like a storm.

"A bed for the night," came the reply.

"Go away!" Lulle stared at the door.

"I'm on my way home – to Pärnu."

Lulle swung around at Mama. Mama shook her head.

"He'll freeze," Granny muttered. Lulle took a step to the window to tug aside the curtain.

My legs were light as string as I sprang across to the door and heaved open the great wooden bolt. “Siina!” Enn yelped. Hardi grabbed the back of my jacket as the door swung open and a man ducked under the lintel. Dark blood streaked his sleeves and blackened ice dripped from his hat and eyebrows.

Murri pranced back and forth excited, lunging, snarling in a maddened frenzy.

I gaped. Juhan!

He tugged off the fur and his coat all the while looking around, at me and Mama and more warily, around the room. He stripped off his gloves and hat and bowed.

“*Kaaslased*,” he said, his blue eyes returning to Mama and me. “Thanks.”

Mama sat back on the bench, her hands in her lap, Lulle lowered the axe.

“You’re a friend and come a way.” Lulle held on to the axe but pointed one hand to the table and tureen. “We have soup.”

I slunk back to Granny who grasped my wrist, pinching my skin.

“I’ve not come so far today, but surely you’ve heard.” Juhan laid his gloves and hat on the side of the stove and lowered his eyes. “You’ve not been outside? Not seen the blazing sky?” He turned solemnly from one to the other, Enn, Hardi, Helve and Annika, Mama, Lulle, even Granny.

Enn spoke up with a quaking voice. “I did. It was fiery bright. Only two nights ago,” he said as he searched for a sign from his mother.

Juhan sank onto the bench, took the heel of bread and dipped it in our soup. He tore at it hungrily. “The sky burned for *versts*, from Polaris to Antares,” he said still eating, sweeping an arc with the bread.

“You’re not *Mustsada*!” Lulle paced. I’d have sat beside

Juhan but Granny's fingers were wired around mine.

"Good god no. But manors were torched," he said.

Mama jumped up. "You've done murder," she growled, me guessing her words they were so low.

"Konstantin Päts had to flee! We're needed. We farm workers. Pärnu friends, too. They knew what was up. I didn't. Not yet."

Lulle and Mama glanced at one another. I knew the look, when they were about to slit a pig's throat. The *sulane* or Kert used to do that but now that, and so much more, was Lulle's work.

Juhan looked at his soup and sucked the bread. A railway worker from Pärnu who spoke for freedom, education and the decent treatment of workers had burned a manor. I tugged Granny's hand and shook her arm. I asked with my eyes.

"So, tell us, Juhan." Lulle leaned on the axe.

Juhan's gaze lingered on Annika but none of us were going anywhere. We would hear it all in this house. He faced Lulle. "Our history will be told after. We gathered like an army, you see. We all brought demands; to the *mõisnik* for a start, for decent conditions and treatment, better than animals, *ja*? And you'd know all about that, yes?"

Lulle stopped swaying, nodded for Juhan to continue. "Of course, yes! Nothing is forgotten."

Juhan glanced at Mama, still as a fish in a frozen pond. I barely breathed.

"They were long overdue, those demands. One rest day a week? Fair rent?"

"So?"

Juhan raised his eyes and hummed – *Manor houses will burn. Germans will die*. "You'd think he'd have taken us seriously. You'd think he'd have listened."

Lulle shook her head. “Don’t suppose he did.”

Juhan sipped the last of the soup. “The men were already decided. They came prepared, I tell you. I didn’t think we were going to … hurt him. Threaten, of course!” He wiped his mouth with his sleeve. “We were ready, I mean, revolutionary songs on every lip. I should have realised.”

“But you dared!” Lulle murmured.

“Dared? Those men pulled up a red flag. Dared? Armed to the teeth, not only guns but forks and rakes and pikes.” Juhan took a knife and stroked it over the bread. “We closed in on him but he stood there, defiant, no fear. Worse, no shame!” Juhan opened his hands to the room as if he were a baron.

Enn and Hardi bobbed on their haunches, their knives loose in their fingers. Helve twisted her braids, her cheeks red. Annika snuggled up to her. I closed my eyes. A drop of water hissed on the stove top.

“Right there on his fine porch, oh so grand, his belly filling out his brocade waistcoat, marked and stained, his silver watch and chain swinging. We watched. The way his breeches stuck inside and outside his boots, untidy, lazy when he might have been a model citizen. Arrogant as a lord but uneducated. Oblivious to our stand. He said nothing, not a sentence, not a word.” Juhan rubbed his hands together nodding as if a bow was too much. “I thank you for the soup.”

“It wasn’t *Mõisaküla* was it?” Lulle asked, barely above a whisper. We knew a maid and a farm hand there.

“Not *Mõisaküla*, no, *proua*. I know *Mõisaküla* myself. No this *mõis*, well it was grand, the remains of a pergola and a fountain and porticoes. Inside, classic stairs. You know, fine enough.”

Papa once took me to a *mõis* when he delivered an inlaid writing desk to a baron. It was a beautiful place.

Juhan flicked at a crumb on the table. “No. His ears were closed. Not a considerate word for any of us.”

My heart was squeezed like a rag. I could picture an ugly thing now. I felt it but I still had to listen. Sometimes things turn the other way and something unexpected occurs. Sometimes I imagine a happy ending but I was afraid for the baron.

Murri laid her head on the floor beside Granny and me. She kept doleful eyes on Juhan.

“All the same, we waited for his reply. We’ve had it up to here, haven’t we?” Juhan’s hand went to his throat.

“They milk us one way or another,” Granny croaked.

“We all have our stories,” Lulle agreed.

“About time. I’d say,” Granny nodded, sipping her drink.

“He was terrified. I mean, what hope did he have against us?”

Lulle handed Juhan a glass of Granny’s drink. “Nobody to save him?”

Juhan’s eyes spoke.

“Not even one?”

“He had a revolver; still I knew we could take him. His manservant was in the house, the old geezer, peering from inside didn’t need to die too but knew we’d come to open their veins.”

I watched my mother, all ears, torment in her face.

“Went for his pistol, we measured every twitch but he was quick and the one who tried to grab it, a boy younger than me, got it. Shot in front of us, sank onto the gravel, laying still as snow. Well, how mad we went!”

I imagined it. Granny’s fingernails bit skin. She was there too.

“We stuck him, not a man afraid to die after that, though he had the pistol. Mad as dogs. There would be murder. We yelled it and the next minute he was down and every one of us fighting for a piece. For our grandfathers and grandmothers, the beatings, the bruises, the starving and curses, kicked like animals, legs broken for not bending the knee. And for the dead boy. I felt every thud go through me. Revenge." Juhan had gone back to it.

"You got in there, did you?" Lulle whispered. My mother's look had turned sour.

"I did. He knew, even as he cursed. Knew he was done. Finally, his turn." Juhan looked up at us. He was pleased with himself.

"And?"

"The burning?" Juhan lowered his head to his hands. "The place went up like a bonfire at midsummer. One of the best! We had to back off. It was hot as hell! Your son saw it there... the sky ablaze."

"Cruel," Mama said. She looked into her lap.

"Dangerous. For you," Lulle said.

"Oh yes," Juhan agreed. "But god knows we've been flogged and broken, and we've taken it. We knew what we were doing. In the end. His wife and children locked upstairs, the butler staring from the windows. I saw their faces. They saw their end."

"They did?"

"I'm sure."

"Locked in?"

They were! I imagined flames licking the walls, coming at them and...

"But they got out!" I cried.

Juhan turned, remembering me. "Perhaps they did," he paused. "Perhaps they escaped out the back and we'd have let them go free. Over the fields. We're not murderers."

"They'll come for you when the police get wind," Lulle murmured.

"Maybe they will." Juhan looked around, a smile testing the

corners of his mouth. "But the Baron Otto von Budberg, did you hear?"

"Who?"

"… harnessed like a horse. Forced to drag the plough. Did you not hear?"

"No! Was he strong?" Granny twittered.

"Not at all. Needed a lashing." Juhan wiped his mouth. "Made him eat hay."

"Ah, ja, paid for his sins," Granny agreed.

"Ugly."

"*Jah*! *Budberg. Noh, jah.*"

We all laughed at that because finally there was a joke after burning and beatings. A man tied to a plough and made to eat hay. The grown-ups laughed, Helve and Enn and Hardi and I too. Though it wasn't funny, not really. I knew that but I let myself go with everyone merrily, with what was supposed to be a joke but when it was quiet, there was a sad silence and Juhan restarted the dirge. Lulle, Maarja and Granny joined in, picked up the words, we children too, though most of the time we were all ears and wide-eyed as they sang;

"*The nobles are dying, the manors are burning,*" like a funeral hymn, a mourning song of doom. "*The forests and land will be ours,*" they sang, Juhan drowning the others out.

7. The Hay Loft

When I opened the door that night I had never expected to see Juhan. He might have been in Tallinn protesting, or Peterburg, working and meeting, anywhere but Metsajärve.

I lay beside Granny who had begun to snore, and her cat, Kiisu, purring. I was desperate to know what Juhan and Mama were talking about. They sat close, whispering as if they had plans but I couldn't hear. I was sure of one thing, that I would not let Mama go marching or burning manors with him. I would make the most enormous fuss in the world. She would have to obey.

Eventually Lulle returned to the room, covered the pot of oatmeal and removed a candle. "There's an old fur hanging in the barn," she told Juhan. She didn't notice me. She slept with Kert. There was a cradle with the baby at the foot of their bed and no more than a hard narrow bench beneath their window. Enn and Hardi had gone to the kiln room, warm as a roast, the kiln fired up to toast the rye grain to keep it. It had a nutty toasty flavour better than anything I knew. Helve and Annika had gone to sleep in the store room. As soon as it was spring they'd get up with the sun. In midsummer, the sun stalked the dark in the best days and nights of our lives. We all wanted them to last forever, not only for flowers and leaves and fruit, not even for the longed-for sun but for the light! Life-giving, precious light. Plants flourished, grass grew tall and thick, rye flowers blossomed, birds never slept. I wanted to lavish love on everyone.

So now we were paid back; the sun too bashful to rise while snow and ice lay ready for ambush.

The Hay Loft

I snuggled with Granny and listened to Mama questioning Juhan. He shook his head. She refused to believe him. Finally she jumped up. “You must have known!”

Juhan’s answered quietly. “I did not. I understand that you can’t know how it was.”

Mama laid her head on the table. Juhan picked up his coat and scarf and opened the barn door. “Goodnight, *proua*.”

Goodnight, *härra*.”

I laid my head in Granny’s lap but I watched Mama staring at the guttering candle. She rose and walked back and forth, arms folded.

“Innocent victims. That’s murder, Juhan!” She said to the room.

Granny snored. I lay still, my eyes closed. I pictured the baron’s children escaping from the back door of the house before it burst into flame, fleeing over the fields to safety, somewhere.

Out of deep sleep Granny sat up, coughing a tobacco-laced fit.

“Siina. Bed. Now! Take the candle.” I was banished to the cold gloomy store room.

I kept my stockings and woollen underwear on and slid between the cold sheets. I would count to a hundred, ten times before I crept out to call Mama, tell her I couldn’t sleep, no matter how annoyed she might be.

I lay waiting for her, tired as I was, but could not sleep. Time stretched ahead of me like a long frozen river, winding and sliding toward a faint, white, iced dream. I imagined I heard the pinprick peeping of *tihased,* the minuscule tits that flocked and fed in blurry clouds. In my half sleep, men stormed and shouted, sliced others with spikes and blades. Juhan, Juhan whom I trusted, ran chasing the baron and his wife and children across a snowy field while overhead the sky blazed red, yellow and fireworks' green.

I willed Mama to come but I could not stop shivering. Granny's half-finished blankets were piled on the pine trunk beside the window. I crept out of bed to where the full moon lit the meadow, the snow, smooth as an ironed tablecloth where domes of firewood were stacked like silver thimbles. At the far edge of the meadow, fir trees lined the forest boundary. Bears and forest spirits waited to devour children there. Wolves could turn a woman into a wolf too. They were more cruel than any *Mustsada*. Forest spirits could change a human into a tree or animal. They lost everything human, their families, ancestors and worst of all, their entire histories.

"Mama, come," I said to the window. Wishing to at least see a wolf stalk from the forest. The frozen meadow was still as a framed painting.

In Pärnu, street lamps would be lit on the promenade. Mama and Papa paraded me some evenings, greeting tea-time women, bridge–players, Papa's factory workers and travellers. Betrothed couples strolled arm-in-arm, introduced friends to one another, stopped to talk and laugh. Mama would wear her white crocheted scarf over one shoulder and Papa, his moustache combed and scented, gave her his arm. Babies, new coats, hats and well-behaved dogs were admired. Young women, even schoolgirls out in uniform, giggled and smiled, coy, for men.

The moon sank behind a cloud. My teeth chattered. I pushed open the door into the main hall. The kitchen was empty and dark as a Cossack's beard. I tiptoed past Granny's cot and opened the door to the barn.

"Mama?" I whispered. Moonlight sliced in from a high window. "Mama?" I called to the emptiness. Stolen? My mother stolen! Stepping deeper into the musk and manure of sighing, lowing animals, into hushing straw, I shuffled and breathed in the dense dark.

"Mama?" A warm draught on my cheek, a bristly nudge and the animal smells. "Mama?" I hunched away from the breath and slimy nostrils. Trampled, killed, and eaten! A wolf, a bear devoured her bones!

But whispering.

"Mama?" Hissing, a *sosistamine* in the matted dark and Juhan's growl among beasts, ghosts and fairies where I fell. Juhan and Mama together, a moment later, three of us heaped up in the soft warmth, Mama giggling with Juhan and me, sprawled on top, in dismay.

8. Sledding

Jutta told me stories when we were in the *saun* as she dipped and poured hot water from the copper ladle, rinsing soap from my scalp until my hair squeaked. Streams skimmed over my face, shoulders and feet. The wooden sauna floor shone like stone. Water grumbled down the pipes but Jutta's stories could take me far from the *saun*. She told me once about a family from Tallinn, (perhaps they were from Petersburg, certainly not Kihnu Island). They had gone galloping over Pärnu's iced bay, four grand, groomed, bell-jangling, brass-decorated horses in front, a sledge loaded with grandmothers, babies, children and luggage, covered with satin-lined and edged furs. They swayed, the sledge careening its way to the island. Stories get embellished in Pärnu. It was a desperately exciting, romantic story telling until the end.

That was when the long summer days had ended and the sun hid behind weighted clouds while fat, wet snow flurried and sank, stayed a week, another, and so on. Mama, Roosi and Jutta stuffed felt strips between the upstairs' window frames and closed the shutters. Gloom crept in. Mama was moody even in her Italian taffeta, with its black reticella lace though the bodice hung loose on her. Once she had filled it.

Mama was more conservative than my Papa. She didn't consider mass education as much a priority as Papa did. She said that *igaüks on oma õnne sepp* – we made our own good luck. She cared about those born into poverty and railed against the orders to send our soldiers to fight against Japan. On the other hand she complained about laziness. Tidiness was a virtue. But it was Papa who enjoyed reading of suffragettes chained to rails. It was about then that he became more radical and involved in dangerous discussions and meetings.

Winter blasted. One February morning dawned clear and shiny as a silver rouble. Anna and Kristjaan were bored to tears with being inside. Me too.

"Go. Stay together and don't go far. Make a snowman. Take your sled. Be home before dark," Jutta directed. It would be dark by four thirty. Jutta was making bread. I would look after my sister and brother.

Kristjaan ran ahead, dragging our sled, his dark red, felted jacket bobbing in and out of sight. Other children slid along the streets, dragging one another, throwing snowballs. The bay tree branches were naked. Our boots broke the thin snow crust as we chased friends across the park. When we reached the Kuursaal, the band stand, Anna plonked herself on the bench as if she meant to stay.

"Anna!" I imitated Jutta but without effect. Anna was stubborn.

Pärnu Bay is wide and shallow and freezes in particularly cold winters. The ice rolled and rose, flattened and bowled, the waves solid as far as we could see. It was a wonderful sledding park. From amongst the fir trees on the one side of the park I saw movement. Mihkel Oks, whose mother sold vegetables at the market came toward us.

"He always looks at you. Oh! Now he's coming over," Anna said.

Mihkel Oks' skates were wound around his mittens, slung over his shoulder.

"Oh, I know," I said, more curious than worried. Mihkel didn't care what I said. He could be serious or funny, joking without warning and could tell me things I'd never thought of. He knew about stars and what it was like in Africa, could take apart a clock or mousetrap and put it back together. I knew how to behave in a house in a *saksatuba*, but he could find wild honey or birds' eggs for his mother to fry for breakfast.

"His father's a protester but he's nice," I told Anna.

"It's a good day. You coming?" He asked, grinning lopsidedly, dodging behind to see if I had my skates. I shrugged, pointing to where Kristjaan was disappearing.

Mihkel was lean. His eyes shone as if he was hungry but he was afraid of nothing: the haunted alleys between the city walls or being stopped and questioned by a policeman.

"I have to get him back," I said, upset already, trying to sound in charge.

"Hurry up," Anna ordered from the bench where she swung her legs. I strapped on my skates.

Children swarmed, squabbling and screaming with sleds and wobbly skates. Ants and Ulve, inseparable brothers from Eha Street, pushed and pulled a Finnish sled. Ants sat on the chair while Ulve tried to topple him. They fought and laughed until the sled and Ants fell over.

Kristjaan and his red jacket shrank in the distance. "Going to Finland is he?" Mihkel grinned.

"Too far! Get him, Siina!" Anna yelled, holding her hand over her nose. I did the same to remind myself it was there. One afternoon with Jutta we'd seen a man stagger from a tavern in Vee Street. The man's face was disfigured, black from frostbite, holes and pieces missing. "Anyway, he's alive," Jutta had whispered, tugging us away. "He didn't end up iced stiff like a log. Drink!" she had said and marched us on.

The wind shook the reeds, frozen glass spears along the

beach. We stepped onto the sand where snow scattered and beaded. Clouds bunched overhead, the smell of snow plummeting.

I burrowed my head into my collar.

"I better come. Your brother won't listen," Mihkel said.

"I can do it," I answered though Kristjaan's red felt jacket was disappearing where the ice waves, flatter, further out merged into sky. Currents could swirl underneath and throw up giant blocks or open black deep holes. "Come back!" I screamed.

"Hurry," Mihkel shouted, ahead of me already but no matter how quickly we stamped on, Kristjaan's red jacket diminished.

"Wait!" I screeched, imagining I heard ice groaning. "Run!"

Snowflakes drifted, settling on Mihkel's hat. His eyelashes turned white.

"Come, come..." he urged.

Snow was covering the greenish – cream ice. I turned back toward the beach. A handful of dots floated through the screen of snow.

"Kristjaan!" I shouted.

Finally he stopped and turned to us. "Cold!" he said rubbing his arms. "Getting cold."

We stood together. Kihnu Island was ahead, Pärnu behind.

"I wanted to be like a *merikotkas*. A sea eagle!" Kristjaan said. He stretched out his arms. "I'm cold. Let's go back!"

Everywhere was snowy white. The only sound was our crunching boots.

Mihkel took hold of Kristjaan's jacket and yanked him from the ice darker than the rest.

"You're stupid!"

A black line ran under us and into the distance. "It's dark," Kristjaan whispered, spun and stared past us to where the shore should have been but now was nothing but snow flurry. “Milk soup,” Kristjaan smiled. I could see his mouth but not his eyes. His hat was pulled low.

We turned a tight little circle searching for something in the dancing blossoms. Any smudge of shore, hint of land, thicker fog, darker lines.

Every year a child was lost on the bay. Fishermen, warmed inside with liquor, might walk for miles quite lost, disoriented by the white. Some drifted away on ice floes never to be seen again. Jutta told me about the two boys who had gone to fish on the ice a year earlier. When they didn’t come back, parents and friends went searching with torches and dogs, calling out, flashing lights. The long night was bitter with wind. The family and searchers returned frozen. But no boys. The parents prayed. Late next day at sunrise, white with cold, starving, the boys came slamming home. Not a finger, not a toe was frostbitten. The parents gave thanks at the Elizabeth Church. The boys swallowed two bowls of fish soup, what there was of the rye bread, then they toppled into bed.

“You heard about the Peterburg family?” Mihkel asked as we huddled on the ice.

“Of course I did,” I said, not wanting to hear another thing. I’d had Jutta’s tragic tales. Those bankers or merchants had drowned. Their beautiful horses had smashed through the ice taking the family huddled under their satin embroidered-edge furs, the babies and the luggage, the whole lot. They’d have frozen all the way down while they sank to the bottom. “So don’t tell,” I said.

Snow floated and thickened. I kept still though Mihkel kept swivelling this way and that. “I can’t tell where we are,” he finally admitted.

Sledding

"The others were just there!" Kristjaan whined.

"So, follow me!" I said, my stomach churning with dread but we had to move. Crystals covered our scarves and mittens.

I knew how upset my Papa and Mama would be. I'd be blamed for irresponsibility and bad discipline. I would have to face both of them and their disappointment in me.

"Everything's gone," Kristjaan wailed, swinging his arms in circles.

Snow piled up on our little sled and hid its tracks.

"Listen!" I whispered imagining children's voices.

"It's my oilskin talking," Mihkel said cupping his covered up ears. "Nothing."

"But we have to get back. Can't you see anything?" I groaned. I needed to move. My feet felt far way. I imagined ice groaning, cracks opening.

"Are you all right?" Mihkel asked. He put his hand on my shoulder. "Wiggle your toes. Wiggle them hard. We'll get back you know. *Kurat*! Look!"

For the briefest moment I could have sworn, I saw the sun.

Mihkel glanced back to me, then to Kristjaan. "So, this way!" He began walking.

"Why?" Kristjaan demanded but he was already following as Mihkel stormed on with me behind. Kristjaan dragged his sled. White hung around us. The sun had vanished as fast as it had appeared. Mihkel looked back to us every now and again and kept his course.

After ages I screamed in hope. "Anna!" I imagined I could see the curve of the beach. Anna should have gone home but perhaps she was still swinging her legs on the park bench, or frozen to it.

"Annaaaa!" We all bellowed.

"Siina! Kristjaan!" I imagined my ears replying.

In the far distance a shadow was jumping and screaming. “Hurrah, hurrah!”

“Papa will kill me,” Kristjaan grumbled as we came out of the fog onto the beach.

I ran for Anna. “You’re all blue! Are you all right?” I shook her.

Kristjaan went quiet, head down, staring at his feet before starting off to Supeluse dragging our sled.

“He found the sun,” I told Anna.

9. My Camera

Ladybirds alit on branches and window sills. Blue anemones crammed the border along our white wooden fence. Further down Supeluse, lilacs and begonias bloomed in gardens all the way up to the park where white clover spread under the lime trees. Winter had shrunk away.

Mama needed embroidery silks from Pärnu's Rüütli Street.

"I'm going to town. Perhaps I'll stop in Munga Café. You may come."

Mama re-potted an amaryllis Papa had given her. Her eyes were dark underneath and I suspected she had a secret in her, like a painting inside the lid of a closed box. A Russian lacquered box with horses and sleighs on the top.

"I love Munga Café," I said. I'd had a cream puff there when I was too small to say.

At the hall mirror Mama fixed a cartwheel hat, a fantasy in lace over her fair hair. "I do too."

Under the portico of Munga Café Mama smoothed the wide lace collar of my voile dress and tucked my hair under the blue ribbon that Jutta had tied. I expected that when we sat down Mama would ask about my handwriting, my German, my Gothic script, my piano lessons. She'd be pleased. I had a new Czerny piece and was promised a Mozart my teacher once played for me. It sounded simple though my teacher said Mozart was never easy. I'd tell Mama I had a sensitive touch and show her my trimmed fingernails.

I had questions for her. I'd not seen Juhan since Metsajärve and no one spoke his name. I had seen the monocled man. I also recognised the perfume of his moustache as he came in our front door. The Estonian party had been formed in Tartu, the *Teataja* news said so – Mama read it every morning. Soon we were all hearing the word *independence*. Astonishing. For the first time ever. Roosi sniffed at it. Nonsense talk. We were all one, the tsar's people. Cook, on the other hand, flew around in excitement. To my confusion she polkaed me around the kitchen and into the hall. I could easily polka.

Mama and Papa continued arguing. I kept out of their way when they shouted and slammed doors. I heard crashes in the bedroom and I covered my ears. Anna got upset and asked if someone was falling off the bed or out a window but despite the pandemonium nothing bad happened. No-one broke an arm, a leg or crashed outside into the lilac bushes. Anna and I pretended it was normal.

At last we were there, Mama and I in Munga Café at a little round table covered in a damask cloth that reached the floor. I considered myself very elegant. A cut-glass vase of freesias stood in the centre, the fragrance heady and sweet so that I leaned forward to smell them but Mama ordered me to sit still. I felt like being perverse.

"Do the men who disappear go and hide?" I asked as she glanced at the menu. It wasn't exactly a question about Juhan but still, I kept close watch on her.

In a way I didn't want to know where the men went as I expected it would be a horrible, dangerous, ugly place. I also assumed Mama wouldn't tell the truth, the way Juhan hadn't at Metsajärve. He'd avoided the truth.

"You're forever asking questions beyond you, Siina. Listen,

they take them places to die."

It wasn't the words, nor that people were taken somewhere to die, it was the way Mama looked at me, as if I was at fault, and in asking I had made it worse. Her voice made my head hurt. I had meant to ask another question, *how did they die*? But I changed my mind. I would be cooperative. I would be good. For some reason, Mama brightened.

"Tell me about the Mozart," she said, so I explained my last lesson including everything from my teacher's words of praise, my consistent tempo, the improvement in my sight-reading, the label on my teacher's hand cream; she always rubbed cream into her hands at the beginning of the lesson. I described the lanolin fragrance and the cabinet beside the piano.

Eventually Mama pressed a finger to her lips because the waitress, heron thin, her skin as white as the pith of rushes, dropped a curtsey and presented a platter of pastries with raspberries, cream-cheese, chocolate and custard. It was impossible to choose but I picked a fruit tart. I sipped milky coffee from a gilt-edged cup and imitated my mother. I sat tall and eager as a new narcissus, ready to talk about meetings and spies and why a mother would leave her husband and children and flee to Vienna, or how a teacher could be marched off by the police.

Beside us, a hat, a wilderness of feathers. Two women whispered, one with the feathers agitating, pointing to a photograph in an album, the other woman repeating, "Oh my dear!"

"My great-uncle. A volunteer fireman," one said, her finger on a picture.

"Appalling!"

"Unbelievable. Father Gapon was hanged for leading the

rioters," said the other.

The women turned pages, clucked tongues in between bit pickled cucumber and liver *paté* sandwiches.

Mama nodded to them. "Moments preserved. Amazing, Siina, no?"

We ourselves had no camera but Mama did buy postcards from the beach parade, to send to relatives in Dresden and Peterburg.

Mama adjusted her crêpe pin-tucked bodice so the gathers fell from her shoulders and were caught by a silver waist panel. She was secretively happy, her face more rounded, her figure also. Today her eyes smiled. I thought of a painted Easter egg, round firm and full.

The other women raised porcelain cups and sipped while between them in the centre of their table sat a black box camera with a leather handle.

Mama took a bite from a chocolate-covered profiterole. "You understand what it means to love someone, don't you? To completely love and trust?" Her fine fair eyebrows arched.

"You and Papa."

She smiled, I thought, approvingly, only it was as much a smile for a child.

"We have secrets, don't we?"

"I know." I knew that whatever happened I would never give away anything that I shouldn't. Our secrets were like exquisite paintings on the inside lids of precious boxes.

"I can trust you even though you're very young."

I nodded. I understood. I would say whatever she wanted.

On our way home along Rüütli I felt the cobbles, stone eggs under my leather shoes. I'd hardly worn them since summer was so short. When I grew out of them Anna would have them. I dangled the paper package of silks and needles Mama had bought from my wrist, though since the haberdasher, she never paused to look in shops.

"We're not getting anything else?"

She strode on. "I have all I want, *kallikene*. But your birthday is soon. Let's get you something, shall we?"

We paused at the watchmaker's window. A hummingbird was poised mid-flight inside a bell jar and set between an oak encased clock and a camera almost like the one the women had.

For moments I stared at a hummingbird bird, imagining it moved but the camera was what I wanted. Its dark lens eyed me, the black leather case and handle like a handbag ready to carry home. "I'd like it, Mama, if I could make you a book of pictures," I said. I tried to read my mother's expression.

"You're far too young, Siina."

"I'll learn to use it. I'll be awfully careful."

Mama tilted her head to one side to look at me. "Fancy capturing things we love, beautiful things that give us pleasure, things we may lose, things that one day will be gone."

"I'd take photographs of Granny and Murri and Lulle with her new baby."

"You can be far off, yet get close to something and have it with you forever." Mama was already far off.

"I'd take Jutta in her Muhu slippers and Cook with a plate of *sült*." Jutta's slippers rioted with colours and stitching and I much as I hated *sült* brawn, I'd have loved a photograph of Cook with a wobbly plate of grey *sült*.

"You can see with another's eyes, or show someone a thing without forcing them to look at the particular moment you do."

Right away I envisaged an album full of my photographs of so many things I saw only once; a storm, clouds like ships, a swallow catching a dragonfly. Others could see what I saw.

"I'll be very careful. Really, really. It's what I want more than anything I ever wanted. I'll learn to be extremely responsible."

Mama gazed at me as if I were a Turkish puzzle. "With such a box you can also tell lies. The camera takes only what you choose. What you choose to take and what to leave out," she said.

"Oh," I said.

When we were about to cross the street to the Elizabeth Church, two black mares jangled their carriage to a stop and a large be-whiskered man in a fawn morning coat stepped out, doctor's bag in hand. He doffed his hat to Mama and gave me the merest look so I knew I wasn't invisible. Before he hurried off Mama nodded back at him. "My doctor. A great pessimist," she said with a toss of her head with her ribboned cartwheel hat.

Somehow I knew I would get the camera and make an album for Mama. I would find things she loved and treasured and I would learn how to see from behind that little dark eye.

10. The Doctor

Rain had been beating for endless grey weeks, gutters spilled like waterfalls, potholes filled, the neighbour's canvas awnings bellied out. Rain jabbed puddles and sparkled on the cobbles on Supeluse. Rain drummed day and night. Our wooden garden barrels overflowed. The alley cats crouched, drenched and bedraggled under the wood-stacked lean-tos along the street under the sheets of iron rain.

Men were shot in the countryside after the burnings. Cook and Roosi talked though they saw me coming and lowered their voices, then continued anyway. I always listened to what went on. A mother and her son were shot and killed in their *saun* in Altskivi. The police said it was an accident. Perhaps they'd shot the wrong men they said after standing them against a tree and shooting them all. Others accused of burning manors were sent to Siberia. Our lives were unharmed but I felt and imagined danger everywhere.

I sat watching the neighbours, boys in soaked woollen jackets or oilskins, laughing and shouting, kicking a ball down our street.

I held my camera ready. I'd have loved just a peek of sunlight. Mama had bought me the roll film German camera from Rüütli Street. The shop assistant explained the advantages of roll film, easy without glass plates he'd told us, surprised it was for me. It wasn't so very expensive, not until I finished a roll when I had to wait days or weeks for developing. Mama liked me taking photos and Papa approved. He said I would learn patience waiting for a good shot. I'd also understand science.

Summer guests had left Pärnu. Austrians were back in their

dark cities, Peterburgers who came for our ‘quaint beauty,’ our beer and black bread, were home, back in the city of bridges, shut up in winter-misted rooms. Men in panamas, women in lace-brimmed extravaganza hats were now ghosts in silver-gelatine prints.

I’d grown tall since summer. I had my mother’s features, her wide-set eyes and thin skin. I was as tall as Helve and Papa said, fair as a birch. I plaited my own hair and Jutta and Roosi took care of Mama, carried and cleaned, no time for tying and untying mine. Mama had been unwell for months. There were Anna and Kristjaan for them to look after.

I watched the rain snaking trails down the window and peeped through my lens to the foggy scenes. I was tempted to click the shutter but I needed to learn patience. I’d have liked to snap the boys in the street but I knew they’d be smudgy and dark. If I got an unusual picture Mama would be very pleased. If the clouds lifted and the sun shone, she’d get well, get up and we’d go out as we used to.

She’d lain in her darkened room for weeks, not as long as Kert, but I thought of him, dreading what lay ahead. Roosi took Mama’s meal tray in, collected the debris, carried out the chamber pot, back and forth. Once she let me take in the hot stone water bottle but soon shooed me out.

Two crows perched side by side under our awning when a carriage drew up. The horse was a beauty, jet black. Rain streaming off its back. It shook its head and harnesses as the driver loosened the traces. The droshky door flew open, an umbrella popped out, a cloak swirled across the pavement, a leather bag flashed. The doctor.

“Upstairs!” I heard Roosi and the doctor’s galoshes slap slap down the hall, the umbrella clatter into the stand, leather shoes tap up our stairs.

I tucked my camera under my jumper and ran, my skirt and petticoats slapping my ankles, my slippers sliding along the hall.

The last time the doctor came he took leeches, those white fat worms, one by one from a jar and stuck them on Mama. They left bloody pit holes, Mama crying. The doctor never cared. I wished I'd scratched and bitten him but I couldn't. Maybe this time I would. I had to stop him.

I sneaked into the room before he reached the landing. I hid in the window alcove behind the wool curtain. Mama gasped and moaned. Roosi prattled on, a cup to her lips, Mama's hair scraped back. She was a skeleton, her face white as her linen, deep lines around her mouth. If she'd opened her eyes she'd not have seen me.

Roosi disappeared the moment the doctor came in. He opened his bag, laid his instruments; sharp, shining, blades; cutting and squeezing instruments, one after the other on Mama's white counterpane. He stood back to choose something.

I poked my camera through the curtain pretending I'd get him but I could not release the shutter. The little lever would snap like a mousetrap. The doctor rolled down the bedclothes and lifted Mama's nightgown over her breasts. I remembered sucking those white globes. I wanted to push that man away. He stuck a glass cup under one breast and waited. Mama snatched air and threw an arm over her face, crying.

"You have pain?" the doctor asked. "Bleeding?"

Mama nodded.

The fumes recalled my own fevers and hallucinations when I was small. I needed to go to Mama but at that moment the doctor swung around and glanced toward the curtains. He was still a moment before turning back to the bed.

"Hurt?" he asked again.

"*Jah*!" Mama said.

He took bloody pads from Mama's side as she swooned.

"Miss!" he called and Roosi was in the room like a streak, removing the pads.

I wanted to snarl like a dog. Mama sighed a huge sigh that filled me with her pain. She would die this time. I ran at the doctor. "Leave her!" I screamed.

He was huge. He stood over me. I tugged his sleeve so I could reach my mother. "Just go," she whispered.

"*Raus*!" the doctor growled.

"But Mama!" I cried as he grabbed me - and I bit him. He let out a roar!

"*Anschlag*!" He marched me across the room, all but threw me through the door and slammed it.

I slid to the floor, sat with knees under my chin and cried. I tried breathing slowly, the way Roosi showed me when I panicked and I felt better. I had dropped my camera behind the curtain. I started crying again.

I would see Cook. She would understand.

Cook was in the kitchen conducting like a maestro over tinkling, jangling pots and lids. There were pans of beef and oatmeal making bubbling, spitting musical rhythms. Cook's brow ran with sweat. Cabbage smell filled the room. At one end of the bench in a cold bath were the pale bodies of skinless potatoes, the shredded cabbage and razor-edged onion slices beside them.

"Hungry?" she asked offering me *pirukad*. *Pirukad* would solve the problem.

"No!"

"What then?"

"I bit the doctor." I still had some of my rage inside.

"Oi, oi, Siina!" She lowered her face to mine. "Now you're really for it!" She winked and flourished her boning knife, slipped it into a hunk of fat and began chopping. She finished a row of even slices before she swirled back to me. "It's a German fad those leeches and bleeding. Your mother needs a good *nõid*, that's what!" Cook had said that before.

"He's only a doctor."

"Well, he does his best."

Ever since *that Sunday*, Mama had pains in her chest. There were times she came downstairs for coffee mornings and would cough, hold her side and wheeze like a smoker. She'd take to her bed and stay there with headaches and pain. The doctor would be called, he'd come and whisper to my father, and leave.

Cook laid down the knife and steel, went over to the groats thickening on the stove. Onions, bacon and marjoram had been stirred together. I hated the smell. In one move she hefted a bowl of black blood, stirred it, touched her spattered apron to her brow, and swiped her hands down her front. "We each have something to offer, Siina." She pushed up her sleeves and dolloped the bloody mixture into a forcing bag. Delicately, daintily, she opened the soft ends of sheep intestines and began filling them with the blood porridge and at the end of each length, tied it. She secured the other sausage end, her tongue slipping from between her lips, her forehead wet as she concentrated.

"And I left my camera in the room!" I said.

"So now look! You're in worse trouble."

"My mother cries and he can't help!"

Cook flinched, wiped her hands on her apron and looked up at me. "Your mother will mend, darling child."

"But the knives and leeches!"

"It's for the best, Siina. You stay out of trouble. Now, try a dumpling. Come!" I still like dumplings.

Cook was a handsome woman I had heard. Her calves were such that country brides would envy and she had a mountainous bosom. She could dish out soup and regale maids and yard boys with what she knew about them so they'd blush and creep away before too many truths got out. She was fast and clever, chopping and carving, inventing ways to make a different sweet or sauce. She'd guess what was bothering me when I couldn't tell Mama. But I never wanted her work, never. I would not spend my time stuffing bread and blood and groats into sheep's intestines.

"Mama won't die, will she?" I said since I had caught my breath and felt better.

"We all pray," Cook answered without looking up.

Winter froze and snowed. Mama remained in her room. A smell of something masked something else. Jutta was bad-tempered over everything, scolded Anna and Kristjaan and me. Papa may as well have lived on Kihnu or in Finland; he came home late though his factory was only on Aisa *Tänav*. His cabinets sold in Helsinki and Stockholm. He ordered a new striped suit and waistcoat with pearl buttons. Electric lights were installed in all our rooms. Cook served even more wondrous pork roasts, cinnamon melted in sugar and *roosamanna* for dessert. Jutta took Anna and me to Rüütli Street for new shoes and brimmed hats with tulle ribbons. On Vee *Tänav*, we saw father's cabinets. Twenty of his apprentices triple checked their measurements so they never made mistakes, Jutta had said. The scenes they inlaid were like paintings – forests and manor houses, lakes and animals, mountains and clouds.

"They go to Germany and Russia, they do," Jutta said. I also had a table. Tiny leafy tendrils curled around the edges of it in the corner of my bedroom. “He’s meticulous, he is,” Jutta said.

It seemed I had fewer bad dreams but still, soldiers sometimes chased me and my legs turned to wet, flopping flax. I lost Mama in a crowd and panicked but I might swim a river, fly above Metsajärve, or ride Lulle’s horse. I loved those dreams.

It so happened that one morning I woke shivering under my goose down quilt. The cold was icy enough to shatter steel pipes. I had to go to Mama. Her room smelled of Papa’s shaving soap and had the moist heat of his morning wash though still clammy and dark. I could make out Mama’s shape in her bed and I climbed up to an unfamiliar smell, neither Lily of the Valley nor Eau de Cologne. It was something unearthly. I lay beside my mother, my head on her shoulder. “Mama?”

Much later Roosi came in to open the curtains. She stood for one moment, took deep loud breaths and wrung her hands before me. “*Oi, oi*! Poor lady.” She swiped her cheeks with the backs of her wrists. “Poor thing,” she said untangling my fingers from Mama’s.

Papa returned home right away, pounded up the stairs, muttered and cursed, covered his face with his hands then locked them behind his back and paced. Back and forth along the landing he went until the doctor arrived.

Roosi brought Anna and Kristjaan and me to stand in a line after the doctor left. Papa took my chin in his hand, his eyes bright with tears. “Siina, dearest. We shall be brave, no? Anna and Kristjaan look up to you. They always will. We’ll get through this sadness. It will end. Now it is very hard. We will all miss your mother. I will too,” he said, his voice starting to crack. The next moment he had left us and in his study, the door open, poured a drink. He went scurrying downstairs and out the front door. Jutta said he would have gone to look at the sea and breathe the air.

11. Eeva

Spring came dragged by the chains of winter. Buds popped. A snow flurry burned them black. Lilac bushes burst green. Grass sprouted.

I pictured Mama half-smiling, her straw-blonde hair piled high on her head, loose over her ears, her face lit from the window, a shine in her eyes, a softness in her skin. In my photograph she was like the moon on a winter's night. I had wanted her embroidery in the picture but that part of the frame was too dark. The best photographers managed tiny details, jewellery and hair clips, buttons and the edge of stitching; still, I'd kept Mama with us because of my camera. I sat with her, imagined her saying how she and Lulle rode horses, climbed trees and swam like boys. Lulle wanted nothing more than a Tori horse but Mama would have concerts, parties and a piano. She loved Tolstoy and she played Chopin, never church or country songs. When she met my father he flattered and seduced her with his manners and talk of Sisley and Monet. One day they would see those works. He wore a button-down collar, his clothes perfectly pressed, hair and moustache lightly greased. So Mama told me.

Summer advanced, leaves gleamed, lilac and hyacinth burst in our parks and gardens, thriving in the long days and metallic nights.

Papa worked endless hours. Roosi and Jutta scolded us. Cook chose the menus, fish soup and *kissell*. "He doesn't care. I'll make a fig pudding tomorrow," I heard her telling Roosi. That was until Papa brought home Eeva Raud, tall enough to look him in the eye, robust and unflinching and played piano like Chopin himself.

Anna and I curtsied, Kristjaan threw a *Kratzfuss*, one foot behind the other. Eeva Raud offered a box of sweets and Kristjaan stepped forward. Anna and I slunk back, unwilling to greet this new mother.

"Eeva has agreed to marry me." Papa looked from one of us to the next. Kristjaan found a smile. Anna looked at her feet and giggled. I stared into Eeva's deep-set grey eyes and at her spidery brows. Her gaze soon shifted to our furniture, paintings and tapestries before returning to us.

"And soon," Papa said, touching his moustache with one finger. "We must have a woman in our home and Eeva has many things to teach us." He took her hand and held it between his two. Eeva smiled enough to crease the corners of her mouth.

"I don't like her," I told Papa when I squeezed against him on the sofa, once Eeva was upstairs.

"What?"

"She's your *only one* now."

"Behave with your new mother. I know it was quick but now that we're married she will be your mother." His expression shifted from impatience to kindness, just by a hair. "You're all my *only ones*," he said lowering his book onto the table so he could hug me. Perhaps he understood. "Be good, Siina. What do you think, is it too late for goggle moggle?"

I loved goggle moggle. Dinner was long over. In the kitchen Papa and I found two eggs, broke the yolks in a little cup and beat them with white sugar. "Believe me," he said as he beat and the yolk began turning white. "You, Anna and Kristjaan are my *only ones*. You miss your mother. I do too. But you're growing up and I would be lonely. Eeva has no children of her own and she's fond of you already. Be nice."

I wanted to tell him he would not be lonely with us, Anna and Kristjaan and me but instead I looked into the goggle moggle. It was almost ready and my mouth watered. Papa gave permission with his eyebrows. “We go on, Siina, *jah*?” The slower we spooned, the more delicious it was. I dipped with the edge of my spoon and tasted the sweetness

“Did you see the photograph?” I had made the frame myself and put it in Papa’s office.

“I did and I like it very much, Siina. I’m amazed.”

I closed my eyes as I licked every drip of goggle moggle from my lips. I rested my head against Papa’s chest. “Why did she die? She didn’t have fevers or pneumonia. Why?”

Papa twined his fingers in mine. He sighed. “Not fevers but infection. An old infection she had for a long time.”

“Was it...?”

“After the shootings. Palace Square. They think so.”

My heart sank. My fault. If Papa had been there, if I’d told him where we were going, Mama would not have been cut.

“No, no!” I cried into Papa’s shirt as he tensed.

“So it was. Nothing to do now.”

“I’m sorry, Papa. I was there!”

He hugged, he even rocked me. “That’s how it was, Siina. Who can say what other thing could have been. We’re not to know. Finish the goggle moggle.” He pushed the little cup to me. I scraped the sides and finished every drop. So Papa had said it. I should believe that it was not my fault.

Swallows patched their old nests, our upstairs trunks were sprung open, the smell of lavender escaping. Pressed flowers fell from lacy camisoles, shifts and pantaloons. Roosi would soak and bleach the stained ones in vinegar.

“I’ll need a new dress,” Anna said as she rummaged,

discarding petticoats and chemises too small for either of us. Lilac buds fell from the creases of a muslin gown Mama once wore.

"We'll have that shortened and taken in," Eeva said and held the blue dress against me. I cringed. How could I wear my mother's dress? But otherwise, what would become of it?

I looked doubtfully at Eeva. "We'll have to cut so much off."

"Does that bother you?"

I held onto the muslin. "No. I'll keep all the pieces."

"A little scarf," Eeva said. "For your head in summer." She reached to touch my hair but at the last minute I ducked away.

"Oh well." Eeva clucked her tongue. "We won't get anywhere if you're like that," she said and lifted out Mama's favourite shawl, fringed, Venetian.

I knew exactly what she meant but I couldn't help it. I didn't like her a bit.

"She really is our stepmother, isn't she?" I whispered when Anna and I lay sleepily in bed.

"I don't like her much," Anna said.

"But there's nothing for it."

"Nothing," Anna said. "How can Papa like her?"

But that was that, I realised. We could do nothing, so that was that. Anna and Kristjaan and I were no longer important. And because Papa did not want to be lonely we had to bear it and we could not stop his loneliness.

From downstairs I heard the piano; Schumann, like a pianist, a real pianist. Of course Papa would enjoy that. Eeva had probably draped Mama's embroidered shawl around her shoulders. I clambered out of bed.

"Where are you going?"

"To listen," I said and crouched at the balcony overlooking the parlour door.

"When school opens we'll see, shall we?" I heard Eeva say.

School! No more tutors. Perhaps I'd like it. I crept back to bed.

"Anna! Eeva wants to send us to school!" I told Anna.

"No!"

"But perhaps it's good. The children play games together. And sports, and run around outside. You make friends and learn geography."

"You know we have to write and speak Russian," Anna warned.

"Oh, I know," I said. "It could be nice!"

"I don't want it," Anna declared and turned over to sleep.

The last tutor at our house had been a pretty Swedish girl with criss-crossed braids around her head who was forever distracted by suitors. She read her letters instead of teaching us, one letter from a German captain who marched up to our front door and demanded to see her. She was soon gone after that, replaced by a Hohenzollern officer, a very old man who would fall asleep mid-sentence, slumped and sagging in the upholstered chair. He snored into his ashy moustache while Kristjaan opened the top window and leaned right out over the street. The Hohenzollern lectured us about Bismarck and although I understood none of it, in the way he acted, furious and impassioned, I wished I could follow what it all meant. When Mama finally realized what went on, that we'd spent hours looking at books with birds and butterflies, naked Greeks and drawings of people's insides, every detail, she was appalled. Yet another tutor had to leave us.

"Now I know that everyone fights and lies. Kaisers too," I told Cook because our tutor said so. Cook sprinkled handfuls of flour on the pastry board, flattened the dough and wrapped up apples she'd brought in from the outdoor cellar.

"Oh yes!" she instantly agreed. "Men are the worst. Fight and argue and enjoy it you see. Don't you go getting a soldier when you grow up my dear Siina!"

"Nor a rascal," Roosi grinned from the other side of the kitchen.

After weeks without a tutor and no lessons, Mama had found a stalk of a spinster who always wore the same brown silk dress, pin-tucked with lace to the wrists, high collars and a veil on her balding head. She stayed with us for half a year and I loved her because she taught us complicated games and silly poems, by heart, in English. She praised us and I longed to please her. She also had to write letters to her bed-ridden mother in Scotland. We had a chance to hide, leap out and terrify her, and tell stories about Tatars and Russian bandits in the countryside who captured old women for their harems.

"I do want to go to a school," I told Anna who had begun gently snoring. I was unable to sleep, my head lumpy with rag curls. "Anna," I nudged her. "I want to go to school!" I said staring at the strip of light under the door.

Now my father's office light shone where he and Eeva worked together, she signing accounts and invoices, blotting, folding and sealing, and he writing letters to prospective customers in Russia, Sweden and Poland. I would ask him what Mama would have said about school and he would say it was none of my business.

In September Anna and I started school, the end of Gothic script and the beginning of Cyrillic which we soon mastered and sure enough, it was useful for a period in our uncertain nationhood.

12. Chemises

"I look like Asta Nielsen wouldn't you say?" Anna held Mama's hairbrush as though it were alive against her black cascading hair.

"You look like my little sister," I said framing her with my lens in the soft, dull light. Days were darkening, winter was almost on us. I laughed at Anna. I leaned back on Mama's bed and made out I was shocked. Asta Nielsen was a Danish screen siren who danced erotically, in the film *The Abyss*.

Anna pouted at me, her lips full and sensuous. "Imagine, Siina! Rather sordid don't you say? She lassoed the man, gyrated and squirmed up against him."

I was intrigued and repulsed. How indecent. "Who said?"

"Elviira! She knows everything!"

"Tasteless!" I said, yet delighted at the daring.

"Yes, and now she has her photographs all over Pärnu. You see!"

Of course I did. Then what? What would men expect from her? What would they say behind her back, or straight out to her?

Anna smiled, leapt and danced, posed and jutted her hips, threw back her head. She could be melancholy or wild, seductive then ecstatic. Our electric lights were wonderfully convenient but I wanted more brightness for my camera.

"I'd love to see that film. At least we ought to know how to flirt, Siina," Anna said.

"I'm not so sure."

"I have to know how to act. It's not real, Siina. It's art, darling!" Anna and I both knew how disreputable acting was but she still wanted it. I hoped her instincts were right, that she'd not fall in with bad men or get a baby. Actually, she was dignified in herself, regardless of what character she played on the stage, whether she was acting mad, lovelorn, or despairing. Pavlova the ballerina and Sarah Bernhardt with her dramatics were Anna's goddesses.

In fact, I too was curious to see the Asta Nielsen film although I assumed that men would be disgusted to be teased that way.

"Helve's your age and she has babies," Anna reminded me.

"I know, but she loves her cows and sheep. It's her pleasure, the spinning and weaving. All that. Never mine!" Helve would also know what she needed to about making and having babies. I had become curious about my mother and Juhan, what they meant to one another, what they had done. Would I also be like my mother?

It seemed aeons ago that I had run naked on the beach or sat bare-bottomed with my family in the *saun.* But now I could never ignore a man's attention, the steady stares, the looks that seared my insides, thrilling, though often unwanted.

Anna and I were seventeen and almost sixteen and in love, we supposed, with romance. I could swoon to think of falling in love. I knew that some men adored me, and Anna. But while she talked endlessly about the boys who inhabited her dreams, I hated the prospect of being mother and wife. Anna never thought that far. She assumed she was beautiful and would be worshipped. I, on the other hand, would not delude myself into believing that a man's promises and love talk would change me. I intended to stay in charge of myself, make my own decisions. Not fall unconsciously. One day, when I was ready, I would pack my clothes and shoes, my camera and maps and board a train to somewhere enormously exciting. Perhaps Vienna. Perhaps

Madrid. Or Paris. Or Berlin. I'd see them through my camera. I'd look at the streets from the height of the cobbles. I'd level my lens at shoes, at heels, at rain and shimmering pavements. I'd point up to trees webbing the foreground, capturing the sky. I could meet men who cared about my work. I'd consider a husband. I would need to be irresistibly in love to dedicate myself to linen and babies and pickling cucumbers. I would never be like my mother – spoke of politics, freedom and the independence while she dallied with perfume, hats, and bridge.

Anna and I had been sorting through Mama's clothes, her old-fashioned lovely underwear, camisoles, petticoats, a silk embroidered jacket which Eeva had laid out on the bed for us. At the dressing table, her skirt above her knees, oozing a challenge, Anna raised one eyebrow, tossed her loose hair and twisted the lengths in her long fingers. I lowered my camera. "Asta Nielsen may be daring, but I don't exactly admire her. Zinaida Serebriakova, she now, she is exciting."

"Oh, the *artiste*!" Anna lunged around the room. I wished I could be so uninhibited, so outrightly flamboyant. I slouched back in what once were Mama's pillows, the smell of her lingering such a long time after, unless I imagined them, remembered the sweetness overlaid with musk. I would have asked her about the things I did not understand and she'd have explained them perfectly, simply.

"Zinaida's stunningly beautiful plus her paintings are dazzling. Dozens of them, nudes lying all over the place, uninhibited," I said. There it was, the thing I wanted, the abandon, the self-assurance.

"Oh yes, she defies tradition." Anna removed everything and wriggled into a silk chemise. She was unlike me, her curves soft while I was angular, her cleavage generous while I was small. She was unperturbed however she exposed herself while I was self-conscious. She straightened the shoulder straps of the chemise, raised one arm behind her head and steamed a look in my direction. "Darling, keeeezz me!"

"Would you pose naked?" I placed one hand on my hip and cocked my head.

"Would you?" she shot back.

"You're the performer!"

Anna shrugged. "It would depend."

"Don't you get into trouble Anna." I worried that she might waste her life with someone worthless. I wanted her to care for herself and consider her future.

She unbuttoned the back of the chemise, dropped it and tucked her arms into the silk jacket. "Do you see knickers?" She searched under the clothes. I watched her in my viewfinder. "Are you taking me in the half nude, Siina?"

"Shall I? I mean, are we modern or not? May we defy conventions? Would you?" I clicked Anna in the silk top, her legs bare, the jacket covering her dark triangle.

"Only if it doesn't get me a baby," she laughed. I did too.

"Do you know how exactly, actually?"

Anna found lace bloomers and threw them in the air. "Thank goodness!" She slipped them on and posed on the chair, her knees together, the split in the crotch gone.

"What happens when we're naked with a man?"

"Pain, screaming, agony, childbirth!"

I nodded and clicked. "I've heard worse. We should ask Elviira. She's done all sorts of things."

Anna stood still a moment. "I won't care a fig if I'm in love."

It was all *desire* – because women cried their way through sex, howled during childbirth, but fast enough let husbands storm in and fasten the door behind them. I'd heard that. Roosi and Cook must have thought me deaf! But if *desire* took hold, perhaps I'd become Asta Nielsen as well!

Anna covered her face laughing. "You'll be a suffragette and never take your clothes off, Siina! Ha ha! You'll never marry! Oh, ha ha!"

"You can't even guess what I'll do!" I said, very annoyed, not wishing to show it, still knowing she'd spoken some truth. Yet I did know what I would do. When Anna transformed to Lily Palmer, Sarah Bernhardt or Asta Nielsen I would develop into a bluestocking and a real photographer. If I never created anything like Muybridge's leaping men and galloping horses nor Julia Cameron's angelic children, and never took portraits as beautiful as Nadar had of his wife. I would make landmarks. I would learn from Atget's everyday architectural photographs. I was poised for my own moves. I had seen beauty. I understood the difference and transition between reality, the view, and the two dimensional interpretation. I had begun to see what painters were striving toward. Wherever I looked I made a frame.

I kept Anna in my viewfinder, her head tilted as she inspected her eyebrows, pursed her lips, and rested the curves of her breasts on Mama's dresser. She laid her head on her arm and stared rapturously into my lens. Strangely enough she could not know how I could reduce her to a vampire, or transform her into an angel. Only Mama and I knew how a camera could lie.

"Unless," Anna drawled, "You meet someone at *Jaanipäev*!" She sat up rigid and tall, hiding her face behind one hand. "You may fall off your horse!"

"What?" I lowered my camera.

Anna pulled her feet up on the chair against her lace split bloomers, hugged her knees and peered at me, doe-eyed. "I mean we know what happened."

We had never spoken of the night in the barn at Metsajärve. I was almost eight years old, so long ago that the memory had all but faded. Had I really seen what I thought? "Anna, what?" I said as I tied back the curtains from the window. "Give me another pose. Come on."

Anna held her hand over her face. "You know more than I do and you keep it to yourself, Siina. I ought to know. I'm also her daughter!"

"Anna, you were almost a perfect shot!"

"I think she was in love with Juhan."

"No, no."

"And with his child."

"Oh Anna!"

"Plus she died of it!"

"Really?" I moved forward with my camera. Anna lifted Mama's lipstick tube. I clicked.

Anna faced me. "We're old enough to hear it." Mama may indeed have had the beginning of Juhan's baby. It may have poisoned her blood. She may have died of it. What misery that must have been for Papa. What anger at the treachery he would have felt. "Siina, the past doesn't go away though it may disappear from sight."

"But what do we know of people's inner lives, little sister? We can't," I said, watching Anna's mincing steps to the bed where she stepped into her own clothes.

13. *Jaanipäev*

I woke, my heart racing, my skin tingling, not knowing why. Apple blossom scent wafted through the upstairs window. I breathed in deeply. Days were lengthening, buds fattening along Supeluse Street. Daisies strewed the lawns beyond my window.

Cobbles and iron roofs warmed. We shed layers of wool, pushed our boots to the back of the cupboard and found heelless summer shoes, Papa, his white canvas ones.

The air sweetened, the sea breeze cooled my skin. I'd have lain in the sun naked, my long legged bathing suit thrown to one side, but I didn't dare. Everywhere was beauty and promises of excitement, from the filmy, frothing sea to the distant islands snug against the sky, an infinity of blue. I was a stream in the rush of spring; a bottled pickle ready to pop its lid.

Anna and I marked off the days to summer solstice – *Jaanipäev.*

We hadn't seen Metsajärve for a year.

We caught sight of Lulle at her wooden tepee, her summer kitchen, where she was waving, calling, "At last my ducklings!" She stood bare-footed on the grassy slope, her blue blouse open deep at the neckline, her skin, summer-tanned. One chestnut braid was tugged loose over her bosom as if she'd no time to wrap or coil it. A straw-blond, fuzzy-haired grandchild grabbed her cleavage, another sucked his thumb and peeked glass-blue eyes from behind her skirts as Anna and I approached.

"I'd hardly know you anymore," Lulle chuckled. I dipped a quick bob which she ignored. I felt around my neck for my camera. I would be ready this year with the right light for the scenes that sprang up.

The *sulane* – farmhand, watched us as he picked up our bags. When our eyes met he tripped over a pail of water. Anna covered her mouth giggling.

"You set us all off. You with your camera. And such finery." Lulle raised an eyebrow at my beaded cardigan. I wished I hadn't appeared so conspicuous. "Oh, go on, Siina, enjoy yourself. You're young and lovely."

Jaanipäev is the longest, wildest of all the harvest festivals, older than Christianity, a time when the people of the land draw breath after spring sowing and before haymaking's long, pitiless days. Workers, farmers, townspeople, everyone celebrates the summer solstice. There's excessive eating and drinking, singing, dancing, and making love to ensure bountiful harvests. The milky white nights overflow into the sorry next days. Comatose bodies are everywhere, asleep in forests, pastures, along riverbanks, on farmhouse porches and beneath the wide forgiving arms of ancient, sacred oaks. Empty beer casks, warm embers of hundreds of bonfires and the char of old boats burned for good luck and harvests spread from Russian speaking Lake Peipsi, to the furthest westernmost point of the Baltic Sea island of Saaremaa.

From my earliest *Jaanipäev* I had sat on my grandfather's knee rocking in time to the accordion, dazzled by the dancers, enchanted by the singing, eager to dance and sing myself. Kert's brother, my favourite uncle whom Lulle reprimanded for lacing his stories with profanities, would jig me over the grass, my bare feet on the toes of his boots.

Now I was impatient to be with my cousins and friends again. I wondered if they'd notice me, and like what they noticed.

Lulle could read me. "That's Eerik Seppa's horse," she said

nodding to where I was looking to a grey mare saddled with handsome nut-brown leather, tied to a nearby rail. “Eerik’s a sweet boy and his father, Jaan and I are great friends.”

Lulle was vibrant, more energetic than women half her age, my mother too when she was alive. Lulle shone like a polished stone, warm and sunny, more than any of my father’s relatives who only ever criticised. No wonder Jaan Seppa, her neighbour, followed her with his eyes, and his feet, even before Kert had been laid to rest. Jaan and Eerik were bee keepers in the Metsajärve *küla*.

“Are you....”

“What, getting married?” Lulle’s eyes crinkled. “Oh no. We’re perfectly happy the way things are. I know just what I want. I work hard, I have what I need. We sowed more grain this year than last and I still have rye in my bins.” I wondered if Lulle and Jaan slept together but she would never say and however much I longed to ask, I could not.

“Besides, I don’t need a husband. Metsajärve does very well,” she said as if guessing my thoughts. “And look, grandsons!” Lulle removed sticky fingers from the chain of silver coins around her neck. She’d been a widow for eight years. Her arms were more muscled than my father’s. Her grandchildren were darlings. They listened to stories quietly, to instructions patiently, learning how mint differed from nettles, where dandelions grew and when to pick them, where to watch for moths that laid pesky eggs. “I need no more,” Lulle laughed and shifted the baby from one hip to the other.

“They’re bonny,” I said, the boys watching me closely.

Once I had wanted to be in Lulle’s family but now, this *Jaanipäev*, as Lulle, Anna and I picked our way across the damp grass to the bonfire, I was sure that I didn’t. The smell of sun-scorched hay, earth and wood smoke were fragrant and familiar but I should not have to justify my camera and beaded cardigan. I was no longer a child but I was certain of where I belonged. Pärnu's cobbled lanes, ancient city wall, the bay and shadow of Kihnu Island, the seagulls and the salt sea were home.

"Those men..." Lulle said as we passed between men and the boys I knew were watching us. "You and Anna, be sure to take Murri to the hayloft with you tonight."

We all knew how old and deaf Murri was. "Anna and I can bark and bite for ourselves," I said though perhaps we wouldn't, I couldn't quite say.

I fingered my camera in the twilight. My photographs would be foggy though I was tempted. I watched the women, the reed thin girls, the young mothers, buxom farmers, lifting their heels, stamping to the accordion, changing to flat-footed waltzes, to coy wooing routines with men whom I recognised. Some were taller than I remembered, some more handsome and bearded, others spotty, desperately growing whiskers. I hoped they'd like my short hair, my daring skirt above my calves, my black beaded cardigan.

On the far side of the field, men raised steins of golden ale, wiping their lips, gazing from one group of women to the next. A harmonica band played syncopated rhythms. Women's voices, high-pitched like birds in flight rose in laughter. Men's treble notes boomed like swamp toads. I saw a hand squeeze a buttock, one slip under a blouse. I lingered beside Lulle but Anna, eager to know who was who, marched on across the field to the noisiest group. A man traced the line of his partner's shoulder blades with his fingers then kissed her. Bowing and handshaking took too long.

"Beer?" Lulle asked me.

"Yes, yes." I watched Anna entertain several men, then further off across the field men and women climbed on the swing, pushing and pumping it up. My grandfather, drunk, was tied to the platform support bars and encouraged his friends to push him until the platform swung higher and higher, and over the top.

"I know, I know."

"I even did it myself," Lulle winked. "Once."

Girls slid off the platform and staggered into the bushes, sure to vomit. "And I've seen that as well," Lulle laughed.

Anna however didn't need such antics. She merely dangled a mug from her fingertips, flirting and teasing and talking nonsense and men gathered. I doubted she was drunk, but certainly merry.

"Your sister …," Lulle began.

"Is sure of herself."

"She shimmers," Lulle said. "And why not? You're both beautiful. You have so much to enjoy. Be happy!" We had paused to look toward the grannies, a row ranged alongside the harmonica players on a bench against the barn. They'd have seen many dozens of *Jaaniöhtut* like this; the flirting and pinching, heard wild promises, whispers of love and loyalty, proposals. As fast as they flicked yarn from their pockets and clacked their needles, they swapped stories, predicting who had a chance with whom, how long a match might last, how long before love and lust vanished and work tired couples to death. The grannies kept their ears pricked, guessed which farm would fail because a woman complained and complained, or a man slept too much, or drank his life away. They followed every breath in the *küla* – the village, the sicknesses that plagued families, the drink or pneumonia that claimed a parent and left children orphaned. They'd birthed babies often enough to say which ones, having no sooner crowned and yelling to bring down the rafters, would grow to robust manhood. Others who whimpered plaintively and turned their heads away from overfull breasts, the women predicted, would succumb to some critical illness. They'd seen children survive smallpox and blood poisoning and would guess who would be next laid-out in the *saun* before the funeral.

They had reasons to know which man would be cruel to his children and animals and which would bring his wife tea in bed, set up the stove when she was heavily pregnant even when it was her work. They already knew the fellow who shouted obscenities to his empty house, cursed god and the devil, threw his axe across the courtyard in blind rage but would never harm a soul. Neighbours could forgive his madness after his young wife died with a stillborn days after his only son had been lost in Manchuria in the tsar's army. The grannies waggled their heads at the shamefulness of a woman who pressed herself against a stranger young enough to be her son. No one, least of all her, knew if her husband had died at a war front, even though soldiers commonly disappeared.

Lydia, bone thin and flinty, and her sister Elvi, round with thick short legs, were taking in the crowd, nodding and laughing. They'd inherited a farm and had taken it up without a man to lift or stack bins and barrels. Together they improved buildings, thatched and screwed moss between wall gaps, ploughed, sowed, mowed and prospered. Elvi's weight was strength, Lydia read, asked, listened to all she could about animals, cheese, barley, rye and bread making. Country folk, Lulle reminded me, had the instincts from childhood, had read the skies, smelled and felt the soil, knew the colour and touch. Some disregarded the almanacs dating from hundreds of years back.

"I don't really understand," I admitted.

"Of course you don't." Lulle nodded toward a clean shaven

man standing close to the fire, his features lit up. “Is that not Juhan?”

Juhan? It was, but aged so that my heart sank and tears filled my eyes.

“It is, but…!” He’d lived in hell. Shrunken and withered.

Lulle held my wrist hard enough to bruise. I wrenched away. “I must talk to him.”

“Be nice.”

I’d tell him what I thought. I wanted to shout across the field. I also needed to think how I’d say what I meant. He recognised me though he hardly raised his eyes.

“Juhan?” He was a lifeless tree. “Juhan?”

“Siina,” he said, his voice smoky, his eyes carbon. “Who’d know you?” he said, a smile suggesting itself. His hair was as long and leaden as his shirt, his cheeks grooved, his skin slack and furrowed. I remembered a face like an iron visor. He watched me, waiting with all the time in the world.

14. War

In an instant Juhan ricocheted me back to *that Sunday*. He had been my teacher and hero, he'd carried Mama into Ksenia's house but vanished before anyone noticed who he was. Before we knew it, it was the night of the burnings.

He was not as old as he looked, but used up and world-weary. He ran his eyes over me openly, from my shining bob to my leather shoes. I wondered if I disappointed him.

"You disappeared," I said at last, wanting to know from his lips, what he'd say. "Did you march in Tallinn?"

"Tallinn? No."

But he'd survived. "So after the manors....?"

"After...." He looked away from me toward the bonfire. I saw a lone wolf, no hero, even so, he had defiance. I'd seen the same thing in Jaan Seppa's father, so quiet he might have been dreaming. He thrashed around in his sleep the rest of his life, Eerik said. Jaan's father had been captured and held prisoner in Central Asia. If he spoke anything of that time a person would cling to every syllable of understated emotion. He said men could be cruel.

"What would you think, after Siberia?" Juhan said, jolting me back to his stillness, the stare of endurance.

I shook my head but I knew.

"I did better than some." He turned away to clear his throat.

I knew how dangerous it was to speak against authority. I'd heard enough of men disappearing. My father was reticence and patience for reason. He led others because he could plan and act with caution.

"I didn't expect to see you. You know my mother's gone."

"I heard."

"You betrayed her."

"Oh, no." Juhan shook his head sorrowfully, convincingly. I wanted to believe him even when I thought of my mother weeping, telling me about her secret, like a painting in a box, under a lid.

"But how?" I began, only what use was it when she was gone and he so destroyed?

I stretched my arms around his neck and held on to his pine, earthy smell though he was cold as a stone, his arms hanging limply beside his thin, unbending body. I let go and stepped back.

"You look good, Siina, grown up."

"You look terribly tired. You know how she died."

"I do." He moved his weight from one leg to the other. Someone had told him. "She had fire, your mother. We shared dreams."

Deadly dreams. "And look what happened," I said.

He stepped forward, took my fingers and pressed them to his lips. His eyes brightened. I imagined the idealist, excessive in love and recklessness.

"That was a time, wasn't it? We may yet live those dreams. We will get what we want. You will. You'll see."

I shook my hand away. "You had no right!"

"Why? She and I, adults, Siina. When do you have a right? When else?"

"She didn't want to die!"

"We knew what we were doing. Don't imagine we didn't. You'll come to it yourself, Siina. When you're older. Remember what your father said when you joined our meeting? You arrived like a rubber ball." He smiled, his face creasing up like a dried apple.

“I’ve no idea what he said. I was a child.” I did remember. Exactly.

“He warned me. He was a patient man. Is he still?”

“Of course. We lost her and you don’t care!”

“No.” He shuffled.

“Did you betray her?”

He shook his head again. “We’d have been a pair, wouldn’t we?” I couldn’t see it.

“You were once my hero.”

“A sad waste that was. They caught me you know, after the manor burnings. Your father was right. I was no use to you all in Siberia.”

“I believed in you once.”

Juhan worked a slow smile. “I believe in you Siina. You let me in from the cold that night. Up against everyone.”

I stood back. My eyes hurting. “I hate what you did.”

Juhan opened his hands in hopelessness. “Nothing is simple. We choose what we believe. What about you?”

I didn’t know and he recognised it. “I can’t do anything brutal.”

“Good! Be a ministering angel. Patch up afterwards.”

I pulled my cardigan tight as he watched, as if he could read my mind.

“How do you live now? Where?”

He motioned toward the forest. “Not so far from here. I have a cabin. An excellent hunting dog. I do all right. Your mother and I were the same as many, for people of the land and those without voices. You might know that.”

So I was wrong, yet something was strange. “You were mysterious, and together.”

"Romantic for you was it?"

"Of course."

"Your father knew," Juhan said.

Perhaps he did and I chose to deny it. Juhan pushed his hands in his pockets and shifted his worn boots in the dewy summer grass. "Listen to your father," he said and with a tip to his hat, a salute, he shuffled backwards, stooping as if he might bow, giving me nothing at all, not a kiss, not a handshake but like a train shunting. I saw humility and respect. I brushed off tears. He shrank, dragging himself across the field.

15. Ilar

I would not stand there by myself in that field when every person laughed and danced, promises of *Jaaniöhtu* mingling friends and lovers. Juhan was my childhood. I was grown. I'd been mistaken. I was duped and felt foolish. When I looked around not a soul cared that Siina Jürimäe stood alone in a field, heartbroken.

I blinked rapidly, wiped the end of my nose with my sleeve and stormed across the grass to Anna. At that moment, from the far side of the field a car thundered and rattled to a stop. Soldiers clambered out, last of all a fair-haired woman in flapping skirts leaning on the largest of the men. She straightened herself and began waving.

"Siina! *Issant Jummal*! She clutched her man as she came wobbling, he supporting her over the uneven grass to me.

"Elviira!"

"Siina! My god! It's been so long!" she shouted from almost beside me. "What on earth have you been up to? Thank god I found you! What are you doing? Why the camera? Where are your friends? Where's Anna! For god's sakes! Siina!"

"Elviira," I stammered, grateful she'd come to my rescue, at least for a moment and amazed this friend appeared in Metsajärve.

"Darling, it's shock and surprise beyond belief! Please!" she went on and began introducing me around to her soldier friends but at the same time, seemed to be looking for something else, perhaps more interesting. "But you, Siina! And Pärnu! What's going on? What a laugh!" I opened my mouth to speak. "Really!"

She buckled her knees and draped herself against her soldier then pushed him forward. “Dmitri, from Pskov! Meet Siina! Oh! We found each other at Mustvee, isn’t that something?” It sounded wicked and marvellous and Dmitri gazed at me impudently. “And oh! Meet Ilar Jakobsen, Siina! A man of action. *Estlane*!” She laughed, directing a younger, finer-looking soldier at me.

Ilar nodded and kept his distance. Dmitri from Pskov’s broad face widened in a smile as he stepped past Ilar, took my hand and kissed it. Poisonous fish, I thought and withdrew. His look, thick lips and heavy eyes made me queasy. But Elviira liked him and she was independence itself, had never cared what anyone thought. She balanced on his arm, recounted the bumpy ride from Pärnu, the roaring engine, but most importantly, that her shoes, a rare, lovely shade of fuchsia, were now stained and ruined, her creamy stockings too. I admired her transparent floral dress floating and lifting against the outline of her neat small bosom. Elviira clutched Dmitri’s arm and buried her face in his shoulder, giggling. He grinned like a cat.

“Shall we go? Where’s Anna?” she said at last.

I took a step but Ilar grabbed my hand. His grey eyes met mine. Straw coloured hair stuck out under his soldier’s cap.

“*Preili*, a moment.” He hinted a smile.

“We’re school friends,” I explained.

“And you a photographer! So daring, like your friend.”

“Perhaps,” I smiled. “Tell me, Ilar, man-of-action, how is it in the military?”

He backed away discreetly. “You don’t want to know, Siina. The military is one thing, war is quite another. And we’re about to find out, aren’t we?” His jaw sagged.

“Really?”

“Oh, yes. Russia never stops expanding, does she? Always.

You're educated and emancipated." He nodded to my camera. "We'll fight."

"I suppose so. But what are you? Socialist Revolutionary? Bolshevik?"

He drew a pack of cigarettes from his pocket, offered me one, and though I wanted to be sophisticated I didn't want to smoke. I was curious as he rolled the cigarette between his fingers of one hand and searched for matches with the other. "I'm none of those. Too many flaws with men who organise. I'm a cynic, shall we say? Anyway, we'll see how much time we have for party differences once we're at war, won't we?" He began to swing in time with the music as he blew cigarette smoke away from us. "The tsar's no different from the German Kaiser, don't you think? But what does it mean for a soldier? We're dead men." I pitied his look, tortured in the firelight.

"Don't say so."

He flourished his cigarette like a trophy. "Don't be shocked. I'm not. Not the first time death has knocked at my door. Destiny." He dipped his head, consoling, uncomfortable seeing my awkwardness. "Listen, come on to the swing," he said taking my hand.

"You're wishing doom. Don't." We hurried over the grass.

"It's not my doing. It's not me," he said.

"Don't! Be positive. Soldiers come home," I said but hearing doubt.

"Oh, really?" He blew smoke over his shoulder.

I stopped, pushed him and he turned to me, his eyes tragic. "Have the courage to survive! That's how it's done. Come back!" I said.

He stood still, cigarette poised to his mouth, eyes narrowed. He lifted his chin laughing. "You're sweet! I wish it were that easy! What a style you have!" He took another drag on his cigarette.

"Pessimism is wrong."

"You care so much about me?"

"I do."

"How much?" he said sliding closer, his arm circling my waist.

"Not like that."

"But *Jaaniöhtu*! and it's my last." He drew me to him, a hand on my breast and I gasped, my nipple scorched.

"Saying you'll die is giving in. It will kill you," I said, peeling away his hand.

"So make it worthwhile." He reached for my breast again.

"Oh, Ilar." I searched for honesty, hoping I knew how, expecting I'd see inside him, know him from some other time in my life, not with desire, not enough. "I don't want you to die. You're honourable and good," I said and held his hand in mine.

He looked down at our hands, his face grim again. "I don't believe you for a minute, Siina. I once thought we could take control, that people like us could command the future. It's shit. We're drones. Sorry. You're naïve and I'm disillusioned. But say, you'd enjoy a beer?" I nodded and he let go my hand and turned away.

16. Mihkel

I forced spring into my step crossing the grass to Anna and Elviira. They were laughing, unaware of me. When Elviira noticed she smiled and hugged me. "Siina, my darling, you're so stylish! So terribly!" She fingered my cardigan and caressed my camera. "I'm hugely jealous! Plus you've captivated Ilar. God! Look at him!" Ilar was striding toward us, a beer in each hand. He gave me one and we stood together without speaking. I didn't know how to continue. Elviira and Anna however, catalogued men, caught meaningful glances and sipped beer. In that soft light the white of the men's shirts and women's embroidered blouses glowed. I eased my camera out and aimed at the dancers. The bonfire would be a blur of light, the background, the soft amber sun – our world tipping. I tucked my camera back in my bag and noticed a man swinging across the field, meandering, pausing to shake hands, nodding to Enn and Leo, stopping with Aunt Lulle, pushing through the dancers – jammed between a heavyset man attached to a woman tossing silver-blonde hair. I heard Lulle's voice in my head. Completely unsuitable, Siina. The swinging man spoke to sisters Lydia and Elvi.

"Mihkel Oks. You know him!" Elviira squealed. "Pärnu boy! Socialist writer of incendiary prose," she stage-whispered. "Published in Petersburg and Tartu, Siina. Oh, la la! Naughty boy!" She snickered and sipped at her mug. I sensed Ilar moving toward me but my eyes were on Mihkel. Elviira gushed on. "Do you like him? Siina! I'm not sure who you like these days but you're in for trouble either way! Ha ha!"

I nudged her, smiling to myself, keeping track of him until I was sure he was heading for me. Ungainly as ever but tall now, not a teaspoon of his stocky family. He raised a hand and nodded before speaking.

"Siina Jürimäe! A great pleasure!" He trapped me with his eyes as I offered my hand. He kissed my fingers slowly, deliberately, quite unBolshevikly. I trembled, excited. "Pärnu *Laht*, but so long ago." He lowered his voice to a hush. "Marvellous to see you." He dropped his hands to his sides, eyes, cool, blue, steady and magnified by wire-rimmed spectacles. His lopsided mouth was oddly attractive.

"You left Pärnu ages ago," I said soberly.

"*Ja, ja*. I've been here in this *küla* since my father was killed. He was a protester at the Sindi mill you know. My mother couldn't support us. We came here, pitched in with my grandparents, managed." He smiled lightly. "I know your aunt Lulle and your cousins." He padded back and forth restlessly. "And here you are." He watched me the way he used to when we were children, exactly what Anna disliked about him.

"I hear you work in Petersburg," I said and sipped my beer.

"*Ja, ja,* but I come back to see my mother. Say! I bet you have your own ideas about where you go and what you do. Modern, aren't you, and European." He gestured at my camera bag.

"We like to think so. In Pärnu." I expected a smart reply but he laid his hand over his chest.

"Pärnu is in my heart but I love this too," he said with a sweep of his arm. "I'm no *talumees*. I can't do it; culling and killing. I can't eat meat." He cast about for anyone listening and raised an eyebrow in question.

"You're honest."

"I use the noggin," he said, tapping his temple, lowering his head to me, rushing on. "I interview people who think they know what's happening, who expect to lead a revolt or decide that a protest march is no more than a hiccup and war is simply a political move," he said winking. I considered asking all the things I wanted to know immediately. Men wanted to fight. The tsar lived in a cloud and willed his people to die. Who cared for soldiers and their families? Mihkel could enlighten me. He wrote for Tartu's *Vaba Sõna* and Petersburg's *Bourse Gazette*. He knew.

"So you stand somewhere. You're not objective once you see what goes on."

Tartu was a hotbed of intellectuals and radicals and he one of them – an agitator on paper with access to politicians.

"*Ja,* I take a stand but I write objectively! But seriously, will you not dance with me?" He bowed, offering his hand conventionally. I set down my beer and followed him beyond the drinkers.

"Though I'm a shocking dancer," he said, holding me at arm's length, checking me up and down so that my face and neck reddened. The drum urged our steps, he pressed the flat of his palm into the small of my back and held me close. The fiddler grinned at me. "You're what I hoped for, Siina," Mihkel whispered.

I felt warm in every place our bodies touched. I might have melted into him.

He reversed direction, timing perfect, moves instinctive.

"You do dance!"

"Not really. A dancer can seduce a girl. Everyone knows," he said, our hands sweating together.

"You're still on Supeluse? No one kidnapped you? Why?"

"Go on! I'll go travelling when I'm ready. Soon in fact."

"*Primo*!" he said stepping between my legs and I followed, stepping between his, waltzing properly, my legs turning to rubber, hot and cold and alarming, his thigh between mine, my skin jumping. He smiled, unperturbed. “I’d be enchanted to have you visit me. You and your camera.”

“Well, I don’t know quite where I’m going or what I’m looking for. But I have ideas but perhaps like you, I’ll search and find out, look for what I want, to turn into something else. Something monumental,” I said with ridiculous daring then closed my mouth.

Mihkel nodded as we slowed down dancing at half beat. “*Ja, ja*. I know what you mean. You’re an artist and scientist. And you’re alluring, Siina. Of course you know that much. Who else has told you?”

“Who?” I said, feeling a clot forming in my brain. “Oh...” I murmured thinking that I should ask more yet wanting to be quiet, to just be close and go along with the rhythms, noticing that he was holding me closer, firmly, as if he wouldn’t let go, as if he was determined to protect me. “I do want to go to beautiful places and meet people I’ve read about. I mean, see types I’ve never seen, capture them as they are and keep them! Like Pääsuke....”

“The man with two cameras!”

“Prokudin-Gorskii.”

“Photographed in colour! The empire.”

“Beautiful places!”

Mihkel nodded.

I had hoped he would take me seriously and even if he had laughed I’d convince him I meant what I said. He didn’t laugh. He stared looking at me, my neck and shoulders as if he might taste me. “You’ll see Prokudin’s work in Petersburg you know.”

“I do. Plus Margaret Cameron’s photographs. Rain and mist and nudes.”

“Aha! You’d move with the demi-monde, Siina. I’ll be in Petersburg.”” His breath warmed my cheek. “When can I see you again?”

He squeezed my hand. “Come. Meet artists and rebels, nihilists and eccentrics, painters and dancers. You’ll be stunned. Stay with me.” Our waltz started again. Mihkel lifted and swung me in the air. I touched the ground, breathless and I leaned into him. “I’ll show you bourgeois glitter, Hermitage treasures, Vyborg slums, Haymarket prostitutes. You’ll love and hate and fear it all.”

“I know,” I said remembering Ksenia’s promises. “I may then,” I said, easily as if picking a berry from a bush. A circle formed and Mihkel lowered his arms to my waist and tugged me to him.

“That city explodes with adventure. Ideas burst. Akhmatova and Blok, they detonate the classics daily! You’ll light up and burst into flame. No, no! You’ll fall in love.”

I shivered but I felt the dread of *that Sunday*. I could taste sickening chocolate milk. This time it would be different. I would take in luxury with Ksenia, photograph people she entertained, princesses and baronesses, get images of her butler and *isvostchik*, the light and snow, the icicles and atlantids, canals and bridges in sunlight, with fur-muffed women and top-hatted men. I’d get the Winter Palace, the red column with the angel on an ordinary day. I’d take the gold Peter and Paul spire and the Neva in summer. Petersburg was not even a day’s train journey away.

“I’m not letting go.” Mihkel tugged me from the circle. I was giddy and limp and I decided we would kiss. “Stay with me tonight,” he whispered when our lips separated. I shook my head, pleased he wanted me, happy he’d keep me. “I want you for myself.”

"I won't, but I'm glad you're back," I said and there was Anna tugging my sleeve, insisting we take Granny home and find our bed in the loft in the hay barn. It was very late, the birds still twittering, the light, soft and creamy. When Anna gave Mihkel the least glance, he let me go without a word.

In the early hours of the next day, the old dugout boat which had sizzled and sparked for hours was no more than a red glowing bowl, melted tar puddled in the centre.

I excused myself from Anna and Elviira and photographed a group of children playing cats' cradle. With Granny's shawl around my shoulders I listened to the droning of folk reliving old times, telling of when they were young and invincible, of barons who worked them for nothing and punished them for less. Perhaps better times were coming they agreed, their voices eddying across meadows, bursting into song then fading. Grandparents, young people, children joined choruses of songs of overlords sung since slave days, the words less relevant, but the passion as fervid as when they were written. I sat alone on a log, my head heavy with more beer than I had ever drunk but happy because there were also loving secrets being whispered within earshot. Couples lay in each other's arms and slumped together on the grass. I took a discreet shot here, young lovers there, in bliss.

I stretched out on the grass beside the dog, Murri, as a blurred Mihkel appeared; shirt open, hair standing up like a rooster, gesticulating toward me. "I've been looking everywhere!" he whispered closer, not to waken anyone.

"And I have photographs. Difficult light."

He wrapped his arms around me. He smelled of beer and wood smoke. "You know what we must do now?"

I crumpled into him. “Jump the fire?” But already he was standing, a hand extended.

“Dare you? You know what it means.”

“Go on! Get on with it, lovebirds. Jump!” someone’s grandfather blared.

We faced one other, gripping hands, and galloped toward the embers, a few low flames and charred wood, all that remained of the bonfire. We ran perfectly in time, he shortening his stride to accommodate mine, me stretching to match his. I felt a lift from his wiry hold as we flew over the dying logs, the world tilting and singing before we tumbled and rolled onto the grass, still connected. I looked for his face as I lay panting and laughing and he reeled over and held me so firmly I couldn’t breathe. “I never knew if I’d meet you again. I’ve been madly in love with you since I was seven,” he whispered.

I laughed. Being in love for that long was beautiful.

His eyes widened. My blouse had popped open. “I won’t resist you,” he said reaching for me, his hands to my face and kissing me hard.

I lay back and buttoned up my blouse, still panting. “You always made me nervous.”

“I make myself nervous,” he said, a foolish look as he reached for me again. “Now the other thing – yes?” He breathed deeply. “The flower. Come, or your granny won’t let up.”

I could feel myself smiling all over because it was yes to the flower hunt and yes to him and more. Everyone from Lapland to Denmark to Italy searched for the fern flower at summer solstice, to sleep, to dream upon so that true love would be revealed.

We paused at the meadow’s edge where the woodland closed in and there I saw Helve’s little sister, skirt hoisted above her knees, bloomers flashing in the bushes, scrabbling and crawling around with Lars, her lame boyfriend, the two wrestling like cubs.

“Other way,” Mihkel whispered yanking my hand.

Ahead the woods were so still they might have been enchanted.

“Are you searching?” I stepped under the trees in the half-light. Mihkel, dreamy in the silver morning, the boy who imitated nightingale’s calls, who found the sun on the *laht*, edged closer and I drew up to him.

“May I?” he said and as I moved to him he slipped his arms behind me and held me as though I were glass. We really kissed, again and again and when I stepped back he held me by my forearms. “I’ll look after you. I mean it.”

“Perhaps,” I murmured to the rhythm of distant drums and accordions. We danced shambling steps further into the woods, me heady with drink and tiredness but I could let him kiss me more, and see what next might happen. It was the right night. He was sweet and perhaps he really loved me. Whatever the woodsy dark held, I was his. He stroked my cheek, pulled me to him as we rocked together from lips to hips to toes dancing and kissing, my heart flipping, my belly yearning for more. When we stood together our bodies were one, our clothing, nothing. We vibrated, our breathing quickening. As one.

Twigs cracked, leaves crunched. Voices blared into my trance. I sprang from Mihkel. Soldiers straggled, blundering through the undergrowth, two, three, another, more, men on the prowl, Russian uniforms awry, faces red and beery, men drinking half the day and all night, coming at us.

“Oh ho! And look who we have here!” one yelled as they circled. I grabbed Mihkel’s sleeve but he shoved me behind him, stepped forward, guarding me, snarling like a dog.

“Get out!”

They slowed a moment. "Oh, the darlings!"

I gripped Mihkel's belt.

"Our Socialist rebel boy and his honey pot! Well, well!" one of them slurred. They stumbled back and forth. I closed my mouth over panic and surging sickness.

"Get out," Mihkel snapped. "On your way! The party's at the bonfire." He straightened, taller, puffed himself up to them.

Still light-headed, my stomach turning to water, I clung on, terrified, trapped.

"I'll have her," the broadest of them taunted in Russian, jumping toward us, the others leering. Tears came. Every part of me stiffened and closed up.

"No closer, not a step!" Mihkel commanded, his hand held out like a police warden. The soldiers slapped their knees, roaring.

"Or what? What, mouse? What... Socialist? Revolutionary? Anarchist? What?"

The largest, dark-haired, eyes like boulders, swaggered, paced back and forth, advancing. "What! Read to us? Save us? A bedtime manifesto? A bedding one! Hah! We'll show you – mutineer!" He spat, his dark hair in Mihkel's face. Another with a thin beard and black slanted eyes bounded forward and socked Mihkel in the chest. I struggled holding on as Mihkel buckled, flailed at the air and together we toppled. The Asian jabbed practice hits, dancing, jeering. "We'll fix him. He's done!"

"Christ we will!" Another soldier, red-faced, pranced sideways, throwing punches as my fists ached to hit him, my arms, to strike. I imagined running, my body quivering as Mihkel on his knees, struggled to stand. I could never run. They'd catch me, pin me down, beat Mihkel to blood and gore, rape me before murdering us both. Elviira had once said this, exactly so. Mad with drink, hatred of Bolsheviks, men, crazed!

"Leave our girls alone!" the Manchurian shouted leaning over us, as Mihkel unfolded. "Use your revolutionaries for fucking! Free fucking, yes? Well, not here! Bolshie bastard!"

"Oh come on! Where are your girls?" Mihkel reasoned, his voice about to break.

The Manchurian's hands fisted, swinging at his sides.

"Come on! Where's your party?" Mihkel reasoned, gesturing, pleading.

"Keep your Bolshevik revolutionary shit to yourself!" the tall one yelled wrenching at his pants, loosening his belt, shirt open, lunging then, with one hit, downed Mihkel again. The soldier crouched over me, ran his hand over my face. "*Milaya,*" he moaned as I struggled and screamed, kicked and fought. "*Milaya*!" he pinned my arms, licked my cheeks and lips, forced his tongue in my mouth as I thrashed. I sensed others gathering while Mihkel lay still. I whimpered, then sank my teeth into the man's mouth. Howling, he leapt back, lunged again, ripped my blouse, shoved his hand between my legs, grabbing and fumbling, me clawing and biting; then he sighed and collapsed beside me.

Mihkel stood over me, a thick branch in his hand. He raised it and beat Vladimir once again. I wished I could faint. Mihkel grabbed my arm. I scrubbed at my face and jammed my knees together. Fuchsia pink shoes!

"Siina! Oh my dear! Oh my god! What in hell? Darling! Siina! Oh God!" she screamed, over and over. Mihkel lowered the branch. Elviira and Dmitri pitched forward, Elviira to me, Dmitri incensed with Mihkel. More of their crowd straggled behind.

"Vladimir! Dear Vladimir! Oh Siina! How DARE he touch you!" Elviira shrieked.

"Oh my Vladimir! My friend!" Dmitri lurched forward, beseeching the sky. He reached over Vladimir, prodded him, turned his face to the side and lifted one eyelid. He leapt and swung at Mihkel, who dodged. “You’ve murdered him! *Bourgemou*! Tragedy! Murderer!” Dmitri grabbed Mihkel by the throat. “This is our Vladimir! Dead!”

I tucked in my legs, wrenched at my skirt, scrabbling to get up. I swiped at my face and mouth and saw Vladimir, still as a stone. Dmitri, lips and thick eyelids quivering, thrust Mihkel aside. “My dearest friend!” he groaned as his friends crowded in, jostling, making obscene gestures at the other soldiers, fists bunching, shoulder charging. Mihkel swayed, the branch fixed in his hands.

“Stop!” Elviira screeched throwing herself between Mihkel and the others.

Vladimir raised his head.”Shit! Oh shit!” he groaned and sank back into the leaves. The men sauntered and staggered. I kept my head low. One soldier pushed me aside to grasp his friend and grief poured out.

“Oh the sorrow!” he cried. “Will he live?”

“We all die!” another sobbed lifting Vladimir’s limp hand.

“Lift him!” I heard as a hand grabbed mine, pulling me back into the bushes as the men gathered around Vladimir. Mihkel and I pushed back into the trees. We crouched together, became invisible, crept, then bolted for the opening, and the fire.

...

Mihkel bathed my head in cool well-water. We sat on a low wooden bench outside Lulle’s pigsty. Mihkel wrung out his handkerchief and dabbed my face. “You’re all right, aren’t you?” he mumbled through a swollen mouth.

“I am.” I tightened Granny’s shawl over my torn blouse. My beaded cardigan was ruined, my skirt, dirt smeared and ripped.

“I’d have had to kill them all if not for Elviira,” Mihkel said, lifting my hair from my face, tracing his finger around my eyes. I nuzzled his chest.

"How did you do it?" I asked at last, trying to piece back what I could, up until the fuchsia shoes.

"I found a club. Primitive man. I'd fight Sarvik himself for you."

"They landed you a few."

Mihkel's forehead was swollen, red and grazed. He'd have black eyes in a few hours. "I'm quite fine, but you?" He kissed my hair.

"I feel sick and horrible."

"He didn't hurt you, did he?"

"Not really. Thank god for you."

He held me gently, exactly as I'd hoped and kissed me on the forehead.

"We never found the flower," I realised as tears washed up onto my cheeks.

"There is no flower. We knew that. There is love and loyalty."

I very much wanted to find that flower with Mihkel. I knew there was no flower but still, we'd been cheated and I felt unreasonably disappointed. "I know there's no flower but still, it's a belief," I said and cried into his shirt.

"It's superstition. We both know better than that," he said, steadily, as if nothing had happened.

He was right. It made no sense to assume a future based on a ritual yet I felt that we'd had a bad omen. "You're right. There is no flower, but there is love and loyalty," I sniffed and wiped tears.

"They wrecked your blouse."

"I have another. I don't care much about the blouse," I said but somehow I had to cry over it.

"I'll kiss you better," he said, kissed my shoulder and neck but right then I couldn’t stand a kiss of any kind.

“You don’t believe in omens?”

“Good ones. All the good omens,” he said.

I rested my head on Mihkel’s chest and cried for my blouse. “How could they? Awful, awful! I’ll be all right,” I raged as Mihkel stroked my shoulders.

“Yes yes. Awful awful. Say, your friend, Elviira, she really loves Dmitri?”

I shook my head. “She’s not my real friend. We were in class together. That’s all. But she did come in at the right time. I thank her for that.”

Mihkel nodded. “Exactly. Me too. She’s a true friend. But I don’t like her boyfriend. Not at all.”

“Me neither,” I said, shivering at the thought of Vladimir and Dmitri. I couldn’t bear it. “I hope those others disappear into dust. I’ll never trust men like them! Not an inch. Maybe they get shipped to Manchuria.”

“Ideal,” Mihkel said with a reassuring squeeze. “One thing is sure. They won’t bother us again, you can bet on it.”

17. Sarajevo

I hadn't heard from Mihkel for a year, not since we jumped the fire. Archduke Ferdinand, stitched into his regalia so as not to spoil his profile had been shot and killed with his wife in Sarajevo by that time. The tsar failed negotiations with his cousin, the Kaiser, and declared war on Austro-Hungary and the Central Powers. It was only weeks since the great fortress of Lemburg was captured by the Russians, lost after the ignominious, never-to-be-forgotten battle led by Commander Brusilov. German troops devastated the Russians, pounded the Galician fortress and took it.

I'd had several poems from Mihkel that was all. No wonder Juhan had been depressed. Ilar could be dead, as he'd predicted, together with more than four million Russian troops. A bullet through the head may indeed have killed him, though if he was lucky, a graze over his temple could save him. Field hospitals still had food, bandages and iodine. I preferred to think of Dmitri and Vladimir lying dead on some far distant battle field; but, what difference would that make? It was better then that the war be over soon and no one need shoot the other.

I tried to guess if Mihkel had gone to the front for a story or was still in Peterburg. He might have been in as much danger as a soldier. Retreat for the armies was an option I'd heard. Peasants were starving before the war so there was less now for battalions of undisciplined soldiers and every day, even less. Some were unarmed. It was hideous to think of them. Retreating armies would certainly starve. I tried to picture Mihkel somewhere safe doing what he could. If he escaped gunfire, could he kill someone for a mouthful of food?

I didn't want to believe the newspapers or worse, the soldiers' stories, regardless of whether they were embellished and exaggerated. Men were mutilated or lost. Mothers tried to shut off feelings, closed their mouths but still, stories were repeated.

I kept wishing for a letter.

"You haven't said a word about him. Where is he?" Anna asked as we strolled under linden trees between Ammende Villa and the market on Kuninga in Pärnu.

"I can't say. I did get a letter and poems but that was months back."

"Many months?"

"Yes."

"You're so secretive. We used to tell each other everything, Siina." It was true. Once we shared every thought and idea, but children wish to be agreeable.

I hated to think of Mihkel at the front in the killing and dying, a man who'd refuse to cull the herd yet protect me. I blocked out the ways men died, lay unburied, rats, lice and fleas swarming and what went on in the minds of men on watch, the waiting and seeing. Mihkel would not be there but Hardi and other boys from our *küla* were sure to be called up. I heard them call in the muddy dark, bloodied and wounded, my cousins and friends. I saw Mihkel running in an ice-black fog, spinning circles, searching for a sign overhead as Cossacks slashed and trampled, my dreams, my fears, in daylight too. I'd call up the taste of wild strawberries, green forests and sunset clouds instead, river banks and the soft focus of Julia Cameron's, angelic children photographed beneath willows and Roman monuments. Still Mihkel's sad image insisted crowded its way into my consciousness and dragged through my mind.

"I understand," Anna said, sunshine and light, excited by dresses and shoes – and her love, Oskar. So now she would perform in Paris and Berlin, he encourages her. Whatever went on in the far reaches of Russia and Asia, thousands of *versts* beyond Pärnu she rejected.

I didn't care so much for Oskar. Anna knew. We kept our thoughts to ourselves, not the way we used to. Once we said everything. Oskar was more than ten years older than Anna and mad about her but he hardly saw me. She had got a part at the *Endla,* an Ibsen play, and immersed herself. Her looks, her clothes, her stature were all and she cared less about me than ever. I wouldn't pour my heart out to her but I hoped that by not speaking about Mihkel I gave him a chance to survive. I willed him to return. I imagined him tucked up in some hideaway scribbling articles, away from shell fire.

"He left Tartu. I don't know if he's in Petrograd or not," I said.

Anna was annoyed with me keeping my distance. She could be open about herself even when we disagreed. She stopped in the street, raised her eyes to the heavens and circled her arms dramatically. I admired her intensity. "Mihkel is all right. I feel it," she said lowering her eyelids as if she was Helena Blavatskaia in a séance. "I mean it, Siina darling. He is safe." She cast a look at me. Pure. Loving.

I desperately wanted to believe her, that this action could save Mihkel at that very moment. I hugged my sister and kissed her lips. I adored her in so many ways, her spontaneity and vitality, her over-acting, her compassion. "Anna, I pray you're right. Thank you, thank you!" She smiled and hugged me again. For a moment we were the way we used to be.

I really could go to Peterburg. If Mihkel was there I would find him. If he was at the front he had to return to the city with reports every so often. I could even go to the front. Women did. Photographers, nurses, truck drivers risked their lives to save soldiers and our country. Despite howling winds, mud, cannons, artillery, tents bombarded, and droves of bleeding dying men, they went. I would not. But I would go to Peterburg, interview soldiers, and report stories with photographs. That was possible. The bandaged and mutilated bodies, the faces, the expressions they couldn't hide. There was my job. My photographs would be published and men and women everywhere would see the monstrosity of war. If anything could put an early end to it, it would be the revealed truth.

"I've had other letters," I admitted to Anna.

"Good. Hurrah! What?"

"Ksenia, Anna, she writes to me."

"Why would she?"

"She thinks I'm Mama. Strange, no? But you know she's offered me work in Peterburg. A tutor with a gorgeous family."

"What family? Where? You'll never accept. You're studying to be an accountant, aren't you? But really you're a photographer, Siina. I know that much. Think clearly now! You're not a tutor."

I smiled to myself. How little my sister knew me. I'd not told her much either. In fact the position excited me. I'd soon speak the plumiest Russian, Peterburg Russian, and as a German tutor I would be challenged but not too much. Besides, I would see a world vivid and thrilling. A grand capital, one of the richest, most daring and artistic. The war in Peterburg was irrelevant! I was terrified at the prospect and completely seduced by it.

"Heavens, Anna. I can't tell you what I may do. I don't yet know myself!"

"Siina, really! Papa will never allow it. Neither would my husband."

I smiled to myself and walked on.

"Siina, what are you grinning about! Tell!"

On the street corner of *Aia tänav* a newspaper boy with a sack of papers over his shoulder held a copy up to his chest; *German High Command uses chlorine gas bombs at Ypres*. There was a photograph of soldiers in a trench facing the camera. Staged. Blatantly. Some photographer had lugged a camera and tripod, glass plates, chemicals, a magnesium flash, developing chemicals and a dark tent there. We saw the conditions in a flash, even the posed, glorified scenes. No writer could match the subtleties of the picture. The men, propped up as they were, were shadows, exhausted with fear exposed. We saw the shape and depth of the trenches, how useless their supposed protection was. Photographers could choose their subjects and disregard what they didn't want although there were clues to the truth in every frame. One soldier gave another a haircut, one shaved before a glass hung on a dead tree. Their demeanour suggested a country holiday, tents pitched for summer, but sabres and helmets ready for heroics. I looked closely at nurses in their white starched uniforms, a Red Cross emblem on their truck, a wooden box of supplies beside the field hospital. It looked hygienic because there were no soldiers yet, none wounded.

"*The Price of Peace and Freedom*?" the boy's newspaper headline read.

"I just wish the men talked to one another. Our leaders!" I glowered at Anna. I predicted her response.

Her large brown eyes blinked slowly. "Siina, it's not for us to dispute. I hate it, of course I do, but there were atrocities in Serbia. Remember! We must act."

I faced my sister. "Don't you wonder why the generals don't

speak to one another? If they could save soldiers dying? Why doesn't it make you furious too?"

"I trust them, Siina. They know what needs to be done."

I gritted my teeth. "We're fighting our cousins, and innocent people die. People who have no connection with atrocities!"

"It's the cost of our lives, Siina. Surely you see that! Liberty has a price. Germany occupied Luxemburg criminally! You know that." Anna swung her knitted bag and gave me another blink.

"But surely, Anna, wouldn't you think there's another way? If you think about it. You see how many millions have died already!"

Anna spread out her hands and shrugged. "Well, they've not found another way. They are world leaders."

"You support the tsar. Haven't you grown up?"

"We are subjects, Siina. We can't afford to lose or back down. We all need discipline and order. That's civility." She strutted ahead to the market.

"To fight like animals," I said to her back.

Anna sat down on a park bench and folded her hands on her knee. "You're going to Peterburg to find Mihkel, aren't you?"

"I am. Then Dresden, then Vienna."

"In this war?"

"Yes," I said because the war would be over within weeks or at the most, months and once again we'd travel, be as wealthy and happy as we'd been before the Tsar Nicholas and Kaiser Wilhelm spoilt our entire civilisation. "I'd like your photograph, Anna," I said as sunlight fell across her face, bands of light and dark giving her zebra stripes. Behind her a wall was stippled with brilliant greens.

"Of course," she agreed squinting into the sun.

"No squinting," I ordered.

"No ordering," Anna returned but she smiled charmingly and whatever frustration I felt with her, she could ignore it. She held her hands above her head naturally and smiled through slit eyes, an oriental look, seduction, allure. "The thing is, Siina, we must stand up to keep what's ours," she explained as if I had no mind.

"What do you count as important, Anna?"

"Whatever there is to count, Siina, it must be done. Stop trying to be so clever. You're neither a man nor a world leader."

18. Saun

One could scarcely see the pine-log *saun* amongst the trees, the tin roof in the shade of lindens, their leaf shape prints. On the farther side flax and reeds grew thick along the riverbank for geese and goslings to hide from osprey and *merikotkas*, sea eagles. Inside the steamy little room, carved ladles hung overhead, Kert's handiwork, and stacked on high shelves, bundles of flax ready for soaking.

Anna and I sweated, our skin pink, runnels of sweat down our faces and breasts and backs as we breathed cedar and surrendered to the heat.

"Am I selfish to feel so content?" I sighed. My skin prickled and soon would be awash with more sweat.

"But why him?"

"Oh, you needn't like him, Anna. I do."

"Well I don't."

I stretched out on the top seat trying to picture him, his lopsided face coming and going. His letter and poems lay under my pillow, unfolded and folded so many times that the paper had worn thin on the creases and almost split. "I'm happy, Anna. He's safe."

"You don't stop about those poems, do you?" Anna said stretching on her back on the lower shelf. She lay with her arms under her head, relaxed here, more than anywhere else. We could say what came to mind. Surprising things.

"I'm too happy to argue," I said.

"Well I'm jealous of Helve's acceptance of her life, her utter contentment. Her babies are lovely too. Little darlings. I could be more like that, don't you think?" Anna sat tall, spun on her bottom and looked up at me. I agreed, at least my mood did.

"You do want more, Anna. I do. But I like what you're saying. The simplicity and acceptance. In theory, but you Anna, do not suit simplicity."

"True. Actually I want big roles. Lead roles. I want to be good."

"Leading lady, in fact."

"Oskar's wife, mother of four beautiful children, and scintillating hostess of occasional bridge parties with important people."

Helve and her sisters were uncomplicated. I was sure neither Anna nor I could be like that. They were happy to be warm and fed, have a good harvest, a man, and babies. They were intimate and attached to one another, even more than Anna and I. They were not afraid to make demands, speak directly, without apologies. The natural rhythms and pauses of their lives suited them. Yet for all of that I did not wish to be them. I would be separate, go off alone, and perhaps never marry, if I chose. "I intend to see Dresden and Marrakesh and definitely Petersburg. Now that Mihkel is back." I nuzzled the skin of my arms, thinking of him. "I will take astonishing, wonderful shots and in the end, a collection."

"So you will," Anna said turning onto her stomach. "I see you there, your pigskin bag and camera, perhaps Mihkel, in a bar filled with poets, musicians and artists and you the only photographer, perhaps the only woman."

"Perhaps." I sat up, my hair stuck to my scalp; sweat puddling in the small of my back, behind my knees and between my breasts. "I may go sooner than you think."

"I'll miss you terribly."

"You won't. You have Oskar. You'll never be lonely. Has he sent you more flowers and jewellery?"

Anna snorted laughing. "I can't say."

"He's shorter than you!"

"Never mind. We'll be in love for ever." Anna slid off the bench, cracked open the door and dashed across the grass, naked buttocks gleaming, dark hair stuck to her back. If I ran perhaps I'd not notice the shock of cold water. Late summer had crept up without my wishing to know.

Anna dived into the river, spraying shining beads of that seemed to pause mid-air. I wiped my eyes, sweat dripping, and chased after her.

The earth was still warm, every green thing giving off a scent of ending summer. Frogs still croaked in the tall reeds, a pair of cranes stalked the distant bank before making long graceful sweeps of their sooty grey wings to take flight. The water glazed with chinked reflections. Anna raised her arms, splashed and tossed her hair. The afternoon was turning gold. I dived and gasped, trod water and watched the widening ripples around Anna. She surfaced, flicked her head around and we swam toward the bank together.

Laughter, men's voices, rang out from the *saun* - our cousins, grey with dust, littered with hay gathered there. Anna and I bobbed down, kept moving to keep warm, sensing the air cooling off.

"Oh, the city girls! They'll be damned cold by the time the moon comes up!" I heard Enn.

"Go away! We're getting out!" Anna ordered.

Enn waved our clothes. "Good! Come on! Give me a kiss." There were loud cheers. "Come on! A hug." Enn threw his arms wide.

"Go away!" I yelled, shivering.

"Don't be shy!" Enn taunted. Anna and I looked at one another and shivered.

"It's only us!" Hinrik called.

Hinrik was a clear-eyed, fair-haired Norseman with a sharp nose and full mouth, handsome and good-natured. Beside him, Enn was stringy and awkward but made up for his odd looks with energy and opinions. His voice boomed across fields. He stuck his nose into everyone's business but he offered a strong arm when needed. Anna and I were very fond of him. He had a kind heart and was easily moved.

"Oh damn! It was such a great idea but you won't play!" he yelled. After gales of laughter we heard the *saun* door close, and a moment later, quiet.

Our clothes lay in a heap on the river bank. We scrambled out, clutched our clothes tight and ran for the house.

Lulle looked over her shoulder when we burst in. "Girls!" She glanced to the other side of the room. Oskar sat, his sky blue eyes wide smiling at Anna's naked skin.

Tädi Lulle set up her paraffin lamps. "I told the men you were there. You swam. There's soup and bread. You know Oskar, don't you?" she said as we scuttled.

In the kiln-house we dried our hair and caught our breaths.

Anna held a hand to her chest. "What will I say? He's serious coming here."

I untangled my hair. "Your decision. You must know."

"I do!" Anna smacked me on the arm, peered at her face and hair, her clothes and shoes. She twisted herself at the little mirror, rearranged her hair, tucked in her blouse and sucked in her stomach, folded her hands under her chin. "He's clever and good looking and considerate. I could fall in love, I mean, it would be like diving into the deepest, bluest, purest water! I could let go!" She refastened her hair pins and arched her dark eyebrows and squinted her perfect eyes and lips. A sculptor would never need lie. She slept as if she had some delectable mystery inside. Men would line up outside the theatre door to see her. Oskar would have, too. He sent her chocolates, flowers and once, silver jewellery.

I wondered if Mihkel would think of me as a beauty. His poems were more like private musings than love. He could easily meet some balalaika-playing Russian lovely and forget me. Perhaps he exaggerated his work and spent afternoons reading Buddenbrooks and writing those poems. I tried to picture him tangoing and drinking vodka. He was a better dancer than he admitted.

"Are you sure, Anna?" I thought of my mother and Juhan. I'd been intoxicated by him. If I'd been ten years older I'd have fallen in love.

"I am! I wish we could talk privately somehow."

Oskar and she were a good match I decided. They'd be happy and devoted. She should say, yes. If he'd come to ask Lulle's permission then Anna had to answer.

Oskar had four brothers, each muscular and barrel-chested. They had wide square faces and eyes that darted, before they penetrated. Among them, Oskar was the most intense. I imagined him and Anna with a string of sons like beans in a row. They'd be powerful and successful, noticing what was needed and getting it done. So I imagined.

"Unless you wait, see something of the world first. You are an actress. You may languish and wither in a farmyard making babies and cheese. Don't you think?"

"We'd live in Pärnu."

"He's a farmer!"

Shouts and laughter came from the kitchen. A crowd sat around the table dipping ladles, gossiping, drinking ale. The men from the *saun* glowed, their hair slicked back, beaming grins around the table, everyone clean and soaked, steamed and soaped. There was silence when we entered the room, and all eyes upon us. Enn greeted us to a murmur of agreement. Hinrik invited Anna and me to sit either side of him.

Hardi's wife Minna caught my eye though she didn't smile. She rarely did and I hardly knew her. Hardi had been called up. Nobody could say where he might be. Helve's husband had been sent away months ago but she was talkative, waiting to hear from him, ever optimistic. We waited with her for anything, a word, a postcard a rumour. Who could predict what the next months would bring even when we all hoped there would soon be an end to the war.

"We used to see you here more often, Siina," Helve said, her tone familiar but a little biting. She'd so often lectured and taunted me, always forthright, dismissing my answers quickly.

"I like it here but I'm studying you know," I said. "Your children are such angels." I looked from one to the other, from their shining fair hair, their firm, quiet innocence - two eager boys and a sweet girl. "They're such lovely children. You must be proud."

Helve brushed the youngest's hair from her face. "I am but that's not for me to say, is it? What are you studying, Siina?"

I was studying accounting, a useful subject which would give me a job. I also spent time with my camera and experimenting with light and shadow effects and developing my films. There was no end to what I wanted to learn. I didn't want to tell Helve that. It seemed disconnected from her life and understanding. All the same, she was content, I decided. She knew a great deal about weaving, knitting and dyeing and all of that demanded concentration and patience. I felt awkward describing my plans to her.

"I'll soon be a registered accountant. I may find a job in Pärnu," I said in all truth. I would not talk about my real hopes, to become a paid photographer. Helve's eyes strayed toward Anna and Oskar and we probably all wondered how they felt, being so obviously in love. But they did no more than stare at one another.

Enn winked at me. "He would have crossed the Sahara for this lady! Great timing my friend."

Anna's cheeks flamed.

"Oh, don't mind us! She's used to audiences!" Enn licked beer from his lip. "Don't you go proposing in private, dear Oskar!"

Anna seemed to recover. Oskar pulled a bottle with red and blue patterned mittens tied to the neck from his rucksack.

Enn made to grab it.

"For *Tädi* Lulle." Oskar snatched it back. "I wish to court your niece," he said extremely seriously as he presented it to Lulle who smiled broadly so that Oskar relaxed a little.

"Blackcurrant wine! But Oskar, Anna may speak for herself." Lulle took the gloves off the bottle. "However, I'll accept the gift!" she said happily.

"A wedding!" Granny called from the end of the table. "I'm ready!"

Anna's eyes met mine. She was overcome, smiling foolishly. I wanted to pinch her to wake her up. Whatever she decided, I hoped it would be well thought out but then Anna generally knew what she wanted.

19. Pärnu

Riding the train back to Pärnu, Anna's expressions changed from serene to exuberant. I kept stirring around what Enn and Lulle had said. I thought again of Mihkel. I'd taken a number of shots of our cousins, the river, a stork's nest. I'd been to the church and looked at it differently in the morning light, the massive walls and gigantic spire, impossible to fit in my lens. I hoped my pictures would emerge from my developing baths as I recalled the places. If I had any as good as I hoped, I'd be happy. I'd told no one because no one had asked and I doubted they were interested that I had an assignment. My photographs were going to earn me money. Perhaps the buyer would even give me more work.

When the war was over I wouldn't feel so selfish about getting what I wanted. We had had a year of horrible, frightening news, every day with hideous inventions. It hadn't touched Anna and me but others lost sons, brothers and fathers. Lulle was delicate because of Hardi and Helve's husband and my heart ached for them. Granny was fragile too, when I'd expected her to be invincible. She was human and as vulnerable as I'd never seen her. Enn, outrageous and clownish, had made serious, emotional remarks. I never believed he'd pray.

I noticed hints of autumnal colours as it blurred by. There were beautiful dyed wool shades of deep greens and yellows and golds that I'd not seen earlier. Meadows became rugs woven with dark amber and muted grey. There was beauty in every stone and post and wooden rail in places I'd not seen before. A rock could be a sculpture, a mossy bank, a warm knitted cape. A sense of my good fortune washed over me. My sister was with me. Kristjaan had discovered mathematics. Papa and Eeva were safe and I was sure, content.

Anna sighed and smiled to herself, her head propped against the window, her lips moving while she read lines from a new play.

“Are you infatuated, Anna? What will we do with you?” I interrupted, wishing I could disappear from the realities, the conflicts and inhabit the happiness that came and went.

For a moment Anna looked confused. “I know I am. Is that terribly self-centred?”

“Of course not.”

“Oh, Siina forget about the fighting. Men do it. They’ve endurance and courage and are used to it. Even little boys.” She breathed deeply, as if we were exonerated. “That’s all they want! It’ll be over very soon. You’ll see!”

How perfectly nice it was to be able to tell herself lies. I wished I could also. It’ll be over soon. But what if there was worse to come? What if they’d just begun? And what if Enn, Erik, Jaan and Kristjaan were pitched off in uniforms and Oskar sent off as a doctor though he’d barely begun his training? Better remain optimistic. Lulle would say that, that we had only the option to bear it.

“You may be right,” I agreed because it was possible. “Perhaps so. We don’t know. No one does.”

“You noticed his blue eyes?”

“Yes!”

“He’s coming to Pärnu, to see me at the Endla!”

“So you say.”

“He is what I want,” Anna sighed.

“But Anna - a farmer’s wife!”

“He’s training to be a doctor. You knew that!”

"Studying. Not yet a doctor. But you'll have what you want and I'll be happy for you," I said, unconvinced but optimistic for her.

I deepened my concentration at the forest flying by. If Mihkel had been sent to the front to gather news, I could actually go there. I could drive supplies and write reports. I could take photographs and send back proofs. The horror, not the glory. If Mihkel endured it, I could.

"You and Oskar ought to have a huge, grand wedding, an event we will never forget as long as we live," I said. Anna looked at me in surprise but could not hold back her excitement.

"Really? While people are dying, Siina? No! Could we?"

"Yes, Anna. I mean after all, you'll only do this once and everyone will pay homage to the soldiers who aren't here. We'll give them respect."

"I'm not sure, Siina. No, no. I would need to think about a party when so many are suffering. No, no. I need to think carefully. But I'll see what he says."

"You should. It would be a happy event. Think of Granny. And Lulle. And Papa." I omitted Eeva. "It's a good idea."

"You really think so?" She looked at me in wonder. "But what in the world could I wear?"

20. Chanterelles

The trees partly eclipsed the sun, shading the street. I searched for an angle, a distant, frosted look to show tranquil Pärnu. Children chased one another around the stalls, small dogs ran back and forth, a dachshund yapped at my heels, a horse flicked its head and jangled its harness.

A housewife leaned over a stall to choose potatoes, clean skinned, smooth ones, ones that would boil white and floury to go with sour cream and onions. I saw Millet's Gleaners, the brush strokes in the woman's curves, her headscarf tied under her chin, the even skin of her face, the silky potatoes.

I snapped, I imagined the photo emerging from the bath, darkening, exposed with textures of stone, wood and linen.

"Chanterelles. Here." Anna made a bee-line for an old woman seated amongst baskets. "*Ja, ja*. I see what you want," she cackled seeing Anna approach. "These are the best. I can tell you know what you want. I know a lady's taste. I'll give you the best." She loosed a handful into a twist of paper.

Anna took them and stepped back.

"A fine picking. My secret place. Not the children's. Not the baron's." Her wrinkles gathered in a knot.

"And eggs, *proua*?"

"The baron's. I can find you bacon and I tell you there's less every day. We all know don't we?" she said more quietly. "As they're killing our children, aren't they? They steal men off the land so Wilhelm and our tsar can feed their war machines. See? What do you imagine next winter? My son's fighting!" she spat. "And I'll tell you straight, it's all shit!" She covered her face a moment before looking up at us from under her scarf. “My boy’s in that hell!” She broke down mopping her face with her rag. “Shoeless and unarmed! What do you say about that? Bootless army without guns! I’ll never see him again, will I?” She broke into a sob.

I glanced at Anna and I cautioned the woman with a look over her shoulder. A policeman had stopped behind her.

“What’s up?” he growled.

“Nothing, nothing,” the woman murmured.

“Problems with our army, did you say?”

She wiped her face. I picked up an apple and gazed at it to avoid the policeman’s eye. The woman straightened her boxes and papers and faced the ground. Soon the police moved off.

“I wish your son luck. I pray he comes home safe,” I said gently as the woman sniffed and moaned, babbled, now praising the tsar and his armies. “God save them,” she called for the police to hear. “God save the tsar – *boje Tzaeria Khrani*! Grant them great victories,” she crowed but under her breath, cursed them, praying god save her son and bring him home.

“Safe return to your boy,” I said from closer to her, as Anna grabbed me by my elbow. We knew the boy would need wagon loads of luck.

“You know all Lulle’s boys are called up now,” Anna whispered.

“No!” So Mihkel would be called up too, from the same *küla*. I’d become a babbling woman, afraid for them all, outraged, furious, muttering nonsense. “No!”

“But they must, Siina. We’re all for the tsar.”

“I’m not!”

“What, so you’re a Bolshevik now?”

I closed off my rage and kept silent.

"I know you are," Anna said walking away, her arms loaded with flowers and vegetables in twists of paper cones. She was about to cross between the stalls when a child frothed in lace and frills darted across her path followed by a boy in a sailor's suit.

Anna, behind her flowers saw none of this. The children came hurtling at her and before I could move or call out, the three of them lay sprawled on the cobbles. Mere seconds later the children's nanny came pounding around another stall. She paused a moment, said something to Anna and was gone. Anna stared at her flowers littered on the ground, her vegetables scattered.

"Oh Anna! Are you all right?" I helped her up and we gathered the flowers and vegetables.

"I'm not!" Anna nodded to where the children and parents paused in their stroll and were looking back at us. "How rude!" She brushed grit from her long dark skirt and dabbed at her knee. Her hand was grazed and bleeding, her skirt, torn and smudged. "Look at me! And those children!"

"A touch of iodine when we get home, Anna. You're all right. The flowers are fine, see?"

"My skirt is ruined!"

"But Roosi will mend it." I took her arm as we watched the children's parents cross the park, the man in a blazing white suit, the woman in a lace and knitted jacket. The children ran over the grass, the nanny trailing behind.

"Arrogant! I'm furious!" Anna muttered.

"I am too," I said.

She pinched the folds of her skirt together. "They started the whole mess we're in didn't they! So how will it end, Siina? Will they talk about it? Do you really think they care?"

The baron, baroness and children, the nanny scurrying behind were a picture. I hurriedly snapped a photo. I looked again at the shock of their pale clothes against the haze of trees and grass, a streak of stone path, and took another shot.

21. *En Route* Pärnu to Petersburg

The railway carriage bustled with families, anxious women, howling babies, bickering children, helpless fathers. Grandparents searched bags for an apple or unwrapped a linen serviette that held a block of cheese. A tall man in top hat and cloak, magician or scientist, sat on the wooden seat facing me. He gave me a close look as if he might know me then left off. I watched family negotiations, pleading and arguing, the giving in, the placating, the dozing and the restlessness.

Ksenia had been writing to me since Mama died as if I was my mother. Despite my replying as myself she kept writing about people I didn't know, described soirées, dinners and guests, one after the other in her usual breathless manner and continued to address me as my mother, Maarja. I was delighted that I should meet ensembles of important people but also anxious about if I would use correct manners and perfect German and Russian. I thought about photographing high ranking individuals, even interviewing them, and felt more secure. I would ask to take portraits to send to newspapers and refer to my earlier commission, small but official. In her last letter, Ksenia described an Italian diplomat, a Georgian bass baritone and a merchant from Samarkand. I wondered if she exaggerated – she coloured her world brightly. Perhaps I'd meet royalty and be drawn into gushing myself. From behind my camera I was safe from becoming a goose. I had some credibility. So long as Ksenia did not match me with a prospective husband, a singer, politician or soldier, she had always been so *üleskruvitud* that she lit me up too. She mentioned the real Peterburg again but also the rank-smelling Moika where at the height of summer, women sat on the banks in their underwear as carts and horses drove by. Such was Peterburg. Many faces. Twelve years after *that Sunday*, Ksenia promised we would find the beautiful things.

It's charming and perfectly safe but here, many men will kiss your hand and compliment you. Keep in mind that French manners are de rigeur *but Russian seduction is everywhere and you, my dear, are very pretty.*

Tartu and the Emajõgi River lay behind us with the Kivisild Bridge where Catherine the Great, famously jammed herself and her bustle between the stone pillars. I folded Ksenia's letter and slipped it into my pigskin bag.

A heavily built, blowzy woman sat beside me and glanced at it but carried on speaking discreetly to her children. I admired the way they listened. The softer she spoke, the more they strained to hear. Each child was distinct from the next, not at all like siblings.

My companion looked outside between the distractions of her children. The youngest kicked the boards below the seat while the middle child, olive-skinned, watched me, frowning. The eldest kept to herself with a sullen expression.

We sped through rippling countryside, beyond snow-covered roofs, fields and bog lands, silver-green firs reeling by, birches shimmering, branches glassy. We travelled the coast close to the high limestone cliffs where to the north lay Finnish bogs and lakes. We understood each other, *soomlased,* our cousins.

At the tiled, brown and soot-dusted Narva station our train hissed to a stop to take on boiler water. I needed a cup of tea. Despite the swarming army recruits, no more than my age, I decided to press my way through. The men could have been ready for a day's boar hunting. One of them licked his finger and put it to his lips, staring at me and I looked the other way with an acute sense of vulnerability, alone I was now with so many *versts* between me and Ksenia. A soldier with a pinched expression pushed against my bottom. I clutched my camera like a weapon. Another boy, fair as a swan, smiled into my eyes. I wanted to tell him that war was no boar hunt.

I was glad that Ksenia had warned me. Peterburg was infamous for outrage. Every manner of art challenged the old standards. If an opera or ballet scandalised Paris it had already shocked Peterburg. I knew there was terrible poverty despite mansions like Ksenia's. Men came to the city to work, desperate for anything because there was no employment in the villages.

"Where you going sweetheart?" A bearded chin prickled my cheek. A hand reached around my waist.

"Listen! Why not stand there? I'll get your photo. You'll be proud," I said. The soldier called friends who posed, pushed out chests, tilted heads in different directions, each his own character. I soared with elation for my daring and perhaps a great picture!

I'd seen the collection, the tsar's photographer, Prokudin-Gorskii had made of our empire, the people and landscapes. From Bukhara and Kirghiz to the Urals, Prokudin-Gorskii captured dozens of cultures, their exotic costumes, spectacular settings, faces of women and girls, remarkable in their differences, shining eyes of children, stately women in Muslim dress, the colours of flowers. He used glass plates and three colours, the first ever. The Emir of Bukhara shone in sensational blue and purple silk robe, gold lanyards and belt, his sword balanced as if he were a great tripod over heavy black boots. A fabric vendor, cross-legged, sat walled-in by his carpets. A shaggy-haired Turkoman gazed in apprehension at the distance he and his laden camel would trek over the Great Silk Road with mountainous grain sacks. Three innocent women in fiery brocades shyly proffered plates of berries.

I took courage. I asked another two officers to pose. Politely, elegantly, they leaned against a station veranda post, relaxing against it as if they were photographed just so every day. They'd have played tennis and croquet on an estate where servants ran for the balls. I opened the shutter and standing still as stones, they chased off their smiles. I wondered, and perhaps they did too, if they would recognize themselves in another six months.

"Cholera and god knows what else," my travelling companion was impressing upon her children as they passed me on their way to the lavatory. "Don't touch anything!" I went too, gagged at the chlorinated lime and got out as fast as I could. Ksenia's place would surely burst with bouquets and reek incense, a samovar in every room and clinking silver cutlery with not a smear. Soon I'd be there.

"You are alone," the mother observed when we sat again.

"I have a place already in Peterburg," I said sampling my potato and herring salad. "I'll be staying with my friend on Bolshaya Morskaya," I said.

"Palatial."

I nodded modestly. I wondered where Mihkel was. If he had a room it would be in the Vyborg. I must have seemed love-struck. My companion eyed me sympathetically. I guessed her to be Lulle's age except that Lulle exuded health. My friend touched my elbow.

"You're from Pärnu, yes? Watch where you go. You're fresh out of the nest, it's obvious." She looked at me wearily, her dark, hooded eyes impassive yet worldly and even seductive. "You need to know what men are although you'll find out in good time. Be careful dearie. They think they can have what they want. Men." She said it with a hint of scorn before turning back to her children, each one's expression different from the next. My companion opened a napkin holding sliced bread with cottage cheese.

"And you're from Peterburg?" I said.

She leaned close and I smelled horses. "I am. I've had a few employers and I hope to find another. My eldest, I tell you, her father was the very devil, but what could I do? Still, I've been lucky. I could have lost everything several times over but instead I have it all. Well, I have enough." She jogged her head sideways. "Doesn't hurt to have money."

"You chose well."

"A woman doesn't need to be beautiful, dearie. A head on her shoulders will do her better. Beautiful women don't always lie about doing nothing. Plain women can get what they want, believe me. Men, now they're different. A beautiful man can't resist spreading his seed. You know what I mean? If he gets the chance. Not women though. We have to work things out don't we? A baby doesn't only suck your milk…it will suck your blood."

Her children watched coolly, the eldest child, head inclined with interest, eyes flitting back and forth from her mother to me.

"I'll find my way," I said feeling less than confident but challenged as she measured me.

"Don't trust everyone. You've a trusting nature. I see it."

"So you say. May I?" I took out my camera.

"Go ahead," she said smoothing the wild arrangement of her hair, pushing down a hat of flattened green felt on top. I framed her with the children's heads resting one way and another on her bosom and lap, each child beautiful in a particular way, their mother, serene.

When we arrived in Peterburg it was dark. Doorways were

shadows, alleys menacing. Block upon block of stone apartments stood imposing and aloof, frozen above streets. Canals were banked by three and four-storied villas, a window lit here and there, outside lamps burning yellow. My camera stayed deep in my pigskin bag.

"You're a serious photographer," my companion said.

"I am. I have an assignment for a collector in England. She imagines we're rustic and simple in Estland after she read Elizabeth Rigby. An aristocrat. And a very good writer. Very English. She romanticized our country and people you know. She called us naïve and charming. Fascinated by our impossible language," I smiled. The woman nodded understandingly.

"Of course," she agreed. "Now I can see who you are."

I assumed from her narrow tanned face and her hooded eyes, her mad hair and unconventional life that she should have red boots, love gypsy music and take men in exchange for drinks and money. But she was interested in my photography and we talked about Peterburg and the state of the government as well. I expected that her Russian was as good as her Estonian and I enjoyed hearing her thoughts.

"Science has a say in photography," I said.

"I'm sure."

"Muybridge proved science with the horses' feet. If they left the ground all at once. His photographs proved it."

"Really! Do you see yourself as an artist? Are you *avant-garde*? They'll pave the way, for a time."

"Really?"

"Of course! The likes of the man who photographed the tsar in Paris."

"Anschütz?"

"The Prussian. His moving pictures!"

"His storks!"

"But Kühn's nudes, oh my! My!" My friend's front teeth overlapped I noticed as she smiled to be educating me.

"That's not what I do," I said.

"Of course not, but it's art." She mocked me as I held her gaze. "Do you imagine a nude sculpted in marble is art? Or the *cartes de visite,* those naked women? Only men want to look at them, don't they?" she challenged. "You make something beautiful, I can tell, but remember, nudes sell! If you should need to make a living..." my friend's face wrinkled. She was older than I'd first thought. "Women take those shots," she added.

After photographing Anna half nude, I'd not thought further but thinking it over I wished I could take more. She'd look back one day and see how lovely she was.

I couldn't concentrate on the book of poetry open on my lap. There were still *versts* to go and I was also curious about my companion. "I love landscapes and portraits. Not so much the 'divine' Sarah Bernhardt or those Greek-draped women with butterflies all over the place. Not them. Those temptresses are old fashioned already. I want characters."

"You do?"

"Yes! But I've no idea how to," I said realising I was saying what I'd thought for a long time.

"Of course you'll want to photograph the war. Is that why you're coming here?"

"I won't be an eye to killing. No. I'll interview and photograph soldiers for history, for the records," I said.

The woman gave me a nod before turning back to her children to give them boiled eggs. "Women are going nursing and driving trucks, living in tents on the war front you know. If you believe in him you could be a pawn in your sovereign's game my dear."

"For our tsar? Drive ammunition trucks to kill my relatives?"

"Yes, yes."

"Never."

She stroked her son's hair. "You see beauty, don't you? If your motives are good, you're saved," she said with half-closed eyes. "So our tsar believes too and he can sleep while millions die. He believes he has the motives!" She shook her head. "Only your heart must tell you what's right."

I was lucky to have met this woman. I sat back thinking of my ideals, Muybridge and Stieglitz, Prokudin-Gorskii and Cameron, and now this unkempt woman who understood me.

Darkness had captured Petrograd when our train steamed toward the Finland Station. Shadows were beasts. I imagined thieves and killers in every murky lane. When we reached the platform my friend gathered her luggage and children who quickly muffled themselves up and picked up the smaller bags. For moments we stood beneath the high decorated ceilings in the vast station. The man with the top hat and cloak caught my eye before he shook hands with someone whose pointed beard was exactly like Papa's and whose red-rimmed spectacles reminded me that Piter's city was sophisticated. The two men swept off together like professors, or magicians.

"The cabs are on Botinskaya," my friend shouted as she moved away gesturing to the street beyond the station.

I felt for my mother's cameo brooch for reassurance.

"God go with you," she called, waving, mobbed by her children.

"And with you," I called, frustrated that I had not asked her name.

Outside, snow fluttered like tiny moths around gaslights. I shared a cab with an elderly man. Barouches and droshkies sped by, one upon the next, harnesses glinting, wheel spokes flickering light. A Tatar coachman, swaying in his seat and bearing a black moustache plunged toward us as we rounded a corner. Another carriage with a bearded, sheepskin-coated driver flew on. I was thrown against the man beside me who whispered, “Careful with your affection young lady.” His voice was thick and gravelly and his teeth shone beneath grey whiskers. I smelled wine-breath. He grabbed my knee and I pushed it away but that didn’t stop him leaning against me, continuing to smile. I sat away from him stiffly, ready to smack him.

Foot soldiers, belted and buttoned, caps pulled low and collars high against the snow strode arm in arm along the pavement.

“Cuirassiers, tsar’s guards, the only ones he can still trust!” the man wheezed. “You don’t know, do you? You’re straight from the countryside. I can see it,” he grinned.

“From the town,” I corrected but stopped from going further after all, why should I tell him anything?

A carriage rang by, a veiled woman, a Muslim, peered from the window into the dark street. Men had spilled out from a tavern, laughing and singing, military uniforms and greatcoats drizzled with snow. They jostled under the lights pushing a woman from one man to the next, tossing her like a puppet between them. Her shawl dropped to her shoulders and I saw her face - fierce and angry.

Once we passed St Isaac’s square we carried on to the theatres. Carriages waited for crowds in front of opera houses. Men in beaver hats and trailing coats, women with furs and wide winter coats stepped out onto the granite steps, nodded, greeted and dispersed from the grand doors onto the street. Liveried footmen waited and bowed. I was amazed though I wished to appear nonchalant at it all. I could hardly believe it. The poverty I dreaded was nowhere. Perhaps people exaggerated.

Anna and Oskar had done their best to dissuade me from coming, warning me of dangerous streets, lascivious men and robbers. I had assured them I'd stay with Ksenia and Oskar then gave me permission to leave. I wondered who was mistaken or out of touch.

The elderly man dozed against the door as we slowed at the fourth line, two blocks from the Neva. Wealthy businessmen and nobles lived in Ksenia and Sergo's street. They'd had a textile factory at first in Pärnu but Petrograd offered plentiful and cheap labour. Within a few years the plant in the Vyborg brought Ksenia and Sergo considerable wealth. Ksenia, an efficient businesswoman, enjoyed that work. Sergo liked control. Ksenia amused herself travelling with their son to the Riviera, Paris and Venice, a different place each year while Sergo went about getting the most efficient looms in Europe. So long as labour poured in there seemed no end to their prosperity. *He loves a challenge,* Ksenia wrote, *though he promised he would come to the Riviera. I know he won't.*

The building where we stopped was massive, columned and carved in the front. At first I thought Ksenia must have forgotten me but there it was, a faint yellow glow in one window. They were there.

Come to me right away she'd written*; The Feodorovna household needs you! A tutor darling! They want someone clever, well-mannered, with excellent German. Someone like yourself! You'll love it, I know it. The Feodorovnas are fine people. Think of it! Their eldest daughter, headstrong, intelligent, but oh my! You'll surely find her interesting and no challenge for someone like yourself. Her younger sisters and brother are darlings as well. Besides, I long for your arrival, Maarja* (she wrote). *I'm* *desperately anxious for us to be together again! You and your mother. I miss you every moment. I think of you constantly.*

I waited on the grand high steps thinking of Ksenia's warm rooms; amaryllis and day lilies in pots, samovars everywhere; hot, yeasty *pirukas* waiting for me. So I hoped.

An ancient, stooped butler swung the door open.

The house was still, not a sound from outside penetrated the triple glazing. I waited for Ksenia's son, Lembit, to come running down the stairs shouting, arms wide for a hug, the way he was described. The lobby was silent as a grave.

The butler straightened up, his face white with exertion. "*Preili* Jürimäe, please, *Proua* Borzakov is waiting for you," he said in Russian, breathing noisily, heaving open the drawing-room double doors.

I stood motionless. Ksenia hunched like some fisherman's wife waiting for a boat to return, her hair covered in a black crimped veil, her skirts black, fixed. A bird cage rattled with lovebirds hopping from side to side. Ksenia looked across to the window, back at her hands folded in her lap and after a very long time she twisted her covered face to me.

I tip-toed forward uncertain of what it was, only knowing there had been tragedy. I reached to hold her hands with caution.

"Poor Siina," she said miserably.

"Is Lembit...?"

Thousands in Peterburg had died of cholera and typhus – millions across Russia, children were especially vulnerable.

Ksenia jerked her hands from me. "Lembit! He's well! No, no! Is he? But Sergo!"

I noticed the masses of flowers, full vases of roses, peonies, lilies, everywhere.

"I came from Tartu. I'm sorry. I know nothing about it."

"You don't know? Dear me! Sit down, Maarja. I'll tell you. Tea? A glass of something stronger?"

I stared, my mind blank. "It's Siina. Maarja's daughter. I was seven when we met. Remember."

"You are so like Maarja, aren't you? I have to tell you. The factory. You won't believe it. I couldn't either. I don't want to. The workers, Maarja, they went mad." She paused. "Tea? You've come all that way."

"It's Siina. No, no. Thank you."

"Yes, yes," she said ringing the bell. Her butler returned, stooped at a little distance, and disappeared.

22. Sergo

Ksenia kept hold of my hands. I sat opposite on her Egyptian footstool, my heart sinking into her Persian carpeted floor.

"I knew they were spoiling for it but not that they'd do murder." She slipped one hand away and pushed the veil off to dab her eyes.

"The Okhrana came to my door, my dear. We know what that means don't we? God almighty we know!"

"Oh, Ksenia!"

"It should never happen! Not this!" She dabbed again. "I couldn't believe it either only somehow I had a sense of it! A premonition, I'm sure. But why?" She livened for a moment pushing her veil further back. "I knew it! I was terribly upset the morning he left and for no reason! I've never been a limpet wife, Siina, oh Maarja! Only that morning I was so emotional, so foolish, hanging on him like burdock. I said be careful, I mean, the streets aren't safe, you don't go about in a fur coat in the Vyborg or anywhere for that matter, not any more! He couldn't understand it. But I'm blessed! I hugged and kissed him and he told me I was his precious dove. He did! Thank God for that. You know him. Rock solid. Dependable!"

I smoothed her hands.

"You'll stay won't you?"

"Of course! But isn't Olga expecting me tomorrow? That was what you wrote."

"She'll understand."

"I'm so sorry…"

"Of course we are. I'm so relieved you're here. Thank you,

thank you!"

Somewhere in the hall the telephone jangled. Moments later the butler shambled into the room.

"For *Preili* Jürimäe," he said to Ksenia. She looked at me in surprise.

"I've no idea ..," I said getting up.

"Really? No idea who calls here?"

"Shall I?" I moved to the door.

Ksenia circled her fingers in the air.

I took the receiver. "Mihkel. Mihkel Oks," it said.

"You!"

"Siina! Aha! I'm right! When can I see you?" he laughed.

I held the receiver close as if it were his hand. "I … can't say exactly. Not just yet but another day, of course!"

Ksenia drifted down the hall to stand beside me. I was terribly embarrassed.

"Not now. Something has happened," I stammered.

"What? Something bad?"

"Yes."

"You're all right?"

"Yes." I held a hand to my chest. I wanted to see him. I wanted to feel his arms around me. "Where are you?"

Ksenia wandered closer. "Anyone I know?" She kneaded her handkerchief in her heavily jewelled hands.

I laid the phone in the cradle. "It was my friend, Mihkel Oks."

Ksenia's face whitened. Her mouth thinned. "He knew you were here? Mihkel Oks? The anarchist?"

"Anarchist! Oh no, Ksenia. He is a Socialist."

"Socialist, oh no. No, no. I've seen his writings." Ksenia trembled. Either she would explode or collapse in tears. She held her jewelled fingers to her throat. "He's one of them, Siina! A rabble-rouser, isn't he? You don't want to believe it? I know it's true!"

"But he's not!"

Ksenia wandered back into her drawing room and fell into a sofa. "Siina, poor girl," she sighed. I felt both her pity and her loathing.

I sat rigid in the peacock-blue velvet chair opposite. Nothing I said would change what she thought now. I had heard of men attacking factory bosses, stripping them, hanging them by the feet like pigs, pasting labels saying parasite. I closed my eyes and wished I was somewhere far away, or that we could begin again and Ksenia would coo and laugh as she used to, singing and chattering. Instead she had begun staring at me with hatred. "You can't stay. You'll have to go. Now!"

"Ksenia! Mihkel is from Pärnu, a childhood friend. A good man," I pleaded.

"He could be a Zulu or Laplander, Siina. He's like the people who murdered my husband. You may not stay here a minute longer. I can't think of it," Ksenia's voice clanged.

I turned my face away. "He and I are bound together. In here," I said tapping my breastbone with my fist.

Ksenia shook her head wildly. "The worse for you in that case!" She stared into my eyes. "I was longing to see you Maarja! So looking forward to it. And you're one of them! I can see it now! But you were such a darling child," she said, tears falling as she returned the veil to her face.

"I've known him for as long as I can remember. How can you not believe me?"

Ksenia blew her nose and wiped her eyes under her veil. I saw the pitying look.

"Because you're young and easily fooled, Maarja! You always

were! Even now you don't understand. You don't see what you're in? How I wish my eyes had been open before! Sergo would be here with me. Now! Go! My manservant will see you out. My poor Maarja! Poor thing! Go!" she shrieked.

I denied the guilt and self-pity. Ksenia was suffering, but I was shattered.

She lay back on the sofa and watched her love birds.

"Accept my sympathy. My heart aches for you," she managed.

"Please believe me..." I began again. "I'm so sorry for Sergo and you."

"Go. Don't come back," she murmured at the birds.

I followed the servant's shuffle. He tossed my bags out the door with a snort and slammed the door in my face. I stood in the cold under a dim light that pointed up falling snow.

23. Bolshaya Morskaya

I was devastated. Sergo murdered, Ksenia, unhinged, Mihkel's terrible untimely phone call and me, rejected!

Still tying up my scarf, dragging my coat on, shivering, I beat on Ksenia's door. She had rescued lost souls! Why not me? I shuddered in disbelief. The open arms, my loving friend, my safe place, upturned! I buttoned my coat and tugged my hat low over my head. A clattering from her side gate – so, she was kind after all. Her landau, gold cross, key and red sleeve of Pärnu's crest emblazoned on the door, drew up to the door. I raced down the steps, my cheeks searing in the cold. The *isvostchick*, a huge man enveloped in a bear skin, moustache and beard like an animal stuck to his face, grabbed my bags as I scrambled into the carriage. "Feodorovna...Bolshaya...," I called but without heed. He cracked his whip and the horses jangled as our carriage lights trembled into the night.

I slumped into the velvet-buttoned seat and we jogged along the wide Bolshaya, slowed onto a narrow bridge guarded by sphinxes, over a frozen canal, sped up again as we turned onto Gorokhovaya. It seemed familiar. I prayed the Feodorovna house would be lit. Someone had to be up. Peterburgers loved the night.

Even so, I imagined photographs, natural, close-up, a unique way to open a collection. I wished I could tell Mihkel. I wished I could see him. Thank the lord I could trust him.

Our landau lurched, throwing me against the door as another sped by, so close it trimmed our wheels. Wherever we going, we went like a fire carriage but it seemed away from the Neva now, when Olga Feodorovna's house was close to the palace and almost on the Neva banks. The train stations however, were at the perimeter of the city. Where was he taking me?

“Driver!” I screamed from the window, ice and wind eating my words. “Driver!” I called again, my lips numbed. Surely I was mistaken. We had to be heading to the Bolshaya Morskaya. I felt lonely and desolate though I’d been in Peterburg hardly an hour. A handbill blew by the carriage window. A woman in a high furred hat spread her full skirt to squat in the gutter.

If Mihkel was with me he’d know where we were going. He insisted he was no politician. He observed and recorded but even he would have to choose a position soon. He’d never be able to hide his loyalties and convictions behind his pen. And neither would I. I too would have to come out from behind my lens and say what I believed. But Ksenia was hopelessly mistaken. Sergo had been murdered in a terrible way. No wonder she’d become a little mad.

When the landau stopped alongside a vast Palladian-arched building I resolved that here I would be warmly welcomed. Light glowed from every window of four levels of the Feodorovna house. They needed me. They would embrace me. I was equal to whatever faced me. I would deal with what lay ahead. Tutors were leaving in droves since the war with the Kaiser but I would stay. I shrugged myself deeper into my coat as I stepped into the wind crying from the Neva. My bags landed with a thud on the steps beside the pillars of marble.

“Take care, *Fräulein,*” the *isvostchick* murmured before he turned his back. I snatched up my bag and held it close. The driver passed a fur mittened hand over his horse’s flank, hefted himself and bearskin onto his seat and was gone.

The back of my neck crept. I breathed deeply feeling that someone was watching. A quick look over my shoulder. Behind me, a group of men, coats flying in the wind, faces fixed on me, had hunched together. Revolutionaries or thieves. Nasty men, their hatred palpable. They drew together and skulked closer.

I heaved myself against the doorbell.

"*Bourzhoi*!" one of the men shouted.

I punched the doorbell again. A glass shattered beside me. My heart leapt. I was helpless yet I had to look around.

"*Bourzhoi*!" another shouted as I flattened myself against the door, praying for it to open. At last. It swung wide. A wide smile, a round-faced Russian girl clasped her hands over her tunic.

"Come! It's cold outside!" she welcomed.

"The *Fräulein* from Pärnu," she said backing away, a quick bob of a curtsey, a sideways tilt of her head. "But you're a day early you know. I better inform Madame," she said. Another servant brought in my bags and triple-locked the door.

The hall was suffocatingly hot. I peeled away hat, scarf, gloves and coat. The butler nodded the merest greeting and disappeared.

My fingers curled around my mother's cameo brooch as I breathed slowly before turning to face a massive gold-framed mirror. I straightened my back, lifted my chin and smoothed down my skirt. I tugged on the double-stitched hem of my wool jacket, lifted my hair and clasped my hands. Perhaps I had escaped a wolf pack. A smile was possible. At least I was warm. Colour was returning to my cheeks. The Feodorovna family was sure to be impressed with my intelligence, my loyalty and spirit.

A valet with tea-filled glasses clinked past me on his way up the rosewood stairs, gave me a cursory glance. Another gusted by without seeing me, a silver tray of documents in a gloved hand, his forehead angled to the cherry wood panelled ceiling. At last the round-faced Russian girl, her brightly embroidered tunic over a floral skirt, returned and bobbed a curtsey, beaming me a glorious smile.

"Come, *Fräulein*. It's all right after all. They will receive you since you are actually here." She ushered me into an anteroom. Dark furniture, tapestries and paintings ticked by, an electric brass lamp, bronze sculptures, armour, saints, dragons and stuffed game followed by portraits … row upon row tracked past as I followed the maid along the unending hall. I spoke German to myself, cataloguing, counting the portraits, remarking under my breath about style, colour, composition and pretension. I would delight the entire family too.

"Oh, more!" I said in Russian as we blew along another dark hallway.

I licked my lips preparing to embellish my credentials.

"*Fräulein*, here we are," the maid said with an abrupt halt, turning to me. "Voilà." I was faint with incense as the great doors of the main hall swung open.

To my surprise Olga Pyotrovna was much less than I expected. I stared open-mouthed for too long. Seated in the centre of the room, her children clung to her from all directions, a basket tucked against the hem of her considerable skirts. Her small oval face was in shadow, her hair covered in a soft dove-grey cap. She was tiny and quite without presence.

I approached her when someone else spoke. "Regard. Elle est ici," the disembodied voice said and followed on, to me, in Russian, "Welcome to Piter's city. You are expected tomorrow but no matter. Let us see you, *Fräulein*." I noticed the edge to '*Fräulein*'. I was to be the German tutor so they should not have taken exception to it but all the same, I imagined an undercurrent, almost suppressed laughter at my position. I was, '*Fräulein*,' while Estonian to my core, and when St. Petersburg's title had been changed to Petrograd. But no matter, I said to myself.

I faced the voice, the room so poorly lit that I saw only the silver-knob of a cane and light glancing off a lorgnette at the end of a long shining wand. A woman sat behind it. “Make yourself comfortable *Fräulein*. You’ve travelled some distance today. So now, tell us something about your studies. How many languages, what other references do you bring?”

I was no showpiece and I would not become one. For moments I faltered because immediately my Russian would be inferior. Instead I lowered myself to a deep *reverence*, and presented myself as correctly as possible, equal to whatever game they might play. On such a bleak night I needed to be extraordinary.

“I speak, read and write German, Russian, Finnish and Estonian,” I said modestly. “Languages were my best subjects though I also achieved excellence in literature and art at school. I have completed study and registered as an accountant and was offered such a job in a large company in Pärnu only a few months ago. I enjoy bookkeeping.”

Did I hear a sniff of disdain?

“But really!” I heard from the other corner. “And music? Poetry?” the other voice asked. I strained to see what sprawled on the sofa, a foot stuck from beneath a skirt, lace shawl draped over her shoulders, a wig askew. I felt an eye on me however. “My word!” someone said. I wondered if I should detail my qualifications further when Olga Pyotrovna cut in.

“*Fräulein*!” she said, her voice, thin and childlike, “Please, sit. We have matters to discuss, don’t we?”

“We do?” I was at that moment overcome with exhaustion.

“A glass of tea?” Olga suggested.

“Thank you.” I lowered myself onto a small silver bench from where I could study my employer better although already I was fascinated at how she was sewn into her Prussian-blue jacket edged with pearl ribbon. She half-sat and half-lay on the chaise. The children, unblinking, appeared to be taking in the entire proceedings; certainly they were curious about me. What I'd imagined mounds of rugs were sleepy Borzois. They raised their heads then turned away in contempt.

It was at that moment I noticed, at the far distant end of the room, a tall figure, a man motionless beside a Roman Apollo. A fire burned and crackled in the hearth, almost his height, behind him. Vasily Andrevich Feodorov, I guessed, swayed on his toes and cast a brief look at me. He had a folded *Petersburg Zeitung*, the pro-German newspaper, in one hand. The other he held behind his back. He was quite the idealised man, wide in the shoulders, narrow at the waist, his legs slightly apart, a brocaded jacket fitting his splendid form. I would photograph him on horseback, Bonaparte style, a sabre in hand, raised perhaps, victory in his attitude. He cleared his throat but Olga Pyotrovna interrupted, fluttering her fingers for my attention.

"*Fräulein*, our friend Ksenia Borzakov phoned me this evening. She spoke, shall I say, she spoke about your socialist friend. And so on. We are rather alarmed."

Vasily Feodorov and the lorgnette woman spoke across us in French.

I could only guess what 'so on' suggested but I nodded, eager to deny whatever I should. I swallowed my tea silently, relieved to moisten my mouth.

"A shocking tragedy. We're devastated."

I steeled myself. "Absolutely. I knew Sergo too, from childhood you know..."

"We're appalled as well." She looked more closely at me,

deliberating. “Don’t expect to see your socialist friend while you’re here. We cannot permit it.”

“He’s a writer,” I said more stridently than I meant. “Not a murderer. Never. He writes for Tartu and Tallinn papers... ”

“We will not permit liaisons of any kind for our staff. Surely you would know that.” She gave me a weak, pitying smile and slid lower on the chaise.

My heart rocked with anger.

“Understand? You will not meet your criminal friend. *Verstehen*?” Her voice was sweet. She spoke in absolutes.

I nodded, lost in the rug, a floral one, at my warm booted feet.

“Besides, your time is precious. You may have an afternoon a fortnight for private matters. I assume you have family friends in Peterburg. You are responsible for the children to advance their German. *Bien*? You must devote yourself entirely.”

But my photographs? “I have a camera...” I said uncertainly.

“Of course. We too. You will be shown your room in a moment. You seem hot. It’s late. So, do meet our children.”

My heart sank. I would tuck my camera away; still, I was not about to be thrown into the ice-blasted streets. I would get my photographs and Mihkel would track me down again and tell me what he thought, honestly about everything that disturbed me.

“*Voilà*, my mother-in-law, Irena Alexandrovna Feodorova,” Olga said with her fingertips.

I dropped a curtsey. Irena murmured in Russian.

“*Enchantée*,” I replied, the entire limit of my French and while I hadn’t much use for it, I did feel plain compared to these women squeaking and rustling in their silks and hurling fragments of French around to unbalance me. Now it was indeed uncomfortably hot, the fire sparking, lights and candles gleaming from every wall niche. I wished I could unbutton my jacket or remove my woollen stockings.

"*Charmante*," Irena Alexandrovna replied with an implied nod.

"And my sister-in-law, Natalya Andreevna Feodorova." Olga glanced to the tilted wig.

"*Enchantée*," I repeated.

"You feel up to it? Alone here in Petersburg?" the sister-in-law asked.

"Yes, yes, I look forward to it," I insisted, forcing a great smile.

Natalya Andreevna's eyes were small and unfocussed yet fixed unflinchingly on me. Her body was limp, her head supported. I wondered if it was possible for her to exert herself.

A sound from the basket beside Olga gave me a start. I had not expected a baby in the room. Olga noticed my surprise and beckoned me. I peered in. All nose and mouth, snuffling waking up sounds from a white cocoon. The face reddened and crumpled as I watched.

"Maman!" a child, perhaps two in frilled bonnet and smocked dress and sucking at Olga's hem cried, though Olga ignored her. The child kept a worried frown on her forehead as she looked from me, to the baby and back to Olga.

A boy, perhaps four years old, with gold curls to his shoulders and wearing a dark scarlet dress confronted me petulantly. He ran his fingers up and down his mother's sleeve though Olga did not react. The eldest child, striking and confident, chest pushed forward, brown hair soft and curled falling over her shoulders, cocked her head to one side waiting for a signal from her mother to speak.

"The children have been anxious to meet you, *Fräulein*. Your German is excellent, *n'est-ce pas*? Ksenia said so. We're all impatient to resume studies, the children particularly."

"She's Estonian," I heard, from Irena's direction.

I was aware that spoiled children were rarely eager pupils but these shining youngsters might well be the exception. They were at least curious. They also clung fast to their mother. The baby's snuffling became a loud wail and Olga made a half-hearted move toward it only to be beaten by a buxom, middle-aged woman in a velvet and gold headdress who swept in, rescued the baby and sailed out with the squalling bundle propped stiffly over her shoulder.

"I believe children's language should come naturally. We'll talk about educational subjects. I know they're curious about the world. I believe they should know about science and art – at their level," I said.

Olga looked unconvinced. "Greet your teacher, *Schätzchen*," she said removing her hem from Magdalena's fingers and pressing the child forward, but Magdalena only held on more firmly and eyed me as the enemy.

"Come, come! Look now, your new teacher, Magda! What's this?" Olga continued in French – something about behaviour so that Magdalena's reply brought peals of laughter from the room plus a deep growling laugh from Vasily.

I stood like a fool, but I smiled, hoping at least for one of the children to accept me.

"Now Katya." Olga stretched out to the older girl who tossed her head. "*Mais pourquoi cette dame ordinaire, Maman*?" she demanded, her hands on her hips.

"*Je te dirai un plus tard ma chérie*," Olga shot back though Katya looked steadfastly at me without acknowledgement.

The golden-haired boy shrank closer to Olga saying *no, no, no*, louder as he went. Olga shook him by his arm. "Our

Alexander. Sacha, at home," she explained and he glowered in reply.

"The last German tutor fled," Irena remarked.

"Afraid of shadows," Natalya said.

I sat like a puppet while Olga berated her children over their manners. They stared ahead, bored. I felt dreadfully tired and longed to see my room, hoping to find it cosy and warm, the bed, soft, the pillows, deep. I was famished too but couldn't say.

"Tomorrow," Olga said. "You'll become acquainted, yes?"

"I'm sure," I replied feebly.

"So, meet my husband, Vasily Andrevich Feodorov," Olga sighed on, her head tilted gracefully to the side. Vasily stepped close to me and I stood to greet him.

Dark, sleek-haired, a moustache and beard trimmed like Tsar Nicholas, blue cuirassier jacket buttoned in brass from waist to neck, a uniform, a protector of the tsar, he gave off hints of limes and wood smoke though he met my gaze like an armoured train. I felt the force of a wind tunnel and needed to grab something to steady myself.

Ksenia had written that he was reckless and arrogant. And loved women. Few believed half of what Ksenia ever said. The woman in the carriage from Tartu had warned me about employers as well.

Vasily wheeled, dipped his head and clicked his heels. His large, muscled hands hung at his sides, the newspaper crushed. I looked him in the eye for a moment before I bobbed a curtsey. He was from head to toe, one of the most perfect figures from I'd ever seen, forthright and unshakeable as good-looking people are, and especially so when well-to-do. "We entrust our children to you, Siina Jürimäe. You become family," he said in rapid-fire Russian.

"*Schatz,* now it's late. Come," Olga intervened but Vasily didn't hear.

"Breakfast is at nine," Irena prompted.

Vasily continued to hold my gaze, his eyes softening while for a moment I imagined myself unclothed and resistance to him dissolving. "You can feel safe here," he said.

Perhaps I would, but so far I was overwhelmed with conflicting messages.

My fingers twisted together. Olga was about to dismiss me. "The children will be ready to begin after breakfast," she said. Sacha laid his head on her knee refusing to look at me. Katya frowned. Magdalena sucked her thumb, Olga's hem screwed up in her other hand.

I nodded to the children and bade everyone goodnight in perfect Pärnu Russian.

At the very top of the rosewood staircase the steps became narrower and steeper but opened out to my room, larger than I expected and with a window heavily curtained. I would look outside in the morning. My bed was covered by a mass of furs, while a handsome ebony stand and dresser was covered with embroidered linens. I tugged off my boots and lay back on the soft bed, the bed headboard carved with grapes and dancing muses. Someone had slipped a hot water flask under the covers but the room was warm, more so than downstairs. I would be comfortable. I discovered my bag with my nightdress tidily tucked on the other side of the room and began removing my travelling clothes.

I sat with my emptiness even as my head swirled with so many emotions from all of the encounters of the day.

At least I had some fine shots on my camera. Perhaps Olga was kinder than she made out. Perhaps the remarks between the women were harmless. I may have been too sensitive, overreacting to inane chatter.

I had saved a bottle of Oskar's wine. I would never drink it alone, but this night was different. I pushed the cork in and with a mouthful of *pirukas*, sipped.

In the morning everything was sure to look better. Instead of Mihkel's, Vasily's face came and went when I lay down. He'd been sympathetic and treated me as an equal unlike the women.

I drifted back and forth almost sleeping. Whatever difficulties were in store I was resolute. I would give in to circumstances. I had to. I breathed gently. I would deal fairly with everyone, no matter whom, and keep to what I believed was right.

24. Goethe

My head was muzzy when I woke, my neck stiff. Frost laced the window panes, three deep. Stone walls framed a snapshot of a thundery sky. Already I felt miserable thinking of the months ahead. I would miss the clear winter days of Pärnu, Anna's pointless optimism, even Roosi's common sense.

I leaned into the recessed window to see below in the courtyard. A *dvornik* carried coal into a cellar, crossing paths with a stable-hand wheeling a barrow of straw. A fat icicle dripped onto the tiled yard. Even here I could smell snow.

I dared not be late for breakfast. I unearthed a crumpled dress, changed my bloomers and stretched on wool stockings. I splashed cold water from the ewer, then French perfume that Anna had given me, dabbing my neck and wrists. I parted my hair in the middle and tied on a ribbon. Bohemian. Still, I needed to set my camera on the dresser, the accordion lens stretched, aperture fixed, ready to fly open.

I would photograph the baby's howling rage, the wet nurse, head-dress flying like a sail and Vasily, buttoned, epauletted beside his ancestor's armour. I would pile the children on Sacha's rocking horse and capture their delight. The instant was everything.

I hurried by generations of oily Feodorovna riding the panelled hall. Another time I would inspect them more closely but I hesitated at coloured photographs; Prokudin-Gorskii, they had to be. In a clearer, dark sepia I recognised Natalya Andreevna flopped between gem-studded Fabergé and an ivory-toned Meissen; a photographer with a sense of humour. Irena

Alexandrovna Feodorova, her cane held at twelve o'clock, peered through her lorgnette from a *dacha* veranda. I was certain, given a discreet moment to set her up I could be as clever. Katya and Magdalena, little tots, swam naked in a river in summer's golden light. Vasily slammed a tennis ball, Olga in the background reclined under an endless brim of lace and straw and Sacha was there, scowling at her knee. The last photograph was another style, another lens, a different composition. None were Stieglitz or Margaret Cameron and I wasn't but I could have picked the grasses and felt the weave of the clothes. A voice beside stopped me.

"Ah, the new *Fräulein*? *Ja ha?*" A red face behind a mutton-chop moustache appeared beside me and gave the photograph a close inspection, imitating me. He smelled of boot polish and boiled onions. "Giles Spencer," he said with a tip of his head and a step back, a suggestion of a bow.

"Siina Jürimäe. *Priyatno poznakomit'sya.*" I dropped a quick curtsey.

"*Fräulein.* Charmed. You're from lovely countryfied Estonia. Rye and cheese, bacon and butter. So I hear."

"From Pärnu. It's a small town, not country. You're English. Is it all oak trees and chimney sweeps?" I countered.

He led me by my elbow, the back of his hand pressing against my breast. He chuckled yet he was almost effeminate, the way his shoulders rounded and he eyed me like a fawn. "Too much Dickens I'm afraid."

I turned for the dining room. Olga nodded us a greeting.

"They read Dickens in Estonia," Giles Spencer announced.

"They would. In German?" Natalya Andreevna wrinkled her forehead.

"German?"

"And Goethe? You read Goethe. And Pushkin?" Giles asked.

"Pushkin, Russian, yes."

Giles hovered at the side table serving himself. I had begun my breakfast. The cottage cheese was creamy, the caraway bread fresh.

"'*Happy the man who early learns the wide chasm that lies between his wishes and his power.' Goethe*," Irena quoted, spooning pieces of diced hard-boiled egg onto her plate with marinated fish. She looked up, the words intended for me.

"'*All the knowledge I possess, everyone else can acquire, but my heart is all my own,*'" I said, pleased it came instinctively. "I'm no scholar. Not really," I said. I couldn't be sure where Irena's quote came from. I hoped my admission would not get me fired. But worse, I could not think of Goethe's most important work!

"'*Plunge boldly into the thick of life, and seize it where you will, it is always interesting,*'" Giles quoted.

"So where else have you worked and why did you choose to come here at this time?" Irena asked.

The cream in my coffee had formed oily bubbles. I added sugar because it was expensive. "This is my first," I said, annoyed to have to announce it.

Irena's eyes shifted from Olga to Natalya.

"Our *Fräulein* comes well-recommended," Olga said.

"But she must stay in the house all the time and play with me," Katya beamed gap-toothed, sitting tall, bolstered on the edge of a Chippendale chair,.

I looked to Olga for an explanation. "Enough, Katya. *Deutsch*."

"No! Because we have guests," Katya protested.

"True," Natalya said.

I waited for a contradiction. I wracked my brain for Goethe's *magnum opus*.

"So, Pushkin? Which of his poems do you prefer?"

"*A Little Bird*," I shot.

Irena looked at Olga, then me. "And what do you take those images to mean?"

"It's the bird's freedom. Beautiful. Don't you agree?"

Irena played with her fork. Natalya dabbed the corners of her mouth. Giles looked at me expectantly. "Thinly veiled subversion." Olga leaned forward cupping her heart-shaped face. "Are you naïve, *Fräulein*? Why else did our friend Ksenia banish you? Remember your place at every moment. *Verstanden*?"

25. Sofia Casanova

In the upstairs nursery room Katya copied Gothic script into a brown covered notebook forming imperfect but recognisable letters. For the dozenth time I showed Sacha and Magdalena how to wind their clockwork monkey.

From behind my lace curtains I looked out over the shaggy heads of the bearded atlantids on our building. The rain had paused, and beyond at the neighbouring Nabokov apartment a droshky pulled up. A group of men argued on the cobbled pavement as a second droshky arrived with more dishevelled men who began to threaten the others. A short bespectacled man waved his hands, made furious leaps at a larger man with bundled pamphlets under his arm. Another fellow in a bearskin coat and with a bird's nest of a beard, swaggered up, shook his fist in their faces, then swung. The short man's mouth cracked open in a silent scream. I could not take my eyes off them from behind the windows. Suddenly the men were rushing at each other, restraining and punching, locking shoulders, wrenching and heaving on the rain-glazed street. One man at the edge of the group took out a pistol but before I heard anything I heard my own shriek, before the shot. The man in the bearskin lowered his hand, the gun smoking and slowly, like a moving picture, the brawl ended, the men staggered to their feet. I spun, felt the children at my side, goggle-eyed at me, unable to see the street from our second floor room. An accident I said. I'd gotten a fright. I held my heart. I'd read in *Izvestiya* about a child, Katya's age who had stolen half loaf of bread, hidden it under his coat and was beaten and kicked to death. A week before on Voznesensky

Prospekt, two clerks on their way home had been shot and robbed and left to die. I peered out again. Pamphlets were strewn along the gutter. The men were helping one another up and gathering the papers. The Nabokov front door opened and the men shambled in, arms around one another.

I turned to a rustle of silk.

"Darlings!" Olga swanned across the room only moments after her flowery Parisian scent floated in the air. She paused a moment and ran her hand over Sacha's head before drifting to me, leaned over the window recess. "Good god! Look at them! They get what they deserve. Killing one another under our noses. Animals! But we should have called the street police. Nabokov, the fascists hate him. They'll murder him one day."

"Perhaps he has a vision," I dared say.

"Shooting one another in the street? Murdering and robbing? Vision, *Fräulein*?" They use women you know. Aleksandra Kollontai, I know her but I'd cross the street rather than speak to her."

"She's so unpleasant?" I knew exactly what Olga meant; still I wanted to hear more. Kollontai worked to improve conditions for uneducated women in factory jobs. She had no need to work and was socially above the textile workers. She was also glamorous and well-educated.

"Unpleasant? You're not so naïve, *Fräulein*. She's conceited, and ridiculous to imagine she can liberate and change anything. What, with free love? Prettier than promiscuity? But I can speak out too, because if subversives mean to destroy us, I'll say something and it won't be soft." Olga's rose jacket collar ruffled against her pale face. "I can make difficult decisions. We all can if we must."

It wasn't the idea of protecting her family that came to mind when I looked at her. I recognized a fierce will and drive beneath the delicacy, she could keep a cool head making instant, detached decisions. She was more shrewd and able than she appeared.

"We know exactly who those scoundrels are, those men who stoke up resentment and fire against the people who provide for them. Jews, of course. Whenever they're raided they have guns and bombs and pamphlets under the beds." Olga leaned against the window beside me. "Rabble rousers, speaking for the workers? No. Think carefully before you speak to anyone today, *Fräulein*. They have nerve to go publishing manifestos full of lies. Greed and jealousy drives them. Who on earth would write that?"

Naturally she had Mihkel in mind. Perhaps she and Ksenia had talked about him before. I wondered if they had provided one another with luscious gossip over the years.

"Russians expect their motherland will save them. Even when they're desperate for a real leader," I said recklessly.

Olga's blue-grey eyes sparkled like ice. "My dear we love Russia just as she is. And we adore our tsar." Her hand went to her throat, her rings flashing, her fingers, thin-skinned, manicured with peach enamel. "The war drives the radicals wild my dear, but we're completely in control. You know we are, don't you?"

So we were, in theory.

Olga leaned against the window niche. I excused myself to sit beside Katya and fill in the spaces she'd left in her manuscript. The radical movement had mushroomed since it began more than ten years earlier. Educated aristocrats and intelligentsia, the Decembrists, had been enlightened enough to shift power to an elected body, while the leaders were shot or imprisoned at a shocking rate. Others lay low but there were women who volunteered to be banished with husbands to Siberia.

"She's brave. She cares about the powerless. Many women complain but do nothing. Some are literally caged by their husbands," I said, another stick on the fire.

Olga blinked rapidly. "Is that what you think, what you hear? As for Kollontai, why, let her go on and do what she does with Lenin and whomever else. She deserts her children and husband to write subversive material. She's proud of immorality! I also care about women dragged down and unable to care for children. They are victims. I pity them. It's sad and shameful."

"Yet you don't support her?" I said softly. I'd gone too far even though Olga encouraged me. She rewound the monkey for Magdalena and set it on the ivory table.

"Kollantai's ideas are absurd, *Fräulein*. She asks too much. That the government raise illegitimate children? *Bourgemou*!"

Magdalena tried to climb into her lap. Olga said something in French and Magdalena went grumbling back to her monkey.

"Kollontai ruins perfectly good industries before she dashes off to Lenin or some young lover. Socialism is it? Short hair and no stays?" The fine skin around Olga's eyes creased. For a moment she really did care and was as angry as I as we stood on opposite sides. I could have said that immorality had always been accepted in men but not women.

"Don't you think some people have no choice? If they're born where they are and have no chance for education?"

"And who asks them to have a dozen children and no husband? It's a woman's responsibility, getting babies. Agreed?"

I felt she didn't believe what she was saying. "It takes a couple," I said guardedly.

Olga looked down at her watered silk bodice and brushed an imagined speck away. Her neat figure was fitted into a tailored jacket that shaped her modestly, claiming more than she was. I wished I could tell her that she had proved herself already, bearing four beautiful children, managing the household and family, entertaining guests and keeping herself informed and educated in politics and art. I'd have loved to have told her so.

"Of course, only the woman pays." Olga stretched across the camel-back sofa, her arms limp. "You must know this *Fräulein.* I see that you're not as naive as you make out. You come from farm labourers yet you've made an entrée into our world. You see? You studied. You worked to move ahead." She rearranged the folds of her skirt and Magdalena climbed on the sofa beside her, imitating her composure.

I intended to be composed too but my hands had tightened into fists. "I came here to work. An entrée was not on my agenda," I said leaning against the window bay now. A small boy and an old woman crouched in the street in thin clothes, feet in rags, hands in ragged gloves. They were dragging sodden leaflets from the gutters, turning them over to decipher them. I stood by the warm Dutch-tiled stove.

"So, *Fräulein,* you'd not be interested to know that the gentleman you met last week, Mr Giles Spencer, an Englishman, was taken with you. He never married somehow. A banker. In two steps you could be well-to-do. But you're not interested, or so I suspect." Olga leaned forward, lifting her satin-slippered feet onto the sofa, and wrapped her arms around her knees.

I was surprised and annoyed. Giles Spencer had been present at a few dinners. He was awkward and odd, born in Peterburg, more Russian in his manner than English. He stumbled his way through English phrases and could not describe a single Dickens' character yet Irena and Natalya Andreevna could.

"My parents read literature and are not poor. I was never a factory worker. The girls in the Haymarket are prostitutes, some of them no older than Katya," I said as Olga flinched. Her eyes narrowed and she shuddered.

"How dare you!"

I reacted too, aware I had now surely gone too far. "I'm very sorry," I said quickly. "I didn't mean it like that but I see it and it is tragic. I look at Katya and…"

Olga flapped her hand. "Enough! Stop now!"

"I'm very fond of her and I'd hate to think..."

"You go far too far! You forget yourself, *Fräulein*. Again!"

I held my tongue. I lowered my head and stood before her, penitent. "I'm terribly sorry. It was stupid of me … I mean to protect Katya. I would always do so."

Olga shook her head at me. "So. You need to learn from life but you've lifted yourself up. You have indeed. I may forgive you. Only don't talk about Kollontai being a heroine! She loves her self-importance. And my children! Well, I leave you to reflect on what you have said."

I opened my mouth to apologize again. I dreaded taking the train home before I had begun what I came for.

"Of course," Olga rearranged herself raising her eyebrows at me. "Many are dazzled by Kollontai. Giles Spencer for one."

I might choose to dance with him. I would. I straightened my face. "I find him foolish and insensitive. I beg your pardon. It's honest."

Olga gave me a look of pity. "Oh, *Fräulein*! I'm surprised!" she said tipping back her head, laughing a light pealing laugh and I understood that perhaps I could too. "He ought to have been shipped off to war long ago!" she said, her face turning grave. "Only we won't talk about the war. I'm too tired of it," she said, a hand to her head. A doleful expression returned. Her brother, a young guards officer had been scythed off his horse by the

Prussians less than three months ago. I had noticed her re-setting his photographs from one table and icon niche to the next, polishing the glass with the corner of her handkerchief before she assigned him to the corner with other dead friends. Natalya lit candles before Saint Titus who protected soldiers. Olga kept her grief to herself in colourless silence. I wondered miserably where Enn and Hardi were and if Ilar was alive.

"Though of course Giles Spencer knows a lot about postage stamps," I suggested hopefully. Olga changed her position on the sofa again. When Sacha and Katya came to her she shooed them off.

"Oh, forget him *Fräulein*," she said, so I assumed I'd made up for my blunders, and also because when Katya came to her side again Olga kissed her forehead and stroked her cheek.

A moment later, Duscha bobbed a curtsey and asked to take the children to supper. Olga went ahead downstairs to play another hand of bezique with Irena, who would always wait on the Egyptian chair.

I turned again to the window.

Spring rain blew hard against the glass as a barouche pulled up outside the Nabokov house and a man leapt out, pulled up his collar, his fedora low, and held his arm like a handle to a woman in an orange coat and fur muff. Mihkel's movements. I wanted to beat on the glass but stood back trying to see her face beneath the mass of orange fur. The two clung together but were soon out of sight under our neighbour's porch. It was Kollontai, I was sure from what I'd read and seen in the papers. She was notorious and popular, attractive and effective. The public were curious about her. She was taller than the man – it had to be Mihkel, though I couldn't see either face. I would have to go outside and speak to Mihkel. He'd be surprised but thrilled to see me.

While the children puzzled with a game matching words with pictures, I completed a letter to Anna. I paused to look outside. Rain had turned to drizzle. Men emerged from the Nabokov house, and at last the man, surely Mihkel, stepped out with the orange puff.

Don't be an idiot, were Anna's last words to me. Mihkel and the orange puff linked arms. I shivered and cringed as he swept her into the barouche. Surrounded by equally self-absorbed, self-important men, they rode off into the grey dusk.

26. Kasakad

My hands lay folded in my lap. I leaned forward a touch to smell dill in my soup, goose grease on the roasted potatoes, and the fruit of my wine before sipping. The food aromas overpowered even the beeswax candles. Crystal and porcelain shimmered and around the table, the children shone like berries - Magdalena in a blue and white-ribboned plissé, Katya, ramrod straight in her seat in a cream, pleated skirt and blouse embroidered with butterflies. Shame, I thought, so many outfits she could never wear them all. Sacha like a sailor child in a sharp pressed suit sat on heaped pillows beside his grandmother, Irena. She insisted he use one hand on his fork and keep the other in his lap. Natalya Andreevna Feodorova, Vasily's sister, sat opposite me and prodded her food.

The moment I laid down my spoon, moon-faced Lyudmila cleared my dish and served vegetables with gravy-covered meat. All week the cook had complained about the vegetables and supplies while in Pärnu such a table would have made a wedding feast. Fruit juices and crackling Georgian wine, sour cream and mushrooms smothering roast lamb. Pepper gravy drowned the carrots and peas. As if no-one in Russia starved, as if there were no war. While men in the Vyborg ate cat, and if they were lucky, soldiers got the thinnest gruel of beans or *kasha* once a day. What could I do except say a prayer to Natalya's icons while I feasted, but I didn't believe.

Olga at the head of the table remained static and limp, pressed in by a headache or pain perhaps. Her cheeks were rouged, her lips thinned when she smiled, no more alive than any of her crowned icons. *Women's problems*, Duscha had whispered and

Duscha was one to know. She talked. I wondered if she would say *cancer* next, blaming it on a sexual appetite, Olga's or her husband's. I had heard that women suffered cancers because of that. Too much of it. And *the nature of women*; the pregnancy, the birth. It was because of our emotions too. We were the susceptible sex, Duscha said so though I was not so sure.

I felt Natalya Andreevna gazing at me for a moment too long from across the table. I lowered my eyes but it only encouraged her to tell me in particular, about the great adventure of her life when she was betrothed to an Old Believer, a Cossack from the Don. I still felt burning rage for Cossacks though their music and dance were celebrated everywhere in Russia. I had long since lost any notion of romance about them.

"He was one of the best. Rode as though he was born on a horse," Natalya said as if I'd never heard of Cossacks stampeding across plains. They could pick up coins from the ground as they went full pelt, firing pistols from beneath the horse's belly. Napoleon himself admired the Cossacks.

"Agile as goats," Olga murmured, unkindly I thought.

"So thrilling. They challenge life and risk death! Their own people, their own law," Natalya said, emboldened. I straightened Magdalena's serviette and moved her plate nearer to her.

"And the music! One would have to be soulless not to be moved. The rhythms, the tambourine. My heart sings even now!" Natalya held a hand to her throat and lived the time and place again.

Olga rolled her eyes. "My sister-in-law." I felt a tremor of sympathy, even pity for Natalya. She wasn't old. She might still have married and had children but the memory of her hero overshadowed everyone else.

Even so, I could not bring myself to speak. I focussed on

Katya's plate as though that was essential. Cossacks remained a nightmare for me.

"Yes! You see! Everything I wanted and loved. I'm a rebel myself. In here." She tapped her chest again though I refused to look at her. From the corner of my eye I sensed her manner and movement. "You think I need all this?" She spread her arms as if she might fly off. "I don't!"

I didn't mind acknowledging Olga who shook her head but said nothing.

"Who else can live like that, nothing but grass and water? Men of iron and women of fire! I still see them, even now, as if it were yesterday," Natalya continued. "Do you not know this *Fräulein*? Have you never heard?"

"I have seen them too. I was in Palace Square on Bloody Sunday," I said laying down my fork. "I see them in my nightmares," I said to a table suddenly fallen silent.

"Ah but the river Don and the vineyards and orchards, the grassy banks, the Azov Sea," Natalya persisted.

I could see it. Sturgeon, caviare and Chekhov's own *Cherry Orchard* near that sea. I could picture Natalya, dancing to exhaustion but now, however many snuff boxes, wigs and diamond brooches she had, she retained her illusions; a Cossack girl, barefoot who could be bought and sold and who danced through it all.

The mushrooms were divine but the cream was not fresh. Neither was the lamb.

"But you were hardly born! I'm disgusted by protesters. What do they achieve commemorating that day? They simply drive themselves mad. And everyone around them," Natalya said.

"They need to accept what happened. Put it in the past!" Irena added.

"I was seven. And I still see Cossack blades and people screaming in my dreams." I surprised myself. The table fell silent.

"It was a tragedy. Dreadful but now the protest it … no no!" Natalya said looking at her plate, shoving her food around.

"The real cost of empire, *Fräulein*, what do you think that is? How is your wine? Refreshing?" Vasily asked.

"My mother died from her injuries. She was stabbed in the side. Her coat fabric entered her lung," I said, without blame, merely a fact though I felt my insides shake.

"And more than one courageous, progressive tsar has been murdered by hysterical crowds." Vasily gave me an intimidating look.

"My fiancée was courageous," Natalya said.

I imagined him, bearded, bristling with ammunition, whirling a sabre over his head. Heartless. Even so I could envision fields of wheat, the river Don, the Azov Sea but not Natalya there. "I'm sure you've fond memories," glad to take respite from the way the conversation had gone.

"Fond! No, blissful!" She sipped another mouthful of wine, tossed her serviette over her plate and slightly staggering, went mincing around the table, swaying from side to side, humming more and more loudly as she went. There was no music but she sang a low-toned, unearthly pitch, another character beneath the wig and beaded dress. Her cheeks turned pink, she flicked out a handkerchief from her pocket, glanced around with pleasure and made another circuit of the table. Olga and Irena ignored her but the children twisted in their seats, giggling. Katya's peas spilled onto the Persian rug, Magdalena and Sacha scrambled down from the table and followed Natalya, kicking their heels and stamping. Magdalena wobbled as she spun around imitating Natalya's tune and taking tiny steps like a Georgian princess. The long wide skirts were missing from the picture. “A woman is never too old for this dance,” she called over her shoulder, waving her handkerchief, gliding around the floor as if she were on ice. Vasily smiled. Olga rolled her eyes. The children giggled and pushed until they were ordered back to the table and Natalya held a hand to her chest, panting. For a moment I had glimpsed the other Cossack tradition.

“Never ask for advice in your life, *Fräulein*! Because you’ll regret it the rest of your life,” Natalya said, throwing a look at Vasily, recovering her composure.

I patted my mouth with my starched serviette. Magdalena plumped herself back beside me, Irena reprimanded her but Magdalena smiled back regardless.

“Chaliapin will sing at the Mariinski,” Vasily said unexpectedly. His voice boomed, trained for shouting orders. He waved his silver fork, tiny in his large fingers. “A gala event. We should go.” He glanced at Olga. I caught his perfume.

From the corner of my eye I saw Olga frowning, shaking her head.

“He’s a genius,” I said remembering Mihkel’s promises, wondering if I would see him again or if he was too busy with the orange puff. He had promised me Chaliapin and Stravinsky, the Winter Palace and Nijinsky.

“Chaliapin is arrogant, and madder than his directors who are totally bizarre.” Irena Feodorova looked around. Her grey-blue eyes were startling in her grim face. “He demanded he do Mephistopheles half naked. Another Nijinsky, he thinks!” she said, wobbling her head, arching her high pencilled brows.

“Why?” Katya squealed.

“His audiences weep with ecstasy,” Olga said laying her fork on her plum cake.

I knew that audiences had been stunned at Nijinsky's sex when he refused to wear anything, not even flimsy shorts over his tights and he was henceforth banned from the Imperial Ballet. I wondered if it was art, ballet, or a new form of revolution that he promoted, or himself as art itself. I desperately wished to see and decide independently.

"Chaliapin is a genius and prodigious! He was dragged from the worst misery in Kazan, my dears. Amazing he reached manhood at all! Tried to kill himself, you know. Poor man. From that part of the world," Irena said, looking significantly at her daughter but Natalya was still in her world.

"Conceit with no respect for his superiors. But genius. We must hear him – Olga, *ma chérie*?" Vasily said.

Katya squared her shoulders and tipped her nose up at her father. She widened her eyes. "*Moi aussi, s'il vous plaît! Vous me permettez?*"

"Please, please, Papa, *Est-ce que je peux*?" Magdalena mimicked, her voice even higher.

I was sure Olga would not go and I longed to. She would go to bed early, her cure for headaches, rest, sleep and certainly a drink of something soothing. Lyudmila told me how Olga suffered from women's 'mysteries' especially after the last childbirth. Vasily gave her a look of regret as she passed her hand over her forehead.

"But take Katya. Why not? Our *Fräulein* will look after her. An evening to remember for our darling." Olga's voice was as tired as her eyes.

I restrained my delight. Inside I leapt for joy. Katya turned to me, her mouth wide open, her eyes popping. Irena lifted her chin and closed the mouth. Lyudmila sprang forward to rescue a water glass.

"It would be my pleasure," I said rather too quickly. Natalya Andreevna began staring again. A woman reminded of her tribal background, thrown over by her Cossack lover would be alert to an Estonian German tutor accompanying her employer to the opera.

"In fact the tsar himself will be there. Our box is not so far from his," Olga remembered as she speared the plum cake. "You may even meet him, *Fräulein*. He with his elegant family. Think of that!"

Lemon and honey, plum and egg sauce melted in my mouth. I set my fork across my gold-rimmed plate. I smiled graciously.

"The thing is, Chaliapin is to be created 'Soloist to his Majesty' tonight," Vasily said, dabbing sweetened cream from his moustache and casting an airy look around, also, for the briefest moment, at me.

"Chaliapin is *Boris Godunov*," Irena Feodorova put in.

At that very moment I decided it entirely appropriate to drink to the bottom of my wineglass and taste every drop from the Crimea or wherever else those grapes had grown. I was already quivering after my first sip and Feodorovna dinners always teetered on the brink of drama. I replaced my glass on the broccato tablecloth and raised my head to Olga. She propped her chin in her hand and held her wine glass in the other. Crystal cuts twinkled. Her sleep-laden eyes shone moist in the candlelight. Angel and mortal, sacred and profane. Beautiful, privileged and miserable. I desperately wished for my camera.

"Thank you, Olga Feodorovna."

"Go, go!"

"So, come! Dress!" Vasily flung his napkin on the table and beckoned Katya. He fished out his watch, the type with ruby bearings. "Dress her warmly and prettily," he instructed Grunya who struggled up onto her puffed-up legs. She'd been perched on the low bench beside us all evening.

I was dying to hear Chaliapin but half an hour's notice to get ready was impossible. Besides, what would I say to the tsar and a poker-faced tsarina? *We love you, Little Father but we far prefer our own government in Estonia. And the people in your streets, Majesty, the wretched souls who stand in the snow, have you considered how they freeze and fall where they are, from hunger? Please! One or two of your gold-framed saints, a Brueghel or Velásquez so scores of your people can live! And, Ruler of All the Russias and Prince of Estland, our boys long to return home to their families and farms. We despise your bloody wars!*

I would say no such thing. I'd be incoherent if I reached within metres of the tsar. Vasily would never again bring me near the Mariinski or in sight of another nobleman or friend, and perhaps not even back to his house if I used the moment to speak anything at all.

Katya slithered from her chair with a *merci beaucoup* and bounded upstairs with a maid at her heels and Grunya lagging after.

Irena Feodorova pursed her lips at me. "My dear, do you have anything at all to wear?"

I did! I had a velvet dress. "I do. An evening dress," I crowed and forgetting the imperative 'thank you' myself after a meal, I followed the trail upstairs.

I held up my dress before the gold, crackly-edged mirror in my room. Ksenia had sent the dress to me in Pärnu. It was figured silk velvet with gold embroidery on the neckline, tight sleeves and soft pleats at the waist. The skirt was neither old fashioned and full, nor scandalously slim-fitting and Bohemian. It was elegant and I had longed to wear it. What was more; Ksenia had given me the matching bag, big enough for my camera.

I wore that dress once when I was as slim as you, she had written. I slipped it on. It was loose, sliding from my shoulders, clinging to my arms and draping low at the front. I had no underwear bodice that wouldn't show so I wore none. I had minutes to do my hair so I pinned and stuck combs and tied ribbons. I had neither jewellery nor silk flowers and only peasants went without curls and nets. I brushed and twisted handfuls of my hair, jabbed in what I had and trusted it to heaven. Parisian and Viennese fashions would be paraded. Petersburg dowagers and noblewomen, wives and daughters of bankers and industrialists, people the Feodorovnas entertained would flash diamond tiaras and peacock plumes but I would simply smile, elated to be wearing Ksenia's dress, thrilled to hear Chaliapin and ecstatic to be in the Mariinski! I raised my chin, flung Mama's floral wrap around my shoulders and threw open my bedroom door.

Downstairs Grunya kneeled and tucked Katya into a white fur hat, coat and muff. Katya looked up. "See! She is coming!" she shouted.

Vasily lifted his brilliantined head to me.

He had changed to cuirassier dress-uniform, a tight-fitting belted jacket and trousers high around the waist, hugging his thighs. His gaze ran from my head to hem. I wanted to be appreciated. My neck and shoulders felt his eyes, and all the way to my German leather boots. He now noticed me as if for the first time. "You're … very smart, *Fräulein*. Fine indeed," he finished and with both hands, smoothed down his glazed moustache.

It was terribly improper for him to contemplate me so boldly but I returned his look with as much assertion, even pausing on the stairs, advancing with the sort of drama that Anna would have in the Endla Theatre. I allowed my wrap to slide down my shoulders as I stepped into the hall, close to him, his eyes still on me and only then did I draw up the folds and cover myself.

When I reached for my coat, Olga and Irena came strolling through the hall toward the library, their heads bent together, a snuff box in Irena's hand.

Olga paused. "*Fräulein,* take my coat, really. It must be minus twenty out there," she said and I heard; *pauvre petite* or was it *bêtise*?

27. The Mariinski

Katya tweaked my wrist when we sat in the side box of the Mariinski. “Tell me the story, *bitte, Fräulein*.”

What could I say to an eleven-year-old about a tyrant who murdered a child?

“Watch and listen. It’s about the music. The story is terribly sad.”

To either side of us, balconies filled with uniformed officers and women, costumed and coiffed, powdered, laced and bejewelled. Embroidered silk coats, *crêpe-de-chine*, Belgian lace skirts, Georgette gowns swept between the aisles. Women paused and postured as I had pictured them, hair threaded with ribbons and pearls, glittering in necklaces, ivory arms and shoulders bared. Unmarried women like Lipizzaner horses paraded, pressing along balcony tiers and through circle aisles. I felt isolated as an island off Greenland. Bosomy mothers in black velvet coats and sequinned hairnets followed two steps behind daughters or leaned on husbands’ elbows. Factory owners in black jackets, silk ties, upright collars, smiled, bowed, offered hands, kissed cheeks, smiled and laughed. I was bedazzled and amazed. Nowhere in the world was there such elegance and sparkle. And nowhere such bleeding and starvation outside the walls. The proletarian opera lovers in the orchestra seats, the clerks and unimportant merchants, artists, musicians and writers mingled with the Bohemians in loose flowing dresses and shapeless layers, as self-conscious and fashionable as the bourgeois they disdained. In the streets beyond us peasants starved and girls Katya’s age were sold.

The Bohemians greeted one another more loudly, gestured more openly and exhibited more passion than the audience in the circle and balconies put together. I marvelled and gaped, thrilled and overwhelmed. There was far too much velvet-silk and fur and too many diamonds and I was transfixed.

I leaned over the balustrade wishing I was with Mihkel and his friends. I'd have loved their jokes, the language, the bantering and wit. I was as radical as my mother, cautious as my father and I was desperately curious. I'd tell them what I thought and they'd hear me. In the heart of our empire there would be talk about our hopes for an elected government in Tartu. I could ask anything and hear the most radical opinions, especially what they expected of the tsar. Would there be a giant crackdown on Nihilists and Social Revolutionaries? Would the government ever give housing money for the poor? Were they serious about bombs and guns to make themselves heard?

"Look, look!" Katya shook my sleeve. "Blue ribbons all over the box!" The tsar and family sat behind festoons of blue shining ribbon. I nodded to Katya. The tsar stared around as if he were hunted. The audience whispered, stared at him while he sat stonily, his daughters also, his starched impassive tsarina as well. Perhaps they denied who they were, that they were the leaders of an empire and city steaming to rebellion.

Vasily nodded to his tsar who dipped his head minimally in reply.

Below us in the stalls I noticed an angular stance and gesture. Mihkel! He clove the air with one hand as if rallying rebels. The orange puff was beside him.

"Someone you know?" Vasily leaned across Katya to me.

"No one."

"Ah, but that is Mihkel Oks. The revolutionary and your

countryman. The woman, she is Sofia Casanova, the journalist."

I fumed. "She is?"

"So I believe. Spanish and celebrated. Makes appointments with Rasputin and interviews Kamenev! I'm sure she adores our politics."

I shivered. I detested what Vasily was saying. I wished I could have contradicted him.

"How do you know?" I said, agonising. It was the same orange puff. I felt desolate to see Mihkel with her, a woman able to dash about Peterburg and interview the political nobles of the moment.

Vasily leaned his head sideways, his face creased charmingly. "I need to know who stirs up trouble, don't I?" He narrowed his eyes beneath manicured brows. "Her family is well-connected so she finds her way easily. She writes for the Madrid press, you know. But she makes us look very bad."

"A journalist must say what she sees. It's ethics," I dared say.

Vasily leaned closer. "Yes, yes. But you're shocked to see him, *Fräulein* and I expect he's telling her lies this very moment. Wouldn't you like to know which ones?" He smiled again while I stewed. Lies indeed. Still I had to peer over the rail once more. The woman was his friend I would wager, sure to be Bolsheviki, probably intimate in the manner of Kollontai.

"Yes. It is my countryman, Mihkel Oks," I admitted though I couldn't see why Vasily cared.

"Tell me about him. Anyway I should enjoy meeting her. Intelligent, stylish, forceful enough to find her way into the heart of the Bolshevik machinery." Vasily gave me a wry smile. "And discreet enough to be invited back."

I shuddered at the insinuation intended to wound me. But I would not allow it.

"But of course they're colleagues. It's the civilised way to behave."

Vasily continued, his voice low as if he was confiding. "She dines with families like our own. Dashes from one party to the next along the Angliskaya Naberezhnaya." He sank back into his blue velvet seat with a satisfied look.

"It's not Kollontai?"

"No, no. Sofia Casanova. Although I'm sure she will be every bit as interesting as Kollontai," he said easing back into his seat and relating the tale of the opera to Katya. He explained that it was pure fiction so she should not be upset.

The conductor took up his baton, the overture began and I heaved relief and fell into the music, glad to lose myself in melodies I knew from childhood. In the scenes of peasants begging Godunov, the music shambled and dragged drawing out the misery that might have been the current Petrograd. The stage tsar turned beggars away just as the reality we had. The opera groaned forward, melancholy, gloom, tyranny. Chaliapin's Godunov was brilliantly performed. Jewel-encrusted from head to foot, the most powerful man in Russia, steeped in tragedy, his pathos convinced me at every moment. I was miserable for him and his agony and felt the entire theatre plunge into his gloom and despair. When he sang '*my soul is heavy*', I felt worse and I could see men in ditches, hungry, shooting, wounded. Were Hardi and Enn facing death, starvation, whichever was to come sooner? Mussorgsky's music tore at my heart and I cried for every lonely fearful moment I'd had and for others' suffering too. I hadn't thought of Oskar for weeks but now I saw him on a battlefield confronting mutilated men, working in horrific conditions, retaining his courage so that the nurses kept theirs, and he a barely trained doctor. A soldier might die in peace or with less pain while a comforting nurse held his hand or whispered that he'd recover. I sobbed selfishly, for what I'd invented, for what I believed was love. I'd been a child in my innocence. I held back my breath and cried.

When the curtain rang down on the first act, I flourished my handkerchief.

"Hypnotic. Dazzling," I explained.

The lights brightened. Katya took my hand. "Are you all right?"

"Oh yes. The music's sad. That's all."

Katya pointed to the ceiling plafond and the enormous crystal chandelier. "Beautiful *Fräulein*, yes?"

I nodded and admired the dazzling light reflecting from a thousand points.

I didn't wish to see Mihkel. I'd rather have faced the tsar himself than speak to Mihkel and Sofia Casanova.

Katya tugged my arm. "Why is everyone running?" she squealed jumping up from her seat.

"*Ich weiss es nicht,*" I said calmly while looking around for a clue, to Vasily for an explanation. The musicians scurried back into the pit.

"*Je ne sais pas*," he said with a shrug. The chorus stretched their arms toward the imperial box singing *God Save the Tsar* – Chaliapin returned to the stage and kneeled.

In seconds the entire theatre broke out in pandemonium. Hisses and boos erupted from the stalls, cheers and applause from the balconies. Tsar Nicholas remained stone. Vasily's face turned grim. "They're going mad! The idiots!"

I tucked Katya's fingers into mine. "Nothing. A show," I said while my heart raced.

"What's happening? Why?" she cried.

"Performing," I said glancing toward our exit, to the floor below where revolvers might next pop. Katya wrested her fingers from mine and plunged across to her father.

"Papa! Why are they shouting?"

"*C'est n'est rien ma petite, rien du tout,*" he dismissed with a toss of his head but he took her face in his hands to look into her eyes. "Really. Nothing."

The crowd surged and babbled. Men grabbed one another. Fists shot through the air. Men shook one another by their collars. A man was punched in the face.

"Because Chaliapin is kneeling?" I demanded unable to restrain myself.

"Yes! You see now! Scandalmongers have been calling him traitor and now, see for yourself! As loyal as Rasputin!"

"But down there…?" Mihkel threw his arms in the air. Those around him took their seats.

"You see! Your friends! Barbarians! Chaliapin is no revolutionary." Vasily slapped his knee as the bedlam went on. "Troublemakers! Insulting the tsar! And Chaliapin!"

Katya cupped her hands around her mouth, thrilled and excited and afraid. "Now everyone is shushing!"

"Because Chaliapin paid respect and those fools insult him! Miserable imbeciles! I'd tell your friend what I think!"

"Please, excuse me," I said. I could not for one moment longer listen to another word against Mihkel, nor myself. I abandoned Katya to her father and fled to the ladies' room where I intended to stay until I knew what to do next.

When I returned to the lobby the opera house boomed with voices. I tugged my wrap around my shoulders and searched the crowds. Far sooner than I expected I found Mihkel with the Spanish woman. They leaned against a column of cavorting muses and nymphs directly in front of me.

Mihkel's moustache and beard had grown wild. He looked like a factory worker or woodsman rather than the intellectual I remembered, and nothing like the man I danced with at *Jaanipäev*. The man who had saved me from ravishment and had sent me beautiful letters and poems from Peterburg.

The Spanish woman no doubt had a battalion of hairdressers and beauticians; her skin was perfect though her eyebrows were heavy and natural. She was dark and short but before I heard her speak I could see how intensely interested she was in Mihkel, and he in her. A vivacious aristocrat. An extraordinary woman. I lowered the wrap, raised my head and touched the curls falling from my collapsing hairstyle. I reminded Mihkel of who I was. "Good evening," I said, smiling at them both and offering my hand first to her.

"Charmed!" she said.

"At last!" he said in Estonian, his eyes holding an embrace as he reached for me with both hands. "*Armas* Siina!" His gaze slid over my shoulders and bosom and for a moment, I fancied his colour darkened. "You're luminous!" he laughed. "Please, meet my friend, my colleague, Sofia Casanova," he said, as if he'd remembered himself and formality, and even Sofia. She was no beauty and not even the sort of woman I imagined to be my competition! Her dark abundant hair was wound in complicated rolls but she had a softness I'd not expected. She would speak for herself too, I was sure of it.

I could hardly be surprised, seeing her, that Mihkel was captivated. He was barely twenty and she had to be close to fifty but there was a great deal of something else about her.

She extended her hand to me. Her eyes smiled. I felt she could be my sister or aunt, the companionable way she greeted me. But she was a socialist. She would snub the bourgeoisie and insist on equality in all classes. But not Bolshevik, at least, I hoped not. All of that was a fine excuse for rampant sex. I knew that much.

Mihkel took my hand, kissed it; unBolshevikly, again, and as sweetly.

Sofia tilted her head. "*Charmante*. Mihkel tells me so much about you."

I struggled. I was so prepared for hostility. "And are you furious with Chaliapin?" I blurted.

Mihkel blazed. "Furious? I'm devastated! He was at the centre of such company, and with the tsar himself here as a witness to how we feel. A moment of truth! He failed us! Depressing and monstrous!"

Sofia sighed and touched Mihkel's arm. "You see, Chaliapin's whole life has been an act, one character to the next. Don't take it hard." Her Russian was unhesitating, her Spanish accent, quaint. "He never meant to bow," she said and turned to me. "Were you shocked also, *Fräulein* Jürimäe?"

My face burned. "*Fräulein*? No, please, Miss Casanova, *Preili*. In fact I had no idea what to expect and I was shocked by the whole thing though my employer, Vasily Feodorov was furious at the protest but delighted with Chaliapin's singing."

Sofia raised her eyebrows.

I blundered on. "I feel sad for the tsar. We all hate the poverty and war but …what can he do?"

Mihkel's expression tightened. "Boris Godunov's hands were covered with blood. Our tsar is as guilty! The country is cracking open to the core, our streets on the edge of anarchy." He circled his hands. "If Chaliapin hadn't given in we'd have some unity but the moment's gone!"

Sofia's hand rested on his arm. I began to wish I'd never seen them. How charming they were and how far beyond their circle was I? Whatever they were doing I guessed it was more than writing pamphlets.

“You meet revolutionary leaders Miss Casanova. How interesting. I admire you. It must be marvellous to investigate our city and write about the disorder so the rest of the world can know,” Mihkel would have said.

‘Ah but you’re a true journalist, she’d have replied. You capture the action, you follow the soldiers. It’s extremely dangerous.’

But what kind of woman could she be, I wondered, to travel alone and always be amongst men whose morals fitted no class.

“I’m glad you have so much in common!” I said instead, my smile slipping away as my wrap from my shoulders did though, I felt sure, less attractively. “Perhaps I was wrong to come here.” I watched Mihkel’s expression.

He released his arm from Sofia’s side and took my hands in his. “Not at all,” he said and continued in Estonian. “Don’t imagine we’re anything but associates, Siina. I’m elated you’re here. Truly,” he said, his eyes laughing.

“While I’m forbidden to see you,” I moaned.

He glanced at Sofia and instantly excused us. “I’ve been following the war in the Caucasus but I’m here now. Don’t imagine anything that’s untrue, Siina.” He held me close, his hand around my waist.

“Oh, now look. Very dashing,” Mihkel said in my ear so I followed his gaze. “How long before he seduces you?” he said as Vasily, his slicked hair gleaming came dodging through the lobby with Katya who bobbed between furs and satins through the buzz, the laughter and chatter.

“Yes. Him.”

"He'll have you for breakfast."

"Stop it!" I said. "I saw you at the Nabokov house. I'm next door!"

"Good. I'll know where to come."

"Absolutely not! I need my job."

The crowds heaved and separated as Vasily advanced toward us. He paused and spoke to an old woman. Mihkel kissed my cheek. "Ah, but we'll find a way," he said as the bell announced the second act. "We'll be together," he said backing away.

"Yes! All right!" I said. He and I had been friends too long to part. Of course I trusted him. I would go out and meet him and he would show me places he'd promised. I'd meet Anna Akhmatova and see the Hermitage. I watched him and Sofia weave through the crowd almost crossing paths with Vasily. A group of soldiers, their caps set backwards made obscene gestures at Vasily's back. I saw Mihkel stop, grab a soldier by the arm, speak for moments before they parted company, as if the soldier had been reprimanded. Sofia took Mihkel's arm and they were lost in the crowd.

I drew my wrap tight. "What was it?" I murmured to myself. "What does he believe and know. Who does he stand for I wondered as I followed after Vasily.

28. Chaliapin

In the last act of the opera I lost track of Boris Godunov. I became more and more obsessed with getting a picture of Chaliapin. Kneeling, I couldn't bear any more tragic chorus or arias, no matter that they were Mussorgsky's. I was devastated I hadn't caught the golden boy on film. Kneeling. I'd have been whisked into the inner circle of *Postimees* and *Teataja* photographers, possibly even *Izvestiya*. And paid.

I shut out the forest and gloomy peasant scenes. I was planning my entry through the stage door. The guards would be like wolves. In Pärnu's Endla I could smile, say who I was and walk in. I would tell the Mariinski guards I was Chaliapin's friend and that I was an employee of *Izvestiya* or *Postimees* or best of all, the *Gazeta Kopeika*, the one kopek paper the workers read.

Perhaps Chaliapin would pose! I'd tell him how loved and glorified he was in Pärnu. Except that I'd be overwhelmed when I came to face him.

Katya had fallen asleep. In the peasants' dirge, a horrible taunting scene I wished she'd not see, she woke. "Is it a funeral?" she asked, her sleep-filled eyes half open. I thought of the night Juhan came to Metsajärve and told us of the burning manors. I was Katya's age. I'd not have brought her had I thought of that, except that Mussorgsky was Russia, and the story was what was to come.

When the final curtain rang down I grabbed my velvet bag, leaned across to Vasily and whispered. "Please excuse me, Vasily Feodorov. I must get a photograph. I shall get a cab home. Thank you so much but really, this is my one chance. Forgive me."

"*Fräulein*?"

"I'm so sorry. Please." Vasily's knees were in my way.

"Yes! I must!" I pushed past him. "Excuse me. I must."

"What, now?" He and Katya were still watching when I glanced back but I squeezed and elbowed my way out in a very Bolshevik manner, marched around the slippery street past one beamed door after another until I came to the stage door lit by a dim yellow light. I pulled myself up, held my camera to my chest like a weapon and confronted the guards. They were smoking cigarettes.

"Siina Jürimäe. *Postimees*. I'm photographing Chaliapin."

The two men regarded me, smirking at one another. "Who? Where?"

"I also work for the *Gazeta Kopeika*," I snapped. "I have an appointment with Chaliapin."

One of them looked me up and down then at once opened the door and called inside. "Igor! A young lady to see the hero – the *one-of-us*," the guard confided with a wink.

I bobbed agreement and followed Igor's broad back. We stormed along the winding passages as if we were away hunting. He turned his head now and again and hummed the melody that was repeated throughout the opera.

A crowd had swarmed Chaliapin's room. I was small and insignificant; sure I'd be discovered as a fraud. Chaliapin stood amongst his admirers, gesticulating, speaking quietly; even so, his voice resonated. He was even larger than I expected and still wore his costume and makeup.

I protected my camera, praying I'd get a moment to speak my lines. At that moment he saw me.

He asked me about me as I set up. I had no plates, no flash powder, no dish or black cape. In my pocket I had string, knotted at metre intervals to measure his distance, terribly amateur.

"Pärnu," I said.

"A lovely town. What do you like to photograph?" he asked and posed even as the throngs milled about. He waved someone a good bye and nodded to another. He leaned against his dressing room mirror but I saw his eyes were desolate like the wretched character of Boris Godunov.

"Nature, people, beautiful things, art works," I told him.

"You'll see no end of sights in Peterburg. Limitless beauty and romance. And despair. Did you imagine you could be in Italy?"

I nodded, searching for another shot. The room was bright with bare light bulbs the length of the mirror and dresser. I braced myself to ask, would he kneel, but suddenly voices rose outside the room. Vasily barged in.

Chaliapin straightened up, and broke out laughing. "Good god! I thought, do you know … for a moment I thought you were the tsar himself, but you're not... are you?"

Vasily clicked his heels together and bowed. "Vasily Andrea Feodorov," he announced and offered his hand.

"Pleasure!" Chaliapin replied as he turned to me. "My photographer, from Pärnu."

"That is, my children's tutor. You've been taken in, Fedor Ivanovich Chaliapin."

I snapped the shutter while they continued. I aimed while they were close though Vasily shielded his face. "Oh! I'm so sorry," I said, but I had my shot.

"Our carriage is waiting, *Fräulein*."

"*Fräulein*?" Chaliapin's makeup cracked with his smile.

I lowered my eyes, folded up my camera and slipped it away. "A photographer also," I said.

"Your tape." Chaliapin winked, handing me the string. "Good

luck, whatever the obstacles. Remember where you come from."

The hallway was empty. The guard kept his head bowed at Vasily but smirked at me. I felt a camaraderie as we hurried down the corridor. Outside on the icy cobbles the Feodorovna carriage waited and the uniformed *isvostchick*, beating his arms and stamping on the pavement.

"*Fräulein*, you are lucky!" Vasily growled as he gave me his arm to get up in the carriage. "Did you imagine you'd walk home? Even getting a cab is not so easy. You have no idea."

"I didn't need rescuing."

"*Fräulein*, you come from a small town. Life in Petersburg can be dangerous."

I stroked Katya's cheek. She lay asleep on the carriage seat but I was the admonished child. "The darling. What a night," I whispered.

"And not yet over," Vasily murmured.

"No!" I agreed, thinking of Chaliapin on my rollfilm, his features emerging when I developed them. I was also relieved to be riding home, not searching for a cab. "I'll never forget the Mussorgsky but I can't believe I met Chaliapin.

"Your camera, *Fräulein*. Let me see it," Vasily said.

"A concertina. Nothing special but I love it." I took out the Ansco.

He took it without a word, turned it over, smoothed his hands over the case then slipped it into his pocket.

"What?"

"I'll keep it."

"But no!"

"How dared you run off? You forget your responsibility!" He glanced at Katya.

"But Vasily Feodorov, it is my camera. Please," I said, my

mouth full of pins.

He ran his gloved hand over Katya's shoulder. "You forget yourself, *Fräulein*. Tutor! What did you imagine? "

"Forgive me. I should never have left you and Katya! How foolish and thoughtless! How could I? But my camera, please."

I closed my eyes. Vasily raised a finger at me. "Restraint, *Fräulein*. Control."

I closed my mouth, afraid of what might come out. Somehow I would get my camera back.

"Listen, forget the angry men and miserable peasants. Dream of the dancing. It was, just as I expected, marvellous. You and Katya must remember those scenes. Explain them, *Fräulein*, in her lessons.

"I've no idea what to say to a child about Godunov. I feel defeated."

"No, don't be."

"I am a good teacher. I also take photos..."

"But this is also a lesson. I keep the camera."

I felt his leg press mine. "I'm truly sorry but it is my camera..."

"You and your socialist."

I was jammed hard against him. "My friend. I have no one else in Peterburg. Not even Ksenia."

"You have us."

"Mihkel's my compatriot."

"I see. And his socialist friend, too?"

"A colleague."

Vasily laughed unpleasantly. Our seat bounced. A car's headlights lit his features, his head thrown back, his chin sharpened by his trimmed beard. He was extremely handsome and his tone persuasive. I was irritated I'd noticed. I imagined a headache coming on. I couldn't answer. I'd never thought of Mihkel with another woman, certainly not someone as sophisticated and educated as Sofia Casanova. I intended to be as independent as she. It wasn't just them together, it was their familiarity and conspiracy.

"You're jealous of her? But you're like her, *Fräulein*. You also wish for self-reliance. But respectable women do not become photographers my dear."

The troika seat was hard against my back. Vasily's thigh squeezed against mine.

"So you say."

"Don't be jealous. I was not laughing at you."

Our carriage bells tinkled across the wide expanse of the Siniy Bridge. We were overtaken by troikas, two abreast and on the near side, the Moika glimmered, ghostly blue. I detested the cold and the granite for as far I could see. Mussorgsky's melancholy music flooded my aching head.

We were at Voznesensky Prospekt – almost home. Vasily faced me.

"You found some pleasure in the evening, yes? How you could pass yourself off as a *Gazeta Kopeika* photographer I do not know. You are brazen."

I smelled lime oil on his moustache and wine on his breath. "I'm desolate."

He settled back. "Loneliness and depression are as normal and acceptable as the ways we try to escape it. We all have moments of despondence. But we have great passion when we're moved – we Russians."

"And I have different moods."

Vasily's teeth glinted. "But a Russian's heart beats. It's not a stone."

I turned to the street. Flakes tumbled like feathers against the lamps as our wheels spun over the packed snow and the horses' hooves thudded on the white cobbles. It was also romantic, even if it was freezing, even when I knew what could lie beneath layers of white. A court carriage whisked by, red lanterns blazing, the privileged inside, bound for an extravagant night. At the corner of St Isaac's square at the Astoria Hotel, we paused as a cab crossed in front of us. A group of men had gathered on the high curb, their fur hats and coats topped with snow. Clouds of condensation puffed under the lamps. The men called out to one another, comrade, general, *tavarish.*

"You see, anyone consorts at the Astoria these days. I can't get used to it, so common."

"So who would you be, were you not born Feodorov?" I dared ask.

"You mean, had I been born on Vasilievsky Island in some typhus-infested hovel? I can tell you! I'd be organizing and getting something done, not dreaming some fairy tale." He tilted the tip of his beard at me. Neither prince nor peasant, revolutionary nor imperialist was immune against charisma.

A couple, their arms around one another's coats, swung toward St Isaac's Cathedral, perhaps Sofia and Mihkel on their way to a bar, the sort where I'd never go.

"You imagine it romantic do you, discussing Marx and humbug with the unwashed?"

"It's heartening."

"Truly? To choose squalor. You advocate poverty and *la grippe*? Cholera... hmm? "

"I expect Mihkel is there."

"Fool. He has a choice. He could do well for himself. He writes well, he's a leader."

"He believes in what he does."

"It will only be worse. Uneducated masses can't control their destinies. They need us to lead. Some are better equipped than others, *Fräulein*."

My jaw set. Of course Vasily was better equipped. He was always privileged.

"The truth is I escaped myself. I mean, why else do we love these charades; dressing up like knights and temptresses, egging Nijinsky on to leap and twist half-naked with his nymphs and pagans? Mad isn't it? Karsavina twirls and frisks with feathers stuck in her head. Why? A few hours of shock and curiosity so we can forget ourselves?"

"I escaped in the choruses. I'm homesick. The music takes me away, but then I plunge with it," I murmured.

"I understand but we don't throw away what we have, nor do we imagine everyone can have what we have. That's a fantasy."

The troika swayed into Bolshaya Morskaya and I could no longer see the glow in Vasily's eyes. "Mihkel believes we can. I do too. Anyway, he lives by what he believes like a proper Marxist. I don't."

Vasily leaned closer. "He chooses poverty and squalor but why should you?"

He was right. I was unwilling to give up silk underwear. I looked forward to roast pork and buttered potatoes, a warm dry bed, a satin covered eiderdown. I longed for beautiful things, and my own safety. Vasily's leg moved against mine. I would gain nothing from a love affair but my leg tingled all the way to my belly. I encouraged him to confide in me.

"I can imagine your naked skin on mine," he murmured in my ear.

The troika bells stilled outside the atlantids of his house. He leaned closer.

"I must speak to you, *Fräulein*. Business matters, yes? Meet me in my study," he said as he lifted his sleeping daughter, handed her to Timur, then offered me his arm.

29. Seduction

I knocked. I waited.

Employers think they can have what they want, the woman on the train had said. The gypsy runaway mother with a blue-eyed, fair-skinned son and red-haired daughter had advised.

I tugged my wrap around my shoulders and opened my employer's door. I would get back my camera.

Vasily sat at a dark wood, carved desk, his face lit by a green-shaded lamp, jacket and lanyards thrown over the chaise longue – shirt collar and cuffs sprung open. Amber light glanced off the facets of his brandy glass. He was older and more tired than an hour ago. "*Fräulein,*" he said. "Sit. A drink?"

I nodded; he poured golden sherry into the glass already in his hand. From the corner of the room I heard Caruso.

"Our children are fond of you, Siina, indeed we all are."

He called me Siina! He brought my drink before stepping back to lean against his desk, watching, displaying himself. I marvelled at his conceit, and his magnetism.

"You know, Olga Pyotrovna suffers from nerves. It makes her tired. Everything and anything overwhelms her. She's glad of your help, as I am." He lifted his glass in a tidy salute. "I enjoyed your company this evening, Siina. Of course Katya is too young to understand opera but never mind that. Thus education begins." I raised my glass to his. "But sadly, tutors come and go devilishly fast. So we will look after you." He slid one leg over the other and swirled his drink. The cabinet with Meissen plates and Fabergé eggs also held a camera, a wooden box camera, a beautiful piece, a field camera on little brass wheels with great bellows and glass plates. Once I had mine back I'd take a shot from floor level, Vasily's boots magnified, his thighs oversized, his head, a pea on a great torso, not to consciously have him appear thoughtless but simply to play with his shape and proportions, though the distortion could hold meaning. "The children are doing well, I'm sure," he said, recrossing his legs.

"But yes!" Of course! Katya was curious, demanding, clever beyond her years, an ear for languages. She'd become fond of me and I loved her. Sacha was attentive and eager for approval, often co-operative; he engrossed himself in small tasks. Magdalena was constantly effervescent, desperate to keep up with the others. "They all make fine progress. Speaking, writing, becoming familiar with the Gothic script. They listen and pay attention," I said.

"Splendid. And you? Content?"

I hesitated. "I am, although Peterburg is so big. I hadn't imagined it really. I'd hoped to see it but," I hurried on, "the children are always my priority."

Vasily cupped his chin in one hand. "Life here has become difficult, I know, even though our empire is sound, believe me. A rabble will never hurt us, no matter that workers chant for rights and freedom like frenzied Tatars. They kick up hell but they're fleas on a dog."

I sipped my sherry, thrilled that I had his ear, eager for his opinions whether I agreed or not. "We may see things differently, Vasily Feodorov. If I don't see things as you do it doesn't mean I'll run away."

"Very good." He set his glass down on his desk with a condescending smile. "So brave, but all the same, you're free, you know and must consider your options should you feel in danger. Understand that I can arrange a travel pass any time.

You'll need one to go home." He looked at me from under his brows. "Our German doctor left a month before you came. My wife had so relied on him, an experienced surgeon and general doctor who outlasted many before him. The previous tutor, a neurotic English woman, scuttled off before the Somme offensive. Understandably she wished to see her nephews before they enlisted." Vasily wandered across to the Caruso, propped his elbow on the corner of the Amour player. "Even so, my dear, we could end the riots and establish order in a week. If we wanted. We have control." He lifted an eyebrow as if to convince me.

"So you will," I answered and he came and sat beside me, leaning forward, a forearm on one knee, his face meeting mine.

"You're dear to us and you're very sweet, Siina. I'm drawn to you, your sense of adventure, your intelligence. I've not met a woman like you before. How did you become so bold?" He laid a hand on my knee. I jolted. The heat from his gentle touch sent fire through my body. I couldn't speak though I had meant to. My thoughts jangled around, the only clear one, his hand and the rising furnace inside me. We sat for moments. I endured, in awe. "Perhaps you will become fond of us too," he said quietly.

I laid my hand on his to remove it but he kissed me, his lips soft but his tongue reaching like a serpent as his hand slid away and reached inside my skirt setting my thigh ablaze. His mouth covered mine, I couldn't breathe. Desire ravaged me. I pulled away only to yield again. His breath, hot and musky sent me to meadows and woods, beds and dreams, to naked wakefulness and springs rising through moss. He kissed my shoulders and neck, pushed off my wrap and bodice and tentatively reached inside, stirring something else in me, longing for love and absolute sensations. My head spun. Whatever objections I may have had dissolved. Still, I was in control. My heart raced, I would surrender. My wine glass fell to the floor and I remembered my camera.

"It's nothing, nothing. Let me love you," he murmured.

"But my camera!"

"Yes, yes, soon enough."

Shock and melancholy flooded through me.

Caruso's singing had ended. Sweet sherry and the taste of Vasily's mouth were in mine. "You'll have your camera. Let me love you."

I shrank, dizzied.

"*Milaya, prekrasnyĭ, roskoshnyĭ,*" he whispered, his hands feeling their way up my skirt.

Milaya! No! Vladimir the soldier with his vile mouth! *Milaya*! My stomach revolted. I heaved away. "No!" Rape and murder. Fear, panic, melancholy. "My camera. That's all."

"Oh, yes. Yes, yes," he promised.

"And your wife!" I demanded from out of reach.

"I give my wife everything. I do my duty." Vasily pulled back, a look of dismay.

"She's sick, plus you have four children, yours, forever."

"I know what I am. More than generous," he moaned. "Let me tell you!"

"What? When you have boundless estates, hundreds of servants, move among the wealthiest sophisticated beautiful women. Generous? You expect to get whatever you want, from anyone..."

"I deserve you." He grinned with self-righteousness and insolence.

I wrenched my skirt down. I grabbed my wrap. "Russia hates your sort with your god-given rights!"

He lay back on the sofa and laughed. "One more kiss and

everything is clear."

"You'll return my camera?"

"You underestimate me."

"I trust you to give me what is mine."

"But of course. I keep my promises," he said, a chuckle in his throat as he crept his hand around my back and drew me to him, but cautiously. His shirt smelled of sunshine, his moustache of limes. I wrestled between him and Vladimir's phantom. And Mihkel. I could have laid my head on his chest, my protector, but Vasily challenged everything I believed in. He had my camera, my independence, my chance to go beyond maid, tutor and immediate lust.

"Besides, I love Mihkel," I said, stiffening.

"I love many things about you. You test me."

"And you play games with me."

"*Milaya*," he whispered, closing his eyes, reaching to kiss my neck.

"Only not that!"

"But one more kiss."

"For my camera?"

"Of course, but a real one," he murmured burying his head in my neck, kissing my skin, his hands on my breasts.

"Just one," I said.

30. Gostilitsy

I drifted between waking and sleeping not wanting to open my eyes, not wanting to leave my dream. I felt Vasily's breath on my skin, his mouth on mine, his hands on my thighs, his smell. Lyudmila knocked on my door as daylight coated my room. She brought tea and black bread with plum jam.

"Lyudmila, what happened?" I asked. "You're not well? What?"

"You're late, *Fräulein*. Katya's rattling on about last night. The little ones are with their mother and that's unheard of."

"So, I'll be down in three seconds." Lyudmila wouldn't look at me. "Something awful?"

"The Okhrana picked up my brother. Yesterday," she said biting her lip.

"What! Why?" I sat up pulling my eiderdown with me.

Lyudmila wedged against the doorway. She shook her head. "He's a mill worker, *Fräulein* but he never keeps his mouth shut. He complained about the work and the dangers, the machines. He almost lost his hand! Who cares? Who will they arrest next?"

"You'll see, everything will be resolved," I said. Lyudmila didn't flinch.

"And what's more, yesterday, a tram, pushed upside down, the driver beaten to death! Death! What did *he* ever do?"

Grunya arrived silently, as she usually did, to stand beside us. "That's not all. They're looting shops! Anyone in the way is garbage! I never expected I'd live to see it!" She covered her mouth and wiped her eyes with a handkerchief.

"People are screaming *Kill police! Destroy the government!*"

Lyudmila went on, and shook her sleeve. "Possessed is what they are! Makes me ill!"

I'd have loved to believe what Vasily said: that the government could take control in a moment. Pärnu, I thought. I missed home!

Downstairs I followed the children galloping through the hall; Katya demanding *blini* with butter and jam, Sacha singing, kicking his velvet skirt, Magdalena skipping. I became more fond of the children every day but they'd soon forget me, the moment I left, whenever Olga chose to whisk them off to the other end of Russia, or me to wherever she decided.

In the nursery we began a scrapbook with the pressed flowers we'd gathered in summer. Violets, buttercups, birch and linden leaves. We glued them between waxed papers and I wrote *das Veilchen, die Birke* so the children could match words to them.

"The mistress wants you, *Fräulein,*" Grunya whispered from behind me. I hadn't heard her come in.

"But why?" Was I a schoolgirl caught drinking vodka with university dons?

Grunya could only roll her eyes to heaven, shrug and retake her seat on the wooden bench.

I pushed out my chin, straightened my shoulders and marched down the hall to Olga's bedroom door, dark mahogany, snatched open by her maid. Olga sat at her dressing table in soft, cherry light, powdering her neck, one shoulder bare, a gold kimono slung halfway down her back. Her maid sat down again, close to the stove as she re-threaded a corset.

I bobbed a curtsey.

"Come," Olga, tilted her head. Her hair streamed like seaweed over her back. Her sleepy borzois lay on the Persian rugs at her feet. "What do you think?" she said nodding to a blouse, lace and satin bound, a soft cream, etched like crystal.

"Beautiful."

"Try it," Olga said tugging her collar over a shoulder.

I fingered the lace. "Exquisite," I said.

"Paris," Olga said with a nervous twitch of her eyes I'd noticed before.

"Only…the children are waiting, *Madame*."

"Oh, come on," she laughed.

A pair of men's shoes lay half hidden by her dressing table, a white shirt was draped on the end of the bed and silk pants hung over a chair. "It will suit you and it's absolutely bourgeois. You like it, *n'est-ce pas*?" She smoothed cream on her neck, raised her eyebrows at me and creased her fine skin in a tiny delicate smile.

I paused a moment before shaking off my cardigan and unbuttoning my blouse. Tamara and Olga watched. In my cotton chemise I felt more naked than in my skin at the village *saun.*

"*Oh la la,* no corset, *très moderne*," Olga tittered.

"Why not? Neither do farmers' wives."

"But no support for the back, my dear!" Olga scoffed.

I raised my arms to show my muscles. "I'm not a farmer but my cousins wear no corsets and oh my, what they lift!"

"*Natürlich*! Peasant backs," Olga smiled in return.

"And strong," I said, still smiling while Tamara grinned as she let my arms into the lace sleeves though I turned from her odour, her monthly cycle overpowering every scent in the room.

"You must always wear cream against your hair, *Fräulein*," Olga said.

And *natürlich*, Giles Spencer would propose marriage to such a blouse while Vasily would surely ravish it and Mihkel would whisk me to the opera leaving Sofia Casanova in the gutter for such a blouse.

I turned this way and that before the mirror but really, too much of my skin showed.

"A different chemise, Siina. Please, look in the drawer." Olga tweaked at her eyebrow. I searched between layers of silk, lawn, bloomers, satin-made buds, stockings in cellophane, and in the corner of the drawer, the glinting of a small, silver hand gun caught my eye. I glanced up to meet Olga's eyes in mine.

"Petrograd is dangerous, no? Vermin creep about, yes? Once people were honest and loyal. Today, who knows?"

I felt the gun, its cool silver, but a beautiful blouse would distract me. A buttery camisole looked my size. Tamara winked when I held it up and Olga nodded. I slipped my chemise off as the door clicked open. Vasily angled himself against the door jamb. He studied me, casually, impudently and as much as I tried to cover myself I managed only to fumble, trapped by the blouse, Olga, and Vasily's cool languor.

"Out," Olga finally ordered and Vasily withdrew.

"You see," she continued as we admired the fit and look of the blouse over the chemise. "I appreciate you. My gift. *Oui*?" She raised her hand to her forehead. "But go now," she said and I, still in the blouse, felt luxurious but even more, cheap.

The Peter and Paul cannon boomed midday as I left the room when Lyudmila arrived with a tray of coffee. "Look now, there's a letter, *Fräulein*," she whispered, glancing at the tray. "From home, do you think?"

I took the letter to my room, hung the blouse in my wardrobe and read.

Come home, Anna wrote. *If we ever argued, I'm sorry. I miss you so!*

I laid the letter on my desk and began a reply. Anna would

know what to do.

Dearest Anna, I wrote, *I wonder even why I left! Now I'm in love with two men and beside myself with confusion! You must think I've become a harlot but it's more complicated than that. I love Mihkel, as always, but he never sees me and now, would you believe, I've fallen in love with my employer, Vasily Andrevich! I wish I could sit with you and tell you about this plague! And his wife gives me a beautiful gift. I'm entirely bewildered, suspect I'm being played, but can't fathom it. What would you say if your employer gave you a splendid gift from Paris? Am I cynical? Should I be? Olga seems to like me but I don't understand this! Perhaps you can make something of it. I can't. Tell me what you think before I do something foolish.*

I completed the letter with a description of the opera with the drama of Chaliapin kneeling, and my daring photographic début! I mentioned Sofia Casanova on Mihkel's arm and my jealous admiration of her. I couldn't tell Anna about going to Vasily's study. Not in a letter.

A thumping down the stairs interrupted me. Vasily, bounding down flushed, straightening his jacket, past the dining room, snatched his coat and blew out.

"He'll leave her. For other women, most likely," Lyudmila muttered as she cleared the table.

"He never will," Grunya argued.

A door slammed upstairs. Olga shutting him out.

"He'll be back to make up," Grunya promised as she settled on the bench, her head against the wall.

When the sun cut low across the sky and peeled into the nursery the children performed a play in their cardboard theatre. Katya was director; even the baby in its basket and the wet nurse beside took roles. I was applauding the actors when Vasily strode in glowing, his brilliantined hair shining. He handed me a linen bag. He couldn't stand still.

"We're going to our *dacha*. Gostilitsy," he announced. "Get the children ready, *Fräulein*, help Grunya. *Bien*?" He paused, gave the waxed tips of his moustache a tweak as he paced back and forth in a strip of sunlight. I wondered what was in the linen bag.

"*Oui, Papa*!" Katya bounced.

"And Olga?" I asked.

"Oh no," Vasily said, killing what might have amounted to an impulsive bow. "It's too cold and too far, but we'll go, the children and their tutor." He dragged a chair under him sitting as if he might ride. "I have a few things to settle in the country and it's such a day," he smiled and we both looked out the window at the clear blue sky.

"Won't it be terribly cold and dark? Isn't it more beautiful in summer?"

Vasily raised his eyebrows at me. "Of course, *chérie*," he whispered. "Gostilitsy will be the star of your folio of Russia. Go, Katya, get ready!"

Katya abandoned her witch's hat and cloak. Sacha ran around the room several times to show his speed and Magdalena followed. Vasily, arms folded under his jacket flaps, braiding sparkling, gazed out the window like a field marshal. "I have two days. I've sent a message for them to fuel up the stoves. It's beautiful there."

When he left the room Lyudmila came to my side. "Don't!" she hissed. "The place will be cold as a tomb and the servants all run off to join something…the war or a brigade of bandits. Don't go. *Fräulein...*?"

I opened the linen bag. Inside, my leather case, inside it, my camera. A cane clicking on the wooden floor as Irena Feodorova met us in the hall. "What! With the children?" She leaned on her cane against the *étagère*. "Vasily Andrevich, you'd go cavorting in the countryside and expose yourself and your children to *la grippe*? With demonstrations in the city and offences committed every day one more dreadful than the last?"

"In fact I must."

"Duscha was robbed yesterday on the street."

"And my steward at Gostilitsy is missing!" Vasily countered.

Irena opened her pill box. "You insist?"

"No one has seen our overseer, *Maman, comprenez*? I must secure our estate!"

"But you're needed here! Army officers are siding with the mobs, have you not heard? Your own company…?"

"Indeed, I have."

"Lord protect you, and all of us."

Vasily peered over the balustrade. "Timur! The Orlovs! Are they ready?"

"You're bandit bait!" Irena warned. "So then – if you must, bring back wine and some decent pork."

I stuffed my carpet bag with the heaviest jackets and wool stockings. I wished for furs. I put the lace blouse in my bag, folded neatly, taking very little space. It was bourgeois, but going without stays, that was revolutionary.

When Timur came back into the hall he wore his green livery, gloves hanging over his sash, hat squeezed over his thick black hair. His beard and moustache were magnificent protection against the cold. The horses had been groomed and fed, the sleigh stacked with rugs and furs, a box of provisions at the back, bread and eggs in case there were none at Gostilitsy but neither straw-packed crockery nor games. It was no summer picnic.

I heard a sneeze from the doorway. Natalya Andreevna, her maid with Duscha at her side, stumbled out to watch us go.

"Gostilitsy! God save you."

"Dear sister! Show faith," Vasily chided.

"Vasya! Rumours fly. Men are rampaging through country estates, even burning them. They so envy us."

"So I hear and my steward hasn't been seen for a month," Vasily explained.

"Lord protect you. So, bring back mushrooms and pickles from the stores. Perhaps some venison," she said.

When Vasily came downstairs, his greatcoat thrown over his shoulders, pistol tucked under his belt, Irena called him to sit a moment and think of what he might have forgotten, and so Natalya could give us a proper blessing.

"Take charge, *Fräulein*. They're only servants," Irena said.

Natalya lifted her face to Vasily. "Keep to the roads, Vasya. It's late to go crossing rivers and lakes dearest brother. When I was young and riding with my betrothed Cossack we took extreme care crossing rivers and particularly in the thaw but on some occasions......"

"*Chère sœur, l'arrête! Cela suffit!*" Vasily growled.

"Yes, you've heard but remember to keep to the roads because I remember when….."

"*Oui, ma chérie*," Vasily agreed.

I waited in the foyer. I wore a fur-lined bonnet with leather trim, and the woollen gloves Anna had given me. Grunya kneeled on her arthritic knees to hook the buttons on Katya's boots, one after the interminable next. Sacha demanded that he bring his sled and Magdalena cried and begged to come but she was to stay home. I spoke words of comfort but Olga soon called from the couch where she was cutting the next page of her romance book. “Do not concern yourself *Fräulein*. Grunya will watch her. Now go while it’s fine and still light!”

Outside, Timur’s Orlov trotters stamped snow and breathed out smoke. More stamina and courage than any other horse, Timur had told me more than once. “See, look at the neck, high and strong, the croup, wide and powerful,” he had explained as if he’d bred and birthed them himself. Their backs steamed as Timur set long winter traces in case they tumbled into a ditch or disappeared in deep snow; they’d have a chance to recover without panicking and tangling. We’d have to stop at least once and change their places before Gostilitsy, it was more than three hours’ ride. As we moved from the courtyard the dogs ran back and forth barking madly, desperate to come with us, though Timur had tied them up. They continued baying and whining as the Orlovs walked from the yard, the sled runners cutting the surface of the hard-packed snow, then onto Bolshaya Morskaya. Soon our troika bells were tinkling along the Embankment and I couldn’t help smiling at Vasily. He pressed his thigh against mine as if perhaps I understood that the journey was about me and nothing at all about the estate, nor children filling their lungs with fresh air, nor the peril of the *dacha* and servants and food stores.

A grey sky hung over Vasilievsky Island after we crossed over the Dvortsovaya Bridge. Snow dusted broken carts, untidy yards and broken-shingled roofs along streets where Tatars cried *halat, halat* for old rags. Hunched-over men dragged sleds of firewood, women sold cone twists of chestnuts on street corners and I looked for signs that their struggle had some success.

Vasily rested his hand on my knee on top of the bearskin. If it were Mihkel I’d have laid my own hand on top, or invited his hand beneath the bearskin. Now I didn’t know what to do. Vasily was still my employer and on reflection, I had to be wary and without expectation that he'd give me any quarter.

As the houses spaced out we advanced into more forest, emptier roads and deeper snow, passed carts and sledges and left neighbourhoods of slapped-together apartments and the smoke and oil of factories behind us.

The sky remained clear and a cold wind cut across our path. Vasily leaned against me until I was about to complain when he asked, "Are you comfortable? Are you warm?" and drew his chin into his neck to look at me, all objections perished.

Though my hat was pulled low and my scarf high my eyes watered. I'd been watching snow flying from the horses' hooves wondering what we would find in Gostilitsy, how I'd amuse the children in the bleak cold and what I'd do should Lyudmila's warning come true. Bandits and robbers were certainly about and there could be no guarantee of stores and supplies in the countryside without the presence of a steward. My face had grown numb. I hitched my fur collar up and touched Katya's cheek to feel its warmth.

Vasily's hand stayed clamped on the bearskin over my knee. "We'll stop for refreshments. Something hot. Very soon." We passed open *versts* of snow-covered meadows and thatched roofs, smoke puffing from chimneys, soft yellow lights promising warmth.

"In summer we dance all night when we come here," Katya recalled.

"I catch frogs," Sacha squeaked between the furs.

"And grown-ups play tennis. You must come! You must! In summer, *Fräulein*," Katya demanded.

"I'd love to," I agreed. The war would be over by summer, the tsar replaced by a responsible civil government and I would play tennis at Gostilitsy, drink Crimean wine from a crystal glass and lie on a rug under an oak tree. I couldn't tell who would be by my side. Mihkel, because the estate would belong to us all. Or to Vasily. I would be his wife or mistress. Or none of any of that.

"The war will be over and order restored," Vasily said. I'd been lulled by the rhythm of the swaying sleigh and the Orlovs running, two speeds; the steady pounding of the centre horse held by the shafts while the outside horses, attached only by their traces, galloped as wildly as my heart. The low roof of an inn at last in view, lights eking out the faintest glow. Timur slowed the horses, drew them in between a veranda and covered woodpile, leapt from the sled and went around clearing the horses' muzzles from hoarfrost, wiping their coats of icicles and changing their places.

I unbuckled my pigskin bag. My camera. "Wait, wait, please!" I called, emerging from the bearskins, stamped my freezing feet, stood with my back to where the sun glimmered, and arranged Katya, Sacha and the sled to fill my viewfinder. Vasily posed without directions, stood on the sled runner, a fist punched against one hip as Timur's head appeared above a horse's back. I clicked, raised my head to see them and clicked again. I felt the thud of hooves and turned to see where snow scattered. A dozen horsemen came thundering to a stop under the distant trees. They reined in their mounts and rounded them together in a shadowy clearing. I turned my camera on them, curious, apprehensive, but not entirely undaunted. One horse was tethered to another, a rider bound at the wrists. I clicked, watched a moment longer, and climbed back into the sleigh.

The soldiers, in ragged variations of Russian uniforms, circled their prisoner.

"*Svoloch*! Dogs!" the prisoner shouted, lifted a bloodied,

beaten face before a rifle butt was slammed against his back. He slumped forward. I heard his groan, squeezed my eyes closed and held Sacha and Katya to me, hiding them but we'd already seen something we shouldn't. Timur and Vasily worked hastily changing the horses, Timur talking quietly, Vasily returning to the sleigh, his hand at his waist, and revolver.

"Papa! Dinner!" Katya cried, struggling from my arms.

"*Chérie, non*. Food at our house and we'll be there soon." Vasily spoke firmly as ever though my skin crept and Katya never questioned him. Timur lashed the horses and our sleigh sped away. I turned in my seat to look back to the outline of a figure swinging between the trees, the horsemen galloping off. Vasily's eyes burned in rage. I reached for his hand but he shook his head, nodded to the children, and ignored me.

"My neighbour's overseer. I think so," he murmured.

"For resisting? For not joining?"

"Exactly. It's what's left. Deserters, Siina. Cowards. Bolsheviks, so they imagine themselves. A mission to destroy us and everything they cannot understand."

I shuddered and turned back to the road, straight and flat behind. Vasily wove his gloved hand into mine and we watched the children sleeping.

"They'd punish you," I said.

"Absolutely."

And you and Timur are no match for all of them especially with your children and their tutor in the way, I thought. I tried to see further than the nearby trees, into the forest we were passing. I could not detect a breath to move the trees or any movement on the ground.

The horses had gained new wind and they galloped between the dense Siberian firs and we emerged into a clearing and descent, our troika bells clamouring like mad.

“All our land. Our forests,” Vasily said, pride in his voice.

“We’re there?”

“Oh, not for another hour.” He leaned to Timur and yelled instructions and we turned from the road and skimmed over a frozen river. “This will save us a good few *versts*.”

“Your mother said ….,”

He nodded. “Exactly.” He pointed to open meadows. “Not so far.”

Forest was cut on both sides of us.

“War needs fuel,” Vasily growled.

For minutes the sleigh creaked as we ground up an incline before a valley opened out below. Balsam poplars had made an avenue to the frosted, snow-bundled gardens below. At the centre stood a stone manor surrounded by the winter-white bones of an orchard under a light mist spreading over the river.

“Gostilitsy!” Katya cheered.

Granaries and the half-moon entrances of cellars were arranged some distance from the manor. On the borders of the snow-covered meadows wood sheds and storehouses would be stacked with grains, meats, wines, cheeses and ales though the manor house was obscured now behind a high stone wall. We travelled beside the riverbank buffered by snowy quilt as the river wound its way to the village and there, to barren miserable houses. A child staggered with a bundle of sticks on his back. An old woman dragged a sled loaded with grey sacks. Ahead, a frozen oilskin covered a dilapidated doorway. I slipped out my camera for the record.

“No men?” I noticed.

“Of course not. I should be guarding the palace instead of

leaving green young soldiers there. We've as good as lost the western front my dear. Revolutionaries dare oppose the war and incite desertion to complete our destruction. Poor Russia." His look was black.

"No negotiation?"

"No! What negotiation? With Bolsheviks!" he glared.

"Well if not now, when all is nearly lost, when?" I cried, as furious as he.

"A soldier fights for the motherland," he snarled. I expected he'd choke.

I thought of the man swinging from the tree and felt the hairs on the back of my neck rise. I never wanted to see anything like that again.

As we sped on down the slope we felt the troika's traces slacken and Timur lean on the brakes. I now saw the massive manor house surrounded by sack-covered statues and countless outbuildings. A tea house rose up, laced in ice, a Moroccan fantasy, an ancient rock and mortar chapel capped with onion domes and more.

"One of our family chapels."

"Your *dacha*! This palace, Feodorov?"

"The Feodorovna country seat." He almost smiled. "A little joke."

"I was born here," Katya chirped.

"*Glückliches Mädchen*," I said.

"*Ja, wir sind alle hier hatten die glücklichsten Zeiten!*" Katya said. I glowed with tutorish pride.

Vasily touched Katya's cheek. Sacha sucked his thumb as though he could milk it. Timur slackened the reins and the horses circled to a stop at the Greek columned front of the house. Vasily swung around to me and swept an arc with his arm. "One star in the cluster of our estate. It belonged to Peter the Great's physician."

Leeches and bleeding. My mother's deathbed. The estate was so vast that all I could do was to breathe in the cold air and breathe it out, slowly. I pictured it in summer, hundreds of servants, field hands, foresters, labourers, the villages of the feudal system, the bewildering endless management and all of it, his. Vasily's.

"Three generations? Your servants were slaves."

Vasily signalled the man at the manor steps to take the bags before he glanced back at me.

"What?"

I thought of granny at Metsajärve, the *Jaanipäev* songs of slave rebellion built into every line.

"What did you say?"

"Nothing. Thinking aloud," I said.

The steward's wife, Masha, stood with her two sons under the arched doorway. The boys, thin and nervous, came forward awkwardly, nothing of our smiling Duscha or Lyudmila.

"Catherine the Great stayed here on her way to Peterburg." Vasily lifted Sacha from the troika.

"With the hundreds of her entourage."

"She could have been killed. When the roof caved in only hours after she left, they punished the overseer. Hanged him," Vasily said coolly.

Masha stood like a stone before him, gripped her layers of coats in the ragged windings on her hands, her head set at an angle to Vasily's fur-lined boots.

"Come. The stoves are lit," he said to me because smoke indeed curled from a half dozen chimneys. "Tell me, what happened to Grigory," he demanded addressing Masha at last.

I sneaked out my camera and felt for the satisfying resistance of the shutter release. Light glossed the ice, sharpened Vasily's buckles and buttons, deepened the shadows of Masha's layers of jackets and shawls in fine contrast to the manor house in the background. The dull light of a late winter's day.

"Come," Vasily gestured, then to Timur, spoke of hunting.

I turned back to the road that entered the estate. Nothing moved. Whoever had come for Masha's husband would know exactly who had arrived at Gostilitsy today.

Inside, Sacha, still in his coat and hat, curled up against the tiled stove. My room, I imagined, would be freezing like the tundra.

Katya dropped her muff and hat on a chair and went directly to jars of preserved spiders and reptiles set on shelves against the wall and with confident familiarity, took a number of them down and lined them up neatly on the table to inspect them. I asked Masha for chocolate and warm bread and soup for the children. I found a glass by the bubbling samovar. Masha muttered to herself and disappeared.

"My great great-grandfather did these. He was a famous scientist," Katya explained as she turned jars over, held them up to look from underneath. Soon Masha returned with bread, pickled cucumbers and barley soup and I sipped hot tea and, unable to resist, opened a new letter from Anna.

Tartu, December 1916

My Dearest Siina, We all miss you! Come home now! I can't imagine what keeps you there where people are shot in the streets, drivers, women and children, chased down and beaten, and Bolsheviks are hung from lamp posts! I'm afraid for you. Do noblewomen really sell linen and opera glasses on street corners? Get on a train and come. Tartu is peaceful, though refugees keep pouring in from Courland, and there are soldiers everywhere. We do suffer as well. The Germans are arrogant; expect us to be grateful for their Kultur! They've taken over Saaremaa and Hiiumaa, did you know? Isn't it enough that the Kaiser bombs and blasts us without you taking up with revolutionaries? Really! I can't bear to read another word about killing. I don't read the papers. God help us! Lists are posted, on billboards here you know and I do not want to see your name! It's not neurosis but I miss you and worry. You can't shut yourself up all day and night can you? Pack your bags and your precious camera! I know how stubborn and argumentative you can be.

"Papa!" Katya jumped. Vasily stood in the doorway, the overseer's son, a boy in his teens, at his shoulder.

I folded away my letter as Vasily sank in the armchair on the canvas cover, stretched his legs and dug a cigarette out of his jacket.

"Katya may even follow her ancestor's footsteps. He was a serious scientist," he said exhaling smoke.

I circled the room beneath a mounted boar and deer high on the wall above the fireplace, a cased eagle and bearskin. A Kandinsky painting and a Leon Bakst drawing, works I had seen in journals, hung on the wall beside.

"I should take those to the city. I'm fond of them. Olga's not. She thinks they're rubbish but I like the new. Stravinsky and Scriabin, tradition breakers." He smiled a tired, piqued apology for a smile.

"Traditional trophies beside the language of revolution. You want both?"

Vasily leaned forward over his knees. "Of course. The best of everything, put simply. These pieces speak for the future, like it or not, revolution or no."

Masha brought Vasily tea from the samovar.

"And your overseer?" I asked quietly when Masha had gone.

"I don't know." Vasily watched the door close. "Grigory may have volunteered. Who can say?" He took a bottle of wine from the cabinet. "A glass of our own. Yes?"

I nodded. "Oh yes, please."

He poured, held his glass up to the window. "Colour's good," he said, came to me and clashed his glass to mine. "Are you warm Siina? Masha will find us something very good for dinner."

I nodded and sipped the wine. "But what can you do if you can't find Grigory?"

He tossed back his head. "What can I do? Close up and batten down. Remove our treasures to the city. What do you say? What have you heard?" He narrowed his eyes.

I shrugged. "People are fleeing over the Urals aren't they? Running off to Paris? What would I know?"

I imagined the road from Gostilitsy and the bands of deserters and Vasily's paintings, crystal and furniture loaded onto a sled, slipping through the forest between bandit gangs.

"It changes meaning, no?" He gestured at the paintings, his ancestor's reptiles, the trophies. "What is a life? A painting, hectares of land or jars of preserved reptiles?"

"Or ideals?"

He swirled his drink. I saw how little we agreed.

"Forget the rules. Who the hell cares? I'm glad you came. You think for yourself and I love it. You argue the point and I enjoy it. You're so completely alive," he smiled, so openly that I believed him completely.

He was certainly carrying the weight of something; his tsar's stupidity or his own uncertainty.

"I need to speak to people in the village about Grigory,

whoever I can find. Please, see the children to bed. I'll check the stores first thing tomorrow. Later, Timur and I will go hunting. God knows it will do me good to kill something."

He patted his waist where he kept his pistol and when the boy appeared at the door, they strode away.

I felt my pocket for Anna's letter.

I heard a man and wife were shot and mutilated near you by the Obvodny Kanal. The crowd even tore their coats and furs off …well, enough. You see why I won't read the papers!

I leaned my head back in the chair and the hairs on my neck prickled.

"*Fräulein*," Masha said from behind me. "Please." She offered me tea and an apple pastry.

"*Issant*! I never heard you." Masha could appear so soundlessly that she unnerved me.

She set down the tray. "And I don't answer to you," she said before sliding away.

I drank the tea and finished my wine. I almost hesitated before biting into the pastry, a vision of medieval poisoning somehow flashed through my mind but it was very good pastry and I felt better after I'd drained my wine glass.

I hear a rumour that you and Mihkel fell out. I'm not exactly sorry. I know you can do better, I mean, a man of stature, like Elviira's soldier or someone like him. They jumped the fire you know, though he was sent to Galicia and hardly anyone returned. He was killed. Elviira has a new man. So, I heard Mihkel's woman is a writer and neither beautiful nor rich. True? Don't be heart-broken, Siina. I'm so sorry to hear about Sergo. It's tragic and appalling. Poor Ksenia.

I took a deep breath. Poor Ksenia, oh yes, but wrong! Anna was infuriating, mixing fact and fiction! Wherever was she getting her gossip?

It's quite exciting enough here, but not insane. I mean, servants don't kill employers! And there's uproar over our future. Jaan Poska and Konstantin Päts are saying we shall have our own government. Some say it's nonsense but I believe it. You should be here. There are urgent developments despite the war and Petersburg's stew. Tartu boils with debate. In the evenings wild ideas are dealt like cards. We speak Estonian in the theatre and between cocktails, tango and what some call jazz. They say we'll have our own professors in the university.

I took a second pastry and sipped scalding, Russian, *caravan tea.*

I miss Oskar, and the months fly by, four before I'm due. My middle … well, you ought to see! Friends tell me I glow! I recovered quickly from my miscarriage, I don't spend any time thinking of it. Women whisper about awful, endless labour and ghastly births. I hear it. I know women die in pain and bleeding but I won't think of it, even after Mama …. I long to see you because you give me courage. I'm so anxious for Oskar. If he survives typhus and flu and cannons I'll kiss the soles of his feet. We've lost more men than ever before. A hundred thousand called up! Ammunition is gold, men don't get proper boots. Isn't it unbelievable when they started off with such blazing success? I fear Gorky was right; we're entering the first act of a worldwide tragedy, God help us! We do get farm produce, not much, nothing like when you were here, but butter and eggs, for a price. We manage. We'd be neutral if not for the tsar, wouldn't we?

Oskar doesn't speak about the war when he's been home. Just as well. It's decent of him to keep it to himself.

How do the Feodorovnas treat you? I can't understand there's still a high life while the city disintegrates! Tell me about Giles

Spencer and the other exotic barons, ones with false legs and ravishing dark-eyed Circassian brides young enough to be their granddaughters. That sort. And the dowagers with their hearing trumpets and travelling snuff. That too. Do not marry an Englishman, Siina. He'll never understand our humour or discretion, nor will he have read Dostoievsky. And one more word. About the languishing porcelain-faced Olga, so beautiful is she, so that fourteen year old schoolboys stand still in the street when she passes? Is it true? And is she interesting or smart or a just a face? Is Vasily as desperately handsome as women say and an outrageous rake? Write me Siina.

Katya nudged my elbow.

"I'm very tired and hungry. I'm finished with the jars."

"My dear! One moment." I held Katya against my knee and she laid her head on my lap. She closed her eyes, convincingly weary.

I skimmed the last lines of Anna's letter. Losing one baby didn't mean anything, she said. She felt only weak, a great clot of blood, not even the notion of a child. Anyway, there was a good chance, the grannies said, there was something wrong with it. This time she was healthy as an ox from the moment she conceived. I had to be there for this baby, and for Anna, I determined. Whatever happened, I would comfort her and do what was needed, to make it easy, to add my support.

Katya murmured into my knees.

"You'd like soup and apple pastry?"

"Yes."

Sacha also woke by the stove.

"Come, eat, then bed," I said.

Their room was warm. I inspected the beds for demon bedbugs, found no signs, tucked the children in wool and fur and they fell asleep the moment they closed their eyes. Lulle would have approved of a room as cold as a vegetable cellar though I didn't.

The German clock chimed eleven when I awoke on the sofa. At some time Masha must have set the table with candles, wine glasses, a Limoges dinner set and food in covered dishes.

I needed to reply to Anna to tell her the truth about Mihkel, explain how we were forbidden to see one another, that Giles Spencer was a curiosity I'd never dream of marrying and that there was nothing heroic in being a victim in a street protest that I stayed in at night and took a cab when I went out.

Vasily and Timur had not returned from the village and it was almost midnight. Ice crackled over the windows. Darkness covered Gostilitsy Estate.

I cringed to think of losing the men. If I dared drive the sled, the children and Orlovs back to Petrograd I'd go the exact way we came, even across the iced river.

I caught a movement outside the windows, a light and blurred shadows. Horses. I shook myself awake and peered more closely. I heard slamming doors and stamping snow before Vasily appeared throwing open the pocket doors.

"Thank god …!"

His face dark as death.

"What's this, a meal?" He glowered at the table, a platter of pickles and marinated mushrooms, the ham we'd brought from town, boiled cabbage and potatoes and champagne thrust in a crystal bowl filled with snow. "Dinner? What's the matter with her?"

"No bear paw soup?" I said, intending to lighten his mood. I didn't. He ignored me.

"She never was a cook," he fumed, tapping a finger to his

forehead. "I'm sorry. Shameful … but well, never mind." He waved the boy to come and tug off his boots. "So, time for a slug of champagne. I think so!"

"And Grigory?" I asked, my glass filled and bubbling, Vasily, beginning to warm up, his colour returning.

"Grigory? Nothing! A gaggle of women and a seven year old boy with fairy tales. Waste of time. God only knows the truth but I can see it in their eyes, measuring me, deciding what to say, butter him up and say what he wants. Well, I'll hunt them down whoever they are, the cowards."

"I need to sleep. I'm awfully tired," I admitted.

Vasily's voice rose. "God! Why? It's so early and you've not eaten. What, are you nervous?"

"Should I be?"

"Of course." He smiled under his eyebrows. "We're getting to know one another, are we not? And we have some way yet to go."

"I don't think so." I frowned.

"I'm joking. Really, I'm teasing. Let's drink to something, yes?"

He'd say me, I knew it.

"To you," he smiled.

"To peace!" I raised my glass.

"To Russia!"

"To *All the Russias*!"

"And have some more," he said beckoning the boy to pour.

I pushed the ham and cabbage around my plate. I was more tired than hungry but I felt guilty with the boy eyeing my food. The potato was good but the ham, stale with a bad smell. At least I could drink wine to cure whatever rot there was in the food. One more time Masha appeared, this time with cherry tarts but however tempting they looked, I almost gagged on the rank taste.

When Masha slid away silently, closing the door, noiselessly, Vasily jumped up and locked the door.

"Come," he said, noticing that I'd stopped eating. He held out his hand. "I've something for us. He led me across the room to the canvas covered sofa. "Sit. I have halva!"

My head swam from the warmth, the wine, the food I'd managed. Vasily never took his eyes off me. I expected him to be engrossed with his estate, the danger we were in, the troubles impossible to ignore. I'd assumed I would be a mere passenger and fleeting amusement. Perhaps I was more. I was certainly intrigued by him. I watched him, wondering constantly what he was planning. And if I was in it. Anna had said that falling in love was terrifying, like plunging down a well, deep and irresistible.

Vasily sat beside me. We bit into the halva, enticing as a Persian veil dance. My eyes had become lead-lidded, my heart thumping away with euphoria, with what I supposed he was thinking. I longed to touch him, his eyes smiling as he fed me halva.

"Forget the others Siina," he said, kissing me. I let him. I kissed him too, amazed at myself, at what I felt. He searched my body for something he was determined to have.

"We shouldn't," I said without conviction.

"But I'm nobody's." The candlelight had softened the angles of his face, the lines around his eyes and his features, close, enlarged.

"You belong to Olga," I said, though neither of us believed it.

He shook his head. "I don't. We're leagues apart."

"What will become of this?"

"But nothing!"

"Nothing!"

"Now, wait. Wait!" he whispered leaping from the sofa, taking up his jacket, feeling in the pocket.

“Why…..?”

“For you,” he said, setting a parcel, tissue wrapped, something soft, weighty and somehow wicked, on my lap.

“What?” I looked back and forth between him and the package.

“My esteem for you. Proof. Open it.” An innocent package in cream tissue tied with silver ribbons. I watched him as his eyebrow rose. “Go on.”

Something pretty, something tempting and surprising. He was full of anticipation too as I unfolded the paper to a yielding, sparkling, glittering mass of light. Diamonds! I lifted it, unravelled a belt, white satin, tapered with silk tassels at each end. I draped it over my hands feeling the weight of the slippery beautiful thing.

“Unbelievable! Amazing! Are you...?”

“Yes, yes. For you.”

“But…”

“Don’t say it. Olga has more diamonds pins for her hair. ”

“Are they really….?” I couldn’t stop gaping.

“Diamonds. Yes. Yes. Oh yes.”

“Good god!”

“Mmm.”

I held the belt this way and that. I stared, beguiled, at the stones. I couldn’t put it down. Vasily took it and tied it around my waist.

“Really…I can’t.”

“Of course you can.” He leaned over looking into my eyes. “You love it.”

I blushed. He saw through me. Completely. Security. Money. A studio. The Orient! “I like it.” It had to be worth thousands of roubles, tens of thousands! The whole length of belt, encrusted.

"It is a rare piece."

I swallowed. I could accept. Did he mean it? Was he testing… or teasing?

"It's completely astonishing."

"Yes, yes, a prize piece, Siina."

How my heart beat, galloping for the consequences, the assumptions made which I would agree to. I'd keep my part. First the blouse, now this. And he, smiling like a wolf, his hand on my thigh, his breath changed and insisting. I did want it; such a belt with diamonds. And he did want me, to kiss me, then more, the next part I could easily guess.

Even so I was in charge, how fast and how far we'd go, wondering if the belt would free me. If they really were, really, diamonds. They shone with fire.

I flounced around the room, the belt loose over my lace blouse. I felt like a child.

"Absolutely sure?"

"Of course. You're worth every stone." He was gulping, practically licking his lips, ready for mine, the lust, the thirst. He dived over to me, took my head in his hands, kissed me gently and as much as I allowed, until more urgently, desperately, hurting me with his bristles, his mouth forcing mine. I let him, faint with excitement, the yes and no we'd been through, the yes and no in my head for so long. I could please him though I shocked myself at my desire, at his, at our easy rhythm, our union, him fierce and me, dizzied and rapt. "Be gentle," I said, which he understood exactly. I would not resist this time. I undid the buttons of my blouse so it wouldn't tear. We'd come together without conflict, though seduction and siege, were part of it.

Moments later we were on the floor, murmur upon murmur,

he in the lead one moment, me the next until we lay curled under the rugs and furs, naked. Above, the chandelier glowed. I'd been helpless against nature, beyond control, my wits vacant while passion took me. So married women, society women, nurses and shop girls knew it. Anna knew. Elviira certainly did, I mused, Vasily's hands still caressing, his lips still brushing my skin.

"You do love me," I whispered,

"I do." He nuzzled, pressing into me, our skin, our honey, glued together. He laughed, his lips buttery. "Your body knows. We're sweethearts. That this was written in the heavens. That you came to me to know me and me to know you. There was no other way, no avoiding, no resistance."

I lay in his arms, the chandelier milky with light, the candles burning down. "Does it also say we can love whom we fight, whom we disagree with? When you're a rich aristocrat and I'm a revolutionary?"

"You're no revolutionary," he said undaunted. "You're a thinker. Humanitarian. That's a wonderful thing. I have obligations, you perhaps understand that, and few choices. There are ways that bind me."

"But I mean it. We strongly disagree, don't we?"

He continued to smile. "Don't you see that under the heavens we're one? That our thoughts and opinions are blessings, that we have the freedom to disagree but we're one?" He rolled on his side, leaning on his elbow to look at me. "There is always compromise between ideas and action, always, everywhere. There's idealism, or some version of it; reality. Can you believe how much I care? That I'm kind? This comes with love. I lay it at your feet to hear you moan because I love you."

We must have staggered along the frozen hallway to his bed, the belt tied around my waist again. Walls pitched and swayed while we entwined. My body ached for him, to wrap myself around him. I opened. I disappeared. I might have been on the moon or under the ocean. I might have been drugged, enchanted, become a bird or an angel. Or light.

Afterwards I dreamt. Music played. Eagles flew. Vasily and I swam together, two eels in a river.

31. Hunters

Masha could have been knocking on the door half the night for all I knew. I scrambled up, my head propped up, heavy and aching. I grabbed my jacket and opened the door.

"The children are downstairs, *Fräulein*. Here's coffee." Masha hardly turned her head but most likely saw how slowly and carefully I moved.

"I'll be down in a moment."

"The men have gone hunting. The children are behaving badly. There's breakfast and there's no more," she said shuffling away.

The smell of fried bacon and onion greeted me in the dining room. More amazing was the painting on the wall behind the mahogany dining table. A Makovsky I was sure; a bride surrounded by attendants, a painting more like an unfinished sketch, blues and golds roughly brushed in. I adored it, the light, the delicacy, powerful and romantic with realism in faces, costumes and details in pearls, laces, wondrous headdresses.

"You're taking us sledding. You said yesterday," Katya shrilled. Her plate was already empty but for a few crumbs. "May I have more?"

My food had been served for me.

I propped my sick head with one hand and reached for coffee with the other.

"Have some of mine," I told her as I tasted bitter dandelion and acorns in my cup. Vasily had expected we'd be bathing in cream and raspberries. No doubt they once had.

Sacha, at the other end of the room, rocked like a Georgian

Cossack on a wooden horse twice his size. "And hunting? When do we go?" he demanded.

"The men go. You wait till you're grown," I said looking at the forest beyond the barren garden.

A crack of gunfire made me jump. Another blast. I sprang to the window. Light snow was falling. The men were somewhere in the forest.

I scrubbed at the *jäälilled*, the ice flowers on the window pane. I was unreasonably nervous. Vasily and Timur had gone hunting since they were boys and Vasily was a soldier. What foolishness for me to be so jumpy. They'd taken the dogs and Grigory's boys.

"Fill the stove ma'am?" I hadn't heard Masha approach but here she was again in her felt boots and with the same sullen look.

"Yes, of course. We're here all day."

"I want to talk."

Olga would have sent Masha off for that tone but I listened, it was only decent.

"You're not them so you should hear me." Masha said from beside me. She smelled of goat. Her clothes were all but rags, her manners offensive.

"I'm listening." I said looking over her shoulder to where Sacha paraded a regiment of wooden soldiers and Katya was making a drawing of a newt in a jar.

Masha stepped closer. "You're German aren't you? Because my children have been sent to the front. My eldest boy was killed you know, in Prussia. I still have my two young ones, my lame duck, and just as well he is, but you being a German, *Fräulein*, you'd know about that. Only, our sons are fighting yours."

I couldn't speak for a moment from the shock. "I'm not German. Estonia is colonized by Germans, Masha but we're part of great Russia. I'm Estonian, never German," I replied rationally.

Masha leaned forward. "Millions are dead, *Fräulein*, and my son." Her arms hung at her sides but she boiled like a kettle. "We've been loyal to the tsar and the Feodorovnas for as long as I can remember our parents and theirs before them but it's finished you see. Men came here, officials from Peterburg, *Fräulein*, and they've been to the front so they know something, they do. You can't say I don't know what's going on now, can you? We'll get bread and peace and land. They promised."

I stepped back. "They have no land or bread to give, Masha," I said reasonably.

"Ah, but they soon will have. And we weren't born to be servants or slaves. We'll rise, *Fräulein*. We will."

I couldn't bear to look at her. She mangled Russian worse than a German trying to speak Estonian.

"Vasily Feodorov is a good man but he's just a man. Always want more, don't they? Greed, you see!" She stood far too close to me. She was small, but wolverines are small and dangerous.

"You and I have no quarrel Masha. We're both servants," I told her but her expression never changed.

"And how is Olga Pyotrovna, *Fräulein*? Ailing? I expect she is." Masha smiled through missing teeth. "Never lifts a finger not even for her own does she? I can't understand it. I looked after mine, five of them, only I've lost my eldest you see." She wiped her nose with her sleeve.

"I detest the war too," I offered.

Masha shuffled to the window. "The wolves are hungry you know. Everyone is. We all want to eat, don't we? My boys are young, but they know the forest, better than our master, I should say. They have to be careful. Wolves are hungry, and guns go pop."

My stomach shrank but my fists tightened at what Masha was engineering as she folded her arms over her brown shawl and stained blouse, the neck soiled and marked, the colour of her crumpled, repellent face, her eyes like stones. “And I’ll tell you what else. I’ve made the last meal you’re getting. You see there’s nothing left. You’re all greed and waste you Petersburgers with your dancing and feasting, drinking bubbles and eating caviare, starving your servants and feeding your horses champagne!” She made a lunge toward me as if she might grab me around the middle and I dodged to the side but she recovered and stood sucking on her wet mouth. “But not for much longer.”

“It isn’t like that,” I gestured, weary, despairing because I’d never convince her it was not my doing if someone in Petersburg fed a horse champagne from a bucket.

“You live on our backs that’s what it is. We’re to gnaw the chaff and leavings are we? Poor people have to steal or starve, that’s what.”

“What are you saying? What have you been up to?”

But Masha was already denying what she suggested. “I know nothing,” She backed away hanging her head. “But it’s been a terrible winter for wolves and servants.” Her pellet eyes almost disappeared. Her nostrils flared. “I know what’s next because when we rise, you’ll learn what it is to be like us.”

“Don’t be silly,” I said in a voice as calm as Timur with his Orlovs.

“Those men said we’d get land, everyone would, and bread. They said.”

“Masha,” I reasoned. “We’ve all heard such stories. I understand you’re ready to trust them, but if we destroy everything we have what will there be? Can’t you see that?”

Her nostrils rounded like bullet holes. “So you say. So you

say, *Fräulein,*" she jabbered, removing plates and cups, knives and forks. She sidled out the door and kicked it shut.

I followed her to the hall. In the kitchen the shelves were empty. The cupboards, too.

"Where is the food?" I demanded, taking Irena's advice, standing taller, imperiously.

"You can see for yourself there's nothing."

"Oh no. Where?"

"Stolen, *Fräulein*. That's what I'm saying. Apples and flour, that's all. Not much is it?"

I searched the pantry. "But what about you and Grigory? You have to eat."

Masha opened her mouth to laugh and closed it, sniggering. "Oh you needn't worry after us. You never have. We're not ones to waste. Who peels their potatoes all to one size? And right now, well I have to attend to the animals, see, so I need to do to that. It's just I won't be doing any more for you," she said and turned her back.

When I returned to the drawing room Sacha was absorbed with his soldiers, Katya with a book. I wished I had a silver pistol in my pocket like Olga's in her underwear drawer. But Masha was busy providing for herself and her boys and wouldn't bother me and the children. It made no sense, I reasoned.

I had stuck a sugar cube between my teeth and sipped tea when the door slammed and Vasily, white-faced, stormed across the room and threw down his gloves. Snow melted on his moustache. A patch of blood marked his sleeve. He slapped his record book on the ormolu table. Timur stood at his shoulder.

"We've been ransacked! Masha!" he bellowed.

Katya and Sacha slunk across the room to sit on my lap.

"*Svoloch*! Animals! I'll whip their hides. You'd think Mongol hordes rampaged through my estate. We're stripped!"

I looked down but when I raised my eyes Masha was in the room her boys peering from behind her, bloodied hands hanging at their sides.

Masha slunk forward, the smell of rancid fat with her.

"What happened?" Vasily growled, taking time to breathe and feel his wounded arm.

Masha glowered, first at me, then at Timur and Vasily. "I know they done it. They're starving," she said in a voice quite different from the one before.

"Good! So tell."

"Won't."

Vasily rocked forward. "You better. I punish treachery."

"I won't." She ducked her head and shoulders and stared at the floor. "Don't care if you beat me. Been beaten before."

Vasily stepped back. "Damn you! Tell or be sorry. The police will deal with you for robbery and you'll wish yourself dead. Everything's gone. Our grains and wines, our meat, honey and jams! Not a bag of flour, not a bean or grain." He pressed a dark look at me. "You see what they are? But I'll track them down, I'll bet my horse! Masha! Tell, and make it better for yourself."

I glanced behind Masha to the window. A buck, head twisted to the side, blood stuck to its winter hide, lay on the snow.

"The neighbour's place was burned to the ground. Nothing but ash," Vasily said.

We were to have taken wine and bacon back to Petersburg. Olga wanted jams and marinated mushrooms. We'd bring back the deer at least.

Timur glared at Masha. "Tell. It belongs to us all."

But Masha didn't hear. She was steady, giving nothing away and for all the foul smell and murdered Russian, rag-bound feet and missing teeth, she held some power.

She lifted her chin to Vasily. “It’s coming, Vasily Feodorov. The End. For you and all yours. We know it. Everything of yours will be ours,” she said, her chin raised, looking Vasily in the eye then quickly, down again.

He peered from beneath his brow. Timur glanced sideways. Sacha and Katya sat as still as the milk before them.

“You think so? You really think you’ll drink wine and eat pasha every day? They’re bloody liars!” Vasily wheeled around to the boys. “And you’ll see! Your liberators are villains and bandits and wherever Grigory went, I guarantee he’s wishing to heaven he was back here. Listen, you’ve seen only the beginning of a catastrophe! You’ll curse you ever heard of Bolsheviks once you get a whiff of what they do.”

I listened to my own breathing.

A crack like a gunshot in the room. We all started. Katya’s preserved reptile had rolled in its jar across the table and fallen to the wooden floor. Formalin spread its poisonous stink across the room. For another moment we were still.

“Tell us who’s responsible.” Vasily flicked his riding whip, and turned his fury to the boys.

“You’d have to kill us and we’re tough,” Masha returned.

I edged closer to the window. Timur ran his hand down the horse’s neck as it stamped and snorted and shook its head. The centre one chewed on the soapy bit that forced her head up.

I felt Sacha’s hand fit into mine and Katya lean against me. I stepped into the hall, handed Katya her coat. I dressed Sacha.

The buck had been tied to the back of the sleigh, the antlered head removed for Masha and her boys. I turned away from the bloodied severed neck. Katya wanted to poke it but Sacha clung to me and peeked from between his fingers. He’d never been so affectionate.

Timur inspected the hind quarters of the young Orlov tied to run behind the sleigh. He shook his head. No, she wasn't lame but there was something wrong with the way she moved.

I wrapped Sacha's scarf around his collar, tugged Katya's hat over her ears and arranged the furs in a nest in the sleigh. I wanted to be home.

Vasily climbed in last of all, grave and moody. We'd brought all there was in the kitchen, beets, a bag of apples and we had the deer carcass.

"What happened? Why are we leaving? When are we going sledding?" Katya went on until Vasily cut her short but to me, enumerated the supplies that had gone. Barrels of ale and honey, sacks of potatoes, beans and corn, wines from French appellations, all stolen. He fumed, describing his once laden barns and winter stocks, though I could hardly imagine them, filled with grains, meats and preserves with desolation everywhere. His futile anger told me not to ask further. Instead I watched ahead clutching my pigskin bag with my camera. I'd not get a picture until they changed the horses and for more than an hour we'd speed through the forests. We climbed the uphill easily before bursting into a furious pace on the flat, bells jangling. I watched the glistening haunches, snow tossed aside, glittering. The horses worked forward, onward, swaying a rhythm, three points, streaking over windblown ice, Timur bellowing, "*Davai*!" Get up! He cracked the whip.

Vasily had ignored the blood stain on his jacket but now he bit his lip and held his arm.

"How did you get that?" I asked wanting to wipe away the marks.

He rocked his head. "Nothing. Could have been worse. A

misfired shot. The boys are stupid," he said though I guessed something more sinister.

"Really?"

"It's nothing. At least I can trust Timur." He smiled ruefully. "It's something isn't it? Saved me you know. I was only a child. He killed a bear. One thrust of his spear. I wouldn't be here now otherwise. It's good to be able to trust someone. Anyway," he said with a wave and a grimace. "We're home soon. You know what it is to love your home, and it's so for me too. I won't give up what we have. It's been ours too long." My heart went out to him.

"I do know." In fact I didn't want to feel it just then, not when everything was coming apart and I was far from home. Anna taking charge of me, because she cared, the smell of Lulle's *rehealune*, even when the ovens were cool, were dear and too far off. I was where I'd chosen to be yet unsure why I'd come. But now I had a perfect shot of Timur, beard and sheepskin coat, snapping the reins and Vasily, the wind tearing his moustache, his red cheeks and nose, rifle clutched at his shoulder. My camera was deep in my bag. In the wind and swaying, flying along, I didn't dare take it out.

"I prefer it like this, nothing between here and Petersburg. Oh, a gypsy caravan, nothing more. I love it," Vasily smiled. He was equal to anything now, after the hunt – primitive man, his land, his kill. "It's here I belong. Never Bolshaya Morskaya. Gostilitsy, whatever they do to it, it's here I love."

When you've been robbed blind and could be strung up around the next corner, I thought. When it could all be gone tomorrow, cut up, razed to the ground? We're lucky to be alive, I thought, but Vasily was saying what it was, what he'd fight for.

"Whatever the losses and heartache, there is always *matyushka zemlja*. Motherland," he said.

I nodded knowing he could read me.

He kneeled down to watch behind us as the path narrowed like a tunnel under the trees, closing together, covering us from above. Snow-laden boughs brushed the troika sides. The centre horse under the painted *duga*, forged on, head high, the overhead firs blocking what little light there was. The snow lay deeper and wetter here than in the open, and slower under the sleigh.

From behind we heard scrabbling and growling. I twisted in my seat. A flurry of grizzled fur and wolves bounded from the woods, darting at the nervous, straggling Orlov at the back. The wolves nipped at her uneven gait.

Vasily swore, jumped up on the seat. "*Chort poberi*!" He swung his rifle.

The sleigh wallowed with the drag of the faltering Orlov with the wolves snarling and diving at her, and away again. The pack doing its work.

Timur flung a look over his shoulder and snapped his whip. "*Davai. Davai*!"

Katya and Sacha, thrilled and terrified, bobbed up and down and clamped onto me. The young Orlov whinnied.

A blast from Vasily. A hit. A wolf yipping and careening to the side, writhing on the snow between the others that still swerved and dipped. Vasily worked the bolt, again, aimed again, cracked another hit. Another wolf staggered, then stretched out on the road, in moments, far behind. The Orlov galloped for its life, ragged, throwing its head, whinnying. Timur would have to slow for her to keep her feet but it would give the wolves an advantage.

"Gently, gently," Vasily crooned to the horse while he reloaded and a lone wolf charged alongside the Orlov, its hackles raised, grimacing, going for the Orlov's neck.

"No!" I screamed as jaws opened and teeth snapped. My

pigskin bag flew, missed the wolf, but distracted it. Vasily swung his rifle, the troika lurched and jogged, the path curved. The shot flashed wide, the wolf pitched itself again at the Orlov. Vasily reloaded, taking forever. I dreaded the grey falling, dragging us all down, tipping over but Vasily blazed. Another shot struck. The wolf rocketed forward, yelping, back legs flying. It went head over heels, and lay still.

I sank back into the seat. Katya wrapped herself around me with, "*Frau! Frau! Frau!*"

The troika danced out of the tunnel of trees onto harder snow and we surged away, the wolves behind fighting over the dead one and Timur shouting, *Davai*! but less urgently, more encouraging so the horses slackened to a steady pace and the Orlov behind kept her feet.

I turned to where I'd thrown my camera.

"Your camera and your bag! Shame," Vasily commiserated.

Not only the camera, but the shots, and Mama's bag. "We might have lost her." The spare grey still foamed at the mouth, hoarfrost sprouting from her nostrils as she cantered on.

"I'll get you another camera," Vasily promised as we emerged into the open.

When we came to the frozen lake, Vasily leaned forward. "Cut across, Timur."

Perhaps it was shorter, but deeper in the forest and we'd been warned about it.

"We'll be back all the sooner," Vasily assured me but I noticed his chest heaved and his eyes stayed on the trailing Orlov. I couldn't ask.

Lake ice slipped beneath us. Timur was eager to change the horses. "On the other side," Vasily urged. "Keep going."

I heard creaking.

"It's breaking!" Katya popped up from the furs like a hunting ferret.

Vasily rose on one knee and leaned on the troika rail. "Nonsense." I did hear ice groan. I thought of us all, horses and sleigh sinking, six horses and a loaded sleigh but Timur cracked and whirled the whip and the horses, terrified by the thunder beneath them, spurted on.

I saw Anna, her baby a little girl, swimming in the womb. We had to get across the lake. I had to get back, to my sister.

The sleigh bumped over the lake edge, Vasily settled beside me and laid his arm behind my neck. "You don't make a fuss, do you? I tell you, if for some reason I have to get out of the city, to save Olga's nerves what do you say? Would you come?"

32. Bezique

Laughter greeted us when we blew into the hall on Bolshaya Morskaya. The women were playing bezique. It must have been uproarious. The wet nurse sailed past with the screaming baby but it was Grunya who welcomed us with prayers of thanks that we were alive while the whole time Magdalena chattered and swung on her arm.

"Wolves tried to get us! Papa killed them!" Sacha screamed.

Grunya untangled layers of fur and wool, shaking her head in amazement.

"Papa shot a deer. It's all blood. The ice cracked and we nearly drowned!" Katya shouted. Olga swung around, a finger to her lips, flourishing her hand, a Royal Sequence.

"*Tranquillité mes chéris!*" she shushed and turned back to Irena and Natalya.

Grunya was gasping with the effort of undressing Sacha and stopped to breathe, a hand to her chest. "I'm so glad you're back my darling pet."

Vasily shrugged his coat into the butler's open hands. "It's all true my dears," he told the women who continued their cards though his mother looked up.

"Exactly! What did I tell you?" she scolded.

I hadn't said a word nor had anyone asked if I was cold or collapsing. I realized they wouldn't have cared had I been eaten alive or disappeared under the ice but finally Olga laid her cards down.

"But you're here now so no more fuss," she said but she did open her arms to her children. "You're terribly cold," she said touching their cheeks with the back of her hand. “Hot chocolate, Lyudmila. And their house shoes, Grunya.”

Vasily kissed Olga on the forehead as she picked up her cards. Natalya swept across the room to the icon of St George to say a prayer.

I dragged myself upstairs trying not to be offended.

Lyudmila came upstairs with tea for me. “They were ransacked were they? Timur told us. He said you sacrificed your camera for his Orlovs.”

“I did!”

She lowered her face. “This poor old woman was struck down and killed *Fräulein*! The police went mad. We know Cossacks can crack their whips but this was the police! The Cossacks turned away. Did you hear?”

“I did.”

“Now who will protect the tsar? The police can’t!” Lyudmila stood firmly, her feet wide apart and looked down the hall.

“Shall I tell you what I saw in the country?” I took a step toward her. “I photographed them Lyudmila. A man beaten, bound, hanged from a tree. I got them on my camera but it’s gone.” I dared Lyudmila to look away. “They hanged him. We were there.”

“It’s too horrible. When I think of my brother, not knowing even…,”

“I’m so sorry. They were army deserters, bandits in soldiers’ uniforms, criminals on the run. And the photos in my camera. I’m so angry. I can never prove their crimes now.”

“And who’s next?”

“Exactly.”

“We’ve no food,” Lyudmila said, rocking in the doorway, her palms together.

“Vasily will think of something or Irena Feodorova will. They’ll find a way.”

Lyudmila opened the door and slunk away. “At least someone killed Rasputin,” she said over her shoulder. I sat on my bed wishing I had the pictures of those men in their uniforms. Whoever found my camera could piece together my life but much more likely, all my photos would be lost forever.

33. Spy Camera

Natalya Andreevna was gone.

"Where? Why?" I demanded.

"Back to the Caucasus. Back home," Duscha said with a shrug. She set down her mop on the stairs to my room and wiped her hands on her apron.

"How could she? Did someone go with her?"

Duscha pinched the end of her nose in her fingers. "Alone, oh no. Lyudmila went too."

"Only the two?"

Duscha looked at me from under her dark brows. "*Fräulein,* how else? Who else would go?"

"But why?"

"Who knows? Not me."

"I need to know," I said edging past her, stepping around the bucket and carefully down the stairs that were still wet.

Irena fumed flicking pages of the *Izvestiya*. Olga pored over *Jane Eyre*. They looked up when I came in.

"You poor dear, your camera gone. Shame," Irena said.

I stood rigid and did not curtsey. I could feel the temperature drop.

"*Fräulein,* tell us what you saw. Street fights? The police won't come any more you know."

"Gostilitsy carved from ice. Breathtaking. I got wonderful photographs."

Irena nodded. "Naturally. The countryside is beautiful. Did the wolves frighten you?" Irena lifted her face and almost smiled.

"They did."

Spy Camera

"So you enjoy your hobby, *n'est-ce-pas*?"

"Absolutely. And Vasily Feodorov gave this to me." I held up a brass framed handbag, filigree curls along the edges, a padded tapestry body, a gift from my employer. Irena stared in fascination. She stretched up. Olga too.

"What a notion. So now you become a spy."

"I most certainly could." I passed them the spy camera. Irena opened the catch and probed the tapestry pouch. "Even room for powders. You might have used it on us but you've lost your chance." Her grey eyes smiled.

I assumed they'd not been discussing me, saying French harlot or German tart because they could have amused themselves over me and my *hobby* camera. They handed me back my new apparatus and I excused myself before they could dismiss me. Katya and Sacha were sure to be getting into mischief in some unexplored corner.

In fact I found Katya cross-legged on the library floor, a medical book and scissors beside her, paper intestines and severed muscles, cross sections of bones and sliced body parts littered around her. Bourgeoisie guilt or a young Dadaist I thought smiling to myself, but only for a moment before I tried out my spy camera, then removed the pages. I admired the exquisite detailed line illustration of a foetus, the curves of the baby like a nut in its shell with organs, blood vessels and heart so clear and defined. I folded the pieces away into my pocket and began to reprimand Katya.

"Books are as precious as jewels. These are irreplaceable," I scolded though Katya's look remained triumphant. "Go," I ordered and she went ahead to the nursery where we had pages of script to write.

The afternoon when we sat together, Magdalena with her

dolls, Sacha with his slate and chalk, Lyudmila came and beckoned to me. We stood before the window watching snow dance.

"*Fräulein*, I wonder why you stay. If I could, I'd go to my family, I would. Every day something explodes or is ransacked. What keeps you? My brother was attacked in the street yesterday. He went to my parents with his eyes bloodied, lucky if he'll see again!" She frowned, wiping her eyes with her fingertips. "The police are always somewhere else even if they do care. So we should believe. He was speaking to a German book seller, can you believe?" Lyudmila shuffled and looked at the floor. "Don't spend your time here any longer, *Fräulein*! Go home to your sister! Natalya Andreevna has gone."

"So I heard. Where did she go?"

"A man. She ran off."

I smiled. "Cossack?"

"So I believe." A smile crossed her lips, mine also.

"But your photographs? Are you really spying?" She looked around warily in case she'd given something away.

"Spying? Not at all! I like to take photos discreetly so people don't pose. I like capturing expressions, surprise, delight, genuine emotion. You've seen my pictures."

"But people say..."

"What, that I'm a spy? Silly."

"So you say."

I stayed at the window. Snowflakes stuck on the pane. A man came hurtling around the corner from Gorokhovaya *Ullitsa*, a mob at his heels swinging sticks and fists, gaining on him until they landed a blow to his shoulder and cut him down. I cried out, bit my lips, meaning to run to the telephone but mesmerised, waited to see what would happen. "Police!" I cried to the empty room. The men beat him as he rolled around, covered his face still they kicked and heaved him side to side, all over him like flies on meat until suddenly they scattered, as fast as they'd arrived.

"Police!" I called again running down the hall to the telephone, peering again from the hall window out on the snow where the body bled into the white.

"Police!" I cried into the receiver, giving my name and address twice over. Waiting. They would come, the woman told me, tediously. No, she couldn't say how long. They had other calls too. Far too many, thank you.

Irena came clicking with her cane into the hall. "What?" she snapped seeing me with the telephone.

"Murder in the street, Irena Alexandrovna! Outside our door!"

Irena jumped. I moved the drawing room curtains aside and we saw the lump. I wondered how long before he died. He might still be alive. Perhaps they'd save him at the hospital.

"Do not go outside, *Fräulein.* Stay here. We cannot interfere with rabble. I insist you stay."

I grabbed my coat, tucked my camera in the pocket and in the other, felt for the pistol Vasily had given me – a tiny semi-automatic pistol, an Austrian, centrefire Kolibri. "Keep it out of sight," he'd said, "But most importantly, do not lose your nerve. If you need to then use it. You'll need protection before long," he said. Heaven only knew if I could in fact shoot anyone.

I stepped into the wind. The street was quiet. The body lay still. I circled it, caught the reek of alcohol, musk and excrement. I pressed my scarf to my nose and leaned over. The man lay on his face but perhaps his heart beat and perhaps he breathed. I moved his head, imagining something horrible. He was cut, black and blue and swollen. I tasted and held down bile. His eyes had puffed like eggs and closed tight, his face red and raw, his nose flattened. “Sir! Can you hear me?”

A sound behind me, a muted thud. My hand went to my pocket. I jerked around. A boy stood behind, younger than me.

“What!” I clutched the gun. His eyes moved like arrows.

“Give me your money or I’ll have to shoot you,” he panted though I felt calm.

“I have nothing,” I said holding out open hands. He’d see I was honest and back off. A boy as young as Kristjaan but desperate, thin, not full-grown but with a pistol.

I shook my head watching him tremble. “Don’t! Put it down. Look, I have no money, but I can get you something to eat,” I said staring over his shoulder to the yard gate. “Put it away,” I repeated as though the gun were a toy.

He hung his head, licked his lips as if they had dried, his eyes starving. “What? Soup? Meat? What?”

“Yes! Yes. Meat. Soup. Put that away. You wouldn’t want to die for a bowl of soup!”

I stared in a trance as the yard gate cracked open. Timur stepped out, one silent foot following the other into the street behind the boy who turned as Timur raised his gun. I heard my scream, “*Nyet! Nyet!*” and the boy, only feet away from Timur gaped in shock, his body leaping at the crack of fire before he slumped like a sack.

“Timur! No!”

He stood there, his sheepskin coat not yet buttoned, his eyes blazing. “Inside, *Fräulein*! You’re asking for death yourself out here! Get inside!” I backed away, wishing to save the boy now but Timur stooped over him before he turned away. “The police are coming, *Fräulein*. Get inside,” he stormed.

“He was hungry,” I mumbled.

“And he’d have shot you.” Timur grabbed me by the elbow.

"So now there are two!"

"Should I?" I said slipping my camera out.

Timur shook his head in disgust. "Well why not?" I took the photo.

That afternoon Irena offered me a glass of schnapps. She did not chastise me for disobedience. "Our world is changing, *Fräulein*," she murmured, watching me, sipping her own tiny glass, licking her lips. "We'll hardly know ourselves a year from now, what do you say?"

I didn't expect a conversation with her but she had addressed me as never before.

"I dare to hope for peace and prosperity for all Russians," I said as she raised her glass again and I drank too.

"I foresee the unforeseeable," she said as I considered a provocative reply but we both turned at the sound of the telephone bell.

"For the *Fräulein*," the butler announced.

"Siina! It's Mihkel. Meet me? Please."

I held the telephone like a live grenade. Irena would become a bombshell at the sound of his name.

"Where are you?"

"Meet me at the Stray Dog. What do you say?"

"When?"

"Tonight? Say yes."

I breathed carefully, quietly as my heart raced. "Yes," I said shivering because what else could possibly happen, and I was sure to regret it if I missed an opportunity. Men were challenging our social order. Momentous changes were being decided.

"I've finished a massive piece and I have a moment before the next. I'm longing to see you! *Noh*? *Jah*?" There it was. Simple enough. "You'll take the tram. Meet me there!"

Elena Stasova travelled by tram, Vera Karelina, educated and upper-class, travelled alone. Of course I would. The Nevsky was lit.

"Speak Russian! I'll come."

"Michailovsky Square! Go in. I'll be there by nine." I whispered into the phone, my eyes on the hall doorway.

"Goodbye!"

"Be careful."

I set down the phone as Lyudmila approached. I wondered what she'd heard.

That afternoon, Katya scratched away on her Gothic script, Sacha made illegible letters on his slate and Magdalena set her dolls in a row, chattering in French while I answered in German. In another hour I would be free.

I glanced into the drawing room when I came downstairs. Irena was hidden behind the *Izvestiya* newspaper. Sofia Casanova's name leapt at me from the front page. Irena sipped some clear liquid from a small glass. I remained in the hall and heard her dissect the news with Olga.

"The Vyborg workers have committed murder. They lynched the manager, tied him to his chair and threw him in the river. They'll never get away with it. It makes me shake."

"Galina Gromenkovna is taking her family to the country. They'll wait there until this is all over," Olga said from further back in the room.

"We ought to go. Come back when everything's better," Irena said. "It does not get better. We need to think about what we'll do, Olga.

"Gostilitsy," she said and I made an entrance, my hands clasped before me like a schoolgirl.

"I'm going out later," I said. "Meeting a friend."

"Oh really? Estonian?" Olga's smile creased her sublime features.

"My sister's friend. An actress from Tartu."

Olga and Irena exchanged glances.

"We're meeting at the Astoria."

"Yes, good. It's lit there. Dress plainly and you must take care *Fräulein*."

Irena went back to her paper, Olga to *Jane Eyre*. I left without a curtsey.

Bolshaya Morskaya was lit all the way to the hotel Astoria and St Isaac's, and beyond to Nevsky Prospekt where tramcars slid along to Michailovsky Square. I sat at a window in the tram, no different from women workers as grey and plain as I. Workers bent heads together as they spoke yet I was nervous as if a mark of living with a maid who served tea and dinner on gilt-edged plates and wine in crystal glasses on ormolu tables had been stamped on me. I tried to believe that the gun in my coat pocket would give me confidence but after seeing the boy shot, I was shaken. How was it that others carried on with what they did, travelled every day, seemingly oblivious to bullet-shattered houses, excrement in the streets, rubbish piles everywhere? Couples clinched together under their coats, going like rabbits in public. Beggars sat in doorways. Women who once might have been respectable had degenerated into tramps. It was nothing like the day I arrived. I heard Lyudmila's question in my head and thought again about Pärnu!

I turned from cracked, smashed shop windows and the filth of the street. I looked around the tram. I could have been a worker too, a secretary from some little business, a mother, returning from shopping on the Nevsky. Marketers still sold goods, wine shops traded with a strongman in the doorway.

I straightened Lulle's scarf around the collar of my old, dark, plum overcoat, suitable for such a night. A man with grease lining his wrinkles and pores propped his head on the window pane, jolting from his daze every now and again. Sailors lounged against the exit. One of them, Mongolian featured, stared unblinking at me. I caught his eye but instantly resolved not to look at him again.

At the Kazansky Bridge three soldiers got on, tall, fair, their features familiar. They stood further down the tram, bantering, laughing. When I got up they followed.

On the Griboedova, the dead black hulks of barges slumped together, bound in ice. Lights on the Italian bridge glimmered in the direction of the Stray Dog. I knew exactly where I had to go. The bells of the Kazan Cathedral rang eight times from the direction I expected. Lyudmila had described the location of the Stray Dog. I could get my bearings between streets and canals and memorised every turn. I anticipated hot coffee in the *Brodjachaja Sobaka*, otherwise a glass of something; wine or vodka. I'd discover the *avant-garde*, snap photos of them; listening to their ideas, their predictions in every syllable and nuance. I assumed pessimism and sooner or later, the fall of a city.

I focussed dead ahead as I walked beside the canal. On the Italian bridge, workers in soft coats and caps loitered, the red ends of their cigarettes like eyes in the dark. How could they know I was going to meet my true love? I thought of Vasily even as I longed for Mihkel. It was Mihkel who truly loved me. So I told myself. He and I were bound together even if we hadn't found the fern flower. He and I need never argue over a person's rights, an ethical dilemma. I would know the minute I saw him how united we were. Tonight I would hear the music of Anna Akhmatova's poetry. My boots slid on an icy patch of the pavement. A broad-shouldered man in a long leather coat strode toward me, looked me up and down as he approached. I jerked my head as if to warn him, that nothing would stop me. I would see Sofia Casanova again and I was eager to reunite. I'd perhaps see Esenin himself and the beautiful and wild Karsavina. I fingered my gun, ridiculously, it was very small and I had no idea if it would maim or kill a person. If I had to, I would point it at anyone who tried to stop me making my rendezvous.

The soldiers caught me up. I quickened my pace. They also.

"Going our way?" one of them said in accented Russian.

"No." I said, resisting a sideways look though movement caught my eye. A swarm of rats disappeared into the gutter.

The second soldier came to my other side. "But we're going yours."

I glanced at them, men my age, a softness about them.

"I like the scarf," the blond one said. "My sister's got one like it."

I stopped and turned. He seemed familiar. "What do you mean?"

He bobbed like a child. "You're one of us," the shorter one laughed. "Didn't mean to alarm you miss, but you're Estonian, aren't you?"

"*Ja*!"

"*Olen Võrstjärvest*," the fair bristles said.

"*Pärnust*," I said.

"*Elvast*," the heavy one said.

I giggled, rather relieved. Fine looking men. I smiled, perhaps too much. I nodded toward the café lights. "I am glad to meet you. I'm going there to meet a friend," I said looking at the Stray

Dog.

"*Noh jah*. We'll join you."

"Tell me about your battalion. Have you heard of Lars and Hardi Jõgeva?" I said.

"Maybe. Say more. We'll wait with you, all right?" The tallest one's eyes twinkled. I was appreciated and safe.

"I'm Siina Jürimäe," I began....

Garlands of flowers threaded through the handrail leading down to the café but did nothing to mask the stench of toilets. I gagged but went in with my friends, glad not to wait in a garbage littered street, the papers, spat sunflower seeds. Trees and shrubs had been cut down or destroyed. It was cold.

The roar of voices burst the moment I opened the door to Stray Dog, packed with soldiers and sailors, men in drab, moth-eaten, worn-to-threads coats, women in berets and wool caps puffing fogs of smoke around the arches of the cavern. Couples leaned heads back laughing, drained teacups of coffee and drank pineapple juice, sitting close, nose to nose. The toilet overpowered the smoke and perfume smells. Some of the women looked like prostitutes. They were the *avant-garde*? I stared, rather obviously.

"Let me buy you a drink. Wine?" the blond from Võrtsjärv offered.

The Elva soldier nudged his friend and cleared his throat. "You'll be lucky if you get vodka."

"Vodka. Anything," I agreed.

The shorter Estonian sat close to me. Friends and relatives, food and drink. Be careful I thought. Wine I could feel in my blood. Vodka I could drink till I was senseless.

"Will we drive off the Kaiser? Are we safe here? Where is

your family?" I began, excited and loud.

The Võrtsjärv soldier filled my glass. The other men looked at one another. "*Kuule*! It's all for nothing, don't you know? Thousands dying for this bloody tsar! You'd think he and the Kaiser could hammer something but they won't! They're cousins!" The soldier tapped his head to show what he meant.

At once I decided to ask no more.

"Plus, anyone can tell you lies, miss and there's gossip enough right here in the city, in this room. I'll bet you. Opinions are cheap, sweetheart." He grinned. "And there are youngsters dead keen to rush out to fight. Can't understand that myself." The dark browed Estonian tipped back his drink and flashed a disparaging look at his friend. I didn't care any longer.

"Beg your pardon if we're blunt but you asked. You don't have a brother out there, do you?" said the first soldier.

I shook my head wanting to talk about anything else, anything.

I looked around at the faces, Russians, Tatars, Georgians, unshaven, unwashed, beaten, half starved. Uniforms and workers, men who carried out orders. I loved the diversity and down-to-earthiness. I forgot Irena, Natalya, Olga and Vasily. I sipped my drink, welcoming the burning flow down my throat, the sensation all the way to my belly. My friends drank quickly though that didn't lighten their moods.

On one side of the room I caught sight of a familiar face. Sofia! "I know you," I cried out and unwedged myself from between the table and bench. "Remember me?"

Sofia slid along her booth. "Siina! Of course! Meet my friends," she said indicating the men opposite, dour and resistant, regarding me casually. And salaciously. A man with a scar on his cheek smiled intimately. Not one of them stood to take my hand.

I turned back to the luminous, Sofia. "I hoped to meet you again," I said, trying to understand her place among her friends, an older woman, practical yet stylish. I marvelled at her magnetism, her particular attraction. By the attention she had from people around her she could have drawn swarms of bees. She held a cigarette elegantly and tapped it into a filthy saucer.

"I wanted to meet you, too! Mihkel talks about you non-stop." She turned on a winner's smile. Her eyes sparkled like the crackle of a Repin oil painting. Her dark curved brows rose up or drew together. She couldn't sit still.

"I admire you," I said. "You make your way with such panache," I confessed. "You tell the world about this struggle. It's not easy, nor safe. I wish I could do that."

"Ppfft! I write for Madrid, that's hardly the world. I'm no different from you, Siina! You left your home and family, *n'est-ce-pas*? You carry a camera and you know how to use it. You see!"

I shrugged. I had come to earn a living and experience adventure as well as to find Mihkel. Of course I planned to use my camera but so far I'd been thwarted, though I did have a diamond belt. I needed to decide how to explain that to Anna. As if she'd believe the story.

"We had no choice but to flee Poland. Out of the frying pan. You see?" Sofia said blowing smoke circles overhead.

"Poland?"

"Oh yes. After Spain."

"Terrible," I agreed. The man opposite poured vodka again and motioned with his fingers for me to drink.

Sofia leaned across the table to me. "I'm determined to see what's beneath this volcano and who is actually setting it off." She winked at me and threw a sideways look at our companions.

"Are you sympathetic to socialists?" I said quietly though I couldn't be sure of the discretion of the culture here.

Sofia screwed up her face in a not-so-pretty expression. "I'm appalled and disgusted the way these Mensheviks and Social Democrats can't piece anything together. They're destroying one another when they should be building utopia. They're like children with tantrums!"

"So, you're not one of them, I mean," I lowered my voice, asking more kindly. "I heard you are sympathetic to them." I tried to appear nonchalant but Sofia's eyes flashed.

"Indeed I am, and where I'm from *privilegios de casta* demands we take our responsibilities very, very seriously."

I loved her outrage. I snapped my camera, wound spy film and snapped again. Her eyes shone.

"We approve of common decency, *mais oui*?"

"Common decency? Who does not?" I squeezed her arm. "I should love to join you on an assignment. With my camera," I said, encouraged by her enthusiasm and my glass of vodka.

Her eyebrows jerked up. "Marvellous! This week! Come!" She leaned closer. "I have a very exciting *rendezvous*."

I pressed the shutter again. Sofia… intriguing. "Certainly," I said. I noticed her attention wandering from me. Something on the other side of the room.

"Don't dare look now!" she warned so I immediately twisted my head around to see a man in the doorway, unruly beard, Persian lamb-skin collar on a heavy wool coat. Our eyes met. Mihkel beamed.

For a moment I imagined Vasily without braiding and pomade but in a worn, dark coat and workers' hat. He'd have stood above everyone, grand, charismatic, speaking socialism.

Mihkel gazed at me even as he barged through the crowd,

stopped briefly at the Estonians, embraced a friend, another, ripped off his gloves and reached around my waist and quite openly kissed me. “You came! I was worried about you. Perhaps I should have come....”

I touched his hand. “No need.”

He trapped me in an embrace, a different man from the one at the Mariinski.

“And I worry about you,” I said.

“I’m all right. We’re both here, aren’t we?” His face darkened. “Though my friends go to die.” I realized he’d not greeted Sofia. “But see, she’s here too. Akhmatova. She’ll read, I’m sure.” Mihkel nodded at Sofia and she to him as we looked toward a tall thin woman with the famous bent nose and astonishing eyes who was seated several tables away.

Mihkel took my fingers and kissed them, there before all those people. He spoke in my ear. “Listen – you see here, Tamara Karsavina danced on this table,” he grinned. “On a mirror.” His fingers tightening around mine.

“You saw it?”

He opened his hands nonchalantly. “I saw nothing! More’s the pity, but I heard the uproar,” he laughed.

I shrank. Did he expect me to be that sort of seductress and entertainer?

Akhmatova was leaning on her elbow in deep conversation with the man beside her, the poet, Nikolai Gumilyov. Her glossy, bobbed hair hung over her eyes, her scarf draped around her shoulders, Bohemian style. She was the same age as me to the day. So it was possible to achieve that much, so young. But I’d also begun my collection.

“She’s radiant,” I whispered to Mihkel who was sitting back to admire her.

“Yes! She stands for justice and equality, women doing what men do; free love, Kollontai’s ideals.” He smiled indecently at me. “And she detests Bolsheviks.”

“I too!” I said, heartened to hear that. Akhmatova got to her feet, rearranged her scarf and began.

"I heard a voice. It called, consoling,
It said to me: “Come hither, now.
Abandon your forsaken, sinful land,
Abandon Russia, leave forever.
And from your hands I’ll wash the blood,
I’ll draw the black shame from your heart,
And with a new name I will cloak
The wounds of misery and loss."

Her voice was soft and unassuming and at first I thought of my sister Anna except that Akhmatova’s tone was gentle while still powerful, not forced, not dramatic. Everyone in the room gave her power and she drew it into herself then gave it back. I felt it, a charge through the entire audience, simply being in the room with an extraordinary artist.

When I heard *Abandon your forsaken, sinful land,*

Abandon Russia, leave forever, I wanted to both go, and stay. It seemed too easy to go, yet the *wounds of misery and loss* were pain I didn’t wish to know. She summed up what many of us thought but could never articulate. She was both reassuring and depressing, confirming our doom and the sense of disaster I had felt from the day I arrived, even if I denied it.

Mihkel reached for my hand and spoke with his eyes. “We’re in it, Siina, loathe, fear, or welcome it.”

A pause, glasses chinked and low voices resumed.

I reached across to Sofia and shook her hand. "Call my number. Say you're from Pärnu, please. Anyway, I don't care what they say, don't forget me! Morskaya 965."

Sofia nodded, her eyes eager and agreeing. I couldn't wait to see her work, and to meet people who would look directly in my lens. I had a chance to ask opinions and my photographs could go to *Postimees* and *Teataja* who were bound to publish. People would learn who was responsible for the suffering and what we stood to lose.

Outside the Stray Dog, Mihkel wrapped his arms around me. Snow blew around the corners of the dark city buildings and over the cobbled plaza. The wind whisked the stink away from the Stray Dog.

"Let's walk," Mihkel said. "Come to my house, for a while."

It was late and somehow I had to get home though Mihkel was persuasive. I'd seen him so little I hated to say goodbye. Besides, I wondered how long I would be in the city, how long anyone would stay when they had the chance to leave. I felt rather carefree as well, warmed by the drink, and secure with Mihkel who was eager for me. I couldn't go back just yet. The Kazan bells rang two.

"I'll show you how I live. It's not so far," he said. Earlier he had seemed tired but now in the cool air he was alive. "I share with a Latvian in a fine old building. He's never home you know. I see him when he's asleep," Mihkel grinned. We walked to the end of the building where a queue had formed. People simply joined queues without asking why. We turned off and hurried by. The stairs went up three floors to his room.

The room was small and Spartan, far smaller than mine on Bolshaya Morskaya.

Mihkel laid my coat and hat over a chair and poured vodka

into a stained cup. I glanced around the loaded book shelves to a desk piled with papers and a bed littered with notebooks, handwritten pages and boxes of pamphlets.

"Printing press under a blanket?" I smiled. He didn't.

"I'm not so suicidal, Siina. Come, sit." He patted the bed.

"Researching," I asked. "Tell me, please. What do you do? I hardly know you. Except that you said you're an ideas man. What does that mean?"

"Oh god!" He flopped back on the bed and lay stretched amongst his papers. "A dissertation? God's truth, where to begin." The spines of Marx and Hegel, Kant and Lunacharsky lined his shelves.

"Are you Bolshevik? Something else?"

"Honestly I can't say." His eyes were closed. I'd not have been surprised if he'd fallen asleep right away. "Look Siina, Social Democrats are not legal so since I don't fancy the police on my doorstep, I'm practical. But as you ask, every group has some merit, and any number of drastic flaws! Who would want to be idealistic? And the people driving the factions – good god! They're mad, while others are merely almost mad. Mind you, there are some completely brilliant, but hopelessly, impossibly impractical! Or without charisma…you see? A mess! The entire movement has such a dream but how to…?"

I nodded. I was interested and I'd have loved to fathom the specifics of each group, what they stood for and how far apart were the ideals, but I'd meant to find something concrete about my true love! "You've told me nothing about you," I interrupted.

Mihkel raised his head and looked at me. "You know, I've had a few too many political meetings this week. Can we talk about your dresses or the opera? What plays you've been to? Please? "

I wriggled on the bed. "I hardly know what you think and I

want to. I want to know what you believe. I wonder about you. What does *he* think? What is *he* doing? It's what I think about!"

"Really? Well, let me tell you about today. I feel like running away from it all. I do think that once in a while. Run very fast." His eyes were tired. He dropped his head to his chest. "The mob mentality is stupid but I must do something. With you, Siina, I feel mighty! I can deal with anything, thinking you'll be here. Even when I don't see you."

He played his fingers along my thigh and I felt the warm delight. The sort of hero-worship I'd pitched at Juhan. I wanted to lay down and look at him, like a cat, have my belly scratched and stroked. "I want to know that you're a good, kind man."

"I am," he said though his hand didn't yet reach for my hem.

"And you still want the fern flower?"

"We better go back for it. I want it. Though you're like spring to me. You lift my spirits to stork nests. Think of the view from there, from some raggedy twisted nest, all the way down to the river." His breathing deepened as if he might fall asleep.

I smiled to myself with the effect. "I've hardly seen you," I said gloomily. I'd seen Vasily. And been with him.

"You make sense to me. You fill my dreams," Mihkel said sleepily.

I lay beside him. He rolled toward me and wrapped his arms around me. "You make me certain of everything."

"You too," I lied.

"Can you love me? Do you think?" He sat up, reached over me and stroked my face, my neck. He fingered the top button of my blouse hesitantly.

I had every right to please myself yet I agonised. I'd done wrong.

"You're thoughtful and intelligent. I love that. You're lovely.

Do care about me?"

I hugged him, wishing to absorb him.

"Be with me. I'm incomplete."

"Though you'll stay here."

"A little longer." He held a hand to his head, eyes closed.

"Such awful things go on in the name of equality." I was thinking of the factory boss tied to a chair. "Men are so cruel in the name of freedom."

He shook his head. "I know, I know!"

"Though it's your position and ideal…"

"No." He squeezed his eyes closed.

"You said you were in here." I tapped my forehead. "You'd never let such a thing happen?"

"Could I stop it? We're not animals, Siina. We're reaching for something. I must do what I believe. There are costs."

I lay back smelling his sweat, familiar and reassuring. "I want to stay too," I said as the fortress bells of the Peter and Paul prison rang three.

"I believe we can do something. I'm not here for the madness of war."

"But you'd not want Russia to lose?"

He laid his head on my breast. "It would mean a chance for the Internationale."

"You could be shot for that today."

"With half of Petrograd? Better to be lynched for something decent."

I murmured agreement.

Mihkel lifted his head. "So should I ask about Vasily?"

"Oh no. There's nothing," I smiled wishing there was not.

"So we forget all that?" he asked, his breath, alcohol.

"Do revolutionaries have children?"

"When they find partners."

"For a better world?"

"Absolutely."

"Yet they don't believe in marriage."

"Marriage is good."

"And fidelity?"

"For me. Certainly. Yes."

"I've not really decided how to live," I admitted.

"But you have your camera," he said and I felt a surge of happiness as if everything could be solved and as my head swam I wanted to plunge headlong into a river, naked so I could feel every sensation possible, the deep Metsajärve water, the tide at Pärnu beach could rush through me.

"Because we jumped the fire," he said in my ear.

I tasted wild mushrooms on his moustache and strawberries on his tongue. I closed my eyes and smelled summer woods and saw streams in sunlight and felt long wet grass under me, somewhere near home.

34. The Tauride Palace

It was Lyudmila tapping on my door whilst I was still trapped between sleeping and waking, floating, dreaming, before reality murdered bliss. A rap, rap, rap but not the normal touch. Somehow muted with long pauses.

I crawled from my bed. Lyudmila, a finger to her lips, pushed me back in my room. "What …?"

"*Fräulein*!" her eyes popped. "Get yourself ready. There's someone here for you. Go!"

I rubbed my eyes. "Lyudmila … ?"

"Your man. Downstairs. Creep out now before they're up."

My heart pounded. Lyudmila was never one to fuss.

I glanced outside. The street was snowy, the sky overcast, a grey March day. I fossicked in my tallboy for underwear. "It's Mihkel, yes?"

"Go," she whispered.

"What's he's thinking. *Jummal*!"

"He said to hurry."

"But the children!"

Lyudmila looked sheepish. "They're busy helping me pack, *Fräulein*."

"Pack? Why? Where are we going?"

She avoided my eye. "We. *Fräulein*. We've been packing for days, all the children's things."

"For god's sake, why?"

She covered her face with one hand.

"You're all going somewhere?"

Lyudmila glanced over her shoulder. "The other side of the

Urals, *Fräulein*, as soon as we're ready."

I held her by her shoulders. "Gostilitsy?"

"Oh no. Further. Further. We're packing the heaviest clothes."

I rummaged angrily through woollen stockings and underwear.

"I'm sorry."

I buttoned my skirt. I couldn't blame her. "Because the tsar abdicated? Is that it?"

She nodded vigorously. "And because the military is taking orders from the workers! Everyone's leaving. You must know! Selling jewellery and the most beautiful priceless furniture though it's rather late for that; you get nothing. They're going to Sweden and France, anywhere. Use the kitchen door, *Fräulein*. He's out there."

I tugged on another layer, my boots, and buttoned my jacket.

"And not to forget your camera." She opened the door.

I crammed on a hat and tucked my camera in my pocket.

"*Voilà! Je suis prête*," I smiled.

"Oh, but *Fräulein* …"

"*Oui*?"

"You have a travel pass?"

I paused in the doorway. "No I don't!"

Lyudmila peered both ways down the hall. "He has one in his desk," she whispered. "I saw it. Better not go on any protest march. Hear!"

"Oh come on."

"Only, after last month's horrors…. Mensheviks! They goad their workers on. Please, *Fräulein*, you never know who the troops will shoot next."

"I've no idea where I'm going!"

Lyudmila gave me a push. "So if you're going, go!"

The Tauride Palace

A droshky waited across the street. “Siina!” I heard.

A man in a civilian overcoat with a Persian lamb collar leapt from the droshky and stood for a moment on the high granite curb.

“Mihkel! You’re crazy!” I said before he grabbed me and without a thought we were hugging. The moment we were in the droshky we were kissing.

“Come.” He dragged himself from me and to the driver called, “Tauride Palace,” but without the blow on the *isvotchik’s* back the way Vasily would have done.

“Tauride Palace? Oh! The Provisional Government? Sofia has an interview and I’m taking photos? I don’t have a good camera. Only this little spy thing! Damn!”

“It’s not that.”

More likely, I considered it would be a demonstration even though the police were turning on one another, joining revolutionaries or royalists. Demonstrations were suicidal. I knew that as well as Lyudmila.

The driver whistled. The cobbles ground away beneath us.

Mihkel shook his head. “Estonians are demanding home rule. You didn’t know? Really? Where have you been?” He waggled his finger reprimanding.

“I do want photos!”

“Stop.” He pushed a brown package at me.

“What?” I began unwrapping. The feel and shape of a camera. Where? How?”

“Never mind! People come and go from my place. Who knows who they are and why they leave things behind!”

An Afco…a beautiful new one. I opened the case and unfolded the bellow lens and its little stand. “But film?” I didn’t dare hope.

"In the bottom of the bag, *tibukene*." He grinned. "Tartu, Tallinn and Pärnu papers want photos. Wherever you can sell them. You decide!"

"How? Mihkel! But listen. Lyudmila told me something."

He pushed his cap back from his hair. "Go on. But I have something to ask."

Cossacks passed us, cantering across the bridge to the Vyborg side.

"Imagine," he held my hand, "Cossacks disobeying their sovereign!"

"Their own laws."

So, they'd been convinced they should support the workers. They rode through crowds, whips stowed, smiling, winking, protecting the revolutionaries.

"But you had something else to tell me?"

"I do. I'm going back to Tartu. Come! We're about to make massive strides at home. We must be prepared. They need us. I must go. Immediately! What were you going to say …?"

"Olga and Vasily, all of them are leaving without me."

He held my waist. The roar of music, the hordes of people surging was deafening.

"What!"

I reached for his ear. "They're going! Getting out! Olga and Vasily. All of them!" I shouted, my voice cracking, upset they were abandoning me. "You think they know about us?"

Mihkel spoke into my ear. "His business to know. Probably filed papers. Don't worry. They won't get a chance."

I jutted my chin. "That's it?"

"You have a travel pass?"

I nodded; planning how I'd steal into Vasily's study and snatch it. Whatever he'd said before, I couldn't trust him now.

Nor Olga.

"Of course I'll come. I need to be back for Anna's baby," I said, though a ball of anger stuck in my chest while Mihkel held my hand, kissing it, oblivious to what I might be feeling.

The closer we came to the Tauride Palace the thicker the crowds. Fair men and women waved blue, black and white flags. Bands pumped rousing songs. A boy beat a drum as the fervour built, the sound of Estonian all around. A motley platoon of shabby workers in expropriated army jackets and caps guarded the colonnaded front of the Tauride Palace. A garrison marched in formation.

"Thousands!" Mihkel said, elation brimming.

Uniformed men, workers of all kinds, clerks and businessmen, women like me, workers from mills and factories stood together.

"We have work ahead," Mihkel said.

"So, let's go," I said.

He pulled me close as a worker in grey tatters slapped him on the back. "*Kaaslane*! *Tere*, Mihkel!" Mihkel answered with the same fire. Others waved. "Didn't happen overnight, did it? Been waiting years. You know it don't you? Jaan Poska, back and forth like a rubber band, meeting, demanding, negotiating. He'll be commissar, you'll see, and we'll get what we want!" Mihkel flooded with emotion.

When the national song began I realized it was the moment. I untucked the new camera. Men and women wiped tears, men's bearing was proud, their look, overwhelmed. It was cold and grey for a spring day and the light was dull but I recorded it. I glanced back and forth to the ranks of police and guards, a peaceful crowd with neither madmen nor rioters carrying our message to the Provisional Government.

Women held one another around the waists; men took their

hats off to sing. I clicked, turned my lens on Mihkel's face, intense, nostrils flaring, eyes burning, his every nerve reaching toward the thing we believed in.

35. Flight

I had to leave behind my books, clothes and shoes. My room was stripped, walls and shelves bare. I set my bags down beside the door.

"Take what you want," I said pointing out the box to Lyudmila. Galoshes and talcum powder, preserves and dried herbs I'd brought but hardly used. I dared not risk taking them now. There was no way to know, but at any time I might need to run with all my belongings. My spy camera was packed with unexposed film and photos, my diamond belt held together with a variety of knots around my waist, the beautiful unexpected Afco from Mihkel with new rolls of film, tucked inside my carpet bag.

"This is for you," I said giving Lyudmila a photograph of the beach in Pärnu with Anna and Kristjaan snuggled together on a rug on the sand. It was one of my first shots.

Lyudmila hugged me and I fancied she sniffed. "You have your pass, *Fräulein*?"

"I don't," I admitted, continuing to fold underwear and socks. I wrote a note to Grunya and put them together. I left my boots for Duscha.

Lyudmila gasped. "But no! There's no one about, *Fräulein*. Vasily Feodorov left yesterday for the front."

"What!"

"He never told you?"

"Not exactly," I recovered, but Lyudmila had caught me and was kind enough not to show it. "Get it now," she whispered.

I placed my bags inside the front door ready for a hasty departure should I need it.

Lyudmila watched with approval. The walls of the drawing room were denuded; icon niches empty, paintings, statues, armour and candelabra were gone. I looked back along the hall and up the stairs. The children's voices upstairs, but no other sound. I turned the door handle to Vasily's study.

Olga, in her dark green, velvet dressing gown, her hair in a cotton cap, skin the colour of oats, sat behind Vasily's desk. She looked up as if she'd been expecting me. "*Fräulein*, my dear," she said, the smile of an angel.

For the briefest moment I considered spinning a long tale that I had come looking for her with some question but her expression told me not to.

She leaned back in Vasily's chair, her hands clasped loosely on the desk. "I must tell you, everything is arranged. We're leaving today and you must go home, or to friends, wherever you can." She held the pass. "You'll need this."

I felt as light as gulls' wings. I couldn't believe how easy this was. "You're all leaving..." I began.

Olga nodded. "In fact Vasily Andrevich has had to leave already but we will find our way. But we have friends and contacts everywhere, of course. We will soon unite." She gave me a look that dared me to think I had any possible influence. I felt entirely helpless and unwanted.

"I beg your pardon, but your husband suggested some months ago that should I need it, he would supply me with a travel pass … if perhaps I should need it..."

"Do not explain." Olga raised her hand and moved from behind the desk. She draped herself on the sofa beside the Amour. Her mouth was pinched, the skin beneath her eyes puffed, but she remained the Meissen nymph, fragile and brittle and now, as she scrutinised me I was unable to dismiss my shame and guilt. My betrayal of her. I felt her reading me. Why had she given me the transparent blouse? How easily had I been manipulated. "Who would have guessed so many of our police would go over to the revolutionaries, *Fräulein*? Did you? Even the Cossacks. I'm astounded," she said, pressed her lips together and continued to observe me as I felt myself wither. She was assured and pointed even though she'd made no accusation. I was being lowered into a trap and I was, without a doubt, guilty. At least, I reflected, I'd been honest with her earlier. We'd spoken honestly about our positions.

"I had no idea. I'm shocked at every step the revolutionaries take but I don't know so much, Olga Pyotrovna. I read the newspapers and listen to gossip but I hardly speak to anyone knowledgeable."

"Hmmm," was her reply as she turned on her hip, lofted her feet onto the footstool and held my travel document in her hand like a handkerchief. "I ought to trust you, *Fräulein*. You've been straightforward in the past and I give credit to my instincts, but Mihkel Oks' name pops up in too many questionable places. We can't trust him so it would be convenient to know where he is. For your own good. For your safe travel."

I felt as transparent as blown glass.

"So here it is, *Fräulein*. Your passage home in exchange for his whereabouts."

My backbone prickled. I shifted on my feet unable to process a single thought.

"I don't see him. I'm going home for my sister, Olga Pyotrovna."

"Really?" She narrowed her eyes. Her lips thinned.

I nodded, swallowing my words. "I came to get the pass. I have no idea where Mihkel is. I must go to my sister."

Olga dangled the document. "He's dangerous, *Fräulein*. Has he seduced you with lies that he's a patriot? Do you have any idea how dangerous such men are to us? They find their way you see. He has."

How could she know more than I? She stared coolly and persuasively. I pictured his face and the sound of his voice, his evasiveness, his promises to explain more later, that all would be revealed, but not yet. That it was dangerous to know too much now. "I don't know. Please. Give me the pass. I'll not trouble you a moment longer. I'll be gone. I haven't the least idea where he is or what he's doing. He interviews people and writes articles. What harm can he do?"

Olga tilted her head and drifted toward me, tottering slightly. "I believe that you know precisely where he lives."

"No." I shook my head but even so, I felt trapped.

Olga folded up the pass and slid it in her pocket. "Pity."

I glanced around the room. In one pocket I had my camera, in the other I fingered my tiny gold Kolibri. I drew it out. I raised it at Olga's face. "Give me my pass."

Her eyes blinked rapidly. She stifled surprise. "How dare you! You'd never use that silly little gun. What is it, a toy? Besides, you're no murderer!" She wobbled. Her mouth twitched. "Timur!" she screamed.

I inched closer. "I must go home. I can't tell you where Mihkel is. If I have to shoot you it's part of this whole disastrous calamity," I croaked. Olga held her hand over her pocket, stared back at me regaining her poise and breath.

"Timur! Here!" she screeched and backed away, step by slow step. "You are perfectly capable of finding your way home," she enunciated pedantically. "Brutality has become everyday fare and no one can be trusted. No one. I must take care of my family just as you must yours. Timur!"

My hand trembled uncontrollably. I'd never fired the gun but I followed Olga's steps, the tiny Kolibri shaking. "Give me the document," I whispered, losing my voice, my fingers twitching. Pop!

Olga leapt, hands to her face, blood trickling down one cheek. She looked at the blood. The document fell to the floor. I gaped at her, horror-stricken. "Oh god, oh god! I'm so sorry!" I ducked for the document, clutched it to my chest, and fled.

"Timur!" Olga screamed as I ran. "Murder!"

I snatched up my carpet bag from the hall, tore open the door and jumped down the steps three at a time.

Timur was bent double on the pavement over his Orlovs still in harness, their carriage tipped over. The horses were collapsed, all three of them, disembowelled, the stench of their innards and blood striking me like a blow. I gagged, covered my face and froze beside him. Tears streamed down his bloody, craggy face.

"Timur! Oh Timur!" I shuddered, my hand over my mouth as vomit grabbed my throat. "Who could do this?" I gagged, murmured to him, words muddled as tears flooded. Another scream came from upstairs. I hesitated, turned to Timur to reach out to him but he was convulsed with grief. I had to keep running.

I set my bag down on the train platform between my feet. My spy camera lay in the top of my carpet bag with my travel pass tucked in the side. In my coat pocket I fingered my dangerous Kolibri.

Thousands were fleeing Peterburg. Anyone with any means was finding a way to escape starvation or massacre. Riots and bloodshed, looting and robberies, opened prisons, and above all, fighting between Soviets and Bolsheviks, Lenin's war cry rousing people to seize what they needed, would very soon destroy the city.

The Nicholas Station boiled with bodies, desperate, distressed families waiting as carriages disgorged the wounded, Red Cross nurses, angels of mercy, lined up to receive them. My camera offered no comfort to wounded men but one day my pictures would count for something. People would not be able to deny the horrors.

A man with bandages over his face, blood dried though fresh was leaking, didn't need to know. I snapped. A boy, whose eyes rolled in his head, unable to faint though surely willing himself to, reached up to me. I laid a hand on his arm. "You'll be all right. You're very brave. Look, the nurses are here," I said and framed him, a young hero.

I stepped up to a man on a stretcher, his trouser legs tucked under him and what was left, blood cake. I wanted to run and least of all look at where the legs should have been. "I'm alive, darling. Can I take you for a beer?" His head waggled with a crazed smile.

I managed a kindly smile before I lined him up for a full body shot. "Not a beer, sorry, but I can take your picture. Do you mind?"

"Go ahead," he gestured. "Only don't you go out there, will you?" His look turned sour. "It's a hell, a bloody, horrific hell."

I stood dwarfed by the massive, dark iron train, the wheels shoulder high, empty cattle cars behind waiting for a fresh load of men for the front. Women in head scarves, men in pantaloons with wide belts, country people, waited. Porters in white aprons, barrowed and hefted. Mihkel was nowhere. Women in hats, a feather here a veil there, grey and mousy unlike a year ago, no one preening or flashing. A year ago Brusilov had convinced

Russians they would win the war. Another campaign like his was all they needed.

I looked back along the platform, my arm quivering, ready to wave at Mihkel. Olga and Vasily were wrong. Ksenia too. He was no leader of rabble and revolutionaries. I agonised over Olga. I'd shot her in the face, her limpid, sad eyes, blinded. I couldn't have, I argued with myself. The Kolibri's bite was like a mosquito I'd heard.

Steam billowed. The train hissed and groaned. I was sick with panic. I scanned up and down the platform. Minutes ticked. If I saw him I'd burst through the soldiers with carbines over their shoulders, bright-yellow cartridge pouches packed with bullets. I'd fight my way between officers' brass buttoned coats and maroon-frocked secret police. If only he would come in the very next minute. My heart thumped. My hands sweated. I climbed aboard. The train whistle shrilled, pain shooting through me.

Buy your ticket, I'll get mine, he had said on the phone and now, now it made sense. Only now, I wished I'd argued we should meet sooner. Get aboard, I'll be there. I'll be there, even if I have to race the train. Trust me, get aboard. We have to leave, he'd said. So, he'd arrive at the final second. That was him. I forced the carriage window open. I leaned out as a head of steam let loose its blast. The guard stepped back, assessed the carriages, held his flag up and flourished it. Someone's pocket watch chimed the hour. Doors slammed. The guard's whistle shrilled. Carriages jolted at the couplings.

I hung out the window unable to feel abandoned, but as we creaked and nudged into motion I stilled myself, ready to accept whatever lay ahead. Olga had been wounded, had sent the police to arrest Mihkel, I decided. She'd discovered his address and marched him off to the Peter and Paul fortress. If he survived there it would be a miracle. I longed for a miracle. I hugged my carpet bag and allowed myself to drift in grief.

36. *Vabadus*

I never expected to sleep but in the end I did so, dreaming frightful dreams of a guard standing over me, demanding my pass. I put my pistol to his head and clutched my spy camera bag. When I looked for my pass it had gone. I tore seams open with my teeth and fingernails as the guard came closer, his red bulbous nose in my face shouting for me to get into the next carriage and lie beside a dead man.

I stirred when the train pulled in to Yamburgh station at the ancient fortress town on the river Luga, twenty *versts* from the port city of Narva. A knot of pain filled my stomach. Mihkel had deserted me or worse, had been captured by the Cheka. I was almost home. While he was a prisoner. To the west of the Narva River I would hear Estonian again, transfer to another train and head south for Tartu and Anna. She would be thrilled to see me. I would throw my arms around her neck and hold her and not let go.

I dozed. I woke. Pärnu could not have changed but Jaan Poska was to be appointed governor of Estonia since the Tauride Palace rally. My photos of that day could have been published. I would have work.

I was desperate to get to Tartu, then Pärnu. After Petrograd our small towns were familiar and more wonderful than any number of Nevsky Prospekts. I kept control of my thoughts. I resisted checking my diamond belt and the knots.

I couldn't guess how Mihkel would survive. Deprivation. Starvation. Torture. He seemed insubstantial unless he was declaring himself. He was entirely self-possessed. Perhaps he was sitting on the train ahead or even in another carriage of my train. Or Olga had called the police who found him and locked in the Lubyanka. She'd sent them after me for robbery and attempted murder. Preposterous! A noblewoman pursuing an employee over a graze from a bullet? Perhaps not. The police would not possibly bother. Unless Olga had been seriously hurt. They'd hound me all the way home. There was chaos everywhere. There were far more important issues for the police. I'd disappear like so many others had. Loyalties in Petrograd bounced like tennis balls, from one far end of a court to the other. Everyone was obliged to alter his allegiance several times a day.

If only Mihkel were to show! The ache in my heart would cease. I'd close my eyes and dream of how we would live together. If only I could see him again!

I opened my Aino Kallas novel and lowered my head. The guards did come, twice, to check my pass. Once past Narva, soon, I could sink back and breathe, although there was nowhere safe from the Cheka.

If Mihkel was right about Lenin coming to Petrograd any day and if Stalin had returned, if political prisoners were released with criminals, the city would go berserk. Anna's and my beliefs were not so far apart. I dreaded Bolshevik power but I was glad to see the tsar's end. His reign had been hideous. I dreamt that Anna and Mihkel agreed that the two people I most cared for became friends.

I shifted on the hard wooden seat feeling my bones. I closed my eyes as the locomotive built steam and the wheels gained traction. I sent Mihkel strength. I prayed he'd been lost only in his writing.

"The Russians are retreating," I overheard from the man with the chiming pocket watch. Outside a *mêlée* more chaotic than in

Petrograd erupted. Someone entered the carriage, someone with a meandering step leaned against me as if the carriage was that crowded. I opened my eyes.

"I told you I would come," he growled, kissed me on the lips and drew back. His eyes clouded, his mouth grim.

"Are you all right?" I whispered, wary of rejoicing.

He took my hand and smiled with sagging eyes. "I came to say goodbye."

"What? What?" I stared into his grey eyes wanting to kiss him and lay my head on his chest but in his face was a permanent goodbye. He nodded to the door. A guard stood on the other side, arms folded over his chest.

Mihkel kissed my cheeks and forehead, then my lips. He squeezed my hand. "I can say goodbye, nothing more."

"But why!" I snatched at him. "Why!" I leapt up.

"They don't like me. I've done nothing wrong, nothing specific. It's the tone of my writing. Nothing I can do about it, *kullakene*. I could try to escape of course but they'd like that, and I'd be sure of a bullet in the back. I won't make it that easy. But who knows, I may even talk my way out of it." He smiled, but only with his mouth. "People survive. You can't know what can happen. They release people on a whim, if they've had warm *kasha*. On a good day."

"No!" I grabbed his sleeve and held on. "Don't say it!"

"I failed you," he said, his eyes showing the fear of an animal bound for slaughter. "I was afraid they were waiting in Petrograd but not here, not this far off."

"Because of me?"

He looked at the floor. "I've seen you. Lucky me. I can live by it now."

I couldn't believe any of it. I glowered at the guard at the compartment door whose eyes never left us no matter how we kissed or whispered. The carriage swayed as we raced across marshland. “No,” I objected remembering Granny’s words: *Those who lose their way in the boglands forget what it is to see the sun. They become lonely and godless and lose hope and no longer dream. They forget what it is to be human. They become libahundid.*

“I will not lose hope because there is a chance.”

“Yes,” he encouraged, smiling his lopsided smile while I saw the dark sunless places they’d take him; cold, windblown deserts of prisoners.

“I’ll come too.”

He shook his head, eyes glistening. “Oh no. Wait here, that way I’ll survive.”

“But I could be with you,” I begged. He smiled, smoothed my forehead and forced a weak laugh. “You’d really do that?”

I nodded.

“But you can be here doing what I can’t. There’ll be bleak days, Siina. Take your own advice and don’t give up. You’ll see; there’ll be something great ahead.”

I couldn’t look into his face. I wanted to reject everything he’d explained, pretending we could go backwards and really escape.

“The Bolsheviks are in chaos. No one can agree. Lenin didn’t believe he’d see a revolution but *Eesti*, oh we’ll do something.”

“I love you desperately.”

He looked into my eyes his face bright with surprise. “Good,” he said and gently kissed me again. “So we’re meant for one another,” he said as the door blasted open.

“Going!” the policeman barked. “Now!”

Mihkel kissed me one more time, our hands fast together. “Trust me, whatever, from whomever you hear anything. Be brave. Don't listen to gossip." He released my hands and turned for the door.

I held on. "One thing," I called, the guard glaring but uncomprehending. "Keep this for me," I said and slipped my mother's cameo in his fist and without looking he buried it in his pocket. Two men grabbed him under the armpits and marched him out. I slumped on the wooden seat, held my breath, then wept. I saw from the carriage window how they dragged him away. I wiped my face but through my tears watched him, limp as a weed, dragging his boots in the Narva dust.

As our train gathered speed I saw him struggle and relax. In the moments before I lost sight of him, a car loaded with armed men careered around a corner spraying bullets. Gunfire ripped through the mass of guards under the headquarters' portico. Police raised revolvers with both hands, others dropped like stones. Mihkel ran, dodging bullets, pounding between iron shacks and stone walls, guns blazing at him but he kept running until he disappeared.

37. Lars Tartu

I found my way through the crowd straggling from the train as it shrieked its departing whistle. On the platform soldiers greeted families, a woman inseparably clinched to her man, a child, fur bonnet flapping over her shoulders shouted “Papa! Papa!” rushing at him until he swept her up and hugged her tight.

The last carriage of my train shrank into the powdery distance, the tracks disappearing like a mirage.

Relief to be home, to hear my language, see familiar fair, solemn features, striped stockings and lace scarves clashed hard against my misery. Even so, I could breathe deeply, feel the cool Tartu air on my skin and vow that I would be equal to whatever lay ahead.

On the opposite side of the station bare trees lined Maarjamöisa *tänav* leading to the town and the river, Emajögi. Snow danced above the cobbled road. Figures faded into milky shadows. I smelled my childhood in the winter earth. I had nowhere to stay.

If just one trusted soul offered me a place to rest my head I’d collapse into dreamless sleep. I thumbed through pages of my address book. There on the back of an envelope in Mama’s neat Gothic script I read; “Aksel Piim, 22 Veski *tänav*, Tartu.” Dear, dear cousin Aksel! The last time we met he was a thin boy, far better at music and languages than me. He would never remember me, a little girl, unhappy and withdrawn at my mother’s funeral. Although, I allowed myself to imagine the warmth of his stove and the taste of creamed mushrooms and onions. He would certainly have a room, a bed with linen smelling of lemons, a soft quilt and a down-filled pillow.

Veski Street was only minutes away. I could be there before it was completely dark.

If Mihkel was free I wanted to wait for him here. But I had promised Anna I would be with her when her baby came in Pärnu. She'd been relieved to hear I would be there. Oskar was far off saving lives and dressing ugly war wounds. So much for the war that Anna predicted to be over! I needed to decide what to do. Tomorrow. Tomorrow I would think.

Light glowed from windows along Maarjamöisa. An old man limped ahead of me when I turned into Veski. A dog barked from behind a wooden fence.

Mihkel could be on a goods' train under sacks of chaff, or jammed in the back of a truck between sheep and cows. He was resourceful. He would know how to escape. I marched on briskly, gripping my bags firmly. Two men in a doorway called out something I didn't understand. I prayed for someone to be home at number 22 and that we would know one another.

"Siina Jürimäe." Aksel Piim's face creased and his eyes widened behind small, wire-framed glasses that glinted in the light of the doorway. He seemed older than I expected. Perhaps he was tired or unwell. He held a cigarette between his teeth and a wet wooden spoon dangled from his fingers. I quickly explained from where I'd come, and how. He listened in a detached way and stood aside. "Come in, come in," he murmured closing the door.

Warm air and the aroma of buttery fried onions wafted from a further room.

"Stay as long as you like," Aksel said immediately, directing me through the house. I expected that his mother would have hung the bleached landscape paintings that matched the worn rugs. "We don't stand on ceremony here, Siina. We all know how things are, don't we?" At the far end of the hall he showed me a tidy room with a narrow bed and a puffed pillow. "My mother's," he said removing his cigarette daintily between thumb and forefinger. "Doesn't approve of a man taking a few drinks."

I set my bags down, ducked to look in a mirror, and to my alarm, saw how wretched I was. Had I been less than polite I'd have toppled into the bed. "Tea or dandelion wine?" Aksel asked as we came into the sitting room.

I sank thankfully into a low uncomfortably sprung chair. "Wine, please," I said.

Aksel squashed his cigarette into a sooty glass dish and leaned cautiously back into a leather sofa. "How was it? What exactly were you doing? Why so breathless and anxious, Siina?"

"Anxious? You would be if you'd been in Peterburg! I can tell you, I'm very relieved to be home."

"Exactly why I never went there, you see." He smirked. "But you must eat. You're wrecked." He brought me mushrooms and wine and we toasted one another. I finished off the food too quickly to taste it. I was very tired but Aksel was kind and I could not excuse myself just yet. Behind him I saw the kitchen bench stacked with dishes, potato peelings, egg shells and newspapers. I ought to have helped but still, I sensed that I was welcome. Mama and Lulle had always spoken of Aksel with admiration, a poet, a composer, a pianist but in asides, they whispered that he was a pathetic alcoholic.

"I tutored little aristocrats," I said sipping my wine. "The tsar's young cousins."

Aksel was smiling. "Indeed. Just as I heard."

"An education for me," I said remembering Gostilitsy, the towers and lace chapel, the forests and *versts* of lakes and meadows, the opera and Akhmatova. "I saw unforgettable scenery and met astonishing people. I have photos of spires and hoar-frosted nostrils of Orlovs. I have Akhmatova and Chaliapin," I said rather satisfied with myself until Mihkel appeared amongst the images once more racing and disappearing down an alley.

"Indeed. But sad too," Aksel said noticing my mood change.

"I lost touch with my friend. Mihkel Oks..."

"Is that so?"

I lowered my eyes tears dripped. "It is so. And I should love to stay here because this is where he'd return but I must go home to Pärnu. For Anna's baby."

"Ah, the lovely Anna." Aksel topped up his drink. "Who's her leading man these days?" He threw me a mischievous look.

"Dr. Oskar is at the front, Aksel. Somewhere," I said searching for a handkerchief.

"Poor dear girl," Aksel said and sank deeper into the creaking leather.

"So you know what's happening here, I don't," I said after another sip and a pause.

Aksel nodded. "Of course. But you must have heard. Frightening where you've been, of course but astonishing too, I'm sure as much as ever! Peterburg, and you feasting and cavorting with the privileged. What would you care about us?" he said, again mischievously.

"I did care! I do care!"

"Well, I question what you've been doing although you will have had a wonderful time. Nothing too good for the owners of Russia, or you."

I'd never again see such extravagance and hopefully, never such poverty and rage. "Of course it was excessive. Crimean wines, cherry sauces, profiterole mountains. I'm glad in some ways," I said but trailed off and sucked at my fork for the mushroom taste. "Thank you, Aksel. This was more wonderful than anything I remember."

Aksel raised an eyebrow. "*Ja*? You photographed people. Those in gutters and those in tiaras? Soldiers and cuirassiers?"

Despite my weariness I began feeling rather hot and annoyed but did not want to argue with my host. "I used my situation wisely, so I think. And it was incredible," I said as Vasily's face appeared to me, the gold braiding of his uniform, the slick of his black hair, my lace blouse, my diamond belt. "I lived well. It's true."

"Indeed. While our world burned you were flying high. But you are here, Siina. I'm glad. For good reasons. More wine?" He raised his glass.

"Yes."

"Of course and for Anna."

"My photos will do good. People will question the war, and know what there is at our back doors."

"Some will Siina. Perhaps. You had adventures. The Hermitage, my word, I was there long ago. The Bouchers! The Watteaus. Monet and Bonnard! Oh yes!"

Aksel surprised me. "I never went there. The walls are all moaning and crying. The dying and the wounded, Aksel."

His eyes flickered but he continued to sip wine and like an old man, put his feet up on a chair. "Please, help yourself to what you need, my dear. I go to bed early and I sleep late."

"Thanks. I'm awfully grateful," I said picturing the bed and pillow.

He laid his head back on the armchair, his eyes closed. "I'm sorry, Siina, we don't have a prayer. *Tulevad meid päästma? Ei tule!*" His voice rose. "*Ei tule!*"

"We'll save ourselves!"

Aksel shook his head gloomily. “Yes? How?”

“We mobilise. I hear of it, don’t you?”

Askel nodded absently. “We will declare independence. Very soon. We’ll see who has courage.”

“And you?”

“Who cares?”

“When the Germans force the Bolsheviks out, *voilà*!” I said.

“You believe that? Very progressive, Siina. You noticed the surge of returning soldiers? Can you imagine a revolt against Russia?”

“Imagine victory!”

“Imagine death.”

“Imagine peace and independence!” I said.

Aksel drained the last of his wine. “Imagine us in chains.” He edged himself forward, narrowing his eyes at mine. “Think now. The Germans are done for. They have their own revolution at home and they’re tired to death of war, fighting White and Red armies. Who can win when a man must shoot his brother and cousin!”

There were hideous atrocities on both sides, of course I knew, still there had to be an end. “Jaan Poska, he must negotiate with the Bolsheviks, surely!”

“Pah! A head of government is a fine title. We’ll see. Better you choose between Russians and Germans, Siina,” Aksel snorted.

I lowered my eyes. I expected his wine glass would slip from his fingers. “We’re punished one way or another,” he groaned as he shambled across the room to re-fill his glass.

“You’re not sympathetic to the old order at all? I’m afraid of the Bolsheviks,” I said.

Aksel shook his head in despair. “We all know about empire.

The Whites will demand order and class and that will never feed the people."

"But surely you must believe in equality and justice. We have the intelligence and will to create that!"

"I don't know, Siina. At least we can speak our minds here today."

I found myself smiling. "Our own state, despite millions against us when we're practically unarmed!"

Aksel raised his glass. "*Vahva*, Siina! One more and I go walking. Listen, I prepare my own dinner. Oh look, an egg. Have it for breakfast!" I followed his gaze to the kitchen and considered a coffee on the Raekoda.

I opened my eyes to breaking dawn and lay still as soft light misted my room. Home. No fighting, no shooting. I would see Anna, soon. Perhaps Mihkel would find his way to Pärnu. I raised myself up, listening for Aksel. Nothing. I bounded out of bed, dressed in an instant, tucked my camera in my bag and tiptoed to the front door.

Along Vanamuise *tänav* the air was biting cold. When I reached the town square I photographed students and soldiers, housewives and schoolchildren. I took the red stone university buildings, the creamy baroque and mannerist town hall in the background and icicles against a clear blue sky, at the same time, straining my ears for gossip, reading faces of soldiers and townsfolk and observing uniforms, listening for promises, opinions and plans. I photographed everyday folk, the exact way they were. There would be trouble because there were so many ways for trouble to come. Even so, there were possibilities to the independence Papa had spoken of so often. I longed for it.

Soldiers grouped and moved off in mismatched army caps,

jackets and coats, men from Finland and Latvia, Estonians in half German uniforms, Balts and Russians, impossible to identify but our spring of independence was welling up, murmuring, bubbling about to roar and deafen us all.

Cafés and restaurants did brisk business. Shoppers brushed against officers and sergeants searching for souvenirs, cigarettes, postcards to send home. I could produce such postcards and earn a living from this stream of population, or in a time of peace, tourists, students and academics. Mihkel and I could live here, near the university. I stepped past a soldier riffling through newspapers in six languages. The next shop advertised electric curls from a frightening contraption of electric wires. My curling tong would suffice for my short hair, a while yet.

The window seat in the Café Kuldpesa on the square was vacant with a view of the town hall and the surrounding shops and market. I stripped off scarf and coat and slid onto the velvet cushion, ordered an anchovy sandwich and creamy coffee. Waiters whirled back and forth with teetering trays balanced like circus jugglers'. My waitress however, resembled a grown-up Katya, tall and self-possessed; her hair plaited and parted the way Duscha's had been. I drank my coffee and watched a child with a wooden gun chasing another in the square. At a table opposite to mine a moustachioed man with a blue silk cravat caught my eye. He was far too dapper for a Russian spy and too well-oiled and coiffed for a Tartu academic. I avoided his glances but sensed him continuing to watch me then suddenly he was standing before me.

"You're new here, *Fräulein*. I can be of service," he said in clipped German, snapping a quick bow. "I know Tartu very well and I'd be honoured to show you the sights."

I shook my head, smiling to myself. I might have asked him to sit and explain why he wasn't in uniform. I could have accepted a drink and asked him what he expected to happen next in Tartu. I might have heard new theories and gossip and contradictions to Aksel's forecasts. "I also know my way here," I replied in German, unable to stop staring at his hair. He bowed more slightly this time and backed away.

On the far side of the square, laden farm carts clattered steel rimmed wheels over cobbles and delivered boxes and barrels to the market. Farmers and housewives bargained before exchanging precious vegetables and grains for money. Maids with baskets hooked into elbows haggled over potatoes, beans, carrots and beets. Loaves of sour, dark rye bread in neat rows soon vanished. I photographed pretty young women and their baskets of vegetables. I kept my eyes open for a familiar face, for Mihkel's shape and movement.

Beyond the market the Emajõgi, frozen solid, was a river of stillness with sail boat masts laid flat for the winter, scows, white from to gunwales to wheelhouse and decks weighted with ice. I photographed them from the bridge and then the river bank and closer, from the solid river. Many crossed from one bank to the other. The light was gentle and took my last frame close-up of fringes of ice hanging from the gunwales of a small boat.

Mihkel had rowed us here one summer, the banks thick and green with trees and sail boats passing us. We had dodged between tarred barges and gleaming steamers, the sky darkening, a summer storm brewing. Mihkel teased me about my manners, called me classy, yet insisted I was a libertine beneath that surface. I didn't want to disappoint him but he was wrong. I refused to say that I couldn't get his jokes. When the storm broke, my cloche got drenched, my dress wringing wet, clinging to me. Mihkel, after rueful glances, lent me his wool jacket, soaked but warm.

"You're not one of those who think photography will end painting, are you? Some have no idea about art," I had said, wanting to impress and hear his opinion.

"Ah, no! It's the future! But painting won't die," he'd said in a blink and I loved him just for that.

Walking back to the town square, my gloved hands warm in my pockets, I noted my bearing; toward the street where Mihkel once lived. It was ironic that I dared not speak his name though I might have walked beside his best friend. Women's skirts were shorter than ever, rayon stockings glossed our legs, we painted our lips red, but talking political alliances was as private as love. More private than sex. Ice crystals blasted a sudden haze and I shrugged further into my scarf and I sheltered a moment beneath the apothecary portico. From here I had a view of the town hall, the Russian tri-colour snapping in the breeze against a clear sky but I'd used the last of my film. Our blue, black and white flags were tucked away in pockets or folded in drawers and cupboards all over Estonia, waiting for the moment it was safe to bring them out.

Up the hill, *Musumägi*, past the ancient sacrificial stone and down the other side I found the house where I'd seen Mihkel. I knocked and waited.

"*Jah*?" A tall man wiry blond hair opened the door. "*Tere*," he smiled.

"*Tere*! I'm looking for *härra* Oks," I said instantly. The man was a friend, so I decided. He was younger than Mihkel, wore a striped collarless shirt and the soft jacket of an office clerk. His mouth almost smiled but his eyes laughed as he appraised me.

"Who's asking?" His pale eyes, more Finnish than Estonian in their Asian lines, shifted to glance over my shoulder. His cheeks were pink above his jaw-line in patchy smudges. He lounged against the door jamb.

"A friend." My ears burned. "Pärnu."

"*Noh, jah*, come on in." He stepped aside and led me to a dark sitting room. Books, files and brown paper parcels covered chairs and tables, quite the same as Mihkel's Peterburg room. Lace curtains sifted the air, a touch of family.

"Lars Valge," he said, a click of his heels and a little bow. "I'll make tea."

"Don't go to any trouble I can't stay," I said for politeness. In the kitchen, a large woman in a striped skirt stood at a stove, a small child on the floor beside her.

"No trouble," Lars called. "I'd like to hear about Mihkel." He gestured to the padded bench seat then disappeared.

Voices drifted from the kitchen, a woman speaking quietly, Lars saying something about Mihkel, the child piping sounds, hardly words.

I inspected the bookshelves. Freud's *Interpretations of Dreams*, Lenin, Rosa Luxemburg's *Social Reform or Revolution*, H.G. Wells. A wooden mug decorated with poker work stood on an embroidered table mat. I searched the framed photographs for a familiar face until the chink of china interrupted me. Lars set down a teapot, a gilt rimmed porcelain cup and saucer and a rye open sandwich with fish paste. I leaned back on the wooden bench and felt at home.

"We've not heard anything for a while. You saw him last," Lars said.

"We?"

"We. Socialists."

"You destroyed the assembly in Peterburg." I remembered from the newspapers.

"We did! Mihkel and others," Lars said.

"So. They're after his blood."

"Well, we're not so popular." Lars continued to smile. "Lenin's first meeting and he lost control, imagine how mad he was."

"As an axe!"

"Yes."

"But do you know where he is?" I tried not to be too eager.

"You were at the Winter Palace rally – the photographer."

I blinked. "I was. I am."

"Yours appeared in the *Postimees*."

I nodded approvingly.

"If you have more we are interested."

"I have no darkroom. Nor chemicals."

"We can arrange that."

"Each picture has its own price."

"Naturally."

"So... Mihkel works for you?"

Lars smiled cheerfully. "Oh, no. He is one of us but he won't be pinned down. Too independent. He's a threat and provocateur, Siina, a menace to everyone except us." Lars smiled more openly.

"You'd publish my pictures?" I asked. He knew my name.

"Of course! Together with Mihkel's articles. We expect he has some."

"I saw him after the rally," I said at last. "We met on the train. They dragged him off at Narva," I said placing my cup so that the little feet set into the curve of the saucer. "Although, it seems you know everything already." I cocked my head at him and reached for a handkerchief.

Lars set his cup beside mine. "We expected Narva."

I stared at the buttons on my boots. I would never make a spy.

"But we don't know who took him and you do. Someone was

informed. You saw."

I heaved a sigh, hot and angry under Lars' fixed gaze. "Well, they were uniforms."

"Of course. What sort of uniforms? Russian? German? Reds?"

"Russian. I didn't really look."

"CHEKA? Military police? Whites? Feral Bolsheviks? A pin, a badge? A star?"

I shook my head. "I don't remember."

Lars' smile vanished. "It's nothing. Never mind but it would help. We'll have to guess. Only you must know that an Estonian in a Petersburg cuirassier's home with a socialist agitator friend would attract attention. You would have overheard gossip. Did Vasily Feodorov join the Whites? Who did he support?"

"Why should you care about Vasily? Lenin was after Mihkel, you said!"

Lars showed the faintest smile around the eyes. "It's information, Siina."

"Wait. He had fur on his collar."

Lars leaned forward and paid close attention. "Anything else?"

"Boots. High boots, like cavalry."

Lars shook his head. "I can't imagine. No badges?"

"Fur on the edges too, on the jacket. Like a woman's."

Lars shook his head. "Not a uniform I've seen."

"The guards were shot. I saw them fall but Mihkel got away. Running."

Lars put his hand on my shoulder. "Running?"

"Yes!"

"Then there's a chance." Lars made his way to the hall telephone and picked up the receiver. "Perhaps," he said and dialled.

☆

38. Anna Pärnu

Pale morning light seeped into the room where my mother had lain before she died, where I had climbed up to hold her hand. I expected to feel her in the room but she'd long been gone. The walls, the linen, the curtains, the blankets where Anna lay, were quite washed out.

"Thank god you came. It's been so long. I thought you'd be sooner. I'm so glad to be interrupted. A moment to ignore the All Consuming One," she groaned.

I squeezed onto the edge of the bed. "I never meant to stay in Tartu so long but I had things to do."

"Things. Things. I know you," Anna said from a sunken clutter of pillows, coffee and sandwiches, embroidery, knitting, patterns and books.

"You ought not make baby clothes."

"Superstitious nonsense." Anna held up a tiny lace bonnet. "Sweet, no?"

"Adorable."

Her face was puffed from neck to cheeks, her skin, unevenly mottled under her nose and around her eyes, her hair wild, yet she was beautiful. Her large eyes shone with a heightened aura.

"Endless hours in labour but the midwife says I'm built for it."

"Fantastic!"

"Earth goddess." Anna rolled her eyes. "Another two weeks, Siina. Are you ready?"

I checked to see if she was serious. "Absolutely!"

She flapped a hand at Roosi who had brought a new tray of

juice, sandwiches and cake. "My god, the mess!" Red juice swam over the white drawn linen, bled through the threads and pooled in the corner of the tray.

"Nothing. It's nothing," Roosi mopped with the tray cloth. "Don't worry."

"Remember Ida?" Anna began. Ida was a friend from school days, restless and daring, married a young German, one leg shorter than the other. He carried a cane.

"Of course."

"Dreadful, horrible birthing time, Ida. Almost died!" Anna rearranged her hair over her shoulders, a woman in fruit. "Two years before she let her husband in her bed! I don't blame her, do you?" Anna showed mock disbelief. "Poor thing could hardly walk after. Couldn't look at her child, sad little mite." Anna tucked the bedclothes around her and wrestled into a new position. "Not me, Siina. Mother Earth. Hands here!"

I felt the kicking. "Should we call the midwife?" I backed away.

"You're nervous," Anna giggled. "Siina!"

I shook my head. "I've no sense of it."

"Neither you do. I wish mother were here."

"Well, *I* am."

"And you better stay. I mean it." Anna reached for my hand.

"For as long as you need."

"Good. Thank god! Oh good!"

Hours of screaming and struggling, blood and pain, sighs and cries. I'd bolt if I could. "Of course. We'll heave the cart together," I promised. "I'll even photograph you both."

"*Issand*! And kill us with your chemicals? We're not a fairground, Siina!"

"Madonna and child! Nobody has done it. Mother and

newborn. Goddess! New life! I've never seen one. Nudes, sirens, breasts and buttocks but not, you know, what you have. The bud of life." I had in fact seen a woman in an operating room photographed but that was different, and hideous. I could have vomited. But Anna and her newborn, they would be spectacular. Beautiful. Earth goddess and babe!

Anna tugged the bedclothes to her chin. "But kindly, Siina and very beautifully, please?"

"Of course!"

"It's gorgeous to have you here, sister. I've been alone for ever."

"Forever. No. But I shall never go back to being in someone else's family, I can assure you! I was neither here nor there. It was strange and sometimes unpleasant."

"And exciting and luxurious. I know. It wasn't your family. It was theirs. Were you any better than cook or maid?"

I wondered what I'd said in my heartfelt letters. "Anna! There's to be an announcement at the Endla tonight. I must go. I need to find camera lights. I'll be back immediately after the speeches are over! After I get some shots. Rely on me, darling."

"Camera! You and your camera. I'd damn well come too if I weren't here cast like a sheep," Anna groaned, folding up the little bonnet. "But first, darling, what's happened to Mihkel? You've still not said."

"We lost touch."

"You gave him up?"

I sensed my control sliding away, out of reach, gathering speed, skating down some slippery slope. "We've lost contact."

"He's a Bolshevik, Siina."

"He's a writer, Anna!"

"But you fell in love with Vasily Andrevich." Anna grinned in delight. "Do tell. Does he wear dress uniform in the bedroom? Is he captivating? How does he begin? French or Russian?" Anna held the baby bonnet to her face like a veil. "Or did *you* start?"

I tossed my head. "Oh, stop. You're making things up. I worked. I was lonely. I heard Chaliapin." I paused to see if I wanted to tell her more. "I did fall in love with him. For a while."

"And he?"

"It was never love."

"He seduced you!"

"He did."

"Well never mind. Was it wonderful?"

I looked into my dear sister's wide brown eyes. "It was. He was heroic and heavenly but it was flattery and advantage. I wanted to believe it was love. He belonged to Olga in every way, their past, children and family. However spoiled she was, he belonged to her."

Anna nodded. "Shame. Sad. Now you feel guilty. Or thrown over?"

"Perhaps. Everything." I wanted to deny that Vasily might have used me. I couldn't believe he didn't care. I was not as modern as Kollontai or Casanova. I felt wretched and disloyal to Mihkel but I wouldn't bore Anna with that. I'd hardly seen Mihkel so how could she understand?

"Maybe I made a fool of myself. But I do love him in a particular way."

"Particular? You mean odd and far away way, dear Siina! But you are hurt. Love can hurt you. I do understand."

Indeed, there was something there about pride and self-respect that I had not completely unravelled. And it would hurt Mihkel. And me, too.

I leaned toward the window and shifted the linen curtain. By the time the lilac flowered Vasily, Olga and their children would be safe in some turreted, onion-domed summer house on a snow-layered plain beyond the Urals. Grunya, Tamara and Lyudmila would be wondering if they'd made the right choices; to starve there since they'd not joined the Women's Death Battalion. Or be shot dead. But really, I couldn't believe Lyudmila would have the stomach for staying in Petrograd under siege and neither would she be welcome in her family, already at the end of their food supplies. Timur would have recovered after losing his beloved Orlovs but he'd never consider an option other than loyalty to the bitter, dire end wherever they went, whatever Bolsheviks or Whites promised, He'd carry the load of three men before giving up on Mother Russia.

"Well anyway, they disappeared. The whole cursed family. Fled. Without saying goodbye. I wish them well," I added quickly.

"You'd never have gone with them, Siina. You're here! But did Vasily Andrevich join the Whites? Did he?"

"He would not! Never."

"So! Hell if they track him down then."

"And suicide to stay! He'd give his life for his tsar but the Whites are not the tsar. They can't agree amongst themselves, Anna. It's anarchy. Well, hideous torture. Suicide either way."

"Oh shame. He's such a soldier. I mean, so I believe," Anna smiled brightly.

I lay my head against the window.

Anna tossed her hair. "That's why you admire Mihkel so, isn't it?" She lifted her voice to her stage character, dramatic and commanding. "Going against all odds. I mean, who knows, sometimes the little man does win."

My eyes stung.

"You're hiding something more," she said.

"Rubbish! I've talked enough. I need to walk and feel myself at home. And I must find lights before the Endla!"

Anna sniffed. "Oh, go on. Go now!" She flapped her hand. "You're angry because you gave up Mihkel. Actually."

"*Kuule*," I swung back from the doorway. "I am upset! Please be nice. Give me a day or two," I said though I'd rather have told her how I felt, what was gnawing at me. She'd be sympathetic if I said how each night I stared into the amber light from the street, a child again and as soon as I closed my eyes I saw Mihkel zigzagging, dodging, running, always running. She'd understand.

I blew my sister a kiss but she had closed her eyes and lain back with an expression that said, 'do not disturb'.

39. Kuusner 24 February 1918

I wrenched my felt hat low and wound my scarf several times around and took up the camera bag with my Afco. I hurried along Supeluse *tänav*. Sandy grains spun from Pärnu beach. Snow would come again. The wind was dropping.

I hesitated outside Mihkel's house before I opened the wooden gate. I rapped on the door. Not even a maidservant.

Chattering groups moved along Supeluse, even from side streets, joining the throng moving into town, an undercurrent of excitement like a song festival, a forest of black, blue and white ribbons wreathing the air.

I caught sight of Papa and Eeva.

"Not home with Anna," Eeva said without greeting. "Left her all alone?"

I wanted to say the same. "Roosi's there. No rush. First baby."

"You're going to the Endla?"

"With everyone. I need to get camera lights first."

"You never will," Papa muttered.

"You and your camera," Eeva murmured.

If I found something better than my Afco I'd be very tempted.

"You're right," Papa said coming to walk beside me. "You must record this night. Our troops are in the square, scouts and school children, choirs and bands, all there. The Bolsheviks are doomed you know. We face tomorrow with something better. Did you believe it would happen?"

"I hoped."

"Lithuanians declared independence. What do you think? There are solutions other than striking and revolting. The

Austrians have chaos. They're going terribly wrong."

I kept pace with my father. "We're following the Lithuanians?"

"A better option. Who would believe we solve anything with socialist hogwash? We should be glad to be so far away and blessed with more sense."

"I hope so Papa. I agree. Peace, prosperity and our own control."

He gripped my shoulder. "And you'll not run off for someone you hardly know, will you? We are so close to getting our own state. You've thought through your loyalties, yes?"

"Yes."

"There are many banners of self-expression, *natürlich*."

"And all manner of socialists," I said wondering if Papa cared that my heart broke, that Mihkel was imprisoned, hurt, or dead. I couldn't tell him.

"You can't photograph in the dark, Siina."

"I can, Papa. Pop and puff."

He waved and I dashed toward Rüütli *tänav* and the Endla. Shops had closed. In the window where my mother and I had first seen my little box camera was an expensive-looking Leica. A shadow of a man turned the lights off.

I thrust my head in the door. "The Leica. How much?"

The man observed me. "I was about to close."

"I'm very interested in it."

"Well I'm selling it for a friend." He glanced at his gold pocket watch but at the same time, switched on a light.

"I need to take photographs at the Endla, for the newspapers. I have a camera but that one, it looks wonderful."

The man reached into the window. "You know cameras?"

"Oh yes."

Crowds surged past. The shopkeeper placed the camera on the counter. “It’s an excellent one. My Polish friend had to leave before the German advance. He had to let this go.”

I looked at the bellows, the aperture settings, the exposure. I searched for holes in the skin and felt the dials turn smoothly. Ran my hand over the silky surface of the red wood.

“And a magnesium lamp! And film,” I asked.

“You know how to use them?”

I nodded. I had used magnesium lighting but not with such a marvellous contraption.

“*Proua* Jürimäe’s eldest, are you? I remember your mother and the little box camera. Andres Kapp.” He made a little bow.

I offered my hand. “*Väga meeldiv*. How much?”

“A hundred roubles. A special occasion. I tell you, it’s all worth much more. The plates and lamp. Of course there are more modern cameras but…”

“I love the glass. The prints are beautiful.”

Andres Kapp put the equipment in a box and I opened my spy camera bag for the notes, gold roubles and silver. He smiled at the sight of them. We knew how unstable the currency was. He was curious about my camera bag and asked if I might sell it but I was too fond of it. If not for the diamonds I could never buy the Leica.

Andres Kapp counted the money. “Right,” he said scooping it up.

“And the tripod?”

“It comes too,” he said. “Plus the Blitzlicht. Magnesium. You know all about them, yes?”

“Yes, yes,” I said instantly. Terrifying explosions were all too common. If the magnesium was dry and caked it could go off like a hand grenade, or not at all. I would discover soon enough whether I needed to ignite it. For now, I need not frighten Andres.

"You may need help," he said slipping on his coat, hefting the tripod over his shoulder, locking the door behind us.

Battalions of Estonian soldiers lined up outside the Endla vibrating in an atmosphere of victory and celebration, surging and humming. Anna had first entered the theatre here for Kitzberg's *Libahunt*, the wolf-woman. Later I would have to describe every detail of this night to her.

"We need to go inside," I said.

Guards in remnants of Russian uniforms, some with pistols, rifles, some dressed like citified gentlemen beside military guards, grouped at the foot of the stairs.

"What's this?" a guard asked nodding at Andres load.

"Photographing for *Postimees*. I need to set up."

The guard, in imperial uniform held his rifle against his chest. He took a step up. "Who are you?"

Andres Kapp pushed past me. "*Noh, fotovõtja, mis muidu?*" The photographer. What else?

"*Ah nii?*" The guard looked us over.

"Friends of Johannes Pääsuke," I said, naming the photographer every Estonian would know. The guard looked blank.

"The film maker. Tartu," Andres responded. I had met Pääsuke, the first Estonian moviemaker and asked about his double camera work. He'd photographed country folk, landscapes, soldiers and the like, ordinary scenes always fresh. "Siina Jürimäe worked with him. They photographed the *Maapäev*."

The guards stood aside. "Go on up! Hurry."

The room that lead to the balcony from where the announcement would be made was brightly lit and surrounded by wall sconces; playwright's busts, prehistoric bowls and one empty - for my light.

"I leave you to fix the scene and make art out of the science. Päts will be nice," Andres assured me. "He's after all a *talupoeg*, a peasant beneath the lawyer."

I glanced sidelong. "Also a journalist."

"He fears nothing." Andres tightened a tripod screw. "He's what we need this moment."

An aide my age, drawn up like a soldier while dressed like a banker, spoke in my ear. "*Härra* Päts is meeting his ministers. He's not here for photography. But if you're lucky he may give you a moment. Not long."

"Would you ask on my behalf?" I said.

The aide looked me up and down. "I can do that."

"Thank you."

Panic rose in my belly. The magnesium lamps were odd, and Konstantin Päts, chairman of the Estonian military, editor of the *Teataja* newspaper, a man who had so far served his country with nine months of imprisonment in Peterburg, was already a hero.

Andres nodded encouragingly. "Keep on."

"Actually I've never used these."

"They will work."

Too much light and I'd get a white blast. Mis-timed or underexposed I'd have nothing at all. I pressed cotton wool around one lamp gutter and set magnesium in the centre. "Light them when I say," I ordered Andres. When I squeezed each rubber bulb, a puff of air would flare, burn the cotton wool and ignite the magnesium for one moment of brilliance, to be followed by billows of blinding smoke.

The aide stood before me and pulled out a silver pocket watch. "Ten minutes. *Härra* Kuusner also agreed. The manifesto is at eight," he said before backing aside.

I smoothed at my hair. I scratched my neck. The aide might light another fuse for me and I'd have a light all around. A poof from above would fill out Päts features rather than weight him with shadows; another from the side would brighten him.

I twitched the tripod the screws again, checked my shutter speed, felt for one rubber lamp bulb, ready to pick it up.

"You left Pärnu some time ago?" Andres asked as we waited.

"*Ah ja*, I have some great photographs from Russia. Yes, Petersburg is astonishing."

"And you're glad to be home."

"Most glad."

"You know the Bolsheviks abandoned Tallinn yesterday."

"I heard."

"I know it's months since the *Maapäev* was declared. It could never hold up against the Tallinn Bolsheviks." Andres narrowed his eyes at me. "You're lucky to be out of Peterburg."

"I know. I know. And what about here? What do we expect?"

Andres opened his hands as if to offer a modest opinion. "A Finnish union, a Scandinavian alliance, a Russian federation. Compromises. The votes say the Bolsheviks are popular," Andres stepped closer. "But they're not! They're represented in Tallinn and Narva, the workers and Russians. Not us. But even if we make a grab for independence we'll be holding on with our teeth." His eyebrows jerked.

We both knew how fast things could change, as in Peterburg. But we were united in a desire for identity. We were not struggling and disadvantaged and poor, pitted against a controlling bourgeoisie.

"It's why we make these mementoes. I wish my friend were here."

"Friend?"

"He'd appreciate meeting Päts."

"We all do. He'll get us through. We're not yet abandoned. We have a chance."

I peered through the lens focusing the glass plate where Päts would sit. "If you had to, Andres Kapp, who would you choose?"

"Either way they'll use us, Miss Jürimäe. I feel you and I have the same outlook."

I straightened up from my camera. "The best have been either shot, or fled. Paris and Vienna."

"The best rush to enlist and volunteer and are killed for their reward. Others scarper as soon as there's a sign of trouble. They're also smart. Cowardly perhaps, but they live."

"It's never simple, is it? Loyalty and circumstance. I'm no better than anyone at deciding."

"Russians suffer too. When you see them close, *härra* Kapp, they bleed and die in awful ways."

"And they'll not stop before they've all murdered one another."

I checked the glass plate again, slid it out and in to the sweet red wood camera. It was large, bulky and heavier than my little box but it was elegant and would outlast many of the others. The silver and albumen prints were gorgeous.

Päts and Kuusner entered the hall. I offered my hand. Andres became official and greeted the men, bowing like a Japanese. He continued his role as my assistant.

Päts, tall, dominating, a superior, deliberate, manner, looked me in the eye and took my breath away. Kuusner, also tall, was more approachable and I fancied, more genuine.

Päts sat and turned his profile and although I was wholly employed with the camera, determining exactly what position would best suit him, thinking of the light and flash and when it should come, I was also overwhelmed to be in his presence. I felt his repressed energy and found him very attractive.

"How is that?" he asked as he posed, turning the minutest degrees to me, then away. Every moment was precious. I staved off panic. I posed his face three quarters to me, found him in my viewfinder, and focused.

For one instant he turned full face. I stared into his eyes, a man who had been beaten and tortured. I saw the skull of long imprisonment, eyes reflecting a stubborn, unyielding will, but tangibly broken and suffering. I pulled back from the viewfinder and looked above the camera. Päts sat in profile, the way I'd asked him to. I held onto the tripod, glanced meaningfully at Andres to steady myself, took a breath and signalled Andres. He lit the cotton in several lamps. I squeezed the bulbs. Magnesium flared. I opened the shutter. A dazzling flash in the room, smoke and smell and god willing, a brilliant photograph!

"You see. Everything went perfectly," Andres told me as we collected our equipment.

"It was good. I'm very happy," I said, bursting inside, relieved.

Outside the crowd had swelled. A bearded man waved his hat, another with a child on his shoulders bobbed the boy up and down. People linked arms.

"You must have a shot of this," Andres said in my ear. "This is the one we need for our children." I sensed a smugness about him and agreed.

I searched for a vantage point. I could hardly move.

Andres pointed to balcony opposite. "If we could get up there…"

"Perfect," I said. A view over the crowd, an unprecedented gathering, flags waving, hope and promise. "Only how to get there...?"

Andres cast about for inspiration. "A moment," he said and went pushing through the masses.

I began counting the minutes, wondering when Anna would call me. I felt a relentless discomfort with her voice in my head. As the speeches came to an end and the crowd began breaking up the street lamps offered light. Andres waving and pointing, flagged me to a building with a shining object.

I elbowed my way forward. Kuusner appeared. The crowd roared and applauded.

"Come, come!" Andres urged, opened the grand oak door and we dashed upstairs.

The noise hushed. Kuusner thrust his chin forward surveying us.

I locked my camera in position, Andres jabbed cotton wool around the lamp gutter and emptied the last spoonful of magnesium powder. "You'll get a flash on the side and nothing but a white burst. I can see you." He picked up the lamp and paraphernalia. "Give the signal."

His footsteps echoed down the stone stairway and set up my lamp at the top of another stairwell above the crowd. He waited for me. Kuusner was in the viewfinder; I raised my hand and released the shutter.

Anna's voice was calling but Kuusner was speaking. The crowd was silent. Our blue, black and white striped flag rose on the Endla flagpole. I saw our landmass, our rivers and valleys, the limestone, the swamps, the tiny villages, the windblown fir forests. Kuusner's voice soared above and we breathed as one.

Never in the course of centuries have the Estonian people lost their ardent desire for Independence, he began. *Estonia, when all splinters, at both ends, will burst forth into flames … Now this time has arrived.*

An unprecedented struggle of nations has destroyed the rotten foundations of the Russian Tsarist Empire ... From the West the victorious armies of Germany are approaching in order to claim their share of Russia's legacy and, above all, to take possession of the coastal territories of the Baltic Sea.

Not a murmur from the crowd but a stirring like the wind in a vast fir forests on sandy beaches. The final words were sung, the song to homeland:

'Long live the Estonian Democratic Republic. Long live the people's freedom', the final words of the proclamation rang out.

Anna let go her agony and Klaara slid into the world and gulped her first air.

40. Klaara

I glanced at Mihkel's front door and raced by. No light. No time.

I wrenched open our front door, a withering sense of doom surging and diving.

"Roosi!"

Not a sound.

"Roosi!"

My camera and tripod tumbled from my arms. I tore off hat and coat and raced upstairs. I paused for breath at my mother's room.

"Anna?" I called.

Anna lay pale as a lily, head to one side, eyes closed. Stains of dark blood all over the sheets. A man stood with his back to me. He held a stiffly wrapped bundle in the crook of his arm.

"Anna!" Still as a pond. I turned to the man, hair disguising his face, and the baby, all but smothered in swaddling, eyes swollen closed, mouth shut tight, skin bright pink. Heart stopping. New life.

The man, his hair blacker and heavier than a Russian priest, thicker than a Lahemaa lumberjack. His eyes were dark even as fire shone.

"Mihkel!" I could scarcely whisper.

He raised a finger to his lips, nodding at the baby.

My eyes burned with tears. "Is Anna...?"

Her colour had bled away.

"Is she...?" I looked from Mihkel to my sister.

"Asleep," he whispered. "It came very fast. A fright. A shock."

"You were here! She's all right?" I steepled my fingers over my nose and mouth and let go the welling tears.

"I'd say she is. The *ämmaemand* didn't get here. She should be. It was fast. Hold her, Siina." Mihkel's slanted smile hid behind the beard.

My tears flooded. I held the stiff bundle as though it were my soul. Mihkel embraced me, the baby, we all three. "I got here."

"I promised I would," I sobbed.

"*Ah ja*, only Klaara wouldn't wait."

"But Roosi?"

"Roosi! She held together in the end. Brave, wonderful girl."

Anna, sighed, nestling deeper in the pillows.

"And you're a midwife, Mihkel?"

"*Talu poiss, kallis* Siina. Farmer's son. We're much alike in our bones and blood." He squinted a sort of smile.

But I had promised. "You came," I managed, trying to see past the hairy mass. "I can't believe it."

"Shhh." He took Klaara and laid her in her cradle. He turned to me and I rested my head on his chest.

"You got away."

"Yes."

"Horse hair?" I tweaked his beard. "There were crowds at the Endla."

"I stayed well clear."

I pulled myself to him, my arms around his neck. "I saw Päts and Kuusner. Photographs."

"*Ai ai!* Siina!"

I turned to Anna. "Darling, sleep," I whispered, kissing her cheek. I tiptoed to the cradle. "She's breathing. Little angel."

"Be proud of your sister. All business and persistence. No hysterics."

"Truly?"

"Magnificent."

I struggled with surges of remorse. I'd longed to be with her. "I'm so completely hopeless," I groaned.

"You're here now."

"I adore her. I can't bear her to be hurt." I wiped my cheeks. "But the midwife..."

The door creaked. A broad-faced, florid woman went directly to Anna, touched her cheek with the back of her hand, stood over her for moments; took her wrist, laid it gently on the bloodied sheets, then padded over to the cot. She lifted the baby out, watched her closely cooing quietly and lay her down.

"Jesus and Mary, crammed like herrings in a can. Jolly well couldn't get through. Nobody could. So how's our love?" she said, returning to Anna.

I steeled myself not to cry. "Bleeding," I said unnecessarily.

"Dearie me! Oh dearie. So pale, poor sweetie."

I glanced from Mihkel to the *ämmaemand*. "Has she stopped bleeding?" I quavered.

"So help me, let's look," the midwife said and together we raised the bedclothes. Anna groaned like cracking wood and I, unused to such things, gave way in my knees to see the quantity of blood, a lake under her body.

41. The Stage

Anna sat upright in bed, tired, calm but no longer wound and bound waist to pelvis. Her colour and energy returned within the month. Every day she grew brighter, every day more like herself. The birth, the midwife claimed, was not so bad. It had been worrying, the loss of blood, but with herbs, cold staunching and her feet raised, she recovered. I watched her, deeply thankful.

Klaara's little cheeks pulsed as she sucked greedily.

"It's another pain, Siina," Anna was saying. "When she sucks and chews… *Issand*, the pain. I can feel blood streaming!"

Close as we were, I wished for some distance. "It's supposed to be good for you."

"Indeed. They say." Her eyes glazed again with exhaustion. "Not exactly bliss, darling. Really, really, really I want to sleep. One of these days I'll even get out of bed. I can hardly believe that!" She gazed at Klaara. "Little sucker, draining me. I will not be attached forever or I'd go quite mad."

"Patience, Anna."

"So, tell. You and Mihkel will get married? Yes?" She stroked Klaara's downy head.

"You know we won't. A ceremony won't make a difference."

"Of course. You're such socialists."

"Bohemians. I'd rather you said Bohemians though they are naughty. I know."

Klaara's hand clutched at her mother's breast as a rebuke formed on Anna's lips. "I don't want you to look a fool when Mihkel throws you over for some neat bosomed little flag-bearer, some sexy little Rosa Luxemburgish type. You'll wind up in poverty and starvation like the rest of them."

"Mihkel will find work. I will too." I bent over my satchel and pulled out the newspapers, *Postimees* and *Teataja*. "My babies," I said, unfolding the pages. I held them up, my photographs of Päts and Kuusner. "So now I am a photographer. I'll find something in Berlin."

Anna blinked at the papers. "Very nice. They're well, realistic. You made a hit with him? He's more than attractive."

"Oh Anna. He's statesmanlike. Charismatic. Yes. It was exciting."

"Of course."

"If you look at the lighting and background."

"I tell you," Anna sighed, "I can hardly stand to be in this nightgown another second." She held one hand over her breast. "As soon as I lose these melons I'll be in real clothes, silk, simple, no fussy crimping." For a moment she lit up.

"Don't expect your life to be the same again, ever, Anna."

"Don't say it. They need me. I know how to run things. A few months, that's all. New plays, new actors. Ibsen's *Hedda Gabler*. So much to do."

"Really." I watched as Klaara's little head rolled.

"I may not play a lead but I will be back. Soon." Klaara flopped like a doll over Anna's arm. "So, you'll really go off, Siina?"

"I think so. I want to see other artists and photographers."

"I understand. I'll learn to drive a car. Fashions are short and I have good legs," Anna whispered. Klaara was sucking again.

"You'll be lovely in drapey things."

"While you'll talk guns and bombs and libertines and lesbians. The Weimar Republic. Berlin. Really. Germany the superior nation. It's arrogance."

"It's also art. Plus anti-art. I'm rather curious."

"What? The rage and desperation? So modern there is no style. That's what I think." Anna shook her head at me.

"It's also thrilling. It stirs us up."

"The Empire hammering *Kultur* and everyone else a barbarian? While you have loyalty to beauty. I know you do. Ballets Russes. Gorgeous bodies. Karsavina. Nijinsky. Yes. I know you're as curious as the rest of us. What do they do and with whom in their spare time? Decadence! What do men do, and women? Don't you find it sordid? I'll think of beauty. The horrors exist but I won't look. I can't stare into the pit."

"Have you had tea with three sugars?"

Anna smiled. "I sit here and I think. We must go to Tallinn. Klaara will love it."

"Klaara won't have a clue," I snorted.

"But I'll love it. I shall get my hair cut. Something stylish and swingy. Something for tango." Anna lifted her eyebrows suggestively.

"Aha! And money?"

"Ostmark, roubles, Finnish or German marks, no point keeping worthless paper. I need a new dress!" I had wanted to talk about Mihkel but Anna was flying too high. "Did I tell you about Max? He has a car. He'll drive." She shifted her hair away from her eyes with one hand. "He's sympathetic with Oskar gone and Klaara sucking and burping and messing diapers all day long. And you, nowhere to be seen while I'm stuck here!"

"Ah so. Do tell me about Max."

"An actor." Anna gently shifted Klaara to her other side. "Sings ragtime. Not so very well but with feeling. You'll love him. Everyone does."

"Not volunteered?"

Anna stroked Klaara's head as she attached to the nipple again. "He can hardly see. Wears the most undistinguished thick glasses, great bottles, poor chap."

"Comes here when Oskar's away?"

"For tea and entertainment. Superb dancer, and handsome! Just laughs, Siina. Nothing political, nothing else." Anna squared away my look.

"And a car?" That was interesting.

"Disgracefully wealthy. Landowners from Swedish days. Own a lumber mill. Of course they'll lose it as soon as these damned Bolsheviks arrive. He's your type though, lavish and smart and talks about everything. He's looking for a wife, so he says." Anna grinned. "Women adore him."

Anna bathed Klaara's head in the palm of her hand while the baby dozed. "You can't have him yet. He's still my friend. You'll soon get to know him when we go to Tallinn."

I imagined the ranks of soldiers, trucks and motorcycles grinding their way through the empty countryside and the miles of forest between Pärnu and Tallinn. Haymaking and ploughing was miserably slow and wearying with so few men. Cattle and horses were scarce. We were in decline.

"Better times are coming, Siina. People say. The war can't last much longer. No one can grow food. It must stop. What do you think, a German state? Better than Bolsheviks."

"I'd hate German military in charge."

"Yet you'd go there!"

"For Hannah Höch's work and the awful Dadaists." I tried to sound light. "Yes."

"God give you strength."

"We need to be relevant, Anna. Dadaists are piecing snorkels and helmets, wooden legs and air pumps together so strange but then you see the meaning. They tell us something. I mean, we need to admit to what goes on don't you think? Or you'd rather a Boucher's pastel and a Fragonard's pinky fleshy shepherdess?" Anna hung such reproductions, gold framed in her bedroom.

"I like them. I do." She rearranged her emptied breasts. "Otherwise I'd go quite mad."

"But how can we deny mistakes and crimes?"

"Oskar's overdue." Anna held Klaara over her shoulder. "None of them left in the south so he can't be there."

"He'll be back. Delayed, re-routed, who knows?" I blotted out images like worn pictures, soldiers at railway stations in sodden grimy blankets, eyes dead, a leg dangling, a face blackened and burned. Mothers or sisters would nurse them, the head injured, the immobile, the minds and memories gone to hell.

"I'd take care of him. I'm practical and extremely efficient when I need to be," Anna said, reading my mind.

"I know you are."

"He'll be back. I can almost, you know, sense his presence. He's close."

I felt it too, him near, wanting to speak to us.

"He'll be home soon."

"I thought you'd know. He'll be proud to see his daughter!"

"Proud of you both."

Anna laughed lightly, a sound I'd been missing. "She's honestly the best curtain performance I've had," she said gazing love at Klaara.

"So, Tallinn?" Enough I thought, guessing about Oskar.

"Soon."

"I'll need to buy film. It's a chance to show my pictures around."

"Not your clunky glass plates?"

“Film’s the thing. Easy and light. Lovely rolls. No messy goo.”

“Great!”

42. Waiting

Mihkel continued to steal into my dreams. I would reach out but he would slip away fleeing with a moaning wail. I would pursue him deep into birch forests where he would vanish. One moment he would be wading into Pärnu Bay, me straggling after, screaming the silent scream of dreams, his bobbing head visible, the next, he was gone leaving only ripples.

Some mornings I would awaken feeling his arms around me, his breath on my cheek, even his warmth. I tried to squeeze back into sleep to hear him whisper and break my loneliness, however hopeless that was.

At the end of a track he had parked his motorcycle and we crunched along the snowy path, crossed the curve of a small frozen stream edged by spiky reeds. On the ridge of the marsh, in the shadow of pines, we found an overgrown hunters' cottage. My hands and face were cold. Mihkel lit the fire. He took out black bread, cheese and a bottle of wine from his rucksack. I set my carpet bag on the wooden bench. It was mere days after the declaration of independence and German armies had occupied Estonia. I knew that Mihkel would soon be gone and I dreaded thinking too long about the urgency of our time together - every moment, precious.

Since the declaration, German troops had reached Tallinn and after that we were held under strict control by the military. Stricter than ever. In the background, in Petrograd, we lobbied for independence. Mihkel and I knew that his life or death depended on negotiations and power, clandestine meetings and subterfuge, the disarray of the Bolsheviks, and the courage and vision of our meagre army.

"All to ourselves," he smiled at last as we leaned together almost kissing. At the moment I expected our lips to touch Mihkel turned and went to the window. He peered outside, ran his fingers over latches and sills with the exactitude I knew him for, inspected the ceiling and the door again.

"What are you looking for?"

"Nothing. I hope to find nothing."

"Good. Come and sit beside me," I thought. Hold me close and we'll thaw, together. I had hugged him as I sat behind him on the motorcycle, all the way from Pärnu. I'd leaned around bends, rocked forward when he opened the throttle, held fast when he hit the brakes, riding as one but once more he was leaving and once more I could say nothing, not a word of regret for his courage, his going to war. I could hardly say anything of my resistance. Men love fighting; they're made for it. Women wait and pray, I'd heard. No, not always.

We sat on the bed to warm it. "Better? We'll soon be cosy," he said.

I nodded. I didn't ask why he was being so vigilant.

"Thirsty?" he said and smiling, pulling the cork from the wine bottle.

He filled tin mugs, pressed the cheese on the bread and side by side we sat feasting like generals. I stared across at the flames feeling my face flush, myself restored. I took off my coat.

"Just us," Mihkel whispered. "I've waited a long time."

"Me, too." For now we were together but again, I had to look ahead.

"We'll come here again after the war. When we've won. In summer." Mihkel smiled but there was unease he couldn't hide as he looked into my eyes and gripped hands. “It’s a fantasy of greens and reds, the marshes and mosses. You’ve seen it.” His voice was rough.

“Of course I have. We always collected berries at Lulle’s.”

Mihkel threaded his arm around my waist. “You’ll be here, in Pärnu, won’t you? You don’t need to say. An empty promise is worse than a lie. I always meant to keep my side,” he said.

“I do too.”

“We can say anything but it’s what we do that matters.”

Vasily’s diamonds were buying guns and freedom. Perhaps they’d save Mihkel’s life.

“I love you, Siina,” he said, his voice hushed with exhaustion and anxiety. “The world has changed. We have as well.” He took my hand and kissed my fingers. “I’ll come back for you. Dynasties fall, nations crumble but we’ll be together.”

“We will,” I said, looking for his mouth, hoping for a taste.

He turned his head. “The bed might be warm now,” he said lying back, taking me with him.

I tugged off my boots. He did too and when we curled up under the covers. I knew he was nervous and I was afraid for him. How I loved him in my head and my heart. I had to be patient, let him tell me when he wanted, whatever bothered him, whenever he chose. I wished I had no doubt. I wanted certainty.

“We’ll win won’t we?”

“Of course.”

“We’ll be together, grow roses and lilacs.”

“And snowdrops. If only for the green tips at snowmelt.”

“And the little bells.”

“But then beets. Plenty.” His eyes closed, his voice fading.

“Where will we live?”

“I don’t give a damn so long as it’s with you,” he murmured, locking me against him.

"Me neither."

We must have slept a long time because it was after midday when we woke. Mihkel stepped outside. I snuggled at his warm pillow and felt something hard. A Browning pistol. I felt its weight and held it as he would. To kill. I wished for no more mystery about him. A soldier needed a handgun with spies and enemies everywhere, within bunkers, in farmhouses, in forest cover. The enemy could be Estonian or Russian, Latvian or Finnish, a communist sympathiser. I punched his pillow back into shape and rolled away.

Mihkel brought tea, bread and cheese back to bed. He walked with an easy looseness, happy, content. The cottage had warmed, the bed too. For the next three days we lived on love, as we say.

Tihased twittered and darted between bare bushes. A doe ran across our path and squirrels chirped in the trees. Mihkel and I held hands and kissed like hungry lovebirds.

After the war I said, I wanted a studio and a darkroom with lilacs outside my window. He said a room with bookshelves, a table dedicated to a typewriter, a garden with beets in view.

We sipped mugs of tea by the fire while it died on the morning we left. I was dazed with love and heartbroken at once. Mihkel was agitated, distant, more remote by the hour. I never knew what he was listening for in that hidden place. I was unsure that he heard even me.

When we stepped back into the forest the day was clear and sunny, the sky so blue there can not have been a speck of dirt in the world. "How did you find Anna at that very moment?" I asked.

"Oh that," he said wearily and walked on.

"But really, Mihkel!"

He stopped me with a grim look and spoke quietly as if the enemy lurked behind every bush. “Let’s not question, Siina. It’s difficult times. Who comes and goes and who stays and why, oh how that can go on.” He shifted his rucksack then took my hand as if to reconcile. “Simply knowing can be dangerous.”

“But who can question you if not … me?” I persisted.

“No one,” he replied instantly.

He might have told me something right away but he did not.

43. My Studio

The days drift like silk balloons some dark, some radiant, golden. Since the end of our war for independence we have settled into our lives with determination. We keep traditions we have always kept, despite the many overseers in the past. There's a will to build up our culture so that music and poetry blossom. We talk about our land and our people. And we are in a modern age. Industry develops, we are proud to have gained the freedom to speak and write our language, to revive Kalevipoeg, to mark ourselves as Estonian in spite of the costs. We honour those who gave their lives for this. We are grateful to them. I look for Mihkel when I go out. I see someone who looks and moves like him.

Many of us have lost a man in the war – a son, a lover, a husband, a father. The fighting in the war against Imperial Germany was horrific, the conditions unspeakable, so now, with independence, we count ourselves lucky. But between those who suffer there is some consolation in being able to speak of it, to feel empathy.

I wait for Mihkel. I will not lose hope.

In our lust for this freedom, we love nature and many forms of beauty. We célebrate our present lives. Trees are green, blossoms full, grass deep. Men laugh loudly, waltz fast and learn new dances. Women flirt, shake hands firmly, hold a gaze with a challenge. Skirts are shorter, legs longer, heels higher. I invite myself to friends' homes without waiting for an invitation. We are conscious that nothing is permanent. I make decisions quickly, though I think things through. We sing old songs and speak with emotion but we're wary. We all are. We all know. We may yet keep our borders or possibly go backwards in our history. Poets and storytellers, writers and composers bring us together. We venerate our trees, our coastlines, our hills. We re-read Liiv, Koidula and Tammsaare. Our ancient runes and sacred trees are venerated as if we belong to another century yet we have expressionist artists who carve bold unerring lines on wood and impressionist painters. Our musicians and composers are our demigods. But always, we are on guard.

In Russia murder followed by execution continues - famine and slaughter; the Kronstadt sailors shot for keeping the promises of the revolution. My optimism is for us. For us. I am home. I believe the sun will shine on us, that we will have abundance and control. We share an intensity for the nationalism we've craved for centuries. Seven. Now we are ourselves. Whatever happens next will not affect the quality of this golden time.

Oskar and Anna have a beautiful three bedroom apartment with two balconies near the park where a statue of Lydia Koidula is to be erected. They have a maid but no cook. Anna has become a hostess with flair. She experiments. I never know what sort of *pirukas* or *paté* she will make but I find out when I visit. I see her often. Her house has become a hub for artist and actor friends. She's secretary for the Endla Arts Committee, promotes and produces but no longer acts. Her husband disapproves. Occasionally a politician, a diplomat or playwright may come to dinner. There are people I offer to photograph and many are willing. Now and again they approach me. I prefer character studies to formal poses and many of my subjects appreciate this artistic style. Now that I can better control technique and understand the chemistry and science, I am free to pursue greater variety. What I can create is limited only by my imagination. I make art, fuelled by the inventive photographers, Man Ray, Roman Vishniac, even Rodchenko and Lissitzky. I would almost give up photography for the colour of Kandinsky. Debate over art and photography continues but is irrelevant. I've found my métier and nothing is more satisfying.

Anna encourages and actually admires my work. It's wonderful for us to be so close. She's my dearest friend.

The doctor is in demand everywhere, in clinics and villages from Pärnu to Tallinn. He's experienced after war. He's loved and admired, a doctor with his skill, gentle and intelligent. There are fewer men after the war. Women are attracted to him. I see him tired and drawn when he gets home. I understand why Anna must keep her own interests alive for both their sakes.

I have discovered and bought a studio and apartment, both; the studio with huge windows looking out onto Rüütli street and upstairs, an apartment with a tiny kitchen but quite enough for me – plus a charming parlour and a cosy bedroom. I have what I want. I wonder what Vasily knew when he gave me the diamond belt. I wonder if he ever thought of me when he escaped across the Urals or wherever it was he went. I wonder if he would care to see my studio and apartment, if he would take any interest in the photos that make me happy. I show my best, most original work in the windows and further back, have drapes and painted screens to transform the room to an Italian loggia, or an Egyptian throne room, depending on my customer's fantasy. I may make a more screens, possibly Rome or Venice, a seaside or Swiss Alps. I'll wait and see what is fashionable.

My work evolves. I make goals as ideas and images spill from my mind. A young woman tints my photographs for customers who can afford them. She's more than talented and experiments with pen and paint. I keep an eye on her as she doesn't take criticism and has her own often remarkable ideas which don't always suit our clients. I feel somewhat uneasy around her and wonder who she spends her time with. It's business so we don't ask about private matters.

I can't say when I'll see Mihkel. I can't possibly know. So many have died in the fight for freedom. So many have disappeared.

But I have Klaara. She's grown from a scrambling blur into a somewhat prim, fastidious child. Anna brings her to my studio often and Klaara loves staying. She's just five, frantically curious, listens to what I tell her and never stops asking questions. She's at a beautiful age. I read to her, tell stories and explain the world - oceans, mountains, stars and comets. I'm very patient, more so than her mother I suspect.

"I want to stay all day," she tells me when Anna leaves. "Mama talks and talks and talks, until Papa takes his bag and goes. It's always like that."

"People need a doctor, darling and he must go to them. He makes people well you know."

"I do know," Klaara says tucking her skirt daintily around her knees as she settles into my blue, woven wool armchair. "I've even been with him, *Tädi*! I saw a dead man once! I like being with Papa." She pauses and looks very serious. "I like being with you too, *Tädi*," she says, a private admission. I bend over to kiss her brow before going to make hot chocolate for her, coffee for me.

The last time Anna brought Klaara, she stopped to gossip. "I can only stay a moment, *kullakene*. One little chat," she breathes as I close my studio door and put up a sign.

"Perhaps you've heard, Siina?" She grasps my wrist as we go

upstairs. "Be a dear and go down Klaara, will you? The costumes, can she, Siina?" I nod. "You can try them on."

Klaara slinks off. This is familiar.

"So. What now?" I pour schnapps for us. It's an hour after dinner. Anna draws a cigarette from a silver case, her fine white hands unlike mine which are brown-stained from developer nitrates. There is no need for me to comment. It is either new love, heartbreak or Oskar's absence, all sufficient to fill an hour or more. I set my schnapps on the arm of my chair. "Tell me darling. I can't wait."

"Someone wonderful. Federico. He's altogether different! Italian! Spontaneous, darling and he sees into my heart." Anna holds a hand to her pleated crêpe de chine blouse.

"Ah so?"

"He'd never lie to me." She pauses to light a cigarette and exhales blue smoke. "He's a little naïve and rather younger than I. Yes, yes, I know."

"Really? How old?" I ease back into the sofa feeling a tiny bit jealous. Anna takes meticulous care of herself. Plus she has our mother's ageless look.

"Not sure but I can add, darling. Oh, what does it matter?" She flings her cigarette arm to demonstrate. "When you find fulfilment."

I hold a sigh and glance at my mantel clock, gold and mauve, exquisite. Dresden. "Anna, I have an appointment in a few minutes. Portraits."

"Yes, yes, I don't mean to stay. I know. I know how it is. I'm terribly busy too. I found a new play. Experimental. *Outré*, Siina. We must be bold. It keeps us alive." She screws her cigarette into my silver ashtray and brushes her skirt, a pencil mustard and grey; she snatches up the matching jacket and slings it over one shoulder. "You'll have Klaara then? I'll be gone a week. Oskar is away, bless him. Klaara beseeches me to unchain her from the nanny. Poor darling."

"Absolutely. Does she have little friends?"

Anna lowers her head to look in the mirror. She daubs her mouth with a bright lipstick in a gold case then tucks it away. "We don't hob-nob with families who invite children."

"Is that so? Federico knows you're married?"

Anna shoots me a glance over her mustard collar. "Siina, we're already very close and yes, he knows me altogether."

I don't envy Anna's life at all, even when I have no lover. I observe. I wait for the almighty and predictable crash. I will hold her in my arms when she falls apart. I wish her happiness. She will swoon and cry, but in love she's radiant.

"Go on now," I tell her. "Klaara and I are the best of pals."

She turns back and forth, unable to leave. "Well, she's company for you."

"Exactly."

"I know you need her. But you're holding on to the past, Siina. I can listen. Whatever happened with Mihkel, I will understand. It's hard to be alone, Siina. I feel for you." I know she cares.

I'm depressed, remembering what I said when we got back to Pärnu, as Mihkel was leaving. I wish I could forget it, but it returns and returns.

Anna leans toward me, inclines her head, her voice softens. "It's not your fault, *kullakene*."

"It is! I was stupid!"

"But we all are, darling."

"He was so secretive. How could I stay silent?"

Anna comes and sits close to me. My customers downstairs

will have to read a magazine. Anna shakes her head. “Siina, there are always those moments, disagreements, anger, tests of love. He should have said something, at least an indication I mean ...”

“But **I** said I didn’t trust him! Of all things!” I bow my head in shame. I do not want to cry. Once the flood gates burst there will be no end. I hear Anna’s sighs. I sniff and brush at my cheeks. “Some sort of goodbye! ‘Come back safe. Have courage!’ I ought to have said!”

“I know. Poor Siina. Darling.”

My eyes fill with tears. I sniff loudly. “What more could I give at that moment other than my resolution?”

Anna looks pityingly and I remember Mihkel’s expression. How he refused to say anything at all about his moves, and how I pressed and pressed him. I’m ashamed. I pushed him away. He was dressed in uncoordinated military leftovers and I presumed he would go to Tartu. Estonians were meeting illegally for the next move – forming independent troops to fend off the coming invasion after the German occupiers were likely to withdraw and the Soviets, surely return. He would duck bullets, hide and ambush, not waste a single shot, supplies were that low. He might have said Tartu at least. That would hardly have pinpointed his position. If only he’d said something. If only I had been quiet.

“How can I trust you if you don’t tell me!” I had finally burst. “Please, Mihkel! I’ll wait forever but just, you know, give me the least clue!”

He gave me a despairing look as if I’d betrayed him. “You must know what is happening, Siina. You’re an intelligent woman.”

“No, not really!” I said and he kick-started his motorcycle, rolled it forward and with a black look over his shoulder, rode away.

I rephrase our goodbye over and over and despite the fact that nothing has been heard, I believe he is somehow, somewhere alive, perhaps wounded, lost mind, lost memory. The war of independence took so many, but I think of him recuperating beside a lake or in some garden shaded by grand ancient oaks. Rumours still go around that he was a spy but how can anyone know? Such whispers turn to silence wherever I go. Spies never give themselves in, even after death. I will wait.

I can disappear down the hall beyond my studio to my dark room. New ideas flood when a stack of prints dries or the moment I roll new film in my camera. The work is slow, developing and exposing. There are noxious smells, but magic emerges. More light than expected, more blur, less light, more clarity. Movement, a deliberate fogging - each photograph carries the memory of the instant just as Mama once said. The particular feeling I have for each is like the cloud passing from one side of the moon to the other. I have a great deal to learn. With every photograph I discover something about myself, and a great deal about this culture and world. I stay awake.

Vasily, I have decided, will be reunited with Olga. They've forgiven one another and live on the edge of a cultured though less flamboyant society than Petersburg, now Leningrad. Perhaps, Paris. Perhaps Buenos Aires or Venice. He will be a shabby replica of his former self, though always aristocratic. Likely he has a young lady friend, *Parisienne* or Argentinian, sensuous but discreet. Vasily's sort always finds a way to live well, dine elegantly, travel in style, side by side with dynasties similarly devastated.

I accept that I am alone but I am used to my own company. The hours vanish in my dark room. The struck-match smell of sulphur dioxide and bisulphate, the toxic scent of hydroquinone, the tarry sweetness of the developing baths engulf the room, and my imagination leaps. Images surface and remind me of someone, a happy meeting, a birth, a funeral, a still pond. Uninvited ghosts haunt me.

Even so I have an urge to flee. I have dreams of places where ancient monuments are inscribed with mysterious writings and beyond them in the milky distance, mountains turn blue. There are places where stories appear so vividly that I believe they describe my life. Perhaps I shall find my way there, re-ignite myself where I have no past. Berlin or Paris. Dresden. Cities built with brilliance and spirit, despite present troubles. When the air is clear, I will go. I have something of Anna and my mother, a capricious streak. When there is not enough here to keep me, I will allow my fire to burn brighter elsewhere.

Timeline for Russia and Estonia 1905-1926

January 1905: Russian revolutionary uprising, 'Bloody Sunday,' in Palace Square, St Petersburg. Sympathy strikes in Estonia. Estonians work toward political autonomy.
November–December 1905: Russian government declares a state of war in the Baltic provinces.
December 1905: Baltic German manors looted or burned. Estonians shot without trial.

August 1914: Russia declares war on Germany. World War 1 begins. 100 000 Estonians conscripted. St. Petersburg renamed Petrograd.

August 1915: In Russia, food and fuel supplies are scarce, war casualties climbing, inflation mounting.

August 1916: Severe food shortages. 8 million Russian men have died in the war.
December 1916: Chaos and mutinies on the war front. Harshest winter in memory. Russian army brought to its knees. Estonia becoming a centre for lively exchange of ideas, advances economically and culturally.

March 1917: Tsar abdicates. Estonia hopes for Home Rule. Estonian soldiers return home to mobilize for independence.
September-October 1917: German troops invade Estonian islands. Russia is losing against the Germans in the war.
October 1917: *Coup d'état* in Russia. Bolshevik government is not recognised by Estonia.

February 24 1918: Republic of Estonia is declared, Provisional Government headed by Konstantin Päts.
February 25 1918: German troops occupy Tallinn and remain until November.

July 14 1918: Tsar Nicholas and family are assassinated.
November 1918: Red Army offensive on Narva on the Estonian Russian border.

January 1919: Estonians aided by the British fleet and armaments; Finnish troops assist and force Bolsheviks to retreat.

February 1920: Tartu Peace Treaty signed. Estonia becomes a republic. Soviet Russia recognizes Estonian independence. Minorities guaranteed their own language, culture and religion.

1921: Estonia joins the League of Nations.
1922: Stalin becomes General Secretary of Central Committee and Russia, USSR.
1926: Baltic German manor houses are nationalized, new settlement farms established. An independent state flourishes.

Glossary

E = Estonian; F = French; G = German; R = Russian

ämmaemand, E - midwife

Anschlag, G - plot

armas, E - dear

arrête, F - stop

barouche, F – 19thC fashionable horse-drawn carriage. It was used mainly for travel in summer, though it had a retractable cover for protection from weather.

bezique, F - card game for two originating in France

Birkenholz, G - birch

bourguoise, bourgeois, F - Philistine, middle class who control capital, derogatory term

bourzhoi, R - bourgeois

bourgemou, R - exclamation, expletive

cartes de visite, F - one's likeness photographed for a visiting card

CHEKA, R – Secret police created December 1917

chérie, chère, F - dear, darling

chort poberi, R - 'go to the devil'

Courland, F - region of Baltic, 1561 to 1795 - Latvia

cuirassier, F - originally a mounted soldier wearing armour covering. Tsar's lifeguard regiment

dacha, R - country house

davai, R - go

droshky, R - Low, four-wheeled, usually open carriage.

dvornik, R - janitor or groundsman

ei tule, E - (they) won't come

Elvast, E - from Elva

Endla, E - Pärnu drama theatre

Estland, G - Estonia

Estlane, E - Estonian

elle est ici, F - she is here

fotovötja, E - photographer

Fraülein, G - title for German tutor

Gazeta Kopeika, R - Workers' daily newspaper in Russia (1908 1918) bought for a kopek.

glücklich, G - lucky

halat, Hungarian - fish

landau, G - city coach drawn by a pair of horses, with facing seats and soft folding top.

la grippe, F - influenza *R*

halva, R - confection of honey, ground nuts, oil or butter. Arabic origin.

Issant, E - my god!

Härra, E - Mr. Title.

Igaüks on oma õnne sepp, E - everyone is responsible for his own good luck.

Isvostchik, R - Droshky driver, coachman

Izvestiya, R - newspaper controlled by Mensheviks and Socialist Revolutionaries until October 1917, then Bolshevik.

jäälilled, E - snowflakes, (literally) ice flowers.

Jaanipäev, E- -midsummer

Jaaniöhtu, E - St John's night. Midsummer eve

je suis prête, F - I am ready

jummal!, E - God!

kasakad, E - Cossacks

kaaslased, E - companions, comrades

Kalevipoeg, E - The Estonian national epic based folktales about the eponymous giant Kalevipoeg.

kallikene, E - darling

Glossary

kallis, E - dear, darling

karukene, E -little bear

kasha, R - buckwheat grain or porridge also made with rice, semolina, millet or oatmeal

keiser, E - autocratic ruler, emperor, Caesar

kissell, E - fruit and beaten egg-white dessert

Kolibri, I - Italian, ladies' handbag pistol - fires 2.7mm cartridges, rather ineffectual.

Kopek, R - coin, less than a penny equivalent

krautzfuss, G - Low bow, German style

kullakene, kurat, E - the devil, exclamation

kuule, E - (imperative) listen

küla, E - village

laht, E - bay

laht, bay, - cove

libahunt, E - werewolf from Estonian folk legend

loomulikult, E - of course

lumekellukesed, E - snowdrops

maapäev, E - Estonian National Council which appointed Konstantin Päts premier in 1918

Mädchen, G - girl

merikotkas, E - sea eagle

milaya, R - darling

möis, E - German manor house

möisnik, E - baron

muinasjuut, E - fairytale, fable

näturlich, G - naturally

nõid, E -, healer, witch

nuhk, E - nose (literal) spy

OHKRANA, R - Secret police established following Alexander II's assassination, replaced after 1917 by CHEKA.

olen, E - I am

Orlov, R/E - One of Russia's horses, the epoch of its horse breeding

päästma, E - to save

pääsuke, E - swallow

Pärnust, E - from Pärnu

pirukas, pirukad, E - pastry with filling of cabbage, bacon, raisins

Peterburg/Petersburg, R/E - St. Petersburg. Peterburg, *E* familiar form

Postimees, E – Estonian newspaper which became first daily newspaper in 1891.

preili, E - Miss, young lady

prekrasnyii, R - beautiful

privilegio de casta, - Spanish, concept of stewardship, expected from the privileged, landowners.

priyatno poznakomit'sya, R – pleased to meet you

Proua, E - woman, title, Mrs

raus, G - out

rehealune, E - barn threshing floor

rond de jambe, F - ballet term, a step

roosamanna, E - delicious fruit dessert

saksa, E - German

saksatuba, E - parlour, named for German style

sarvik, E – devil from Estonian legend

saun, E - sweat room dedicated to washing and relaxing, for ceremonial washing of brides, birthing place, bed for the dying.

Schätzchen, G - my dear, darling

soeur, F - sister

soo, E - swamp

soomlased, E - Finns

sosistamine, E - whispering

suffit, F - enough

sulane, E - farm hand

sült, E - head cheese, brawn

svoloch, R - dog, derogatory term

Tori E – horse bred to resist Estonia's harsh conditions

tädi, E - aunt

talumees, E - farmer

talupoiss, talupoeg, E - farm boy, farm boys; young farmer(s)

tänav, E - street

tatikud, E - boletus mushroom

tavarish, R - comrade

Teataja, E - Estonian-language newspaper founded in 1901 in Tallinn by Konstantin Päts

tere, E - hello, greetings

tibukene, E - little bird, chick

tihased, E - tomtits

üleskruvitud, E - wound up

uulitsa, R - street, avenue

vabadus, E - freedom

vahva, E - brave, spirited

vastlakuklid, E - white flour, sweet dough filled with whipped cream. Named for *vastlapäev*

vastlapäev, E - Easter

väga meeldiv, E - greeting, pleased to meet you, literal- very nice

Veilchen, G - violet

verstehen, G - understand

verst, R - 1.067 kilometres

Zeitung, G - German newspaper

Konstantin Päts - The most influential politician of interwar Estonia. Served as the country's head of state, condemned to death, later headed the Provincial Government. Arrested and deported to Russia where he died in 1956.

Johannes Pääsuke (1892 – 1918) - the man with two cameras – photographed more than 1,300 shots on glass plates in a national ethnographic project across Estonia.

Mustsada, E - Black Hundreds, ultra-nationalists in Russia; extremists.

Tales for Alyonushka - Children's folk tales.

Sergei Prokudin-Gorskii - Russian, first full colour photographer contracted by Tsar Nicholas to photograph the Empire.

Decembrists - Russian revolutionaries, primarily upper class who led an unsuccessful uprising in 1825 and whose martyrdom inspired succeeding generations of Russian dissidents.

Lubyanka - Headquarters of Russian counter-intelligence, in 1919, taken over by the CHEKA; also a prison.

Acknowledgements

I have many people to thank for inspiration and advice as I researched and wrote this story.

Thanks to my sister Lee Chisholm for endless encouragement – and to her book group for thorough reading; brother George Carr for meticulous editing; Jamie and Dougal Scott for cheering me on; Lisa Roberts-Scott for reading; Kerrie Scott for supporting.

Thanks to my Seattle family and friends: Pille Mandla for patient, meticulous explanations and translations; Elga Mihkelson for close reading; Enid Vercamer for many discussions of pre-Soviet Eesti and the social fabric; Taimi Moks for reading, her honesty, awareness and coffee; and others who gave me generous time to answer many questions. Thanks to my Seattle Writers' group for strong critique; our clique at Joe Lerner's for robust editing.

Thanks to my family in Estonia: Mai Mandla in Rakvere for details of life on the *talu*, the dress, culture and everyday behaviour; Tiina and Peeter Nõges in Tartu; Lembit Idvand in Pärnumaa; Magda Kurismaa, Ülo Tõnts and Katrine Veanes' father in Tallinn.

Thanks to those scattered in other countries: Mirdza Peterson, Gold Coast QLD, for enthusiasm and absolute confidence; Robert Blobaum, Eberly Professor, University of West Virginia, for reviewing the Baltic history; Maret Kivisild in Vancouver BC; Paul Vaigro in Ponsonby NZ for precision and Robert Jackson in Aesch CH.

Thanks to my wonderful Waiheke writers who brought me to the finale!

And to Bruce Scott, for unfaltering optimism, loving reassurance and technical help!

The Author

Ingrid grew up in Auckland in a tumultuous extended family, her parents having fled Estonia and Russia. Her childhood was immersed in Estonian language and songs from her mother, grandmother and great aunt with revelations of war and the longing for independence. Her father hammered out Rachmaninoff, mourned the demise of the Russian peasant and sometimes danced Cossack style.

Ingrid lives on Waiheke Island, NZ, where she awakens to birdsong and where creative works flourish.

Leaping the Fire is a work of fiction based on the lives of her family, in particular of her adventurous great aunt who fled various dire situations during her long life.

Made in the USA
Columbia, SC
07 May 2017